VOYAGEU

BOOKS THAT EXPLORE CANADA

Michael Gnarowski — Series Editor

The Dundurn Group presents the Voyageur Classics series, building on the tradition of exploration and rediscovery and bringing forward time-tested writing about the Canadian experience in all its varieties.

This series of original or translated works in the fields of literature, history, politics, and biography has been gathered to enrich and illuminate our understanding of a multi-faceted Canada. Through straightforward, know-ledgeable, and reader-friendly introductions the Voyageur Classics series provides context and accessibility while breathing new life into these timeless Canadian masterpieces.

The Voyageur Classics series was designed with the widest possible reader-ship in mind and sees a place for itself with the interested reader as well as in the classroom. Physically attractive and reset in a contemporary for-mat, these books aim at an enlivened and updated sense of Canada's writ-ten heritage.

OTHER VOYAGEUR CLASSICS TITLES

VOYAGEUR CLASSICS

BOOKS THAT EXPLORE CANADA

COMBAT JOURNAL FOR
PLACE D'ARMES

A PERSONAL NARRATIVE

SCOTT SYMONS

INTRODUCTION BY CHRISTOPHER ELSON

DUNDURN PRESS
TORONTO

Project Editor: Michael Carroll
Copy Editor: Nicole Chaplin
Design: Jennifer Scott
Printer: Webcom

Library and Archives Canada Cataloguing in Publication

Symons, Scott, 1933-
        Combat journal for Place d'Armes : a personal narrative / by Scott Symons ; introduction by Christopher Elson.

(Voyageur classics)
Originally publ.: Toronto : McClelland & Stewart, 1967.
ISBN 978-1-55488-457-5

        I. Title. II. Series: Voyageur classics

PS8537.Y523C6 2009   C813'.54   C2009-903250-3

1   2   3   4   5   14   13   12   11   10

 Conseil des Arts du Canada Canada Council for the Arts ONTARIO ARTS COUNCIL
CONSEIL DES ARTS DE L'ONTARIO

We acknowledge the support of the Canada Council for the Arts and the Ontario Arts Council for our publishing program. We also acknowledge the financial support of the Government of Canada through the Book Publishing Industry Development Program and The Association for the Export of Canadian Books, and the Government of Ontario through the Ontario Book Publishers Tax Credit program, and the Ontario Media Development Corporation.

The photographs on pages 42 and 400 are by Christopher Elson.

Printed and bound in Canada.
www.dundurn.com

Dundurn Press	Gazelle Book Services Limited	Dundurn Press
3 Church Street, Suite 500	White Cross Mills	2250 Military Road
Toronto, Ontario, Canada	High Town, Lancaster, England	Tonawanda, NY
M5E 1M2	LA1 4XS	U.S.A. 14150

   ANCIENT FOREST ™
FRIENDLY

INTRODUCTION:

Siting *La Place*

BY CHRISTOPHER ELSON

> It's all a question of seeing — of eyesight on site.
> — *Place d'Armes* (125)[1]

> I left several lives behind ...
> — Interview with Tim Wilson[2]

Scott Symons, one of Canada's most remarkable and controversial cultural figures, passed away on February 23, 2009. He was seventy-five years old. "My life is a sketch toward a life I'll never have time to live" is a phrase he often used with his friends and in interviews. Symons's life was indeed a remarkable one — abundant, excessive, troubling, exigent, and colourful in the extreme. The fruitful and destructive tensions between his lived experience and his artistic project lie at the very heart of his literary reflection. *Combat Journal for Place d'Armes*, first published in 1967, was the inaugural statement of this unique sensibility, a work worthy of republication and reappraisal.

Reaction to Symons's passing in the media was predictably ambivalent. Although he had fallen nearly silent in recent years, the echo of decades of greater and lesser social controversy and the received critical judgment of an overweening and unrealized artistic ambition with which the name of Symons had come to be associated were the dominant notes of the necrologies and articles published in the wake of his death.

Martin Levin of the *Globe and Mail* referred in his blog to Symons as a "potent and scathing presence" in the Canadian literary life of the 1960s and 1970s and noted that "I never met Symons. And somewhat regret it (I think)." Film director Nik Sheehan's appreciation of Scott in the March 12, 2009, edition of *Xtra!* characterized the late author as "an uncompromising artist, a difficult friend and a giant of a man." David Warren's column in the February 25 *Ottawa Citizen* engaged the same terrain, differently: "Scott was, in the best Byronic tradition, 'mad, bad, and dangerous to know.' I was honoured as well as inconvenienced to know him well. I loved him, and wish him success in his new vocation." Warren contributed in some further measure to the appraisal of his artistic accomplishment: "With sex out of the way, Scott's topic was Canada: the dignity she had, and had lost. Paradoxically, he was a true son of that Rosedale heritage, very proud of its accomplishments, and painfully ashamed of its decline into trend-conscious mediocrity." Sandra Martin's obituary in the *Globe and Mail* gave a very thorough account of the complex life lived while emphasizing the view (widely held) that Scott Symons had not established the necessary distance between autobiographical exploration and literary characterization and narration: "His life was his art. Alas, it was not a masterpiece."

Who was this writer, this man capable of eliciting such admiration, uneasiness, excitement, fascination, and condescension? And what does his work mean for us today?

Hugh Brennan Scott Symons was born on July 13, 1933, in Toronto (between Orange Day and Bastille Day, as he once delightedly said to me). He was one of seven siblings, the son of well-established members of Toronto society. His father, Major Harry Symons, had been a star quarterback, a fighter pilot in the First World War, and was a writer himself, winner of the inaugural Stephen Leacock Prize for Humour in 1947. His grandfather, William Limberry Symons, was one of the architects of Union Station in Toronto and a major contributor to the dwellings and character of Symons's beloved Rosedale neighbourhood. On his mother's side, the Bull family legacy and its English connections were deeply influential for Symons. His grandfather, Percy Bull, was a near-legendary figure in Toronto, known by many as the Duke of Rosedale, a cantankerous "rogue male" and a member of the Mark Twain Society.[3]

Symons attended Trinity College School (TCS) in Port Hope, Ontario, where he met his lifelong friend, Charles Taylor (son of E.P., a *Globe and Mail* London and Beijing correspondent, and author of *Six Journeys: A Canadian Pattern* and *Radical Tories*). In a 1997 Vision TV interview with Tim Wilson, Symons remarked on the quasi-Benedictine character of life at TCS, and trembling with emotion evoked the impact of having attended Anglican chapel twice a day for five years. The sense of life as ongoing liturgy, the conviction of its sacramental character that permeates *Place d'Armes* and other works, had its roots in that environment. He also recalled with scorn the anti-intellectualism of the establishment boys there. For Symons, "jock" would always be synonymous with cultural underachievement — personal and national.

After a year in the city at University of Toronto Schools following a gymnastics accident, Symons attended Trinity College, University of Toronto, and took a B.A. in modern history, studying with eminent Canadian historians of varied ideological stripe such as Frank Underhill, Donald Creighton, and Maurice Careless. Like many other university students of his generation, Symons was a summer officer cadet with the University Naval Training Division. He self-deprecatingly referred to himself as "the least pusser cadet they'd ever seen." But he took real pride in this affiliation and had great affection for the Royal Canadian Navy, which he always cast in later years as a Dickensian universe of improbable and touching characters.

Scott took a "gentleman's M.A." in English literature at Cambridge University from 1955 to 1957 where he studied with F.R. Leavis and was influenced by tutors such as Dorothea Krook and Basil Willey. While admiring his tutors greatly, he claimed his real education in England was in the King's College Chapel, at Evensong, in the Fitzwilliam Museum, and with relatives in London. In March 1958 he married Judith Morrow, granddaughter of the president of the Canadian Bank of Commerce. For the next three years he and his wife were to move between journalism jobs in Quebec and study at the Sorbonne, where Symons received a Diplôme d'Etudes supérieures and where he became close to the Christian existentialist Gabriel Marcel and a regular at Marcel's salon. Symons once recounted for me the humorous but bittersweet anecdote of how he fell out with Gabriel Marcel. He and his wife put on a skit about a small accident they'd had and a police officer who had caused them problems, a sketch they thought amusingly showed French stubbornness and unwillingness to admit ignorance in the face of obvious contradiction. The renowned philosopher, dramatist, and music critic found it too clichéd and insulting, and they weren't invited to return.

The Paris interlude was intended to bolster a deepening relation to the French language and to French Canada. Symons and his wife became collectors of French Canadiana, particularly of rooster weather vanes. He claimed to have been shot at by an angry farmer as he tried to steal one, with his wife saving the day in the getaway car. There is no doubt that they became close to the burgeoning intellectual and cultural scene. In a 1963 speech in Winnipeg, Symons stated without hyperbole or irony, "we witness in French Canada what is perhaps the most talented, the most purposeful outburst of creative energy anywhere in the Western world today. (It makes the New Frontier group of the United States look like a posthumous Edwardian garden party.)"

By then Symons's intimate knowledge and insightful perceptions of Quebec had been recognized with the 1961 National Newspaper Award for a series written in French in *La Presse* and published in his own translation by the *Ottawa Journal*. The series described the emerging Quiet Revolution.

Symons even sometimes claimed to have coined the term. He had become an honorary member of the St-Jean Baptiste Society, the first Protestant ever so honoured, and was close to the influential editor of *Le Devoir*, André Laurendeau, later of the Bilingualism and Biculturalism Commission. Yet Symons had to move on from journalism. Responding to a mixture of family and inner pressures, he sought and accepted a position as curatorial assistant in the Canadiana Department at the Royal Ontario Museum (ROM).

From 1961 to 1965, Symons worked at the ROM, becoming chief curator of the Canadian collections, and was an assistant professor of art history at the University of Toronto. He and his wife had a son, Graham. Symons was awarded a visiting curatorship at the Smithsonian Institution in Washington, D.C., and was also made a research associate at the Winterthur Museum, the principal American museum of the decorative arts. Charles Taylor's *Six Journeys* contains an account of a public talk Symons gave at the Smithsonian about French-Canadian and New England rooster weather vanes, and the comparative properties of those "cocks." "His audience, who listened in absolute silence, became aware that he was giving a lecture on comparative eroticism," writes Taylor. Symons's unique take on the life and liveliness of objects and his exhaustive connoisseurship didn't go unnoticed in the United States, and he was offered a position at the Smithsonian. He declined, citing a "date with the Canadian Centennial."

Indeed, somewhere between his sense of the disparity between the dominant accounts of Canadian history and what the objects were telling him ("furniture doesn't lie") and his shock at the adoption of a new Canadian flag designed by a committee and first flown in February 1965, Symons came to the difficult decision to leave behind his life of privilege and cultural achievement. There was also the matter of his increasing interest in the erotic beauty and sexual attractiveness of men. Somehow this erotic turn was connected to his concern with the loss of national character, purpose, and potency. This sense of personal and collective crisis had to be dealt with; the urgency became simply irresistible for Symons. In 1989 he recalled the decision to quit and head for Montreal, a move that he always called a *démission*, no doubt because the French word retains a sense of mission rather than simply conveying the fatality and fatigue of resignation:

> I contemplated for at least five years before I did what I did that it would have to be done. I kept waiting for other people to do it. Why should I, who was happily married, had a lovely home in Toronto, a lovely farm full of Canadian art and culture, a Curator of Canadiana, a Professor at the U. of T., a Visiting Curator at the Smithsonian, have to do it? I did not leap with any glee. There was a sense of vocation and a sense of civic action. One can laugh at it, one can praise it, but it's genuine.

Place d'Armes, published in 1967 by McClelland & Stewart and here republished by Dundurn Press, captures this precise moment in late 1965 and its break with life success, career competence, bourgeois heterosexuality, and social respectability.

It is nearly impossible and perhaps unnecessary to sum up the thirty-four years of Symons's life following his decision to leave behind his Toronto world. It is fair to say that whatever judgment posterity may have about the decision itself and about the literary work that it permitted, the "demissionary" himself lived out the full consequences of his act in the years that followed. After trying for a time to hold his marriage together in the context of his now-overt bisexuality and need for a sexual life including men, Symons broke definitively with the marriage and lived a great passion with a young man, John McConnell, who at the time of their meeting was not yet eighteen. Flight to Mexico ensued, where the lovers were pursued by the Mexican Federal Police at the instigation of their families in Toronto.

Symons liked to joke that the Canadian Honours System saved his life when he won a prize for best first novel and returned to Toronto to collect it. He was able to finish and publish *Civic Square*, begun between the writing of *Place d'Armes* and its publication.[4] This second published work was an extraordinary, unbound book-in-a-box, the Toronto counterpoint to *Place d'Armes*, again centred on a public square and seeking to deepen a sense of Canadian meanings through close attention to our built heritage.[5] An internal exile with John McConnell followed: he spent time in British Columbia in the lumber woods and embarked on a "furniture safari" that resulted in the writing of *Heritage: A Romantic Look at Canadian Furniture* in the west coast Newfoundland fishing village of Trout River.[6] Eventually, Symons's relationship with McConnell ended, and in a movement of shock and reconstruction he spent time in Mexico teaching at PEN workshops in San Miguel de Allende and eventually settled in Morocco, which he had earlier visited, almost accidentally embarking for Marrakesh rather than Mallorca on a holiday from London. From those experiences between 1970 and 1974 came the three volumes of the *Helmet of Flesh* trilogy. Only volume one has so far been published — in 1986.[7] (All of Symons's books appeared originally with McClelland & Stewart.)

In "Notes Toward a CV" in the 1998 Gutter Press anthology, *Dear Reader: Selected Scott Symons*, Symons gave a tender and compact assessment of what twenty-three years in North Africa had meant to him:

> [T]he role of Morocco in Scott's life (1971 to the present) has been large. It gave him hearth & haven. Allowing him to take his stand, hang

tough, and bear witness. Armed with fluent
French (Morocco is part of La Francophonie!)
he could live joy (much), sustain his rooted
Canadian meanings intact, and … grow. What
he loves in Morocco is their sense of dance,
music and the pipes of Pan. And their incredible smiles …

There were periodic returns to Canada, often connected to
a writing or media project ("Canada a Loving Look" — *Globe
and Mail*, 1979; "house writer" for *The Idler* in the late 1980s; et
cetera) or the launch of Nik Sheehan's film and my anthology
in 1998, but Symons remained faithful to the nourishments and
the contemplative possibilities of Morocco until forced to leave
by urgent personal circumstances in 2000. He and his Canadian
lover and partner in Moroccan life for almost twenty-five years,
Aaron Klokeid, also separated at that point.

Symons spent the last years of his life in Toronto dependent
upon the goodness of friends, the remainder of a last bequest
from his lifelong supporter and correspondent Charles Taylor,
and what little income he could earn from writing and royal-
ties. He published a few pieces in the *National Post*, worked on a
novella, *Kali's Dance*, based upon his last experiences in Morocco,
and drafted elements of a memoir, none of which were brought
through to publication. His health gradually deteriorated until,
finally, suffering from diabetic brownouts and for all intents and
purposes homeless, his dearest friend, Mary-Kay Ross, was able
to arrange for him to take up residence in Leisure World, a con-
tinuing care facility on St. George Street.

Scott had written that "I quest the right death." I recall him
saying to me in Rasoir, Morocco, looking south over the wall
behind his magnificently simple home (like that of a high Roman
official in retirement) to the brush and seemingly endless dry lands
beyond, "When it's my time, I'll take my motorcycle and see just

how far south I can go. I want to disappear into Africa. No one will ever know what happened to me."

Circumstances are our masters, as Blaise Pascal said. Symons's "sunset time" was to be spent in slow decline in Toronto rather than in an eschatological African road movie. Those of us who knew him in those last years, who visited him occasionally with sadness and trepidation in the dreadfully reduced circumstances of the euphemistic Leisure World, found him to be unfailingly gentle, engaged, unreconstructed, still himself. I will not forget his bravery on the occasion of our last lunch together.

The rest of this introductory essay was originally written before Scott Symons's passing and focuses on the achievement of *Combat Journal for Place d'Armes*.

From One *Place* to Another

New Year's Eve, 2007, Dakar. First day of a two-week stay in Senegal. I dare myself from the Novotel into the unknown avenues, leaning steeply (a very Scott word) toward La Place de l'Indépendance. The newness of the African night, the strangeness of the streets, the rush and flare of fireworks overhead, and the brief, bright volleys of sharp firecrackers underfoot all combine for an uncanny, elevated perception.

I'm thinking, too, of another *Place*, of Scott Symons's remarkable, durable, influential achievement, *Combat Journal for Place d'Armes*.

From one Place to another then, which seems oddly fitting, utterly right. *Place*, with all of the bilingual signifying power that Symons evokes and analyzes in his "novel." A place, a site, a space, spaciousness itself, spaciosity of inwardness in its conjunction with the real. An inner sanctum, *for intérieur*, inner Château, to use the language of the mystics, as Symons sometimes has. As he puts it in Day Five of *Place d'Armes*, La Place is "the inmost world" (146).

Back in my hotel room — after failing to reach La Place, driven here by pickpockets and shady followers. On with the TV, looks as if it will be an Al Jazeera kind of New Year's, but then I see it: the Church of Notre Dame on Montreal's Place d'Armes in the film *The Whole Nine Yards* with Bruce Willis and Matthew Perry, a movie about a Montreal dentist's conflict with his new neighbour, resettled American hit man Jimmy "The Tulip" Tudeski.

There it is, the very church that grounds and founds the extraordinary ecstatic Canadian novel I have in my bag, rearing up on the small screen in this African hotel room. It can't be relegated to a background, not to a mere beauty shot, not even in such a limited, competent exercise of light entertainment. To my utter amazement, La Place really is everywhere. I hear the roar that Symons sung. I did not expect it to come rushing in on Senegalese cable.

Laughing, I remind myself that my task remains the writing of something like an introduction for something cleverly disguised as a novel.

"I have come to sight La Place for others ..." (96)

Place d'Armes Today

Place d'Armes, originally published as a dissonant and dissident centennial gift to Canada from its author, a Toronto curator, professor, and journalist on the run from stifling respectability, is a classic of our literature and one that retains remarkable power to fascinate, to enervate, to confuse, to provoke, to arm and disarm the reader (who is always Dear Reader to Scott Symons).

Expressing a multi-faceted crisis of identity, *Place d'Armes* was written as it was lived in a three-week period in late 1965. It is a text born of the same sense of foreboding that gave us, at almost precisely the same moment, George Grant's *Lament for a Nation*. It may be thought of as the last will and testament of the last British

North American, a High North American Tory who knows that his culture is in stalemate and who is trying to invent forward metamorphoses for it. It is also a founding moment for gay literature in Canada and an open, utterly honest plea for liberty of sexual expression and largeness and generosity in conceptions of love and sensuality. It is a transgressive literary text that plays havoc with generic modes, mixing diary, fiction, thinly disguised autobiography, and cultural commentary. It is a work that even challenges our sense of the book as a predictable, easily definable object and the novel as a recognizable category. Yet there is a narration here, characters, and an effort to find good forms. But they are complex and imperfect forms submitted to the larger necessities of an existential quest. The book overflows with bold and exciting solutions to almost impossible representational challenges.

The overlaid voices and typefaces marking out the various modes (journal, novel, novel within the novel, parodic or documentary asides, and digressions, et cetera) are dizzying, perhaps a little bewildering. The reader must really read this text. And that is part of Symons's intentions. His "narrators" do not do everything for us but rather lead us deeper and deeper into the real and virtual city, the concrete and the symbolic *Place*. It may be said that all culminates on Day Twenty-One in a moment when the fictional creation of Hugh Anderson, Andrew Harrison, himself turns to writing a novel, the main character of which is named ... Hugh Anderson. With this move we have a kind of internal looping, a metafictional recognition of the book's complexities, a mise-en-abime of unity: Symons writing Anderson writing Harrison writing Anderson writing Symons. Day Twenty-Two, the day of the final and definitive communion scene, can only happen after the recognition of this unity and it brings all of those presences together. We might even say that it is precisely that multiplicity, that "host" that is held together, allegorically elevated and held up in monstrance at the centre of La Place in the closing orchestrations of the novel.

Two other points concerning the originality of the book are worth mentioning for readers just discovering Symons. First, *Place d'Armes* is part of a three-book sequence, a trilogy. In *Place d'Armes*, Hugh Anderson remarks upon the necessity of a diptych, a Tale of Two Cities. *Civic Square*, the Toronto novel, the book-in-a-box, hundreds of unbound pages in a mock-Birks gift box, was to follow in 1969. But the diptych, too, required fleshing out, more Body and Blood, another spatio-temporal or conceptual dimension in Symons's constant quest for enriched dimension-ality, an enhanced spaciosity that the language and atmosphere of the mid-1960s allowed him to call "4-D." *Heritage: A Romantic Look at Canadian Furniture* (1970), the third installment in the trilogy, seems like a coffee table book, a connoisseur's treatise, *un beau livre*. But it, too, practises genre-bending. Symons does not so much describe the works of early Canadian furniture-makers as intersect lovingly with their histories, their lives, their characters. It is really a furniture novel, as Irving Layton is reported to have remarked.

The status of the three books themselves as objects has also been much discussed by observers and admirers. *Place d'Armes* was published in hardback in a format that reflected the nine-teenth-century journal used by Anderson in the story, including jacket pockets containing marked-up maps, postcards, et cetera. There is a page at the end that is simply the reproduction of a notebook page with phone numbers, appointments, notes, and lists. Stan Bevington of Coach House Press designed the book and contributed immensely to its originality. In Nik Sheehan's film, *God's Fool*, Bevington reminisces about reading Symons's manuscript (delivered by his wife) and making a trip to Montreal to reconnoitre the routes of the narrator. "When I came back it was really clear that we had to put in objects, that we had to make the book an object, as discussed in the story. We had to make an object that was hard, not floppy. Through discussions with the production people at M&S there kept being obstacles so I said,

'OK, I'll do it.'" And do it he did, earning a later compliment from the ultra-demanding Symons: "Stan still thinks at finger-tips." All of this contributes to blurring the distinction between the finished volume and the process and the means of its writing and its material form. For Symons it cannot be a matter of polished, achieved, closed fiction, something has really happened to someone and something should happen to the reader. Equally, some*thing* has come into the world in that exercise of creativity and life affirmation. And that thing is no dead, remote object, but something to be touched, to be held.

It is difficult to disagree with Peter Buitenhuis's assessment in his introduction to the 1978 McClelland & Stewart paperback, that *Place d'Armes* is a supreme statement of the Canadian imagination of the 1960s. It certainly ranks alongside such other canonical English-Canadian texts as Leonard Cohen's *Beautiful Losers*, Graeme Gibson's *Five Legs*, or a little later, Robertson Davies's *Fifth Business*. And it must also be situated in relation to the most significant works of the period in French Canada, with which Symons was deeply familiar, notably *Prochain Episode* by Hubert Aquin (Robert K. Martin goes so far as to call it "almost a translation" of Aquin's book).

In its unleashed psychic and libidinal energies, its avant-gardist formal logics and hugely ambitious syncretic/synthetic aspirations, Symons's book is certainly representative of some of the decade's wider and wilder possibilities. But *Place d'Armes* is also idiosyncratic, anachronistic, sometimes reactionary, even as it participates enthusiastically in headlong literary (post)modernity. Symons's first novel and his subsequent works find their own way in a negotiation with millennial cultures and the acceleration and transitional qualities of the contemporary. In the early 1970s he remarked that "Today is very exciting, but I don't want to live in it" and asserted that "we're living between two minds today."[8] The moment to which Symons's work belongs is not narrowly contemporary.

(Parenthetically, it is interesting to note how *Place d'Armes* situates itself so explicitly in relation to other works of the 1960s highlighted in the 2005 *Literary Review of Canada*'s list of the one hundred most significant books in Canadian history.[9] "I cry too little for the sensibility" when all our intellectuals moan "too little for their minds" [55] evokes Hilda Neatby's *So Little for the Mind*. The text engages the thought of Marshall McLuhan intermittently, already taking that proper name as synonymous with reading media. *Place d'Armes* also takes note of the recent *Lament for a Nation* by George Grant [though, remarkably, the polymorphous/polyvocal narrator notes that he has not read it and does not need to]. The novel that Hugh Anderson is sketching out in the Combat Journal is referred to by one witty friend as a "minority report to the Royal Commission on Bilingualism and Biculturalism." Mocking but informed reference is made to Stephen Vizinczey's *In Praise of Older Women*. And Hubert Aquin and *Prochain Episode* are vitally present in the text through the figure of Pierre Godin, with Anderson reading his novel, *La Foire aux Puces*, and noting Godin/Aquin's suicide obsession, the liberating power of an "*assurance-vie*" consisting of a bottle of cyanide. It is fascinating to ask oneself if, in the current flowering and multiplication of Canadian writing, there might be such a strong sense of historical moment, of culture and commonly recognized stakes, if one were to examine key works of the first decade of the twenty-first century forty years hence ...)

Academic criticism of the novel (or anti-novel) has come in two waves, so to speak, with some crucial early articles focusing on questions of genre, narration, identity, and religion and a second constellation of concentrated critical interest associated with postmodern critical stances deriving insights into the text from gender and queer studies and postcolonial literary theory.[10]

Two statements will serve to condense the general tone of these interpretative moments:

These sophisticated journals remind us, as does so much recent Canadian literature, that evolution is preferred to Revolution, that what is great in the past can be adapted to give strength to the present. (Elspeth Cameron, 1977)

We would not want to lose a text as rich, as outrageous, as powerfully evocative of its time as *Place d'Armes*, but it is necessary to read it defensively, ready to take up the combat that Symons wants. Its limitations speak eloquently to the problem of writing the other, of speaking from a position of privilege while seeking to efface it, and of the ways in which a jouissance that seeks to undo the (cultural) text may end up simply rewriting it. (Robert K. Martin, 1994)

Each generation of critics, while arguing for strengths and weaknesses of the book, seeks to recuperate the difficult-to-contain text and maintain it in a positive relation to essential and diverse contemporary critical or ethico-critical perspectives. For Cameron it is the secret continuities between the contemporary manipulation of the diary, the production of a radical Combat Journal, and the many earlier historical manifestations of journals in Canadian culture. For Martin it is the desire to maintain a powerful text of transgression, resistance, and pleasure in spite of certain of its apparently politically distasteful aspects.

While each of these clusters of articles provides rich insight into the textuality, genericity, ideological underpinnings, cultural meanings, and consequences of the text, sometimes the singularity of the text eludes the interpretative models imposed upon it. To wit:

Terry Goldie: "*Place d'Armes* only reacclaims the misogyny of Tory heterosexism in a Tory homosexualism."

Robert K. Martin: "One problem with Symons's project is that it amounts to a kind of literary blackface, the performance of sexual or racial identity."

Such statements seem to this reader demonstrably false, over-determined by their theoretical starting points, and necessarily reductive of texts that are infinitely more subtle and idiosyncratic than these reductions allow. But this is not the place to make an extensive demonstration or counter-argument.

By way of further introduction, let us consider just a few ways into *Place d'Armes*, a few avenues traced by Symons into the allegorical Place. The way is fraught with obstacles, but the obstacles also provide the way forward. With Hugh Anderson in the Rapido train, on the Day Before One, we are held trembling at a threshold: "unwilling to resolve the contradictions already becoming apparent" (45).

Passionate Impasse

Impasse. The word and the phenomenon haunt the quest of Symons-Anderson-Harrison. He is constantly faced with and sometimes briefly tempted by the "instant security of stalemate ... the security of impasse" (235–36). In the early going, when Hugh is on the Rapido train en route from Toronto to Montreal, his first unsatisfying encounters with his fellow citizens leave him with the feeling that all that can be attained in his urgent but as yet undefined "sensibility probe" is a kind of "improved impasse" (60), with Canadian decorum serving as an obstruction to feeling, an excuse for the avoidance of life. (Hence also the provocative opening disclaimer, "any resemblance to people dead or really alive is pure coincidence"). But Symons's whole work rebels against the risk of "consecrated impasse" (174).

By the end of the exhaustive and exhausting writing out of the adventure, such impasse has metamorphosed, multiplied, opened up, become "Holy Impasse" (384) and at the precise moment where failure seems most likely, a successful breakthrough into realms of enhanced consciousness occurs. This is a paradoxical exit with no exit. An empassioning aporia, to speak like the Jacques Derrida of *Demeure*, where he analyzes the paradoxical death/non-death by firing squad of Maurice Blanchot in the latter's *At the Instant of My Death*.[11]

Importantly, Symons himself is fascinated by the need for such enhanced passion and by the limited resources of the English language to convey it. In an act of translation that is cultural and spiritual more than it is narrowly linguistic, he considers the French *passionnant*: "there is no expression in English like c'est passionnant — literally it is empassioning" (282).

The work of Scott Symons is empassioned and empassioning or it is nothing. And it derives its passion from the experience and transformation of impasse.

A Text of Resistance

Place d'Armes must be read and experienced as a text of resistance: the book ferociously resists all forms of reductive, identitary thinking. It seeks to preserve sentience, lucidity, the articulation of education and sensibility as against the homogenizing tendencies of our time. It attacks official culture in its various guises, and in particular the obsession with the Canadian identity and its careerist "mechanisms." The intersecting discourses of media/advertising/tourism/business are called into question from the opening pages of the book in a Radical Tory critique of the incipient formations of what we might call today late or information age–capitalism. Symons has an undoubted, instinctive respect for institutions but abhors what large corporate structures, be they private, like the "Mommy Bank," or public, like the federal civil service, can do to a person's openness to life. As he puts it in his brief biography at the end of the volume: "*Status*: A Para-Canadian, released from any allegiance to the Canadian State but obsessively devoted to the Canadian nation." He is concerned with the "man," the human being and the human consequences of accepting such restrictive modes of consciousness and expression, the effects of surrender to the "world of memo" and "mere competence."

It is surely no accident that the "novel" begins with a flat imitation of a tourist blurb about historic Place d'Armes. Symons's initial narrator, Hugh Anderson, is appalled at the ease with which he is able to produce this competent but empty approach to La Place. The false distance that it implies is precisely that reduction of the human to an alienated consumer, of a culture to its merely cultural effects, a reduction that Symons will combat in this book and in all of his published and unpublished work. He knows that the risk of failure is high, as is that of ridicule, but he must try.

> "Que veux-tu? It's my last chance ... my own
> people have put our cultures into national com-
> mittee. They have deliberately killed any danger
> of a positive personal response." (100)

The resistance of the "demissionary" is precisely the existential affirmation of a positive personal response.

Twenty-five years after the resignation from Toronto respectability, the *démission* that became a life mission, Symons recalled the choice in these terms:

> The choice risked my life because it risked my
> sanity. I knew that this was where one had to
> move, to open the doors to male sentience. T.S.
> Eliot said that if he hadn't pursued the path he
> did — a very dry life — he would have gone

22

in the direction of Durrell's *Black Book*. I'd read that before I jumped. At the same time, women's lib was just beginning to explode. I couldn't go to another woman because I already had the woman of my choice. I have always found it odd that I am considered the black wolf of CanLit. I'm a very conservative guy who went to Easter Mass at Saint Thomas's. I'm a quiet person and in many ways timid. I was brought up with a deep sense of civic participation and commitment.[12]

Defence and Illustration

Place d'Armes and all of Symons's published work seeks a language adequate to the kind of heightened experience upon which he gambles all. Symons's language is enlivening, empassioning, neologizing, inventive, sensitive to the evolution of English, forward-looking in its assumed heritage of the freedom of the modern avant-gardes, but rooted in place and in history, and, of supreme importance, in a constant rapport of translation with its nearest other, French.

Some of the strategies utilized by Symons include alliterative punning (e.g., "the Nicean niceties"); discombobulating prefixes (e.g., *impatriate* for *expatriate*); transforming proper names into verbs (e.g., he Michelangeled me); the development of new compound nouns frequently to describe the kind of radical sensorial/emotive/conceptual shifts he intuits (e.g., *umbilink, cocktit, assoul, manscape*); the development of signifying and significant identity abbreviations that can be reused in the novel (e.g., ECM, Emancipated Canadian Methodist).

Aural punning on homonyms is also a favourite tactic of Scott Symons who frequently underlines the difference (or differance) of writing and orality. *Phallacy* is one particularly nice find, pointing as it does to a critique of phallocentrism in a writer sometimes accused of "hypervirility" or even "misogyny." For Symons the male sexual organ is at the centre of the "perceptor set" joining self and world, but it is always, like so much else in this work, set off, relativized, in relation to inner, spiritual connections. And to the truths of language speaking itself. *Phallacy* argues gently against the risks of the narrowly phallic, the too-literally male, the vainly cock-focused.

> Carnal joy, joy incarnate, then isn't joy made by
> carnal manipulation, by mere phallacy ... it is
> a rejoicing at the world I already know ... it is
> quite simply the perception of that world, at any
> moment, eternally. Eternity intersects time at
> the moment, that ...; the moment that you see
> — really see. And makejoy is killjoy. Phallicity is
> fallen ... (267)

At times such punning, neologizing play might seem emptily clever, willfully mechanical or forced, but as Elspeth Cameron has pointed out, "The word play in *Place d'Armes* ... is not mere sophistry. As in Joyce, it is part of the breakdown of fixed forms which recreates the cosmic flux of experience." The moments of maximal linguistic extension and uninhibited inventivity occur at points when the Communion vision, the slipping into 4-D, seems to be at hand (though we must note that the final experience of the work is that of ellipsis, the spent and holy silence of the blank page).

Much of Symons's writing confronts the mysteries of mystical participation in the universe. Examples of sensory shift, even of synesthesia, when one mode of sensory apprehension overlays or replaces another, abound. Some crucial moments occur in the Church when the candles, on various visits, confront Hugh-Andrew-Scott with their roaring. At one point this extends to a

total vision: "The sight of their sound was heaven" (246). This is
an impossible representation, yet one that Symons will repeatedly
endeavour to have his readers experience, sublime failure after
sublime failure.

When Symons refers to himself as a "Canadian de langue
française" (96), he not only establishes a relation to French Canada
that is non-appropriative, respectful of its difference, and respectful of the ground of its attainments, but he cunningly-punningly
situates his artistic project at the intersection of two languages
and indirectly asserts a cultural entitlement to that Other. In particular Symons will push the boundaries of English to capture the
lived consequences, the pull, the feel of quintessentially French
structures, particularly reflexive verbs, creating not-quite-correct
pronominal structures like "I seat me" or "I write me" or "It sufficed him" (394). The relation between self and world is thereby
underlined, rendered slightly strange, heightened or exacerbated;
it is part of the opening that *Place d'Armes* enacts: "I am living me in French, *being* lived in French," he exclaims revealingly
at one point, yet he is "writing me in English" (285). Much of
the singular force of the language in this work derives from this
simultaneous existential translation.

Communion

> I would say that anyone who sat down with my
> three books could have no doubts at the end of
> the three as to what it was I was going through.
> Anybody could see that I was negotiating my
> way through a series of secular experiences —
> of blatantly secular experiences — and trying,
> through them, to find the spiritual. I was try-
> ing to find sacramental reality. And my effort —
> again this is where I'm not a writer — my effort

is not to explain these experiences to the reader,
but rather to put the reader through them.[13]

Symons, through the adventure and the proof of his text, aspires to a quasi-sacramental yet heterodox incarnacy, the Real Presence of Catholic theology passed through very radical modern freedom. He seeks to *make revelation of profanation after having made profanation of revelation*, in a useful turn of phrase belonging to French poet Michel Deguy.[14] "He thought again of the Communion. That was the verity ... of Body and Blood. It was inevitable if not yet completely achieved." (385)

Communion takes many forms in the work, and the economy of ingestion, swallowing, digestion, assimilation, and transformation is operative in everything from lunch dates to fellatio to the close observation of furniture and buildings. "You eat the site till it is inside you, then you are inside it, and your relationship is no longer one of juxtaposition ... but an unending series of internalities. It's like looking at mirrors in mirrors ... or rather crystal balls in crystal balls. That's my job now ... to reinsite the world I've nearly lost." (126) *The swallower swallowed* would not be a bad subtitle for the work as a whole. "Eschew the historic plaques. Eat the building." (140)

In the ecstatic yet dominated orchestration of conclusion, Holy Impasse has become procreative impasse, a substantial transformation, the breakthrough to "4-D," a swallowing that is a swallowing up, total communion. The swirling, poetic evocations of Day Twenty-Two have been read in strikingly divergent ways by critics, but whatever the dominant images might be, the logics of porosity, vulnerability, penetrability, ingestion, and violability are operating at full capacity by this point:

no longer was there any question of details, of
itemization ... all that had gone now ... he was
confounded, in utter conjugation with the body

of the Church — it was militant in him. He
turned — and staggered out ... the Place d'Armes
was outrageously alive in him ... (395–96)

Conclusion:
"You Hate Them Almost as Much as You Love Them"

There are scenes of *Place d'Armes* where "the monster from Toronto"
— as Robert Fulford called Hugh Anderson (and by extension Scott
Symons) in an infamous and damaging review — comes to the surface, notably in the interactions with Rick Appleton, who functions
as a scapegoat for sellout, almost an evil twin, the enemy or at least a
frère ennemi. One cannot deny or downplay the anger and the spleen
in the Anderson-Harrison-Symons complex. But the deep meaning of *Place d'Armes* is a hating through to love, another reinvention
of impasse: "art is love — even an art of hate is love — the optimum
of despair — creating despair in hope of hope" (361).

"'You hate them almost as much as you love them ...'" remarks
a perceptive antiques dealer as she observes Hugh Anderson
devouring and demolishing the English-Canadian customers passing through her store (116). What terrifies and enrages
Anderson is a deadening of sensibility, an increasingly abstract,
technified relation to life, a growing corporatization of society, a
diminishment of honour in relation to career, increasing greed,
creeping amnesia, reduction of potency, smothering of spirituality.
Yet Symons the culture critic is always secondary to Symons the
joyful participant in life. The efforts of the Combat Journal pay
off, in the end. They allow for the transcendence that joy affords
and a true sighting of the richness of the fabric of what is given
in the literal and allegorical City:

I realize that what has been restored to me these
past days is my self-respect. I have gone through

Hell for Heaven's sake ... and found my human
dignity. Bless Meighen's eyes, bless the chalice,
bless the Mother Bank and the Great White
Elephant and the Flesh Market and the Sphinxes
Large and Lesser and the Wedding Cake and the
Greyway and the Front and Holyrood. (368–69)

Symons's text is finally just that, a restoration: last words and
blessing for his cherished, unknown readers, a figural return to
an inner place that can never be fully grasped but which is always
real, immanent in all of life's moments. The final image of the text,
an outstretched finger bursting with life and blood points there.

Place d'Armes is an act and a gift of love. It is a masterpiece
in contemporary composer Pierre Boulez's terms, "something
unexpected which has become a necessity." One that new readers will gratefully receive in this timely new edition.

Notes

1. Unless otherwise indicated, all parenthetical page references
   are to this edition of *Place d'Armes*.

2. Tim Wilson interviewed Scott Symons in Essaouira, Morocco,
   in June 1997 for Vision TV. He was kind enough to provide
   me with the unedited footage of this interview from which
   I have extracted this phrase.

3. In this biographical sketch I make use of the following sources:
   Charles Taylor, Scott Symons chapter in *Six Journeys: A
   Canadian Pattern* (Toronto: House of Anansi Press, 1977, 191–
   243); Scott Symons interviews in *The Idler* No. 23 (May/June
   1989) and No. 36 (July/August 1992); "Notes Toward a CV"

in *Dear Reader: Selected Scott Symons*, edited by Christopher Elson (Toronto: Gutter Press, 1998), 309–14, and "The Long Walk," *ibid.*, 303–08; various interviews conducted with Christopher Elson in 1995 in Essaouira, Morocco; unpublished texts, diaries, and drafts.

4. *Civic Square*, the "book-in-a-box," is the second part of what Scott Symons always referred to as his Tale of Two Cities. Picking up from the formal liberties and material inventivity of *Place d'Armes*, in certain respects it is the most singular of his published works. An unbound book counting in the hundreds of pages, contained within a parodic simulacrum of a blue Birks gift box, every copy was personally signed by Symons and decorated with his trademark flying phalli, an illustration of the movement of Eros. The work connects the High Tory spirit of Rosedale with the emergent hippie spirit of Yorkville and gives us a multifaceted "Torontario." Symons left a copy in the collection plate of St Thomas's Anglican Church in memory of his father Harry Symons. In this book there are many episodes, investigations of sites ranging from Nathan Phillips Square to Mosport Park, from the Blythe Folly Farm in Claremont to Chestnut Park Street in Rosedale to the Toronto Art Gallery's "Op-Pop" Ball. In the 1997 documentary *God's Fool*, painter David Bolduc and curator Dennis Reid speak with intense fondness of *Civic Square*'s ability to draw together "urban ferment" and "rural transcendence." It contains a plethora of lyrical quasi-poems and didactic asides, mini-essays, rants, pseudo-prayers, as well as a polemical history of English literature, a celebration of dappled Country Canada, an ode to cocks (and cunts), a Canada prayer in the mode of an Our Father, intense typologies of Canadian personalities, descriptions of birdlife, the "yella-fellahs," yellow warblers, and much else. Throughout Symons holds nothing of his linguistic playfulness back. One

passage builds to an expression that the author begged the publisher to allow him as title — The Smugly Fucklings.

5. The main character of *Place d'Armes* is in a very deep way the square itself — *La Place*, in Scott Symons's intensely personal usage. The historic public square located in Old Montreal and bounded by Notre-Dame Ouest, St-Jacques Ouest, St-François Xavier, and Saint-Sulpice streets is the site of a range of architectural and monumental forms ranging from Georgian-Palladian to Neo-Gothic, from Art-Deco to High Modernist. A nineteenth-century sculpture by Louis-Philippe Hébert of Sieur de Maisonneuve, situated in the centre of the square, harkens back to the earliest moments of the settlement, Ville-Marie, and the epic character of the establishment and defence of the seventeenth-century colony.

    Harold Kalman's *A History of Canadian Architecture* (Toronto: Oxford University Press, 1994) mentions Place d'Armes in several places. It was the site of the first Bank of Montreal headquarters constructed in 1818–19, and with each addition to the bank's properties, innovative and nationally important approaches were taken. Kalman also gives a fascinating account of how Notre Dame, "the most important landmark in the early Gothic Revival," emerged from the competition among parishes and the desire of the Sulpicians to make a major statement by bringing in a foreign architect (James O'Donnell, a New York Irish Protestant!). Kalman's text provides in a very condensed form some of the same factual, historical information dispersed throughout Symons's more lyrical text and puts Place d'Armes at the centre of Canadian architectural evolution.

    In her foreword to *Montreal Metropolis 1880–1930*, eds. Isabelle Gournay and France Vanlaethem (Montreal/Toronto: Canadian Centre for Architecture/Stoddart Publishing, 1998), Phyllis Lambert, founder and director of the Canadian Centre for Architecture, underlines this "initial duality of religion and commerce" (6). She plays off the very different Place d'Armes and Dominion Square as capacious and generous sites of some of Montreal's necessary cultural and urbanistic accommodations: "The architecture of eighteenth- and nineteenth-century Place d'Armes and nineteenth- and twentieth-century Dominion Square is paradigmatic of Montreal, a city accustomed to change and to accommodating opposing values, able both to absorb the shock of the new and to create the variety of urban structures and infrastructures called for by the twentieth century." (7)

A small pamphlet in the Quebec National Library, apparently self-published in 1968 by philosopher and theologian Michel Bougier, emphasizes the Catholic and French-Canadian elements of the square, including the importance of the International style Banque canadienne nationale building by architectural firm David et Boulva. But it is in considering the church that Bougier is at his most eloquent: "It is sweet and good to find oneself, on some wintry afternoon, in the grand, nearly deserted vessel. Its sombre and contemplative atmosphere encourages one to reflection, to just desires, to good will." Symons's apocalyptic communion must be set against this rather tamer vision of spiritual life.

Finally, perhaps the best single source of information and inspiration relative to Place d'Armes may be found in a text by Maryse Leduc, architect, which accompanies the book of cut-outs of buildings in the square prepared for Héritage Montréal by Conception-EditionsARC and available for purchase online at *www.copticarchitecture.com/a.htm*. Leduc bridges the competence of the architectural historian and the excitement of the urban dweller who finds herself enlivened by the "event" of this phenomenal ensemble of buildings. "At once both contemporary and classic, the square is truly an urban event, a place that enhances the buildings that enclose it. It is a pleasure for the eyes, inviting them to discover there a detail ornamenting a doorway or the grand interiors [*sic*] spaces that extand [*sic*] the square. The views and vistas that the square offers are each as impressive as the other, forming both tableaux and individual landmarks in the city." (2) With its emphasis on the informed pleasure of seeing, on the conjugation, as Symons might have said, of interior spaces with the urban landscape, Leduc is very close to Symons's perception of the "insite" of the sight.

Other sources for those interested in Place d'Armes include Marc Choko, *Les grandes places publiques de Montréal* (Montreal: Editions du Méridien, 1990); Madeleine Forget, *Les gratte-ciel de Montréal* (Montreal: Editions du Méridien, 1990); and Monique Larue with Jean-François Chessay, *Promenades littéraires dans Montréal* (Montreal: Québec-Amérique, 1989).

6. *Heritage: A Romantic Look at Early Canadian Furniture* (McClelland & Stewart, 1971; republished in the United States with the New York Graphic Society), with photographs by the still-prolific John Visser, completed the first trilogy. The book is an anatomy of furniture, a "furniture novel," as Irving Layton is reported to have said. Leonard Cohen told Scott that he had done something very clever, producing a "hand grenade disguised as a coffee table book." The volume's long concluding essay, "Ave Atque Vale" ("Hail and Farewell"), is an account of the "furniture Safari" from southwestern Ontario to St. John's, Newfoundland, taken by Symons and his lover in 1970. It evokes landscape, old, rooted Canada, the personalities and places associated with the most significant finds of Canadiana. Furniture is faith, Symons repeats again and again. The philosopher George Grant wrote the preface to "this splendid book" and noted that in it "Symons shows us consummately that the furniture of any time or place cannot be understood as a set of objects, but rather as things

touched, seen, used, loved, in short, simply lived with through the myriad events which are the lives of individuals, of families, of communities, of peoples." Who else but Scott Symons, reminiscing about a French-Canadian armchair, a *chaise à la capucine*, could persuasively argue, in the midst of intense connoisseurship and curatorial precision, that contact with such a chair constituted a breach of his marriage? "That was in 1959 — my core attained. My smug opacity ended."

7. *Helmet of Flesh* (McClelland & Stewart, 1986; also published in New American Library in hardback and paperback editions) owes its existence to the editing of Dennis Lee, who helped bring the thousands of pages of draft into something resembling a coherent whole. *Helmet I* describes the arrival in Morocco of Symons's alter ego York MacKenzie and a series of wild misadventures which ensue. There is a trip into the High Atlas with a band of misfit Englishmen that cannot end well. Constantly present in the overwhelming Moroccan setting, through flashbacks, letters, and photographs, however, are Osprey Cove, Newfoundland, and London, England. Simone Weil is a tutelary presence here with her spirituality of extreme attention, as she is in the still-unpublished installments of the second trilogy. There are remarkable set pieces in which Moroccan realities challenge and transform the sensibility of the main character, particularly through the experience and reading of carpets, the uncanny attractiveness of Moroccan music, and some crowd scenes in the Medina of a rare descriptive power. It is to be hoped that someday *Waterwalker* and *Dracula-in-Drag* may also be published.

It is important to note that Michel Gaulin has translated *Helmet of Flesh* into French as *Marrakech* (Québec-Amérique, 1997) and that his translation of *Place d'Armes* was published in the fall of 2009 with Montreal's XYZ

Éditeur. The French translation of *Helmet of Flesh* received some excellent reviews.

Excerpts from the unpublished volumes may be found in Christopher Elson, ed., *Dear Reader: Selected Scott Symons* (Toronto: Gutter Press, 1998).

8. *Eleven Canadian Novelists*, interviews with Graeme Gibson (Toronto: House of Anansi Press, 1973), 310.

9. *Literary Review of Canada*, November 2005.

10. In the first group: Elspeth Cameron, "Journey to the Interior: The Journal Form in Scott Symons' *Place d'Armes*" (*Studies in Canadian Literature*, Summer 1977); Peter Briggs, "Insite: Place d'Armes" (*Canadian Literature*, Summer 1977). In the second: Terry Goldie, "The Man of the Land, the Land of the Man: Patrick White and Scott Symons (*Journal of the South Pacific Association for Commonwealth Literature and Language Studies*, Fall 1993); Robert K. Martin, "Cheap Tricks in Montreal: Scott Symons' *Place d'Armes* (*Essays on Canadian Writing*, Winter 1994); George Piggford, "'A National Enema': Identity and Metafiction in Scott Symons's *Place d'Armes*" (*English Studies in Canada*, March 1998); Peter Dickinson, *Here Is Queer: Nationalism, Sexualities and the Literature of Canada* (Toronto: University of Toronto Press, 1999).

11. Jacques Derrida, *Demeure: Fiction and Testimony* (Stanford, CA: Stanford University Press, 2000).

12. Interview in *The Idler*, No.23, May/June 1989, 29.

13. *Eleven Canadian Novelists*, 317.

14. Michel Deguy, *Arrêts fréquents* (Marseille: Métailié, 1991).

INTRODUCTION

Selected Biographical Sources

Gibson, Graeme. *Eleven Canadian Novelists*. Toronto: House of Anansi Press, 1973.

The Idler. Interviews with editors. "The Decade of the Last Chance," No. 23, May/June 1989. "Deliquescence in Canada," No. 36, July/August 1992.

Symons, Scott. "The Long Walk" in *Dear Reader: Selected Scott Symons*. Toronto: Gutter Press, 1998.

_____. "Notes Toward a CV by Scott Symons" in *Dear Reader: Selected Scott Symons*.

_____. "Rosedale Ain't What It Used to Be." *Toronto Life*, October 1972.

_____. "The Seventh Journey (A Last Letter to Charles Taylor)." *Toronto Life*, September 1997.

Taylor, Charles. *Six Journeys: A Canadian Pattern* (Toronto: House of Anansi Press, 1977).

Selected Critical Sources

Briggs, Peter. "Insite: Place d'Armes." *Canadian Literature*, Summer 1977.

Buitenhuis, Peter. Introduction. *Place d'Armes* (Toronto: McClelland & Stewart paperback edition, 1977).

_____. "Scott Symons and the Strange Case of *Helmet of Flesh*" in *The West Coast Review*, Vol. 21, No. 4, Spring 1987.

_____."Scott Symons" entry in *The Oxford Companion to Canadian Literature*. Toronto: Oxford University Press, 1997.

Cameron, Elspeth. "Journey to the Interior: The Journal Form in Scott Symons' *Place d'Armes.*" *Studies in Canadian Literature*, Summer 1977.

Dickinson, Peter. *Here Is Queer: Nationalism, Sexualities and the Literature of Canada.* Toronto: University of Toronto Press, 1999.

Elson, Christopher. "Mourning and Ecstasy: Scott Symons' Canadian Apocalypse" in *Dear Reader: Selected Scott Symons.* Toronto: Gutter Press, 1998.

Goldie, Terry. "The Man of the Land, the Land of the Man: Patrick White and Scott Symons." *Journal of the South Pacific Association for Commonwealth Literature and Language Studies*, Fall 1993.

_____. *Pink Snow: Homotextual Possibilities in Canadian Fiction.* Toronto: Broadview Press, 2003.

Martin, Robert K. "Cheap Tricks in Montreal: Scott Symons' *Place d'Armes.*" *Essays on Canadian Writing*, Winter 1994.

Piggford, George. "'A National Enema': Identity and Metafiction in Scott Symons's *Place d'Armes.*" *English Studies in Canada*, March 1998.

Young, Ian. "A Whiff of the Monster: Encounters with Scott Symons," *Canadian Notes & Queries*, No. 77, Summer/Fall 2009.

COMBAT JOURNAL FOR
PLACE D'ARMES

any resemblance to persons dead,
or really alive, is pure coincidence

To T.W. and J.S.
   without whose love
this book would not have
      been possible

And to all those who have
made this book necessary

Stranger, reconquer the source
                    of feeling
For an anxious people's sake

From NIMBUS, by Douglas Le Pan

Basilique Notre-Dame in Montreal's Place d'Armes.

THE DAY BEFORE ONE

"La Place d'Armes is the heart of Montreal, metropolis of Canada. No visitor to the city can afford to miss this remarkable square where the modern and the historic meet in splendour and harmony. Walk out to the centre of La Place — and stand under the great statue to Maisonneuve, founder of the city, in 1642. On the north side of La Place stands the Head Office of the Bank of Montreal ... popularly known as 'My Bank' to over two million Canadians. On the west side is the Head Office of the Banque Canadienne nationale. The largest financial institutions of English and French Canada respectively: side by side, tower by tower. Yet facing these two ultramodern skyscrapers, on the south side of the square, sits the Presbytery and Church of Notre Dame. This Church is traditionally known simply as "The Parish," the pride of the Sulpician Order who once held all Montreal in fief. The rough stone Presbytery dates from the days of Louis XIV, while the Church, which was completed by 1830, is the earliest example of the Gothic Revival Style in Canada. It is considered one of the finest in America. The lavish interior of the Church, copied from La Sainte Chapelle in Paris, is one of the sights of the city. It is appropriate that the Church is faced not only by the modern Bank of Montreal tower, but also by the old Bank building with its classic pediment and dome, dating from 1847. To the east the square is fitly completed by two handsome stone skyscrapers; the Providence Life Building which will remind you of New York in the Roaring Twenties, and beside it an excellent example of the famed brownstone architecture of the High Victorian Period.

In effect La Place d'Armes is a summary of the entire city. Because to the north and west of it rises the mountain with its new city of commerce and cultures. The Queen Elizabeth Hotel, the most up-to-date in Canada; La Place Ville Marie, the largest shopping and office complex in the nation; and La Place des Arts, symbol of the vibrant artistic life born of the meeting of French and English civilizations in the New World — these are only a few blocks away. While to the south and east of the square lie the great international harbour of Montreal, and the historic Old Quarter, with its unique ensemble of Georgian stone buildings. If you want to wander these curving streets, in a matter of minutes you will be in la rue St. Paul with its modern boutiques and art stores, its antique shops, with the magnificent Georgian Bonsecours Market, once the Parliament of Canada, and Notre Dame de Bonsecours Church dating from the eighteenth century. Fine restaurants will cater to the appetite your stroll whets. Afterwards you can visit the French Baroque City Hall, or the Chateau de Ramezay Museum, once home of the Governors of Montreal; see the first monument in the world to Nelson, or wander along St. James Street, and enjoy the great Victorian palaces of commerce. Don't forget to stroll down to the harbour (only one block south from St. Paul Street) to the great grain elevators and freightyards. To the west stands the Harbour Commission Building, a handsome Victorian fantasy, to the east the Jacques Cartier bridge, while just out of sight is the Ile Ste-Hélène, site of Canada's International Exhibition — Expo 67.

La Place d'Armes — heart of Montreal, old and new. La Place d'Armes — heart of Canada!"

Thus Hugh Anderson tried to imagine how a tourist blurb of La Place d'Armes might read. He sketched it out in full — and then gave up; it revulsed him. Partly because he couldn't really bring himself to do it well, and partly because he could imagine it only too well. He decided to concentrate instead upon his own memory of La Place d'Armes ... trying to recall it as he had known it during the four years he had worked within a block of it, on St. James Street. He remembered the domed Bank of Montreal Building well. Then he had to admit he had never been in it. No, he reflected, not once ... only in the new section. It was virtually the same for the Church of Notre Dame. It had always stood there, as some magnificent Gothic scenario — a fine backdrop for prestige office buildings. Like having the façade from Westminster Abbey, or Notre Dame de Paris, dropped into La Place as guarantee of quality: Episcopal Approval — an Imprimatur for La Place. But he had never been in it ... oh he had visited in it — once, maybe twice — and he always told friends who were visiting Montreal that it was a "must." But he himself had never been to a service there. He had meant to go that Christmas, to the Midnight Mass ..., but he had gone skiing instead. Odious recollection ... (besides — the snow went soft). And he couldn't remember anything precise about the Church inside, save that sensation of Olde Golde everywhere ... the Sainte Chapelle bloated beyond belief. As to the rest — well, the new buildings of the New Montreal hadn't been built: La Banque provinciale, La Place Ville Marie, La Place des Arts. He had only heard about them. And he had to admit that he never, not once!, strolled the Old Quarter. Oh, he had visited the Chateau de Ramezay once by accident; it was a hailstorm. As for the rest ... he really only knew about them through history textbooks, by implication.

With that he stopped, acutely self-conscious, embarrassed ... turned around to see if anyone was looking at him, at his smug self-assertive ignorance.

No one was looking. He laughed small consolation: how the hell could anyone see what he was thinking anyway? His guilt was a private matter. But he had to face the truth: all he really knew about La Place d'Armes and its entourage was what he could have put into a bad tourist blurb. He was victim of the very thing he mocked! To save further discomfit he turned his mind to the job at hand, unwilling to resolve the contradictions already becoming apparent.

The assignment he decided in fact was simple: a short novel on La Place d'Armes in Montreal. He knew exactly what it was that he wanted to do with it. Namely present La Place as a centre of life and vitality in the Montreal metropolis. It was La Place that would, of course, be the Hero. Of that he was certain ... the novel would grow out of that fact. All he had to do was live La Place and he would end with what he needed — a novel that glowed with love, with his own love of his community, his nation, his people. A novel that glowed with love in a world whose final and last faith seemed grounded in hate. He wanted to share that love, and to show that only by that love do people live, really live. With any luck the essential experience would be achieved in a fortnight, perhaps less. In either case he would be home by Christmas. He planned to arrive in Montreal on December the first.

He thought again of La Place ... yes, it was ideal: a historic square, perhaps the most historic in North America, or in the New World for that matter. Three-and-a-half centuries of history ending in 1967 as the heart of a giant empire — Canada — and the site of the first International Exhibition that had ever received world sanction in the New World. No — decidedly there was no other square to equal it ... and he counted off the competitors — Boston, Boston Common, the Liberty Route, the birth of the American Dream and all that. Well, Boston had gone dead. And so had the Amurrican Dream for that matter — (his facile inherited contempt of the Americans — the mere Americans — was all contained in that slurred pronunciation "Amurrican") Or New York — Times Square, for example. Centre of the World. What about that? Somehow it didn't do. It didn't have a heart, or a soul, or something ... something was wrongside-up about it. If nothing else his novel would prove that, by contrast. That left Philadelphia — which had been displaced by New York — and Washington. Same argument all over again for these then. And for Chicago, the Second City. Or San Francisco — excellent also-ran. What about Mexico City? Surely it was a contender. Well he didn't know Mexico City — so it was easy to rule out. That left only his own city, Toronto, with its claim to be the "fastest growing city in North America." Which meant the fastest growing "white city" in the world. Perhaps that was what was *wrong* with Toronto!

Nor could he find any heart to Toronto ... no central Place ... unless one took the new City Hall and its monolithic Phillips Square. Anyway,

La Place d'Armes had a two-century headstart on that … and any sense of dimension in time in Toronto was about to be extinguished by the destruction of the Old City Hall which gave all the conviction and perspective to the New — torn down to make room for a department store. Well *that* told the whole story. He grimaced. No, it was Montreal's Place d'Armes all the way. He felt relieved, and settled back in his seat aboard the Rapido — "fastest commuter train in the world … 360 miles in 4 hrs. and 59 minutes!" For a moment his own smugness conjugated with this triumphant smugness of the train and taking out his little black notebook he began to make his Novel Notes — some for the Novel, but some for himself. The latter would, naturally, be the best — after all he wouldn't be able to present the complete truth in the Novel. So it was important to have complete notes for his own private edification. A kind of private revenge against the restrictions of the Novel itself — a sort of intimacy. The intimate privilege of the first person.

"… *spent the weekend skiing — a sort of final outing before Montreal. Left Mary & the two children to return with friends to Toronto. She is in good spirits & can handle the home easily enough till I'm back…. It all makes good sense. Ran into Jackson on the daytrain from Collingwood … haven't seen him for two years. We exchanged supercilities last time — each politely contemptuous of the other — he of my publishing house respectability; I of his success in the mass media — a televisionary … mass mediocrity! Now we sat together like old buddies, confessing our faults … the vacuity of the media (Toynbee is right — TV is "the lion that whimpered!") & the constipation of the business world. As though each of us had seen through ourselves in these last two years. And come out divested — & afraid. Things have changed. Everything has changed — absolutely. The very nature of reality has changed. Maybe that's why I let Jackson quiz me overtly…. Jackson — "well, you're a square in revolt. We're all squares in this country … I'm a square. But I still don't understand you.*
You didn't need to get fired. Your training was unique.
Experience with that Montreal publishing firm. A book of excellent

critical essays on Canadian culture. A Governor General's award. A powerful family name, a beautiful wife — & you say, two kids. Bilingual. & an appointment at the University of Toronto for special lectures. You were made, man. & we needed you. You didn't need to capitulate...."

I laugh, and remember his public criticism of my essays.

"I can't explain it. But I know what I'm doing. I simply know I had to demission — had to leave. I suppose it was the very fact that I felt I was a 'made man' — that all I had to do was become president of my company, & then die ... or rather die, & then become president of the company. But much more important than that is the feeling that I've been unmade ... that the events of the past few years in Canada have been systematically destroying me, my culture. I have slowly been eliminated — all my faiths.... Take the new flag (one floats by out the train window) — that is as good a symbol as any of the dissolution I feel. Every time I look at that frigging Maple Leaf I dissolve. I simply cease to exist. It's not a question of patriotism — my family's been tangled up with the New World for over two centuries now. It's a question of reality. Take just the visual fact of the flag. It's a non-flag.... I can't explain it."

And then they were at the Toronto Union Station. Jackson was gone ... wishing him well. He was perplexed by their conversation — the complete frankness of it. It made him uneasy. Not because it was frank, but because it implied more to the novel than the novel he had planned. But he didn't realize that yet.

He appraised the station ... a splendid thermal bath. It was in the best style of the period: monumental Roman Classic. And at the same time he regretted its predecessor for which his grandfather had been an architect ... it had been that brownstone Romanesque that Richardson had made famous — full of rough brawn. And inside the station he flinched at the juxtaposition of this muted thermal bath style, like some great banking house, and the constrained jazz of the new billboardings now around the wall. — The ads were representative, he mused, of the new Toronto: a pair of TV personalities "invited" you flagrantly to "Listen Here" — standing at ease in their red waistcoats and their glasses that made them look relaxed middle-class intelligent. Respectable hicks he decided. Or high-class jerks. It didn't much matter. In either case they didn't belong in the station. Not in *this* station, *his* station. Which meant that one day the station would be pulled down. But he didn't dare admit that either. Another billboard boasted the "brightest paper in town" that it boosted. Beside it a forty-foot guarantee of medical insurance. Lastly a cigarette sanctioned by a wholesome lass in tartan. Yes — it was a good cross-section of Toronto-town. Add only the stationwagon perched comfortably over the stairwell — "Canadian built — for quality," and you had the complete picture. The only difference between the Canadian and American stationwagon being that the Canadian had less chrome and cost more. All of this, and the conversation with Jackson, hackled him. He walked over to the ticket booth. Last time he had taken the CPR. This time he would take the "Rapido," the "National" line.

"... *the ticket booth is the same old bronzed respectable — like a bank wicket, but jazzed over now with a fay red-white-blue decor of posters. The attendants the same — a sort of cheap felt blazer, Minute-Man blue with red trims. Look like gas station attendants on a Labour Day parade ... that's it — the new Guild of All-Canadians. And they* are *descendants of the Amurrican Minute Men — same narrow folk culture that produced the car-spangled banner. It's the colours ... those folk hues. This is just a mutation of the same: part Rotary Club cheeriness, part cheerleader razzummatazz, part modern electronix. Christ I hate it: the Canadettes! Preview of 1984. Bless damned Orwell! Just time for a snack in the York Pioneer Room ... "*

He settled in and looked it over ... quickly discredited it as part of the new Canadian kick for their cottage pine past. Simply a comfortable Canadian variation of the American Abe Lincoln myth. It made posthumous peasants out of all their ancestors. He couldn't take much of that. He enjoyed peasants; but he didn't like retroactive peasanthood as a national patriotic pastime. There was something sick in it ... an inverted snobbery. The fact was that the "log cabin legend" simply didn't belong in Canada ... it really belonged only to that initial, and belated, American yeoman tradition in Southwestern Ontario — Grit

Ontario ... Canadian equivalent of the New England Myth that still implicitly dominates Amurrican thought. The thought that Canada, at this late date would be subjected to a pirated and aborted American puritan legend depressed him. And he fled.

"... I thought of touring the new City Hall. Haven't yet. A good idea now ... after all if this New Canada is real and right I'm as much a tourist in Canada now as anyone else. & I can see the Old City Hall at the same time. But didn't have the courage.... The exposure would rob me of the energy I need for Montreal."

Suddenly the real magnitude of what he was doing and of what was being done to him shook him. He hadn't as yet completely allowed himself to know. But every now and then he had a deep realization of what he was really doing — some deep tissue of him opened and he shook from stem to gudgeon. The only thing he could do now was to see someone: people still fortified him. He phoned Beatrice Ellis — he had kept in touch with her these past difficult months. She had edited his book of essays. Had done a sensitive job — and she had told him then (that was four years ago) that he had something much more important to say, that he wouldn't get away merely with his essays. There was just time for a cup of tea together (it wasn't a "drink" — that was what happened in novels; and he smiled.) Beatrice had "died" a few months ago, heart failure, under an oxygen tent — and then been revived and come back to tell about it. She would know. He tried — between the lines — to tell her what he was really doing ... tried to tell her that he knew that the novel was for real. He wanted to tell her of the hara-kiri explicit in it. But it was hard to acknowledge fear to someone who has already died and come back. That strengthened him again. And at 4:45 p.m. he was on board the Rapido ...

"the Rapido! the very name pillages me of more blood. Part of the mediocre anonymity of the New Nation. An evasion of identity. An abstraction. Might as well call it the 'Quickie' — the Cdn Quickie. But that would be too American. At least the CPR has the guts to be the Chateau Champlain ... or the Royal York. Well — the new name matches the new ticket booth matches the new Canadettes in the

booth matches the Respectable Hick matches the New Flag matches
the new entry to the train itself … from the main floor of the thermal
bathroom. I got a new respect for that great arched Roman Bath as I
saw in contrast the board-and-batten triumphal arch all of eight feet tall
through which we went to the train. Red-white-blue archlet — not the
old colours, grim old colours, full of gristle and gut, but these new candy-
floss colours. (Oh, Christ, even the colours of my community are
undergoing a change of life — are being gelded!) At the arch entry a
professional greeter welcomes us in. Rolls out the cheap red carpet for all
of us members of the new lower middle-class Canadian royalty. Pathetic.
Plush for the people.

Why can't I be proud of it? I should be. It is clean, competent, fresh,
proper. It even has this mitigated concern for majesty — the plush carpet,
the stage-set entry, the self-effacing CN impresario to grimace us at
entryway … I suppose because it makes me by definition part of these
New Canadettes. A sort of post-graduated folk-yeoman-king…. Hell
— why should I be proud of it? This isn't what my people spent two
centuries here for! Even if I wanted I have no right to be proud of it!

Dumped my bags on the rack between cars #3012 and 3011
… & slump into a seat — lucky got one by a window, facing forwards
(dislike riding backwards). Ten minutes to go … catch up on my Notes.

… 4:45 p.m., sharp, the station moves away from us … leaving
me exposed sudden to the body of my city … out the back corner of
my eye that becalmed Beaux-Arts bulk, rising like a series of improved
Buckingham Palaces piled atop each other — the Royal York, could
only be she

the long slit unended of Yonge Street — like all our streets —
dissolved only by infinity

with that wedding-cake turn-of-the-century prestige bank at
the lower left-hand corner — Front Street corner: a kind of gaudy
bodyguard for the longeststreetintheworldthatisYongestreet ending only
in our Ontario Lake District. Bank of Montreal, at that!

with its back square upon me, the squat cube of our beer baron's art
centre: O'Keefe

overtopping all these, the soft-nosed phallicity of Bank of
Commerce — circumspect, uncircumcised — 32 stories of Canadian
self-satisfaction

the new National Trust tower, well below

& below again, prickly up these closed commercial shops, the spired
incisions of the old City of Churches — Saints James & Michael &
Metropole

&, last link with the old city, Osgoode aside, St-Lawrence-Market-
where-Jenny-Lind-sang

pinched by the Victorian gabling from Jarvis Street East ... even
gables in Toronto are Presbyterian spinsters' eyes on my wayward
trainside

Gooderham 'n Worts stone distillery — 1832: THERE is
the REAL HOY culture ... Honest Ontario Yeoman — Hoyman
— none of this nostalgic log cabin cult ... but cubic yards of squared
stonework — behind it, the high windows and gratuitous lantern of
Tuscan Revival blocks (if only they would repaint these!)

a minute, a panorama of 2 centuries passed ... to the free flowing
muck of the Don River — where Founding-Governor Simcoe's wife
fished for fresh salmon! What could she think now of this shit-sluice?
Anal canal for 2 million congested citizens! And all the valleyside of it
superways with some guilty pretence at parkland

squat huddle of houses ... one, two, five, seven minutes ... the
Emancipated Methodist Culture of Canada! ... Cdn squatters — our
national smugliness — small, stolid bungalows; unlike anything in the
Yewnited States — smaller, thicker, squalider. Someday we'll clear the
land of these affluent slums — in revenge for the lost White Pine we
cleared first to house them....

a trickle of land ... apologetic almost — extinct landscape!

redbrick belfry & white cornicings cuddle me kinetic to the land
for spring — of course: the Church at Dunbarton — rural Ontario
Ecclesiological — as specifically Ontario as the French-Cdn parish
church is Québec ... want to shout the news out to the traincar ... but
am silenced by the sight of she-man opposite me

glut of bungalettes again — more modern now
the Ugliest City in Ontario — easy laureate: Oshawa — cartown
Queen Anne's Lace, Milkweed pod, St. John's Wort … all the
sun flushed earthenware of Ontario winter garden of the open fields
(want to shout — "do you see these? — look — our winter garden …"
but the eyes in front of me are deaf) — snow-pocked field furrows …
sudden woodland shimmers bronze of wintered beechleaves

at horizon spruce palisade (sharp eyes, like those spinster gables!)
alerts me to the orchard that must arrive & cedar hedge, overgrown, and
hip-rooved bulky barn, stone root house, & same stone foundations to
the blockhouse home red-and-white brick trimmed that completes this
Chateau-fort of our HOYman. Massive, impenetrable, us! Nowhere else
in our wide bloody world but Ontario … Southern Ontario: Home —
damn it, and blessings

more bungalows distress the site — unworthy, unworthy — God
— UNWORTHY offspring

Spiresides — Port Hope … & on the knoll behind, overlording
the factories beneath its notice almost but not quite, Cdn Eton (for
better and for worse) — Trinity College School — vestige of the
disestablished upper Canadian Anglican Genteel State (but choose your
enemy then — this … or the bungalettes! Sweet choice.)

that impasse resolves sudden with the grace notes in conscientiously
squared lines between the great cubed fieldstones that amass an
eternal yeoman stone Georgian home — Canadian Fabergé, these
stone houses: cameos out of rich stone-sown earth to clear those near
generations thrust abruptly by now to be restituted in only a retroactive
nostalgia for tourists and the New Nation: as though killed for a better
Resurrection. Each one still a gem — legacy rebuking the preflab
culture around it … Cobourg … & now the dark.

How well I know this route — our Ontario Front, Niagara to
Montreal — 500 miles of us. Ontario Foundation line, and front
door to our estate of ½ a million square miles. In each town, village,
still, a relative a memory, an echo of community lost under bulldozer
… Cobourg — with its magniloquent Court House — New England

*Meeting House interior compounded with British Raj stonework
exterior. Ontario!*

*Belleville & Trenton ... where the stonework changes from
fieldstone to limestoniness ... from freckles to garrison grey. & the Trent
waterway debouches from Georgian Bay into Lake Ontario. Where
Champlain canoed (idiot adventurer!) four centuries ago to found our
empire. Outside the window, in that dark, all my entrails rolling under
us now —*

*the great slice of limestone into Kingston, that grey canyon cut
by the highway down into the valley of the old capital town of the
Canadas — Kingston ... where I walked that afternoon in November
— to have the pleasure of seeing that unsung Ontario Trinity ... St.
Andrew's Presbytery — the best of Ontario stonework; Elizabeth
Cottage — the loveliest Walter Scott gothic; & (aptly Anglican) Okill's
Folly — the most splendiferous Regency manor — now the residence
of the Principal of Queen's Univ ... all within a few hundred yards of
each other — & was as joyous as if I had walked from La Place de la
Concorde to the Louvre to La Sainte Chapelle; & had wanted to take
a whip to the passers-by who didn't make obeisance to these splendours.
& why not — infraction against beauty is a crime against the state!*

*Of course the Penitentiary ... Child's King Arthur come ironically
true, with its busy turrets ... & the Military College (dare one still call
it "Royal" — because that too will go soon enough — we'll rechristen
it the Federal Military College ... surreptitiously! — and then by
Order-in-Council)*

*the old #2 route thence to Ganonoque's Golden Apple — laden
with stonehouses and flowers spurting out of stone roadcut canyons ....
& that day, it was February 28, when my wife & I sunbathed on the
front porch of the deserted summer cottage, over the Thousand Islands,
after returning from Amurrica — laughing at the legend of the frozen
North (the look on the mongrel dog's face, & then his master's, when
he saw us there!) The Ontario Front ... Giant sentinel Mulleins
stalking the land still in dried khaki above the white field beds. I know
just where the climax oak and the hickory start again, near Kingston*

… Oh, out that window is all of me underfoot. Out that window is inside me, always. That *can't be taken away. Can it? & now it is dark … I can see the Macdonald-Cartier "Highway" (damn the official term "Freeway" — it sounds like some boxtop prize … or, closer to the truth, a come-on to the Yank tourists) and its load of cattle-cars … all bypassing this Front, happily for the Front, unhappily for them … because suddenly the people that made the land disappear, under the asphalt and the speedometer.*

The lights of the great Du Pont factory outside Brockville — and I pray that our lakeside won't become like that of the American lakefront or Toronto … a shambles of hotdoggeral and gimcrap, and factories: because Lake Ontario may be the American back door, but it is our front door. Our garden. Then Upper Canada Village … which warns me that our history is now under glass … or under the St. Lawrence Seaway — and that this is but a sop to our vestigial historic consciences. After all, the Village is under the supervision of the provincial tourist department! QED. Goddam it.

So — I have a nostalgia. For my land, and its people. I'm a romantic. A sin in this era of belated Canadian positivism. I cry "too little for the sensibility," when all our intellectuals moan "too little for their minds." Too bad! I love my land. & damn their dry eyes. Detesticulate.

The home in Iroquois, where we were received for lunch … bad 1920's Art Nouveau with a painting of an Irish setter on velvet over the fireplace — & the look on the man's face, he was from the West, when I told him there was no sound in our East like the prairie meadowlark … I thought he was going to kiss me … but he got me another drink instead, unasked & we loved each other across the ages. & then quarrelled over politics. But meadowlark still sang.

Oh, yes, goddam it — I love my land … & I love my people. Still. Unpardonable crime in this age of "cool culture" & commissions. Or is it simply untenable fidelity? The latter has it, of course. So, I'll love, & go under, hating those who so conscientiously kill my love …

Abruptly I am grilled … a cold sear of bright grilling me

— *grilling my flesh all bloodless bright red — Hate: of a sudden hate has me, has won … carries me off bodiless in triumph. Jerk me forward to catch this rape in the act, before too late — before I dissolve before I detonate. Make notes, ward off the evil eye now. What happened? What in this Hell happened? Go back & piece the evidence together. First — Where am I? & then sink back as I see … the train had stopped, lurched my eyes back into the traincar … Back in? No! — out: train swallowed me out of my land, smothered me away from my earth … dispersed me under the grill of neonessent light, those candy floss red seats — at once compressing and atomizing me. Anteus bereft … Christ — in a hot sweat I need a pee. & heave me into the aisle, into — "Hello Hugh — you look as though you need a tonic" — I look up to find the soft laughing eyes of Jack Greg … we speed to the bar-car. Thank God it's him … someone I can want to see. Fellow publishing house man. Feverish in delight I leech him of the blood the Rapido has just haemorrhaged out of me … squandered. & over a martini I don't want we giggle indecorously about the Great Auk the Royal Ontario Museum has just acquired (both bird-watchers!) Positively clenching the padded seats with our buttockry …*

"God knows that's what the museum needed — a Great Auk! — the one thing all museums need, and lack … " and I catch Greg's lilting gawkwardness out my eye-corner in a feline complicity of joy … we both mould the seat pads in an accredited squirm of delight, harvesting their Great Auk.

Greg — "It was bought from Vassar College" — a burst of sweet gigglement again.

Me — "God — our provincial Auk came from Vassar!"

Greg — "What's more, it was Audubon's Great Auk."

That is too much — we eye each other openly, as silent upon our peak … More laughter. & then the Great Auk has done its service. Has bound us as one flesh, refurbished — & can be discarded, like any dildo. I stop — suddenly aware how nearly the laughter has consummated my self-expenditure. So close to depleting my entire reserve of credulity now, of faith, of available energy. Suddenly wary — I nurse my last ounce

*of resistance. Look around at the bar-car. At this new world of plausible
plush. I'll have to be careful.*

*Joined by two of Greg's friends ... an Englit don & wife from the
University of Toronto. A typical Englit combination — the wife has a
beard, bass voice, & three testicles. She is a TV producer when she isn't
producing hubby. He is a falsetto — visually if not audibly; as slight as
his wife is muscle-bound, no beard because no chin to carry one ... I
bethink me of the Great Auk again ... Thank God for the Great Auk
— after all, the provincial museum is part of the provincial university
— it can do yeoman service therein. Audubon's Great Auk, bought from
the girls of Vassar .... It will just be sufficient.*

*Jabberwocky for half-an-hour, as I keep withholding me from the
decor of the bar-car ... And then the Englits are leaving ... wife carrying
hubbie off by the scruff of his neck. Mrs. doesn't like being in a "beer
hall." Incredible — but so ... But who am I to laugh — because I can't
stand the place either, although for different reasons ... Try to put my
finger on it now — just what is it that this decor is doing to me (because
I cannot hide from me that it is doing something with me, or trying) ...
again — all I can say is compression, into a small space, & at the same
time danger of detonation. A strange kind of ambivalent pressure. For the
moment all I can do is hold me together, hold me at qui vive in face of it.*

*Dinner with Greg ... roast beef (almost rare enough to be
rare), green peas (wizened), and roast potatoes (sullen) — "The
Parliamentarian's Special" quoth the menu! God — the Cdn Nemesis
... A half bottle of Beaujolais scarcely masks it .. Greg laughs — "it's
just a variation on Air Canada's performance — airborne buses. One
and the same thing. You know — this train is really a set piece ... it
establishes the kind of citizen it wants." I know instantly that Greg is
right .... know exactly what he is saying. "You mean the people are for
the car, and not the car for the people — it is the people who have to
'live up to the car,' grow into it — a car made, not to suit the people, but
people being remade to suit the new Canadacar."*

*Greg's right. His perception mates my own — "if these are
Canadians remade to suit the traincars, the Club Car we passed*

57

*through getting here, that's the car for the people who service the People.
The car for the Canadians who are remaking Canadians: the New
Canadian Club for the People's Commissars … with its red carpet,
black leatherette chairs, & the pictures at one end by W. H. Bartlett,
circa 1830, for the permanent English-Canadian Victorian Romantic,
& at the other by one of the young French-Canadian revolutionnaires,
bought with his third consecutive Canada Council grant. The Club
car is the Club of our New Establishment." Greg laughs again, at my
flinch — "You've got it — this train is a very precise political platform
… it's the travel arm of the Third Adam."*

"I don't understand you there."

*Greg: "… the new Cdn Man — the Uprooted Cdn; we used to
be part of the First Adam … the continuous civilization of the Western
World. That was our role in the New World. The Americans left us that
legacy when they became the Second Adam after 1776 and all that. Well,
these jokers (Greg jerked his head to embrace the diner) belong to the Cdn
Grit Liberal Culture … whether they know it or not. They've uprooted,
to rule. Their implicit claim is to be the Third Adam. But they're officially
'modest' — so no one says it. They just understudy the role!"*

*I laugh — Greg, like me is a hopeless Tory … and I know that,
like me, he voted NDP last time: Tory Radical. Our Toryism is our
culture as Canadians … not our politics. I look behind Greg — there
is a beaut! Cdn Male: age 46?, navy blue suiting, waistcoat (no
handkerchief), unobtrusive glasses, solid … with a face of precast putty.
His conversation is alas all too clear — I don't overhear it; I'm overrun
by its calm assertion: "… they don't put enough force into their speeches,
not enough guts — I ghost write for the Minister of Finance — he's
uninspired … " I can't believe it — can't believe this man criticizing
dullness; it's self-contradictory. For a moment my whole personality
focuses again, all the legions called home by concentrate of contempt.
For an instant I am whole again — alive from toe-tit to occiput. My
whole being accuses these sterilettes. And then I feel the danger of
exspenditure again. Pull in my horn; I'll need it later — in emergency.
"But this train IS an emergency … it is THE emergency, integral part*

*of it...." Greg looks surprised at this outburst. "Oh I'm just talking
aloud — I'll subside in a minute." But Greg is looking at me with a
large understanding, & I blurt on, "this train is as dangerous, as lethal
in its own right as any boxcar translating political deviates to Siberia.
Its tactics are more subtle — but they come to the same thing: absolute
elimination, corporate destruction." Here Greg looks mystified & I stop
... & am vulnerable again, to dispersal.*

*After dinner, back to the bar-car ... alone. I don't know why. I guess
I need a drink. A brandy. Ask mischievously for a Marc de Bourgogne.
There never is any, of course. I always ask just to reassure me there
isn't any .... Only one place in English Canada where I have had a
good Marc. A free seat by the window — my partner in crime discovers
himself readily to me ... after all, we are fellow inmates, accomplices of
the Rapido (there is still something furtive about the bar-car).*

*"My name's Jack Emery — second year Law, Dalhousie .... live
in Willowdale ... I like hockey and theatre. What do you do?" I flinch
... it is the "what do you do?" that hurts. Always "what are you?"
Never "who?". In all my years in Toronto no one ever asked me "who"
— except "who's what." People are expendable in English Canada;
everyone is only a person "ex officio." & now, of course I'm no longer
anything. Except a deserter ... no — better than that — because I
have my purpose: I'm a demissionary. God, here is this law student,
already firmly entrenched in the English Canada Heresy — ex officio
humanism! It's a form of agnosticism. But what chance has he, the
betrayal has been made for him, at birth, by his community. We offer
each other a drink and discuss the new cabinet changes.*

Student — "Canadians think too much about themselves."

*Says it with diffident self-satisfaction — like a Christian who has
just confessed his Fault, & is now fresh armed with a proud Penance. &
that done he unthinking opens up a little ... that is, his eyes open into
mine more ... I nearly fall into the unexpected aperture ... but even
as I totter bar-car catches me & I withdraw in time. I can't afford to fall
anywhere in these surroundings, because I have no control. Draw back,
vetoed again. Stammer something — "we may think too much about*

ourselves, but we never feel for ourselves." That ends the exchange. The best that can be achieved now is a slowly distending propriety — a kind of improved impasse.

He returned to his own car. And waiting to get off wrote his notes with what care he could muster, testing the muted vulgarity of the Rapido. He had to acknowledge to himself that this train *did* set the taste-pace for its clientele. The clientele being those, like himself, in the coach — the Permanent Commoners ... Improved Commoners now, he supposed. And the administrators, the taste-makers, being those in the Club Car. The new élite. The new Canadian Priesthood. Secular Order! The enemy within. The new ultramontanism — with Ottawa as Rome. He'd have to start his own English-Canadian "Quiet Revolution" — against this new Canadian Church ... he, the anti-clerical Loyalist.

The man who shared his seat returned from a later dinner. Young — perhaps 30. Black suit, but with small cuffs. Hair close cropped — but not chopped ... sat silently down, careful not to intrude his eyes upon anyone. Started reading: only the chapter head was visible ... "how to handle a conference." Hugh sank in consternation: "God, the army is everywhere." He went back to his notation ... scribbling furious — "the national government has become our Tastemaker — and the Taste it is setting is disastrous indication of the New Man it is concocting by default...."

By the time he had finished they were in Montreal. Everyone was filing out. Everyone, that is, except a young man three seats forward who stood up, dressed himself with confident placidity, while conscientiously allowing the others to exit. How was it possible, Hugh pondered, to be so correctly condescending as this man was? And then — as he watched the performance, mesmerized — he knew that the youth reminded him of someone. Whom? He stared ... the boy must be twenty-five, hair kempt by comb (not brushed, of course), grey coat unobtrusively tweeded, suit implacably pressed. Standing with his body held carefully at arm's length ... from what? Hugh didn't know. Not yet. The man was obviously a model, for himself — but of what? Bells rang in his ears ... the youth put on his white scarf, his gloves. And then it all came to Hugh with a rush — the face from the picture on the wall of the United Church Sunday School near Collingwood, the skiing village

... that was it: this youth was a Blondbeast for Jesus ... the completed Canadian Methodist! Roundhead with Honours! A variation of the man who had just shared his seat ... and who had looked like (Hugh realized it now), those ads for Canadian Army recruitment: those earnest faces — firm (not forceful), clean cut (but not chiselled), accessible (but not frank). Hugh watched amazed at this performance. Surely there was a flaw somewhere. No — there was none. The young man helped a lady with her bag, carefully withdrawing from her extracted thanks. It was painfully embarrassing to Hugh. God — the kid is going through all the right motions ... like someone from Whitby Ladies' College — the complete Methodist Husband for the completed Methodist Lady. Everything was right about it. For a moment he thought that the only solution was prayer — real prayer. And then as the All-Canadian Good Boy carried himself firmly down the aisle (no organ playing — none could: the Kid would see to that!) Hugh felt an insufferable urge that he didn't define ... he couldn't; he was in situ now — Montreal.

The station clamoured around him — he gazed into the noise, displaced suddenly ... so different from Toronto, from the great thermal Roman Imperial Bath of Toronto Union ... wherein no one talked — except the Highclass Hicks of Listen Hear on the billboardings ... who yapped at the Permanent Commoners convening to their traintimes. These Hep Hicks — "everyone's chum," the pert alert Torontonian.... Well, here in Montreal, it was decisively and disconcertingly different. The station engulfed him now, and he weaved his way through the crowd — "the best-dressed peasants in the world," he thought, as he warped and woofed his way to his baggage. And the best-behaved. And then he realized that while they were a crowd incoherent around him, engulfing him, yet they were no more than in comparable space in the Toronto station. But the whole experience was utterly different. He gazed around the station — it looked rather like a well-organized sequence of American wayside kiosks. There was a percentage of that, and a percentage of shopping centre, and a percentage of "better buy British" to it all. Around the ceiling, an immensely squalid frieze depicting Canada, apparently, because underneath it the words of "O Canada." "Better buy Canadian ... better belong to Canadian Club" — that was the subterranean message ... "because Big Brother is encouraging you." There was that — and the seethe of sound that was a seethe of people. Hugh was too tired to understand all of it now. He caught a cab to a three-buck tourist home near the station ... run by a French couple from Provence — and battened himself down for the night. And as he locked his door and undressed the fissure opened him again and he realized where he was ... remembered again, in deeper measure, why he was there. The train ride had in part veiled it all for him even as it exposed him to it. Had veiled his novel, just as his novel seemed to veil his real purpose. A process of interlocking amnesias. Well, now he couldn't forget. Because he was within striking distance of La Place d'Armes. His rapid breathing as he lay abed informed him that his heart was racing. He reached into his brief case for his book — Boswell's *Life of Johnson* ... somehow he had never read it through. Ridiculous gap ... so he had brought it along. And his hand fell on his Brief Biography. Why had he brought that? His curriculum vitae? What in truth *was* he doing in Montreal?

Brief Biography

Hugh Robert Anderson ... born 1931 ... Toronto ... second son of Colonel and Mrs. ... 117 Crescent Drive ... Upper Canada College, Trinity College in the University of Toronto (History and Modern Languages — French and Russian), St. John's College, Oxon., P.P.E. (of course!) ... Four years with Montreal CBC special features (documentary), six years with the House of Johnson, Toronto, in charge of publications on Canadian history and literature ... lecturer at the University of Toronto ... author of *Essays in Canadian Taste: a Study in the Relationship of the Arts and Politics from 1812 to 1914.* Hobbies: bird-watching, Canadiana, conversation ...

It was an impeccable cursus honorum canadensis. Completed by a wife, (Mary Joan, only daughter of Professor and Mrs. J. A. Robins) and two children, suitably divided between the sexes. In five years he would have been the effective head of the House of Johnson, Canada's most respected and progressive publishing house. He was perfectly bilingual (four years in Montreal had seen to that) and thoroughly respected by French and English Canadian editors and authors.

Hugh eyed the biography quizzically, incredulously ... almost as though he were hiring this man. He was suspicious: it was too good to be decent. Something was wrong somewhere. Then he remembered — it was him. Hugh Robert Anderson. He closed his eyes — the sweat stung in them. The thunder was his heart. It must all be a bad dream.... He farted, and the bland musk of debilitated Parliamentarian's beef (almost rare) assured him that it was for real. He thought of the Rapido-ride down. It had been at once curiously flat, yet riddled with pitfalls. Now he was in Montreal. And he was there on schedule. He looked at his watch ... after midnight ... so it was already December 1 — the first day of his Adventure. That was as planned.

It was indeed for real. It was he, Hugh Robert Anderson who had been fired two months ago — conscientiously fired. It was he who had, quite casually, at lunch one day, finally ensured his firing. Lunch with the President of the House of Johnson ... Richard Johnson, C.M.G., F.R.S.C., LL.D., Q.C. (he had the order wrong — but he could never remember this mutation from the Canadian Debrett's listing really — it was so much easier to have a title, and be done with it — and not this subterranean alphabetic dignitarianism.) The lunch was at the York Club ... ensconced in all those magnificent Italian Renaissance Revival Victorian carvings. Johnson was asking pointedly, "Why do you think we missed that contract with the university, Anderson?" And precisely between a bite of Camembert, that was still, alas chalky (the York Club should have known better — and for a horrible moment Anderson had also wondered if the carvings on the wall were merely plaster) and the happifying recollection that only the York Club served a Marc de Bourgogne, Hugh replied quite spontaneously, almost affectionately, "Because you've got no balls, Sir." It had been so incredibly simple. He himself had heard this reply with interest and incredulity. Then, for one ghastly instant, Hugh thought that he had been wrong, that Johnson DID have balls, at least ONE ball ... and that he was going to stab him, Hugh Anderson, with his steak knife. Hugh even hoped that this was so. It would have restored his faith. He waited, expectant virgin, for the thrust — and once again he even believed that the carvings on the walls were indeed wood. And then he was deceived. The cheese, the carvings, and Johnson, were all putty. The contortion of Johnson's face that Hugh had taken for genuine militant rage (Johnson had been a brigadier), was merely that kind of tumescence that precedes tears. And the president's only achievement had been to control his tears. Hugh looked up after a moment. Everything was in order again. The whole incident had simply blown over. But Johnson's eyes had gone that bald greyblue ... eyes from which one bounced with the false spring of tired broadloom ... eyes that looked neither out nor in — the look of a defeated man who still wields power. A month later Hugh was caught out on a technicality. He received a letter from the president inviting his resignation. He didn't even bother replying.

It was rather sad. He even liked Johnson. But once he was sure that Johnson had no balls, and was inordinately resentful of anyone who did, then the die was cast....

A truck squealed against the curb outside his window. Hugh's flesh shrieked. He was outrageously alive now. Every pore audited the street sounds. He knew that he would get no sleep. What was worse a fever had set in ... all the old signs of strain in him — fatigue, fever, sore throat. He dosed himself with cold pills, aspirins, and settled down to sleep on his fakir's bed of goosepimples. He was still hopeful that he could accomplish his assignment ... could place the Place d'Armes and thus his novel. If he could just rest a bit, shake off this damned flu bug.

DAY ONE

NOTEBOOK

— awake at noon — pills have abated flu-fever. Lie abed, slowly draw me together

— read a little of Bozzy — just to place things a bit.

— Got La Place on my brain

& gingerly out of bed, palp embodiment for self-certification: all intact. Out pipes! Brunch in greasy spoon

down thru the city — Peel St — Dominion Square (is it true that a sparrow hawk nested atop Sun Life Bldg. I hope so!) Pick up tourist map, postcards

— the Cathedral, squatting like English parish church amidst La Place Ville Marie, Sun Life (no hawk in sight) and the Queen Elizabeth Hotel (Fr-Cdns call it Le Reine Elizabeth — even the Queen has changed sex in this goddam country!)

Quebec Hydro — Christ, pull yourself together — Hydro Québec: that's what the "nationalization" was all about — the provincialization, the French Canadianization of the hydro, three yrs ago.

Taxi drops me at edge of La Place d'Armes. Proceed on foot — to reconnoitre. Not much snow — fortunately.

Don't want to see too much yet. Not till I dig in, get some sort of control centre for Operation Place d'A. Otherwise might shoot the whole venture prematurely. Phtt ... 10 years out the window. Mortal expenditure — & nothing to show for it. Except the notes kept while in training, intermittent, these past 7 years, & they are, at best, sketches — undercover sketches!

just take an oblique glance, out the side of my head ... yes — still there! A few changes — one big one : Who is it?

retreat down sidestreet, right under the nose of Target — & set out to find quarters. Sthg nearby — not more than 5 minutes from the Square. I'll have to scout the quarter, foot by foot this next fortnight: reinterpret every map — translate them. All out of date — & more dangerous — all deceptive, deliberately — hiding the Place. Know that from odious experience (that night, in '61 …)

Ethg will be disguised! Masked.

I'll have to devise my own map … prerequisite for safe encounter with Target. Will be tricky — every foot of the way mined.

Can't find right digs — ideally a small pension over the Square. Best facing the body of Target — bull's eye!

Small hotels — five blocks East (Old Directions) … several — in a sub-Square: La Place Jacques Cartier (meaning?) What is relationship between Square & sub-Square — Big Place & Little Place. Conniving. I'm wary tho. Make sure to find out. Excellent proximity.

Question of hotel … which one? Comes down to two: one faces City Hall (Old Style) & the old Market & the belltower of Sailors' Church. The other faces La Place — tho I can't see it from here. I'ld rather face forward blind, than backwards visual. Moreover the seamstress on the second floor reminds me of … no matter

Hotel Nelson. Why? Aside from its relationship to Monument in the Little Place it confronts.

Kick me all day for choosing this hotel. Too much like an old hen. But it is the right one — the one that 1st engaged my attention, my loyalty. Besides, each time I go out I'll interrogate the view from the other, wondering why I didn't take it, & that way get best of each world.

If I'm wrong I'll move (tho I never will! Besides it would attract too much attention.)

Installed by nightfall. Try to read; fail.

Why have I come? I would give anything to know & more not to know!

Squander remaining energy on this why for. Flee to dinner, across La Petite Place. Buy conscience off with spaghetti, soup. Slink to sleep.

DAY TWO

Hugh awoke slowly — dredged himself from bed, and installed himself at his portable typewriter, duty-bound. It had been his faithful comrade-at-arms for eight years. An Olivetti Lettera 22; it had never failed. He had written his first book on it. And ever since. He opened his briefcase, reached in for his Journal, and started to type.

"The morning is deep downcast in me, numbskulled, and my brain bloats against greysky. Catch my dreams by the tail ... reach out to prey upon them. But they are gone even as I reach ... Well, if I can no longer feel, at least I do have time to think. I have reached shelter, a hide-in, and I think I am undetected. No one knows I am here. I'm not even sure I realize I'm here yet. And certainly no one knows why (I like to think that I don't know why — but I know deep in my bone I do, that's why I'm here.) If anyone did know then my Disaster would be disastered. The important thing now is to keep a meticulous record of the assault, so that if I fail at least the ground will have been broken. If I succeed then others can follow; the results will be self-evident. In either case a day-by-day account, in detail is essential. For the novel — and for the Real Thing. I'll keep on taking notes. And then write them up as I can in this journal. Flesh them out ... flesh me out!

Irony: I bought this journal six years ago, when I was still in Montreal, with CBC ... meant to keep a daily record. Never did. And now I'm here, writing it, because I didn't dare then ... didn't dare me. Serves me right. Remember the day I bought it — after lunch with George Carter, at Delmos Oyster Bar,

walked along la rue Notre Dame and down-dropped in to an
antique shop ... one of his clients. All that Canadiana (little
did I suspect then it was my culture in the raw). It was lying
in the bargain pile on a gate-leg table. Picked it up unthinking,
uninterested ... perhaps to look interested, perhaps to protect
me against other purchase — the redflare of cover caught my
eye I guess, the red and black while George talked shop ...
balancing the book in my hand — an old-fashioned journal and
notebook — my hand tested by its heft, substantial. With a good
spine to it. None of that paperback stuff (a paperback culture
has no tiger in its tank — must needs make one up). And open
to the marbleized end-papers ... curls my coil (there's the rub).
Plus a pocket for papers ... containing one reproduction map of
old Montreal and a couple of postcards — one of the Bank of
Montreal, the other of Notre Dame's gut ...

Bought for $1.

George laughed — "You're a symbolist."

"Why?"

"The date — 1867!"

I hadn't even noticed ... But I never wrote a word in it:
fled to the respectability of Toronto instead.

Stop yapping and write!

7:46 a.m. Waking this morning and even last night I was
aware once again that my novel is in fact some deeper assault
on reality than I care to admit. It is ... it is a war — between
reality and me. Maybe it's a Holy War. I can't tell (stop lying
— of course it's a Holy War!) Alright — it is a Holy War — so
this journal which is a diary which is my log-book is really a
Combat Journal. It couldn't be anything else. I should type it
in red.

Must keep a duplicate. In the hotel strongbox to be
forwarded to Eric in case of emergency. I know he'll see to it
that it is published. (Don't let me down Eric — you have no
right to. What I say belongs to my community — to what is left

of it, that is. It is all I have to give. All! And if they don't want it
… well at least they can never say they weren't told.)

Between my notebooks, my Combat Journal, and what I
manage to write of my novel, the picture should be complete.
As complete as I can make it. And if I succeed, then I'll have my
novel from it. Then the rest can be set aside....

But I'm not going to fail. I have no right to do that either.
I am honour-bound to succeed … And I must bind me to my
word. Screwed to the sticking point! I've rubiconned every river
that ever ran, bombed every bridge — just to make sure I've
cornered my cowardice. For the rest, ten years of meticulous
preparation. Of training. Maybe fifteen, if I include those first
years, at the University of Toronto … when I furtively, almost
unwittingly, protected my counterpoint to the Amurrican
Dream. Ten years anyhow. Ten years of tacking back and forth
— but always to the same end. Always the same preoccupation.
What subterfuge it has meant … I always the subterfugitive! No
matter. What counts now is that I've reached my target. It is still
here. That was the work of yesterday. I took few notes yesterday
— even though it was the First Day. The First Day on the site. I
just didn't have the energy; it had all been consumed in getting
to the hotel, into a striking position. I remember now that I had
felt how dangerous my sense of calm was to the whole purpose
of the expedition. Because it is war — and I realized already it
was war, and that any placation was capitulation. Yet I persisted
in feeling calm. And I had to keep telling myself that this
adventure is essential. Of course I knew that it was — even if
for some time yesterday I only knew abstractly and had to keep
sending me mental telegrams, like "EXPEDITION URGENT
STOP NO RETREAT STOP KEEP YOUR COCK UP
STOP." No, I knew well enough that it was essential. That was
it: I was dangerously smug about the fact of the danger. That
was what worried me. Lulled me into a security right in the
face of absolute danger.

And then later yesterday — in the late afternoon, I harvested the exhilaration of recognized danger, and the whole thing was implicitly clear again. I could relent.

... 9:25 a.m. Breakfast at the hotel — while the waitress clucks about this dining room like some pullet over her brood — and I ponder the matter. Really wonder whether I can achieve it. It is mad. This "adventure." I suppose the real question is whether it takes place at all. My fear now is for the adventure itself — because that is the basis of the novel. Amongst other things. And at this very instant, as the oatmeal porridge ballasts my grumble gut, I am denuded of everything except my faith in the possibility of the adventure. Yet even as I fear for the venture I realize that the fear is of no way out — fear of the final extinction of my plans. And once again I realize how serious it really is ... this goddam "novel" of mine. It is a matter of life and death — whether I like it or not. Moreover, if I turn back, then it is automatic death. So I know again what is at stake, and the Adventure, the Novel, simply is. I am dedicated to victory, because I am dedicated to life against death.

In the strain of this recognition my appetite is gone ... because my body is gone — has been nullified by the act of questioning. I have lost corporate credibility again. It is detached fingers that wipe detached mouth as I pick me up and carry me back to the room....At least I can study the map of the quarter ...

As I re-enter my room on the third floor my ear is cocked to the shunt of freight-yards just below the hotel....I am huge again with the dream I forgot this morning ... muster me once more to typewriter before it evades me again ... if nothing else, I can keep the goddam log-book up to date ...

It was home ... in the home I've never built. In my old Toronto Rosedale ... that house, on Crescent Drive, Tudorbethan, with park ground behind it.... the banquet

hall in the basement — wine-cellar banquet hall; vrai cave!
(Virulent in me … every detail — as I hear bells from
trainshunt.) Twelve-foot dining table from Les Frères chrétiens
of Montreal, a drawer for each monk's pewter cutlery … 14
places in all. Generous places. Table with the trestled feet, wide
plank top, and the iron crane drawing out from the end, for
the marmite. Item #377 in Jean Palardy's illustrated *Furniture
of French Canada*. Around it those chairs I could never afford
to buy … those chaises à la capucine, circa 1780. With their
flowing arms joining balustered back and legs, front and back.
And the cherub-winged backslats. Fourteen of them — a
dozen in dark hardwoods — walnut, butternut, stained maple.
Plus two in tiger-stripe maple — voluptuous in the wood's
countercurve to the curvette of the design of the chair itself.
This in the very centre of the room…. Walls white plaster
roughcast. Ceiling high (it keeps getting higher as I recollect
it.) Around these walls — upjutting from every corner and
pillar and beam — the strut of the cave — a dozen Coqs
canadiens, rampant. At the far end immense rocaille hulk of
sideboard — like some purebred milchcow decked out for a
fête champêtre at Versailles. Clawed balled feet. Atop it, large
carved cupboard for eaux-de-vie … straddled by six torchères
that stand four feet each. All in white and gilt. On the left wall,
a huge mural scene, a fire…. But scarce time to take all of this
in, even in recollection, when the guests arrive. Who are they
to be (trains — keep shunting — I would know who arrives!)?
Suddenly candles blare, ignite, and She arrives in sheath dress
that cracks my whip … followed by Him in dinner jacket and
bespectacled smile, teeth wide-eying (High Church Ipana!)
and hair in kempt dishevelled pelt. No Announcements.
Simply an informal elegant investiture of this home hall à la
canadienne … investiture of us, of what we are as citizens, as
people … I serve them un vin d'Honneur — a Bernkastler
Doktor 1959er goldbeerenauslese — in my grandfather's high

Victorian Hock glasses. High Victorian, High Hock, High Glasses … with Chinese waterchestnuts and bacon … serve them from the front seat of the Child's Hearse — lifesize — from Lévis, P.Q., hearse all inordinate with angels and roses and garlands, steep carved pine, white and gold, and all celestially earthy (those trumpetting angels have firm French-Canadian buttocks.)

As I pour the Bernkastler into the onion-skin green of glass diaphanous under tremble of fingertits wine flows down necknape of Tony's hairline, down vertebration into the roothouse that used to be behind Great-grandfather Jameson's homestead at Grimsby (Ont.) … into roothouse and up spat back out at me into the glass of Princess Meg from her left breast that was cut clean from the dress, displacing the Order of the Garder. Eau de vie, I gasp, and kneel to let it tumble my crown…. Scene only interrupted by the Canadian Chairs that come assclasp us all to a stewboat of Oxtails stewed as meet for Mighty Methodists … and serve with a red wine that I grow myself, below the house on the slope behind the Toronto subway just to prove that Ontario wine need not be the red Niagara piss with which we glut our home market … a little red brute strong enough to grapple these tails — secret being, of course, that as in certain small crus of Pomerol, I leave the stems and all in the pressing, to flesh out the wine, give it mastication … un petit vin masturbateur de l'Ontario … l'état de l'Ontario, S.V.P. Till Margaret had been oxtailed, and Tony with, and everyone ordained therein because it is meat and right so to do … and as I look up (the bell of freight train clarifies the site now) I see that the sideboard is 18th century French-Canadian baroque-rococo church altar, Ecole de Quévillon, and that the angels are now suspended from our lowering ceiling, and that Tony is my chair and Princess Meg clutches regally every oxtail to her Order of the Garter, and all we guests concerted shout — "Alleluia, I'm a bum…."

I wake, just in time to curtail an unsolicited harvest of me,
and now, in recollection, remember clearly that as a child I had
been deeply preoccupied with the conjugation of OurBelov-
edKingandQueenandwasthereabeginningnoranendtosaidconju-
gationIwasconcernedtoknow atwhatpointitdi dallen din us, as I
was sure it did.

Then I realized that there is a huge silence resonant in me,
as dream dies on my vine ... the freight-yards are tranquil, and
the bells have stopped.

Sit in this sweet bereavement. Evacuated. Suddenly recall
my tourist map. Bought it yesterday ... but hadn't courage to
look it up. The least I can do now is circumscribe my area. On
earth, in North America, in the Dominion of Canada, in l'Etat
du Québec, in La Ville de Montréal, in the centre of the city,
the old centre, by the side of the St. Lawrence, where Seaway
begins as Lachine Canal, this area. The area — I pinpoint it now,
with precision — bounded by the St. Lawrence, McGill Street,
running up from the river, north-east to Craig Street, then
easterly, past City Hall as far as Berri, down to the waterfront
again. Le Vieux Quartier, plus a bit. Within that a still smaller
area ... bounded by la rue St. Jacques to the north, la rue St.
Paul to the south, the Bonsecours Market to the east, la rue
St. Pierre to the west. Within that — La Place itself, La Place
d'Armes ..... and within that again, of course — but that will
have to wait.

These are the names, the streets; the shorthand for the
reality. I know that. It is the reality I seek. Yet even as I succumb
to the map, looking at it, I feel La Place, the whole quarter,
ebbing dangerously out of me ... And I bitter realize that
I have committed the cardinal sin, reducing the quarter to
this map. To allow this map — even as guide. Perhaps if I slip
out now, quickly, I will catch the quarter, La Place, the bulk
of it, the embodiment of it, before it all folds away into this
map that betrayed me ... in a moment of weakness. Fling

me into parka and beret, sortie out … not with intent to site
the quarter definitively — but to make honourable amends
for having slighted it — for having presumed to reduce it to
a few square inches of map. Running down the stairs of the
hotel, out the door, into La Place Jacques Cartier … up past
the Nelson Monument and the Court House … down la rue
Notre Dame, quickly hurry now … to La Place, the central
Square, noting fearfully already how vague these are become
in me … till I reach La Place itself and enter, unwitting now,
and not till I am half way across it, the buildings flowing past
me, shadowing me, shadows in me, in the corner of my eye,
do I realize that it is already too late. Already I am invisible …
and La Place is detached, receding out of me. Already. Stand,
in centre Square, glaring at the buildings, the Place; and only
shadow. Intermittently a lurch of something more substantial.
But in essence, only shadow … only the remains in me of the
Place. I drift on, across the square, down St. James Street, trying
to regroup me, to pull me together, to substantiate me…. But
I can't … the best I can manage is some sort of condition
midway between incarnation and excarnation. At best I am half-
cocked now … my body is midway — neither here nor there.
Nothing is specific. And then I am at an intersection (which
that cursed map tells me still is McGill and St. James!) In front
of me a modern business building … a sheath-glass tower. And I
am falling straight into it … on pretext of looking for someone
who isn't there (if he is, he's lost). But the truth is. I fall into my
own vacuum! And then, in minutes, shoot out again, like some
electronically processed statistic. My chameleonage complete
now … feel as I felt I was about to feel in the bar-car of the
Rapido. Something has happened to my gut … something gone
out of me. Somehow I have been dispersed … would panic —
but there isn't enough of me in one place now to panic … and
then do panic — and when I stop running, I am back across
the Square (it passed through me absolutely unnoticed — it is

only by looking back that I know that I have passed through it!) and I am having a belated lunch in some plastic-nicolodeon joint ... my remaining embodiment looses its teak timbre from the executive suite of the glass-sheath tower and goes salmon pink along the counterline now ... Soupe du jour et biftek, au point ... The food descends my elevator shaft and congeals in my salmon plastic-pinked stomach — fortunately I can't vomit, can't even feel nauseous: my stomach is artificial now. Soooo ... I've chameleoned to that point. I've decarnated further than I feared. Only the old imitation wrought-iron coat-wrack in the corner, splattered with taches of aluminum paint to modernize it — only that keeps feeding me now, intravenously. And it is out of place, as is my blood. My heart founders. Under these conditions my plans are simply impracticable. How can I share the intensity of joy that the Square is in me, has been for me, always, implicitly, till today, till now, when I actually reach out to prove its joy for the sake of others? How can I write the Novel. There isn't any Place to live, to see, not any more ... it has gone out of me. Worse, the very converse — the same Place d'Armes has become for me simply a bloodsucker — each building a leech, draining me of my remaining corpuscularity. What I had come to see, still vainly hoping to share, not only has failed me, but has turned against me. I am left with an inversion of my verity. Gathering up my encroaching invisibility and my check, I flee — so discountenanced that I am able to walk past target, site unseen — a mutual agreement almost. Slink to my hotel. No — all my tactics are wrong. I cannot give what I now no longer possess — nor can I leave dispossessed. My Novel is out the window. So is my life!

I try to think ... no use. I can't feel anything ... and out of touch, I'm out of mind — out of my mind. For a brief moment I know that I am on the verge of insanity ... Lie down, lie down.

vertebra wrench, open and squeeze clamped closed like accordion, ramming the punch of me from tail to necknape, head threatens to detach — and suddenly bolt upright from the thrust I'm awake to the realization that my body has simply corporately echoed the sound from freight-train shunting in the yards — my ear still thrums bright as the trainbell rams the entire cargo home it freights. 7 p.m. How long did I sleep? My guilt musters me to typewriter ... and for two hours I record this day's disaster of me. Dispassionate, because detached now. Disembodied.

Done — I wonder what next? Technically I'm through — washed up, or washed out. I can go home now. Settle into being a civil servant or university prof or a bond salesman. It's as simple as that. I've just died. Why not accept the fait accompli ... and enjoy my retirement into the Canadian Social Welfare State; climb into the trough, with the rest of the Citizenry. Head reels again ... and I know that this is impossible; I would shoot myself first ... What the hell have I been doing these past ten years, if not evading that issue! That impasse. The All-Canadian Clunk — no, I'ld rather die, again, than say yes.

Out into the night air ... aware that I need food, though not hungry. Wend me through the velvet dark of the humid December night, to the restaurat of Paul-Marie Sanson ... Le Chat Botté, just a few doors from *Le Devoir* on the same side.... *Le Devoir* — our only relevant journal of opinion — the only Canadian newspaper that absolutely had to say what it had to say these past ten years ... and said it. It had guts. And at *Le Devoir* it had been André Laurendeau — the editor. One man, who stood up to be counted. When it hurt ... But for some reason or other no one from *Le Devoir* ever eats chez Paul-Marie. Paul-Marie is a Frenchman ... from Le Midi ... and that, finally, is unpardonable. That he serves the best food in Montréal, that he is no more expensive than the other intellectually or socially chi-chi restaurants nearby which are also reasonably inexpensive, that he is actually only a few doors from the newspaper. None of this matters. Paul-Marie is French, obdurately French. Moreover his decor is neither improved Habitant, nor a clinically clean version of Paris Left Bank. No — Le Chat Botté is simply eternal French bistro in a Canadian Victorian setting that has been here since built ... the mantlepiece settles the period pretty well; one of those carbuncular wooden mantles with knops and finials and chip-carving overall, thoroughly clotted with a grained golden oak finish multiply varnished. By the time of Queen Victoria's Diamond Jubilee it was honourably aged. So Paul-Marie's clientele is English-speaking mainly. Because of the atmosphere and because of Paul-Marie, and because it is in Le Vieux Quartier near such quarantined denizens as *Le Devoir*. A visit to Le Chat Botté for an Anglo-Canadian Respectable is as risqué as a tour along the Red Light lane ... I remember watching them order meals here, many times ... invariably the same — steak after an onion soup, finishing with a crême caramel, or a pâtisserie française. In fact I never was entirely sure what Paul-Marie used to do with his tripes and brains, and bowels, and pigs'-feet, and head-cheeses and illegal game, and all the other pungent extremities of barnyard flora and fauna. The answer I supposed all along was Paul-Marie himself ... as I see him again, now on entry, I am sure of it. Six foot three, he hasn't lost a single one of his 329 pounds. Sitting with his back to me, in front of the TV, eating his blood sausage and terrine de foie de vollaille. Seated amidst the clamour of his oh so empty tables. If possible he has grown even more Paul-Marie, has grown further into himself. The Paul-Marieness of Paul-Marie — absolute self-fidelity. He hears me, and pivots his chair ... impounding me with his 329-pound eyesight, probing me deep for my food potential, for my significance as a man-of-food. Decides I'm insignificant ... and is about to let his waitress guide me to a table, when suddenly his eyes focus on mine ... "Monsieur

Hugh ..." and he is on the instant dissolved from implacable
food concentrate — like some fossilized but pliant pemmican —
into inordinate activity ... in seconds we are safe, in the kitchen,
with its ten-foot stove, wood-stove. Paul-Marie promptly stuffs
it with more wood — which it patently does not need, and
then armed with an outrageously undulant ladle undertakes
a constrained elephantine ballet from pot to pot ... a joyous
war-dance of the foods, in my honour ... digs ladle down to
turnip and gourd and leek and all the bloated enormities from
its international reservoir of innards. Roils the stews, the soups,
the sauces, in a free molestation that would please any voyeur
of feed. High tribute, that. And I am embarrassed by it. On
the centre table a mound of brains that could only be from a
dinosaur, did a dinosaur have sufficient brains to still be dinosaur.
And guarding these, from the far end of the kitchen, perched on
a pair of bar-stools, the lares and penates — King and Prince —
German Shepherds eying me with the same intent I apply to
the food — a fierce friendliness.

I know exactly what I feel ... like the gentle man in
Galsworthy's story of the old custom shoemaker, whom he must
frequent, out of loyalty ... I would eat Paul-Marie's food were
it rotten! "It's changed, Paul-Marie, it's better than ever." The
Frenchman smiles amidships — "on va manger, eh Monsieur
Hugh ... on va manger" — and he masticates each word he
proffers ... leads me triumphantly back to his table, afront the
TV screen, gouges me tablespoonful of terrine, and leaves me,
irritated by the TV, and sad.... God knows I didn't come to
Montreal to watch TV ... offended, I raise a breadful of the
best terrine in the nation to my mouth, hopefully — suddenly
I vibrate, terrine glowers ... it is the voice on the TV. I know
that voice — know it gutwise. It's Jean-Pierre Préfontaine ...
talking political leaders; how often we did that during my stay
in Montreal. I watch the terrine, rich on the bread, and then
lower it to my plate, untouched. That munificent voice of Jean-

Pierre, voice that is what he has to say. Voice from these same
innards that Paul-Marie marinates and steeps and stews and eats,
all by himself (and I remember now that Paul-Marie, too, has
a huge voice, a voice that, once on the rampage in song, turns
your earth upside right.) And then, my terrine grounded, I
concentrate me, almost malevolently, on what Jean-Pierre says
— because I know that he says nought. Now all the questions
are into me again as a great tidal bore. Why does this man say
nothing? Why does he settle for $50,000 a year ... with his seat
on the Royal Commission on Canadian Culture, a face on TV
and a voice on radio? It's all balls ... or rather it's all no-balls
at all. Absolute irrelevance. Jean-Pierre knows that ... knows
that he is saying nothing.... There's the rub. He knows the
impotence of what he says.... The terrine, on my bread on the
plate, catches my eye again — it is the sound of the voice that
does it — Jean-Pierre has started in again ... that is it — it is
how he says it that is inordinately potent, I quiz the screen again
— poor Jean-Pierre, you are left only with the right to hear the
sound of your own voice. Echo of a fecundity forever unused,
untapped.... What happened to you — why did you desert?
Where did you go? What do you see now as you leer out at us
from within your electronic cage? Pauvre Jean-Pierre ...

"Qu'est-ce que vous-voulez, M'sieur ... ?" The waitress
is at my back — and I realize that I am speaking out loud —
apostrophizing the shadow of the shadow of Jean-Pierre, that I
am even imitating his voice ... in French. And that as I imitate
it I eat of the terrine de foie de volaille. It tasted of ... but
even as I rejoice at the empire of taste in this terrine it has
gone. Christ — I'm back at absolute zero again ... headspin. I
hang on to the carafe of ordinaire that Paul-Marie has squatted
afront me. I appall me ... I cannot taste any of it. I know that
— my taste buds have folded — closed down for the night. It
is the sight of Jean-Pierre ... his deliberate demission. He is
posthumous ... and knows it, and accepts it, and goes on living

it warmed by the sound of his own voice ... warming the
last cockle of his heart. I cannot stop me now, watching this
television spectre ... no stop, stop — wrench my eyes out of
it just at the moment when body threatens dissolution again
— just as I see Paul Marie's terrine descending my transparent
gullet — proof positive of my desubstantiation.

And now, eyeballs popped back in, I am reprieved (if not
saved) — a trio arrive, and my instincts apprise me of a Scene.

Young couple. Plus a little Big Daddy. Out on the Town —
the Lower Town. Big-Little Daddy pays. She smiles upon him;
hubby talks for their supper. I listen out the corner of my ear ...
Paul-Marie bounds over onto them, accosts their appetite, waitress
smiles and we convene complicit over Paul-Marie's campaign ...

Me — "what an urgency to Paul-Marie now ... services
them as though they were on Messianic mission, dependent for
capacity to Resuscitate upon a warranted feed-station...."

Waitress — "c'est toujours comme ça. If they leave food
uneaten he is sad ... mopes."

See their eyes skirt the menu ... Big-Little Daddy smiles
approbation. Wife smiles upon husband. Husband talks more
fluently. Thus the bargain is made ... "three filets Mignon, three
onion soup ..."

Paul-Marie knows their lines — plays them out, his feet
pounding time, whole body urgent to the metre, scanning
their food-place ... "et comme desert nous avons pâtisseries
françaises ... fromages ... crême caramel...." He is almost
malevolent ... the "crême caramel" only comes out after a
hopeful pause, and then is said with culminating authority in
the absence of theirs.

I can't take any more of this ... watch the TV an instant.
Reduced to that. Paul-Marie pounces on the kitchen, armed to
the teeth with his orders ... his pots-au-feu bubbling for only
him and me, and now only him — as I am a hit-and-run victim
of TV. The trio play out their night's engagement. For one

unperceived moment, witless, I realize how fine the terrine is
... catch the colour of it out the corner of my eye ... "colour"?
— yes, that is what it is — I see colour on the TV screen, and
realize abruptly I am nibbling the terrine and catching its
kaleidoscope ... catching all the essential out the corner of my
eye. And then it is gone — just as I know it, it is gone ... like
the Place, with the map....And I am gone, in absentia.

They have their crême caramel. My eyes are dry with the
screen or I could cry. I want to go over ... to wheedle. "Excuse
me Sir ... but Paul-Marie serves the only cêpes in town, as a
savoury! Cêpes mesdamesmesdemoisellesmonsieurs! Cêpes!
And un petit vin de paille. And with coffee, he has his own
eau-de-vie, from his village, near Carcasson, it's all on the menu
... in English." But I know if I wheedle they will mount their
high horse and I shall have to take out my knife and cut off the
vestiges of their humanhood, scrotumsacking them with a single
twist of knife like coring dead apple for stewpot....

I am out on the street again. Sauve qui peut! Told Paul-
Marie I would come back later in the week ... that this was
but a tour de reconnaissance. Bandying towards me, short legs,
crooked nose with dilating nostril (left one), deep bruised
eyesockets, barrel chesting over those legs ... a reporter turns
in to Le Devoir. God — how habitant he still is ... Habitant!
But he has just turned my country inside out with his "quiet
revolution" — 150 years too late.

Oh God — that's it ... my country, my eyesight, my taste
... all gone now! I knew I had forgotten something. I had
forgotten everything. And La Place ... I stumble my faith down
la rue Notre Dame, blinkered, saving me again for La Place
d'Armes. Past la rue Bonsecours with its church, and La Maison
Papineau, and the Chateau de Ramezay, and the Hotel de Ville,
and the Court Houses, old and new ... screening them with my
televizor, to evade stumbling over them in my dark. To La Place.
And only there open my eyes, wide opened, to embrace La

Place … mumbling "I've come … I've come … look, I've come back, I promised."

It's gone too. Why fool myself? There's nothing there. Oh, there's something — I see the outlines, delimiting the buildings around La Place. And with an effort, from memory, I can still name them — at least the major ones — clockwisely, from St. James Street side — new and old Bank of Montreal, that pair of skyscrapers on the east side — one with the old Banque Cdne nationale, the other, the old Providence Life Building. Behind me l'église Notre Dame and its Presbytery … But it's all irrelevant now. The veil has come down in me, over my eyes. I am shut off — cannot see, nor hear, nor touch. Look again at the Place — no, it's just a postcard there now, a site through a viewer, and even that is ebbing from me.

So that is it — I came to La Place, to prove possession of it, to fling it in the face of the infidels, to cower them with the reality they have sacrificed, and, at the very moment of proof, find I have already lost it … lost everything.

Stumble up the steps of the Church, can't harm me now, no longer; sit down, go and sit down, enter and slump in the first pew … slump my body still ironclad around my core, body frozen over me frozen in my own steep freeze … ironsides … and dump me here, moribund. My eyes rebut the body of the Church I can no longer see, sweeping over its body — in a reassurance that I am unscathed by it, and even as I confirm the armour-plating I am stabbed … from the right, and I turn stunned to the face of the wound, follow the trajectory of thrust from my flank, across the aisle till I am up to our hilt in the eyeballs of a youth who curious appraises my arrival. I withtract instantly, close the ironclad, close … but I have been penetrated and cannot and look back up again along the same trajectory of sight and am imbedded again in those eyes on me … stumble back out of the Church that sudden flares in me, anywhere … and as I exit, turn to exorcize those eyes and still cannot, and now we are talking under the huge arcade of the entry and walking in the light snowfall that I feel against the hot socket of my left eye windsown.

Down the sidestreet by the Church, and after a five-minute walk the bar closes around us and we are babbling. Deep inside I am taut, closed ... I Know where I am, but I don't want to know ... I Know this is the last remedy, the disastrous prerequisite, but don't want to know. Peer cautiously at the barroom ... there are about 75 of us here ... I glue my arsehold to the chairseat like bitch in heat, while trying to wag my tale in self-deprecatory defence. Seventy-five of us ... from 15 to 50. I'll watch — no harm ... parry an eyethrust from leftflank. Parry and feint. In front of my screen a blondie convenes an entire tableau around him ... watch his progressions ... five other she-males resuscitate at the end of his fingertits ... all engaged in the rhythm of his embodiment.... The rotten French-Canadian teeth, sleezy tights, fuzzy-wuzzy parkas ... all these disappear as I too dance at the end of those fingers, my armour-plate clanking to the floor ... my flank is open now, unveiled left toe twitches, nostril flares and as blond boy quivers his court to renewed palpability, I sudden retreat, on the run, back into my safety of insensibility — but even as I do I am stabbed again, and turn to the boy from the Church still beside me ... Yvon ... 18, in turtleneck skisweater, a snood of dark hair, and eyes climbing all over inside me, as though I am some site ... "insite," that is it ... all that land inside us ... Yvon — shy, but firm — nothing coy. He has just pierced again my flank, emancipated me again from my ironsides ... and I have just swallowed him eyeballs first. The pact is simple, frank, immutable. This then is disaster ... the complete, instant immersion in another. No holds barred. Absolute accessibility. And it is disaster ... consequence of my desertion of all I hold dear — the requisite Disaster....

"Il me faut cinq piastres ... je suis commerçant." My head
roars ... senses close — I turn to grapple with that Judas-kiss....
Everything left in me focuses my deception ... my eyes muster
my accusation, and as I look at him we are imbedded along the
line of looking; his eyes flow into me again, and I accept their
need, and my own.

Walk the greystone street from the bar, the same side of La
Place as my petite place ... down towards the harbour ... along
a grey way of stone houses ... flanked by them each side, till
we are in front of a fine Regency stone home, now for tourists
... up the curving cast-iron steps two flights, from whose top I
can see the white new dome of the Marché Bonsecours, the
rippling cupola of the City Hall ... and if I step to one side,
the towers of Notre Dame, with the Bank of Montreal behind.
The front door is bullworthy — no battering would breach its
stolid convolutions of wood panel and applied pilasters. Inside
everything clean, in place ... a snugglery amidst these Georgian
townhouses that are become everything but what they were —
boutiques, tourist homes, warehouses, brothels, antique shops.
I can only chuckle ... if only the Regency gentlemen of old
Montreal could see this ... or the Historic Sites Committee today.

Yvon's room ... an extension of the bunnycoats I saw in
the tavern. Those parkas canadiens which no English-Canadian
male nor even she-male would be seen dead in alive. A kind of
blatant cuteness. The walls bleu-pale, of dribbly plaster pattern;
crucifix on the wall (after all — I met Yvon at the foot of the
altar!) flowers potted on a low star-spangled coffee table (Air
Canada styling!) — they are plastic, but I scarce note that except
by mental recollection, they seem so right ... live flowers here
would be fake! All warmly cosmetic. Yvon reporting to his
"colleagues" (think that is the academic term) in the basement.

... what the Hell am I doing here? What are the chances of
getting out? There was a murder in this block a few days before
I arrived — my cleaning woman told me all the details ... I

scout the innards of the cupboard — no one there. On the table,
beside the potted plastic flowers three colour photos of Yvon ...
in each one he has the same intent, diffident look. In each one
he shields his eyes from the probe of the camera ... never really
letting the camera see what I have already seen in him, through
his eyesite. How can I possibly believe him conscientious
accomplice to murder. His innocence is so articulate in these
photos ... his self-consciousness.

Yvon back — close the door ... lock it carefully — turn,
look at me ... it is a warm looking. A male prostitute — he
patently likes his métier — his clean bluejeans already taut as
he stands akimbo, gentle, awaiting — nothing slut, nothing
brazen, nothing aggressive, nor weak. He is simply there ... **all**
there. And he wants to be there — that's what he is there about.
What's more, he expects me to be there. I watch this open and
absolute salutation in silenced admiration ... this complete self-
presentation. My presence acknowledges him ... gives birth
to him. God — this métier of his, it is divine. No actor could
approximate this extraordinary gift of self that the $5 conceals.
This boy simply wants to give and to be given. The five bucks ...
give it to him now ... hand it to him saying "You can go now if
you want." Yvon folds the bill carefully in his shirt, looks me up
and down — is it reproach? And then steps forward, unbuttons
his checked shirt and draws my thighs to him gentle and hands
on my back kneads me into him ... I watch us wary ... not a
false move. What Yvon does comes from within him — from
some inner law he follows now flawlessly, while his eyes palp
mine. I watch intently for the slightest failure in that law — at
the slightest deviation from it I would be released, and would
flee ... There is none. This boy is an artist. And he sells his body
the way artists do, only they do it at once remove, on canvas, or
sculpted ... his art is consummate, direct....

Yvon jabs cocked pants now steep into my thighside ...
thrust him back and eat his body wholemeal through my

eyeballs. Still he awaits. And as though unveiling virgin I part his
bluejeans and complete our divestiture, till we are naked in us….
His body proffers so naturally — so freshly — the virginity
lying in the renewed wonder it reveals for him so clearly now.

Imbedded together I man his rood that fulfils my palmed
handling … firm in the hand … the rediscovered heritage. Yvon
eyes always follow me through mine, always completely there,
always implicating my own, so that what is done at manrood is
already assured in eyesite … once only do I avert my eyes, and as I
do the thunder of my ear dies and I am alone. I panic, and my eyes
turn quick to filch him at cockhead, and as they light thereupon I
see his eyes again, ears open, and again I feel steep inside of me.

"Comment veux-tu arriver?"

"I don't know yet."

Yvon's eyes summons us … "Je ne l'aime pas dans le trou…."

I feel my disappointment … because there is a negative in
us now. Then I see his eyes — they are not negative; they are
only the look of a boy about to take Communion. Run my
rood along his, lying us askewer, touching us together for the
first time, thus, lightly, run it along, till our cocklips touch, run
it down the firmed centre of his manhood (simple statistic: he
has 10 fine inches of gift), and slowly creep my cocktip up to
his, his eyes on my cockhead, then his eyes clamped in my own,
we eyesite each other, till with easy implacably concision the
cocklips kiss again and I am inflorescent, bathing his rood in
liquid moonstone. Yvon's eyes close in a Mona Lisa smile of the
line of the lids, and as he lie so immersed in my harvest I gather
his root till it blurt sperm bolts clean up to our breast.

His eyes open, incredulous with wonder … dresses as I
watch him. "Where will you go now?"

"je rentre au club … je vais danser…." Yvon smiles, pats the
$5 … I know that although our conjugation has been tentative,
yet I will always remember Yvon, because he restores to me
an entire world … suddenly he reincarnates me after twenty

years of meticulous self-destitution. For twenty years I have
adhered meticulously to the code of the latent Civil Serviceable.
For twenty years I have flirted with sterility. Now, at the final
moment, I have broken. Yvon breached me at the moment of
final closure. I am free to be myself responsibly ... free to know
the world I have so conscientiously extruded.

For that Yvon is blessed ... I look at the crucifix on the wall.
"I met you in the Church ... yet you are ... you are" (I couldn't
say, or didn't want to say "prostitute") He sees my difficulty ...
as I stumble out my compromise word "you are promiscuous."
Yvon smiles "oh non, tu vois, je suis Catholique."

Wonderful variation of a theme — "non anglised angeli" —
"not promiscuous; catholic...." Out of the mouth of babes.

As we go out, the door of the next bedroom is open. The
same reality to it: definably French Canadien — incredible "bad
taste" ... but incredibly complete bad taste ... nothing out of its
own taste — all of a piece. And that piece is of podgy flesh paste
... a plaster-of-Paris incorporation! Polychromatic! Like those
same plastic flowers hung beside a same Christ. All of life as
some bloody waxy image ... with all artificial colouring — like
margarine, maraschino cherries. Pinks, powdered blues ... star-
dust! It loyally revulses me....

And in a wicker armchair, in the corner....

"Bonsoir Pierrot ... je m'en vais au Rock." Yvon is gentle,
polite ... saving him from a kind of smugness, from a holier
than thou so clearly produce of his fortune with me ... his duty
done for the day. A kind of sainting for sinhood.

"C'est Hughes, Pierre...." For one catastrophic moment I
fear Yvon is going to say "C'est Hughes ... de Toronto." And
bless him for not damning me with it.

Pierrot cocks a toe up at us ... bigtoe, barefoot. Same lifekit
as Yvon. Jeans, plaid checkered shirt — plus a slight cravat, gold,
knotted at his Adam's apple: Little Lord Fauntleroy as good
Amurrican Bad Guy ... Bigtoe eyes me, still cocked (toenail cut

and cleansed … into me. Taken by bigtoe! — as decisive as that unseen flankglance penetrating me in church with Yvon still unsighted. Ears thunder. Sheer lust of life.

"Cinq piastres?" The voice is mine!

"Ouaé msieur … non — sis … c'est déjà minuit pawssé"

"Je reviens tantôt." And I am walking along the Greyway with Yvon, leaving him at his club — Eden Rock (I didn't notice the name when we first came): odious name … en anglais du reste. Yvon smiles — "au revoir … tu étais chic avec moi … tu vas aimer Pierrot … puis il adore le 69!"

And I am at hotel, to my room, for the extra money … and then back along Greyway to Pierrot … it's crazy, but now I know I must honour this lifelust in me, or live still-born. And within an hour of Knowing Yvon (because only the Biblical "Know," with its capitalized "K" describes for me this kind of knowledge) I am knocking at the bullworthy door again. Betrayed back into life again by bigtoe! Pierrot answers … barefoot. Back into his room where the bare-assed Christ bleeds down the pucker-plastered blue wall. Pierrot is reading *Manorama* — not a mag I know, I note wryly … picture spread of other Pierrots. None of them is Pierrot: not that I expected — but none of them carries himself the same as my Pierrot. Something drastically different … in the embodiment. Pierrot senses my thought train.

"Ils sont tous Américains…. Pas comme nous autres … pas du tout." So he knows too.

"Et pas même comme vous autres, non plus." I bless him the condescending compliment — pauvre Angluche que moi.

"They are all Squares" — Pierrot is proud of his comment, and his English.

"And what are we?" I blurt aloud … unwitting expecting an answer — *the* answer. He shrugs … and quietly undoes himself … his shirt aside, and over to his sink, washes hands, feet

"mais jamais ça" he smileblasts into me, patting his hand to his crotch … "je ne le lave pas — pas jusqu'à après … ça goute

vrai comme ça" His smile seconds his point … Yvon's teeth
are singularly un-French-Canadian, almost Ipana bright — but
Pierrot's are indelibly Canayen … like rotted patates frites.

And in the shuddered observation note that I have some
answer to my question — "what are we?" — it is this remaining
capacity for some kind of life-giving dirt. "Pourriture noble" —
that mould blooming on French grapes giving a lusher, richer
wine. Pourriture noble … and again sight those teeth, that
green bloom of fleshbronze. "Ca goute mieux" — Pierrot is
hideously right. Bouquet and body … tang that doesn't come
in an economy bottle. All the difference between.

Pierrot is lying in an open loll on bedface, twitching me
with bigtoe … immense beckoner as my captive eye swallows
it whole and am unawares into his manscape still at ten feet
distance yet touched in a way that nobody has ever touched
me in my own community d'Angluche. Into it and feeding …
guzzling a sheer gluttony. Pierre *is* a slut … and I buy his body …
like over-ripe wine. (Dizzy said — was it in *Coningsby*? — that
any man can like good wine, but it takes a connoisseur to enjoy
bad wine …) watch his body cocking, his hidden Man risen
under bluejeans … bigtoe down and rises rises me slowly rising
with him rising me and in me am over to this manscape standing
high over hawkeying this land this whole nation lying rampant
under my very eye as abruptly I skydive onto this sweet prey,
headfirst beakfirst onto swollen jeans nuzzle into the manmusk
seeping through the closed fly breathing deep into this musk, as
Pierrot grasp my head of hair, probing into my overbrush, then
I am back up to eye this site again … yes, ohhh yes, it is entire
land spreadeagling there entire land I always knew was there,
never absolutely lost, merely out of site, and now is confronting
me hands down to grasp entry opening in earthquake of us
the Man of Pierrot hidden still under winding whitesheath of
underwear I reach in to palm the body that clasps my hand
around and around its trunk to root Pierrot sifting thigh into

my gasp as I bare the massed trunk of him, uncircumscribed
land naked in fullflesh, head down to bigtoe in fierce Ptolemaic
circumference sucking me down down inexorable to imbed me
in this land as Pierrot certain of the way divest me still standing
aside him, till free naked I am fallen back into the land to plow
us under ... running my muzzle over this countryside surging
up on me, alive into this banished world so suddenly restored
whole ... swarm me over Pierrotland from all directions as
this manscape gets on my horse to ride into me from every
direction riding all of us at once everywhere we move is always
everywhere moving to everywhere else in the free fields that
wind unending up our valleyside to peak and back while Magpie
highdives down with Icarus into a blue-skie seat that afterwarns
me now I am in the same world that Pieter Brueghel says he so
rightly saw four centuries ahead of us but we forgot to entirely
believe with him yet is so absolutely here now from the moment
I bury my nose in this burning bush whose 10 inch stalk batters
my nose is hoof of horse from that plowman behind (he doesn't
notice Icarus skindiving below) each furrow cavalcading into this
eternal Campagna worldwide that I bloodhound relentless into
the wideyed distance that is all immeasurable foreground Pierrot
given each brush and rock and clump pummels me roundalay
in my mulburied bush ... as I eat this all edible manscape of
Everyman feeding to my need, famished and it is true then
that we poor Protestants deny the Body and Blood that was
given for us as guarantee for our Sinworthiness ... denying the
world on this Ptolemaic platter only circumscribed here by the
bounds of that dire need I nurture hearandnow while I pangful
recollect divine Raphael's "Disputa" whose very detachment
from all flesh whose very vaunting perspective would cut my
tenuous umbilink with all this land still left latent in me to
plant and plow to belated harvesting as I soar now above the
Plowman all the land white and warm beneath my birth and
soar centred over all circle down and down onto the head of

this brave Plowman whose toe still touches the deep earth still imbeds us all in the land that feeds us as down now onto his head I engulf in my anxious mouth for that manmusk Pierrot said he kept clean for such meet needs while I mouth this landcocked head savouring oh at longed-for last this noble rot to cleanse me knowing how rightly Moutarde de Dijon is gutted from the furrowed land while mere Amurrican hotdogs are clotted with that quickblotted tang that kills all taste of truth in Man so now I savour this sheer landmusk grateful that Pierrot thighrides into me so I grasp his bushimbedded rod striding up and down around its rot articulating my manhood at each gust of lush fleshscape salting me plow deep this landman that plows me to impending harvest Pierrot moaning steep in flush we fondle dandle clasp and run along the hedgerow by our shore I ply and row wondering this Icarean Sea wherein Pierrot has engulfed us both face to cockface and I sink to rise us again sucking huge in me the pod burst from this land spurting seed in our gathering mouthfulfilling with that first citric precision of spermblurt followed by the glut of man splashed in throat and gullet, spermspurt in nostril flaring wide as Pierrot grasps my ebbing trunk to earth of us lying thigh by thigh turning at last only to kiss the mutual musk of seed sown around our muzzle as he lopes last over to the basin to wash away any lost part of our deed as I watch knowing it is the lope I marry land to man in that conjugation all free flesh knows from a world that quakes with every step we take....

Give him his cinq piastres, plus un piastre parce qu'il est minuit passé, plus encore un piastre en souvenir de Pieter Brueghel (and his Icarus) and I am into the night air ... walking with sure stride. Where — where the hell are you going, I ask me? Till I am at La Place d'Armes ... and enter, and stand in the centre, free man with the key back in to the kingdom ... Christ — so that is it ... the veil rent from my eyes, all the Place sears in me, with a lucidity that....

I don't stop running till I am at my hotel. Safe abed....

Ahh — so that is it. The issue is joined — squarely (heinous multiple unwitting pun!): To see La Place, to write my novel, to come alive, again, I must fall, utterly. To share my love I must humiliate me ... must grovel. Stand waistdeep in the shit ... and then sing. Sing, goddam it, sing. I try to sing a little ... what? What shall I sing? I don't know anything to sing. Hit Parade is crap (and "crap" is just shit-substitute: crap is pseudo-shit, ultimate degradation.) And "Onward Christian Soldiers" seems so inappropriate.... "Things go better with Coca-Cola ..." — no good! I'd better do the Christian Soldiers. "Onwaaard Chrissstyenn Sooo-olldyerse ..." Ok — enuff. The main truth is out now — I've got to pay homage, or I'm done. Real homage — call it "hommage" — fealty to my Liege Man. So be it. But who will bless my God-damned soul?

Clock tolls 2 a.m. I feel immense relief now. An immense cleansing.

Surely that can't be right — "cleansing"? ... my dear Hugh, you are out of your mind! ...

Yes, but I'm back in my skin — I've jumped back into my skin ... back into my wits....

So it is a cleansing. That **is** it ... exactly what I do feel. Even more precisely — a purification: now explain that one — no I don't want to — I'd only explain it away. And then I could write a little essay about it — a tract for the times.

Purification — and the need, the intense need now to live again; all because of that accomplished deconstipation ... that's it — a deconstipation — blew twenty years of shit out of me ... opened me up again — tore the veil aside ... and left me whole again, made me whole ... holy: has made a man out of me again.

But you've just slept with two teenage male prostitutes! You are beneath contempt, defiled ... a lifetime of honourable chastity sold for tripe....

No no no — that is not so — and my whole body shines now in the face of my mobilized accusation. What is it then? Have I simply accepted Hell — simply (good Protestant) reassured myself of it … my holy life-insurance? And is this apparent defilement now the prerequisite of Heaven?

And the Place d'Armes … I ran from it … just as I was about to see it again, with ferocious clarity — see it as it has always been, latent in me … Why did I run — just as I was about to repossess it? Why?

Idiot — because it looked you in the eye the way Yvon looked you in the eye. It wanted you … and had you returned its gaze you would have been dismantled again. La Place is a voyeur … it hunts you as you it.

But I couldn't give me again. Not to La Place. Not that way.

Then you will never see….

As I turn to bed I see IT — that map — that goddam tourist map … the fatal flaw … the moment of lack of faith, when I looked at it, instead of the reality, instead of the Object itself. Throw it out. Throw it out! Too late. Pick it up … and those abject postcards I wanton bought — I see it now — as substitutes, as mediators between me, and the Object Incarnate. Notre Dame Church, the old Bonsecours Market, La Place Ville Marie, Nelson's Monument, the Bank of Montreal…. Throw them out! No — insert them into Combat Journal. They are part of the Evidence … for and against. Ah — traitors! You betrayed me…. You led me down the garden path — to smash, against Eden Rock. Well — you can stay now, to stand trial. Stick you in with the rest … over my marbleized face.

Asleep. It is 3 a.m. Preparing me again for my novel. I lunch with Luc Raymond tomorrow which is today. I will begin, right after Luc. These first days simply a false start. Completely wrong — the very opposite of what I wanted. Must eliminate them from the Novel.

DAY THREE

COMBAT JOURNAL

... slowly awake to the clangour of my body ... I'm a brass
band conducted by ... by the Little Square below my window
... my entire body is trumpet and thrum and fife and flute....
blares me. Now I recognize that it is the Petite Place that is
the band, and I the conductor ... my body the conductor. Or
is my body being conducted? Listen with care — no, my first
response was right: I *am* the band, and the square conducts me.
My cock tells me that.... I waken more — am properly awake,
because I hear with ears as well as cock ... sounds funnels direct
in instead of steeping me.

Sit up ... into the decisive sense of physical accretion — I've
grown a cubit. My whole being distended. Savour this increment.
A sudden coming of age. My God — of course — Yvon! No
wonder my body is back now. My whole being shimmers. I
want to sing again ... my gut is a mouth organ. Nature calls —
honour it ... and am sudden bereft of my extension.

At 1 p.m. still expecting Luc at the hotel for our noon
engagement ... curse his lateness. I could have sortied out to
La Grande Place — La Place d'Armes — am ready for it ...
opened to it now. Maudits Frangluches ... they have no sense
of time (but a wonderful sense of timing!) — and I sit in the
lobby awaiting him ... flogging myself with the delay. Watching
the old hens at the front desk, going through the motions
of running the hotel. And then watch more closely ... no —
they're not running it ... they're running with it, responding
to it — they are a mirror of the inner rhythm of the hotel ...

responding like live-wired marionettes as the hotel runs around
them. Their bodies dance the comings-and-goings…. Mouthing
their own mime of the events that swirl us. How does a place
like this operate? Now the black-haired maman bobs and
twitches with an extra flibbertigibbetery and Luc is all around
me bobolarking too and when I finally net him down we have
already crossed la Petite Place, past Nelson's Monument and
down Notre Dame Street to Le Petit Havre, a block towards
La Place d'Armes. Barely in the restaurant and Luc pirouettes
with indefatigable grace at the second table … kissing the hands
of two demoiselles … "de la Galerie Ste-Geneviève … rue
St. Paul …" while I am engaged in evading the glance of two
Anglo-Canadian acquaintances of TV-days at the table beyond.
"You must visit their gallery…."

"Bien entendu" — I acquiesce, still evading, and in the act
caught by the corner of my eye on his young brunette both
of us unwilling but instantly invaded by our glance…. And
introductions done and a luncheon engagement made for the
sake of my Novel, with the brunette, we ensconce ourselves
in the next dining room, unobserved — seated across the
compulsory French Canadian red-checked tablecloth. I await
his first move. It doesn't come. Luc arrived in orbit, he remains
in orbit, and while I patiently attend his play on the chess-board
tablecloth afront me he is all over me….

"Comment vas-tu?" — he is hovering in front of my
nose now, having negotiated every nook of my well-vested
corporation. "Comment vas-tu, Hugh?" His eyes pilfer mine
with their solidity and unwitting I am aflight in our crazy
dance now…. Aflight because I instinctively know that his
"Comment vas-tu?" really means "Who are you … who are you
now, Hugh? … it has been four years since I've seen us … who
are you, who are we … let us be these now, right now … who,
who, who, WHO?" With this, all my whats are filed, and for
five hours we are launched in lunchtide … lunch à la française,

en française. Eating, laughing, gesticulating, talking, alive in
French. And I am all my French Canadianité again ... c'est
ma Francité. Now I take on, chameleon, all those additional
forgotten attributes that are mine by right as a Canadian de
langue française.

Luc — "... wonderful you are back with us ... you will
stay now?"

Me — "I had to come back ... I couldn't stand it any more."

Luc — "stand what...."

Me — "us — my own people ... English Canada ...
Toronto.... I was finally fired ... I triggered my own firing
squad."

Luc — "bravo!"

Somewhere in the midst of this conversation that is the
converse of a dialogue ... that is more truly duet ... we pinion
lunch. Luc pinions lunch....

"Madamoiselle ... qu'est-ce que vous nous suggerez
alors...?" And the eyes of the blond French waitress are aflight
with us and somewhere in the third orbit we find calves brains
with capers, a carafe of white wine, crême caramel (!) ... black
coffee, one armagnac, one calvados and one Marc de Bourgogne,
each (violin-cello, cello, and bass-viol).

Across from me Luc is stationary a moment as his eyes fix
me: "Maintenant tu vas commencer vivre alors ... ici."

"Yes — I must start to live ... I've just been born...." His
eyes are my smile for me. I note for the first time that he has
glasses and that the left lens is held in place by scotch tape. Bless
him. And behind the scotch tape, those innumerable eyes of Luc,
on me into mine, pervading us with unnamed joy. Luc — poet,
cinéaste, Separatist ... French Canadian!

"Yes, I am doing a novel ... on La Place d'Armes...." And
I try to explain again, for my own benefit what it is that I am
doing, objectively ... "I have come to sight La Place, for others
... I never really saw it during my four years here. I always took

it for granted … knew it was wonderful but never why …
never probed my belief that….

"Attendez une seconde … M'mselle — votre vin … il est
légèrement maderisé vous savez … essayons le rouge alors."
She is back moments later with a carafe of red — and we are
refurbished.

Me — "I love it here … in the Vieux Quartier … I am at
home…. It fulfils something in me … completely … demands a
plenitude of response from me … forces me to flower (I could
never say that in English you know … people would laugh!) I
want to communicate that in the novel."

"Je vois bien … eh, mon vieux — et ta femme?"

"She knows I must do this … that I must come alive before
it is too late … I could not do it if she did not have faith in me,
and I in her … if that went, then it wouldn't be worth doing. It
is a question of live or death … tu sais…."

"C'est évident! Mais combien des vôtres comprennent cela?"

"My wife — nearly. And one childhood friend who has
been implicated in my life since I was twelve … and Jack
Richards, because I pave a way for him now…. And Eric
Newman — you know him from CBC."

"Et ta famille … ton frère aîné? Peter?"

"No — he mustn't understand what I am doing … or he is
ruined. He is intelligent…."

"Mais sa sensibilité?"

"… has scared the balls off him. He's like all the rest, all
the good ones … their sensitivity has literally gelded them, for
fear…. After all, he's Personal Assistant to the Premier — balls
are incompatible with Canada-career."

Words flight around us, envelopment. Messages sent
back and forth merely to consecrate the understanding that
existed since we met a millenium ago. My body distends now,
thrums, and a whole vocabulary that I have forgotten returns
in a cluster like sunlight suddenly clotting in my gut after

penetrating my eyeballs. Vocabulary that carries with it all its meanings that my respectable personality has conveniently forgotten — forgotten between the memos, the dictations, the phonecalls, the meeetings....

"The hero of the novel is La Place d'Armes ... and the action is all in the sensibility ... it is an adventure in the senses, intelligibly — thinking at the end of my fingertips."

"Pour un Angluche, c'est rare...."

"I know — you French Canadians will understand it better than my own community. But you'll also have to forgive me for it....

"But it is suicide in your own community ... at least political and social."

"Yes...."

"And it had to be that rather than moral or spiritual suicide — suicide of the respectability instead of suicide of the sensibility ... bien entendu."

"I had to choose — slow death in conformity — or sudden, vehement, brutal life ... had to shock me back into persistence. Pulled the trigger at the last moment.... Another two years, three at the most ... and I would have been sold for a death-time."

"And you come back to us alive ... it is the opposite of the famous *Two Solitudes*...."

"Yes — everything I am doing disproves the *Two Solitudes* ... but that's only incidental. After all, any damned fool can disprove an academic thesis. Besides — it's unkind to disconcert professors. It's like poking fun at priests when it isn't necessary ... one strange thing — since I have made my break, people are afraid of me ... I sense it when I meet them now ... when I meet old acquaintances ... they look at me as though I were suddenly officially dangerous. Obscene. And I sense with that some new power I have with them ... just at the moment that I have given up power as it were. They cringe when they see me, and are fascinated...."

"You are their bad conscience now...."

"Perhaps.... But I'm having difficulty enough clarifying my own conscience without troubling myself much about theirs.

"Mais votre démission les accuse et les rend coupable!"

Luc understands completely ... I feel a surge of release ... I can cry now. But that would be a scene. And maudlin. Whereas I never felt less maudlin and more lucid. Besides, it is no longer necessary to cry, because Luc is absolutely here — totally here — nothing human withheld. Present avec cette présence that I had long ago learnt with my French Catholic friends.... His "présence" — his Real Presence, embodies me again, commandeers my spirit, raises me up. Yes, I had forgotten all that ... yet it is what I have come back for, instinctively ... come back at this final moment, just as I was about to pass beyond recall.

"I can't say it in English, Luc ... typically. But in French I can — 'j'incarne un énorme besoin du Canada français' — just **because** I am English Canadian ... just because I love my own people, my own land, my own citizenship, my own family, so very much. You Canadiens are an essential part of my own will to live...."

"Your novel sounds like a minority report to the Royal Commission on Biculturalism —" Luc laughs....

"Yes — I suppose a little; but that isn't really it at all ... at least I would never write it if that were it...."

The Marc palps my tongue, sheathes it and furrows its wake down my gasp leaving a trail of fresh plowed soil right through to my buttocks.

"Your Jean Lesage hit closer to the truth in a speech in Peterborough — at the opening of Champlain College. He said "You English Canadians ask us always what we want in French Canada.... Well I ask you, what would you deny us?" — there is the crucial question ... and the answer is simple ... the English Canadian can never allow the French Canadian to have that kind of joyful plenitude that he won't allow himself ... the English Canadian can never pardon you your delight in life ... let alone enhance your delight of his own free will ... because he himself is self-castrate. He *hates* your joy. And fears it — it judges and damns him!"

Luc dandles his ballon, inhumes the bouquet bodily, masticates it, and sets his glass down without having molested a drop...."It's all back-asswards you know ... you are the rooted Anglo Canadian ... the Loyalist, the High Tory, and you are here, embracing our French-Canadian Revolution, in the Vieux Quartier of Montreal...."

"Que veux-tu? It's my last chance ... my own people have put our cultures into national committee. They have deliberately killed any danger of a positive personal response. God — they've put the whole nation into Royal Commission. But the truth just isn't at that level, at all. English Canada has just been raped by French Canada, and even at the crucial moment of rape, it unctuously denies loss of its goddam maidenhead. It's been a semi-detached rape....We've simply backed into buggery ... and invoked a Royal Commission to prolongue our virginity."

Luc looks dumbfounded — "but it is the French Canadian who feels buggered by you English ... how can it be the reverse? How can you feel buggered by us? Ça, je ne le comprends pas....You must meet Pierre Godin; his new novel complements your English-Canadian case, but from our French-Canadian side.... Get it — it's called *La Foire aux Puces*."

For a while we talk of the upsurge of French Canadianity ... and Luc confirms what I sense now — that it has in fact been accompanied by a deeper disinterest by French Canadians in English Canada ... in re-appropriating their own munificence they have less need of us in every way ... just at the very moment when we, as never before, need their gift of life.

Luc laughs — "Tiens — we're coming dangerously close to having a 'dialogue.'"

100

And I wince — because he is right ... because in talking thus we have lost something of our realities ... we're aground.

"You're right — dialogue is disastrous ... for our truth; particularly for your French Canadian truth. 'Dialogue' is defeat of you and of what you have to give. Dialogue is detachment and death."

Luc has gone ... dinner is being set. He insisted on paying our luncheon. I dally the last of the Marc, watch the diners arrive, the play about to begin again. And browse his new volume of poems ... and I realize with despair that me and mine, we have never really dared ourselves in poetry, never fully — we've never felt our way right through ... and I know that this failure in words, is a failure in living. No one has ever said us, and now perhaps no one ever will. We've been bought off ... there's that new book on Canada ... lamenting our dead nation. Well, I've never dared read it. Because I'm simply a result of what it diagnosed. Why read it anyway? I know it all by heart already! That's why I'm here.

My day is done now ... reborn in Luc, I subside back into posthumous state now that he has gone. Quiescent — still-born. No Order-in-Council, no national committee, no Royal Commission can resuscitate what has been taken out of me and my land, taken out by Order-in-Council, by committee, by Royal Commissionment. And I damn the ... damn them all. Because they *are* our failure!

"Dialogue" — fuck that ... what we need is a national enema!

That night he ate late, after typing his Combat Journal. Ate in a sailor's restaurant, down at the harbour front, on Commissioner Street, by the wharves. The sailors eyed him as some obscenity — furtively taking him in, and he felt he was obscene. Not because of what he had done. But because of what he was, and what he had never done. He felt hopelessly middle-classed, and his obscenity stemmed therefrom. He knew it. He stumbled out of the restaurant — it was the Neptune — but he didn't even see the sign; left his meal unfinished. In five minutes he was in La Place d'Armes, but all he could see was the face of Luc ... "oui, je te comprends," Luc was saying, "mais c'est suicidaire." His head reeled again — he heard the train bells thunderous in him ... all the same signs. He made for his room again ... running. And abed, got out his notebook to jot ...

"tomorrow, I must make a circuit of La Place ... must situate it all. Must...." And then he was asleep, notebook in his hand.

DAY FOUR

He woke at 7 a.m. ... drenched in sweat — was it claps, or simply the fear of claps — or just the life fever that he was living now. He wrung himself out of his pyjama top, and fell back abed, ruminant — manhandling himself. His stones for him were absolutely touchstones — talismanic. He could rub them like Aladdin his lamp — conjuring up his genie for any place or event or person. It was as infallible as some electronic machine. For the moment he ruminated thus, gently, upon his campaign. Somehow or other things had changed. His initial plans all seemed to have collapsed. It just was not going to be possible to take the Place, outpost by outpost, street by street, converging finally onto the Square itself. No — that wouldn't do. But he didn't quite know what to do instead. That was the rub — and he kept on rubbing. But the only solution he got was the young brunette he had met from la Galerie, with Luc, yesterday at lunch.... Luc's hand-kissing ... but she wasn't a solution, at least not a final one — it only delayed the real issue.

Routing himself from bed — it was already after 9 a.m. — he ducked the flak of cars from below his window. Each backfire, each honk, reminded him again of his absolute vulnerability — his absolute violability. Everything still hurt — still shuddered him, threatened to fracture him, like some plate glass window, into a thousand pieces. Everything was still palpable; sounds, sights, smells — they penetrated him in a perpetual sodomachy that left him a daily raped virgin. Each night renewed his tattered maidenhead — and each day slashed the renewal. "Christ — every goddam bus, or car, or motorcycle can rape me ..." he mused, leaning over the window to locate the trespassing dildo that had just relieved him of his most recent virginity — a small sportscar — suitably red, squealing to a stop in front of his hotel, incising him even as he stumbled from bed.

He had better get into his Novel. He knew that … in minutes he was out on the street. Notebook to hand.

"Down to the bottom of La Place Jacques Cartier … into the train yards — watch the shunts; & sight the bell-engine — it seems so harmless …. Left, down Commissioner Street … the long arcade of grey — & painted across the face of each, the old names … harness shop, dry goods, wholesale, storage … all the old trades. Names worn, replaced by neon signs, or sold out. Up the façades, the angulations of iron fire-escapes…."

He stood taking his notes. Wanted to write down the names. But nothing came. Nothing was happening. It all seemed so pointless. The names. He looked again — it was meaningless. Why go through the motions? The very crescent of greystone itself seemed dull, dirty, fit only for demolition. How could he have ever found beauty in them. He wondered. And shuffled on down….

"on the inside of the harbour fence — looking up at the line of buildings — the old view seen from the incoming boats.
    Past the Neptune Restaurant.
    Past a statue I must examine … Jo Beef's restaurant (excellent modern folk artifact).
    Stone wall, between warehouses and Commissioners Street … miles of it — man-height; best I've ever seen.
    On my left, the huge warehouses, joining the Quai Jacques Cartier to the Quai Edward VII to the Quai Alexandria.
    Superb Georgian architecture of the old customs building in La Place Royale — Garrison Georgian!
    At the end, Harbour Commission Building … Wedding Cake Victorian — something wonderfully plentiful about it … rusticated façade, cast-iron (I must come back to it) — to the junction of McGill Street with Commissioners Street. One corner of my world now — looking back, the view impresses — the long crescent of Commissioners Street seen to advantage from here …."

As he looked back the buildings along the crescent appeared stacked, one onto the other ... as though he was looking "up the street" ... the buildings were amassed, placed a firm pressure on him as he stood like some cornerstone at the corner of the two streets. The pressure gave him life — took the flatness out of him, out of the view....

"... *above the crescent, the towers of Notre Dame, the Providence Life building with its soft gothic skyrise, the dome of the Marché Bonsecours. Behind me, a glimpse of the St. Lawrence — not many glimpses as I walked this Front (that's what I'll call it — the Front ... like the Ontario Front!)*

Turn up McGill Street ... ugly line of office buildings d'un certain âge. They could all be torn down without loss. I suppose the Customs Building has dignity ... massive Britannic Classic — good place to lock up all the wares of other nations ... to clamp down on exotica.

Best thing is the rear-end view of the Harbour Commission Building ... the front was in rusticated stone, the side in plainstone ... but the rear, in natural stone (like Chateau de Ramezay) ... a kind of rubble effect, surmounted by the conscientious dignity of dome and mansarded roof.

Place Youville (must get historic data — wasn't she a founding nun etc?).

Nice firehall at the far end of this Place ... Lowlands baroque I suppose .... Odd, but nice here — such a relief from the Customs Building! That's about it, till the sideview down Notre Dame Street relieves me of these bland enormities ... so much is happening in Notre Dame Street, visually that is. Even more interesting than the view down St. James Street now.

La Place Victoria (a whole circle of smaller "places" around La Place d'Armes ... Places Royale, Youville, Victoria, Jacques Cartier ... they ARE someplace!) With the sudden jut of that black skyscraper to the left of statue to Queen Viccy .... What's its name? Viccy's more interesting — for the first time I feel a need to use my binoculars (my

*concession to a camera!): God — that face, sooo smugly! The Madonna
of the Merchants! That's Her.*

*Behind, a mountain face — not Mount Royal, but the skyscrapers,
new and newer, that efface the Mountain ... the old Sun Life, largely
hidden by the Ville-Marie, Queen Elizabeth Hotel, the new Chateau
Champlain (most recent in the long lineage of CPR's high Canadian
romanticism) ... Hydro Québec. & somewhere snowed under these,
Mary Queen of the World — the Basilica. Then, through a gap, if I
move to the left, the Mountain itself, with giant cross....*

*The policeman, directing traffic, at St. James and McGill —
unbelievable: such elegance, such self-evident delight, such grace ... at
once Grand Seigneur & Habitant. How is it possible to have such a
policeman.... It's ballet — modern dance! The fluency of his gestures.
Makes turning the corner in a car seem an honour, a privilege, a joy ...
an accredited sensuosity! But the drivers merely scuttle past.*

*Down to the lower side of Victoria Square — do the length of
Craig Street, just to circumscribe my area ... seems little of interest —
just the upper backside of my Place d'Armes in effect.*

The modern end of the Star *newspaper ... & further along* La
Presse *(largest French daily in the New World — but since all its crack
reporters left to go to the ill-fated* Nouveau Journal, *they call it "la
compresse" ... and no longer is it termed the "le plus grand journal de
langue française," but "le plus épais"). Typical difference between* Star
and Presse *buildings ...* Star *is clean modern.* Presse *the same ...
but its reinforced concrete has a Pattern to it; and its huge ground floor
windows are tilted, Mannerist.*

*Back-end of the Bank of Montreal: with its truncated classic details
... only half convinced.*

*God, those odious second-hand stores ... every item capable of
communicating the Bubonic Plague ... c'est certain! They ought to be
burnt out.*

*Corner St. Laurent and Craig — view of the old Court House, &
beyond it, the Hotel de Ville, up on the hill to the right. Good contrast:
the "chaste" conservative classicism of the Court (good, clean British*

justice!) & the voluptuous insinuations of the City Hall. Armouries
below. Small houses just beyond, up the side alley — a delight ... each
façade a church altar — RC altar, that is. Expect the Host to pop out.
Wild colours.

Along as far as Place Viger (who was he?) ... Statue to Chenier,
hero of the Canadian Revolution-Manqué (why is everything
Canadian "manqué"?) of 1837 ... shows him as "respectable Victorian
Gentilhomme-Habitant" — complete with ceinture fléchée. A supple
version of a Father of Confederation.

Excellent view of City Hall.

The old Viger train station — red-brick romanticism ... only it's
yellow brick. Snoop inside. It's now a subdivision of the City Hall —
filled with little offices ... Plumbing, Parks, Council of the Arts: all the
functions of the City ... drop in on the Conseil des Arts. Magnificent
High Victorian plush armchairs ... the kind with dimpled seats ...
leather — with tassels! Came from office of Camillien Houde. (Oh,
yes — I remember who Viger was — an early Mayor of Montreal.)

Turn down rue Berri, third side of my outer Square. A run of small
semi-detached houses, rue du Champ de Mars ... more tabernacles, The
Notre Dame Street underpass ... to the CPR harbour yards. Signs
that boat me to Cornerbrook, Newfoundland (direct), the Saguenay
... Bridge over the St. Lawrence (Jacques Cartier) — but much more
elegant, a gossamer traintrack, rising from the water's edge, running out
to a Campanile, half-a-mile away. For loading grain?

Berri Street at Commissioner ... & I look down the crescent
again .... Immediately on my right, Ironworkers' Union building ...
delicious Victorian accretion (I must have a love-hate relationship with
Victoriana!) — round tower with balcony, for Ironworkers' version of
Juliet in the balcony scene. Lunchtime ... & they gather (sans Juliet). I
feel unwanted, & withdraw.

In the trainyards, a sinister yellow-brick castle, with dark trimwork
... a satanic mill! (except that it seems to be an office building).

Down Commissioners Street (it does have an "s" on the end of it).
Sternum of Bonsecours Church. & facade of the old Market

Building: they've filled it with modern offices now ... saved the building,
but evacuated it of all the sights, sounds, smells, colours of the old
Market Place. How typical. A clinical job.

    Along further to my original point of entry ... the bottom of La
Place Jacques Cartier — my Petite Place. Huge grain elevator to my left.
To my right, Nelson Monument (first in the world — 1809) atop that
ridge that runs above the Front ... Notre Dame Street the centre of it.
Backbone to La Grande Place!"

He walked up into the Place Jacques Cartier ... his tour of duty done.
That is how he felt it: he had "toured" the outer circumference of La
Place d'Armes ... had scouted the perimeter of his world. It had been
hellish. And he wondered why. It had been Hell, that is, at the beginning,
when he saw nothing ... saw only the signs for each building or company.
And seeing these signs, he couldn't see the buildings themselves, except
as outlines, as subsidiary facts. Everything had been, quite specifically,
"flat": the whole experience had been flat. Then as he got further into
it he opened up ... it was the Harbour Commission Building that had
first expanded him, then the supple undulations of the policeman at St.
James and McGill Streets. And then (he had forgotten to note it down
and promptly did so) the skyrise of the Providence Building seen from
Craig Street — "it is quite organic, like some sudden tuber thrusting up
in spring growth, after rain." By the time he reached the rowhouses, the
"tabernacles," he had relented — opened up. Somehow he felt inside
these houses that were now inside him. It was disconcerting but specific.
All "Victorians" — late Victorians — must somehow be Catholic he
decided. By the time he walked up into La Place Jacques Carder he was
no longer touring, though he was still going through those motions (and
catching up on his notes). As he entered the small square it was walking
into him as he into it. The experience was precise: what went into his
eyes, went right into him and through, and out the other end of him
and circled round and came back, back into him. He was unwittingly
very much part of what he was seeing ... couldn't detach himself from
it. Could no longer see it as a "tourist" at all. And yet, now that he was
this way in it, he could take notes ... it was all suddenly immensely
personal and meaningful. And *he*, as a result, was suddenly immensely
personal and meaningful. Obscenely so. He had just circled his world

... and his world circled, quick Ptolemaic mappemonde, he himself was encircled ("girdle me a globe"!) in some Copernican revolution of time and place that he didn't want to understand completely.

What had started abstractly had ended intimately carnal. He knew that if he thrust further into his tour — that if he now toured the middle world, that bounded by St. Paul — St. Pierre — St. Jacques — and Bonsecours Streets — he risked some kind of exposé (rather like an unwonted strip-tease) for which he wasn't prepared. Or was it rather a kind of insight. He stepped off the curb into St. Paul Street — a taxi skidded on the ice stopping to avoid him ... tore the pocket off his coat as it shot by — left him stumbling back onto the sidewalk immersed in a broadside of French-Canadian oaths ... "Christ de tabernacle...."

At lunch he realized that everything had closed down on him again. He could only see the writing, the neon signs ... he could no longer see the buildings out the window. He was constipated again ... all congealed inside. His gut knotted and rumbled. That taxi had scared him. Suddenly he felt that he must go to the Square — must confront it forthwith — penetrate it now. Two days ago he had merely shadowed through it. Now he must enter. He left his lunch midway, walked up to Notre Dame Street — noted the City Hall on his right, and relented again long enough to let his body photocopy it, and then turned left down Notre Dame Street, past the newsstand, the shops of religious paraphernalia, the Victorian pilasterings, the gothic pile of the Providence Building on the right as you enter the Place and lunged into La Place d'Armes. Blinking back the half of it, yet entering withall — entering and falling down the near side of the Square, to the upper side ... retreating, away from Notre Dame Church itself. Scouted the periphery, noting the buildings (he had seen most of them from the outer periphery that morning and had recognized them) — but not swallowing them ... he didn't insite them — merely allowed their outlines. Accepting them as facades (whereas before when he had traversed La Place they were merely shadows). He was relieved — "yes —, it's all here, the whole thing ... even better than I could have hoped." Then he closed down his lens and, despite his best intentions and throwing the remnants of his planned campaign out the window, he caught himself unawares entering the Church itself. It wasn't a real entry, of course — for one thing there was only about 10 percent of his perceptor set working — but it was an entry. Almost an enforced entry. He entered, nonplussed at his own action. Sat quickly at the back and slowly established the degree to which he would allow himself to see this now. The degree to which he could see. Sat, and was disappointed — because he only could see 10 percent: 10 percent visibility, 10 percent viability ... 10 percent vulnerability. And watching himself watch he saw the Church arrive on his sight like a bad overblown postcard that suddenly engulfed-the viewer. Only the French Canadians could have done it, he mused ... relieved now at his detachment — it's like some third rate Church ornament, bloated beyond recognition, until it becomes the Church itself. A miniature inflated, like a soufflé, to another dimension. Sat — and quite happily nibbled on the decor, like Hansel might the Witch's Gingerbread House. His tired flesh reaching out to mouth the crumbs.

Then he left, just as abruptly as he had come. Unscathed. Disturbingly unscathed (he vaguely remembered how different he had felt when he had first reached La Place Jacques Cartier that morning, after his tour.) Descended the left flank of the Church exterior, down to St. Paul Street, below the Church. Stopped at La Boutique, and entered (again, contrary to all his plans). He assured himself it was only to reconnoitre. To establish some further outposts around the square, and within the perimeter. That was it. He would only stay a moment — long enough to scout it out — as he had with the Place, and with the Church itself. He would return another day with enhanced perceptivity. This was simply an initial exposure, or imposure. Like taking snake-venom — little by little increasing the dose till you can handle the full bite.

A Grand Tour of the Outer Walls this morning ... along the Front — the Great Crescent ... to the Wedding Cake at McGill and the harbour. Up McGill to Viccy's Place (Madonna of the Dry Drugs!) — along Craig to Viger Chateau, and down again to the harbour. Can't see a thing at first — and then everything starts to see me. Christ, what's happening? First I'm nowhere — then everywhere is me. There's a wizard in the woodpile! Hit by a taxi — scared the balls off me. Scares me right into La Place ... and the Church — just to make

sure: Erewhon! Then La Boutique — how palpable all this
French-Canadian art is — everything is manipulable. Malleable.
Everything touches me. One exception here ... the engraving
by the door ... looks like a filet of ossified fish. "C'est de qui,
ce tableau, s'il vous plaît, Madame?"

"C'est par Robert Jackson." I knew it ... it's Angluche
— I didn't need to ask. And for the first time today, a flush
of hate against my own people ... against their progressive
disembodiment. Flush accentuated by the arrival of a young
couple ... he in long striped wool scarf, she in best Junior
League — a couple from some upper middle-class "Tatler"
society. I know instantly they belong with the engraving by
the door. Watch as much of it as I can withstand ... then flee
on down the street — to the Antique Shop. Specializing in
early French-Canadian furniture. The dealer I've known since
... since I bought this Journal! ... I also bought my first piece
of French Canadiana from her; one of those titan women who
eat men (in contempt) and women (in delight). Her assistant
recognizes me, madame le patron being absent for an hour....
It is sanctuary from the circuit, from those carnivores — that
couple ... fleshkillers, but not flesh for eats — merely deadening
flesh to leave rotting for fossilization. Dazed sit abruptly in
rocker to rest me (Boston Rocker ... but these fulsome turnings,
and the deepening curve of back promise my grateful back
and hands that this is Montreal Boston Rocker ... French-
English Canadian — happy bastard: Franglais! Frangluche!).
Settle back to encroaching contentment, into my hobby of
watching people watch antiques. As much of an art, and a sport,
as birdwatching ... human avifauna! Mostly passerines ... with
the odd great northern diver ... and lots of coots! Settle back
to watch rocking my hobby horse gentle till it stops me in mid-
rock: Christ it's them ... the Tittle-Tattlers from La Boutique,
pursuing me, here, in sanctuary, leaving me no peace of body (as
important as that of mind). Grasp the right underarm spindling

of rocker — alright ... so I must face up to you, deal with you.
Well, I'm ready! Your faces in the front plate-glassed window,
Koala bear-eyed at the reality you espy through this Looking
Glass ... I hubnub the rocker turnings — quick Canadian
chaplet — protection against this infidel. They are edging now
to entry door and all accidental fall in with breathless instant
apology — "may we just look around" — instantly enveloping
us all in this exulpation from the objects that traduce them. Such
a high proclamation of innocence. But you must be lying ... for
us all — pray to God you lie. Clasp the turnings, rock gentle,
watch ... pray! Watch that innocence in action. To make sure....
If it is right, if you are truly "only looking," then we are all
lost. Know that now as surely as ... as I know that your bodies
undermine my own, such complicit disembodiment.

And you can serve besides as introduction to the shop ...
I've not had time yet to appraise its contents myself, just arrived
... I'll follow with your eyes....

They set out — self-guided tour (of course clockwise
... and I remember, abashed conformist that I am, that I too
walked the world clockwise today ... with the current) ...
assistant leaves them be, knowing too well that she cannot
present an object to them unwilling to entertain it yet ...
leaves them alone to grapple with the objects as they can, or
dare. At the first trap now, mantrap ... I watch them, rocking
ceased, bated — watch them approach it, to the right of the
door, five feet to the right, on the first wall right-angled to the
Greyway ... greywall growing out of Greyway, but undressed
stone, rampant stone, offsetting this furniture I don't yet see,
seeing only their eyes as they embody the object, the degree
only to which they receive it. Five feet along, they both
impeccable skirt back at absolute right angle (two steps each)
total of three feet — so that the piece is deep! ... and back that
three feet scout the object to hand, his eyes raised inadvertent
a foot above his head and then along the length of his body

which glance they both follow bodily.... It must be a French-Canadian tall cupboard, an armoire — three feet deep, a little over six feet high and almost as wide. They follow their skirting around its far side, to doublecheck against hidden threat. None. And then they are back to their central frontal vantage point, for safety — square on the piece I still don't see....

God — their bodies must have antennae like bats, sending out radar signals, warning them of objects, keeping them always at detachable distance. Just out of touch always ... about 18" margin — out of fingering range. Instinctively thus (it is their penultimate instinct) knowing the polite distance from the furniture, the object, the reality they survey. So precise is it that I could draw with accuracy a chalk line 18" around the perimeter of this armoire, and up the wall, around its form. A remarkable achievement — theirs, that is. And one that requires a very precise tailoring of personality. Tailored like their clothes: not to fit, nor to define their bodies, but simply to contain and constrain them. Well — at least they don't have clothes off the wrack — they don't look like Prexy Johnson and his Ladyboid!

Released, I rock a little — just to reassure me of my own presence. Because I still have not seen the armoire, they have not presented it to me ... merely evaded it for me. But how can they present it, to me ... to themselves? Too late to sight it, they are moving on ... I can tell — their clothes are moving, moving them ... carrying them off in such worthy acquiescence, out of harm's way ... out of range of the armoire (please ... won't you show me that armoire? — but they are already beyond recall of it and it remains a blank in me ... a blank block against that still rampant stone-rubble wall which reminds my rocker to roll me now) — till the obscene thing happens afront our unprepossessed eyes ... on her left leg, left side of left leg, sagging out visible shriek on flaccid flesh now ... her stocking has fallen halfway down, the net bagging out and I want to shout out the glad terrible news to our apprehension.

But she hasn't even noticed ... doesn't feel it though it sears
my own pantlegged calf on her. How long before she will? And
then I realize, in coldsweat that she won't ... she can't know to
notice. Because those clothes (oh — how uncanny that balance
of them: at once constraint and detachment) are detached from
them even as they contain. Incredible condition ... autonomous
juxtaposition. Withholding but not touching. How is it done?
How? And somehow — as my hands slip around the rocker
turnings again — it enhances the obscenity of what I watch ...
multiple obscenity — in the contraceptual image of fallen flesh,
in this exposed privy garment, in the absolute insensitivity both
of wearer and her companion. And which is the real obscenity
of it I can't yet tell me.

All eyes on them, I miss the contents of the shop ...
engrossed in their elaborate evasion of the objects they have
come to sightsee ... she in the lead. That walk of her ...
waddling highheeled around some box of her, boxed in from
thigh to neck, body boxed in ... like armoire boxed out of
both of them extruded, unflinching. Watch that Walk ... walk
that never touches her — walk from knees down — talk from
neck up. In between only that shut-out armoire, out of both of
them as he follows her Box-Walk. And I know that my failure
to receive the armoire through their insight is their failure is
her Walk that cuts out all with such precise extrusiveness. Watch
in perplexed apprehension ... till they are at the stairs, opening
to the second floor, laden like this first with unabashed objects
rampant all around us (when will you let me see them? dammit
... or do you systematically annul each one you scout out,
dispelling it for ever from you and all who observe you?)

And why bother spying out the second floor if you have
so consummately evicted the first? But they are insistent at
the foot of those stairs forcing the concession from the shop
assistant that they don't want to ask:

"the second floor is open too...."

And with that grant they assault the stairs. Shift my rocker imperceptible along the line of rock, to watch this breach of the upper keep. Because it *is* some kind of assault and battery, some kind of structural dislocation. First step, second … my hip hurts: each step they make threatens dislocation of it in me … as they afront each step crushing it steadfastly underfoot almost as though it hadn't occurred. A circumnavigation that is an extrusion that is an annullment — as with that withstood armoire. Watch her box up that staircase, each step piled until I see carefully built beneath them those stone foundations of the house from the Rapido window … those honest Ontario Yeoman homes of the diligent nineteenth century. Honest stout cubic piles. And this is like watching granite cubes quarried from the staircase…. Granite cubes — cubes: **cubes** … that's what they are … these houses, homes, people, my people … Cubes! Rocker slides warning me abrupt of overtilt. Tant pis — I have them: Cubes. Not Squares at all … Cubes Cubes Cubes … want to rush over and kiss her fallen stocking that his red face has now sited — kiss their Cubes — her Box, the extruded armoire. Kiss this identification of us … but still have the sense to comprehend they would mistake my motive so sit pregnant in their discovery to me. And rock.

Cubes! That's what distinguishes them, you, us, from the overplayed Amurrican Square! Because the Square is in fact two-dimensional … like the façade of Mount Vernon, or the White House … faces resultant from an instant clapboard culture (preflab). The Square, like his New England historic house beautiful (pace Puritans!), has finally been evacuated. Hasn't got the substance of our Canadian Cube … oh, the sweet substance. And adoring I witness this Ascension of the Staircase — this infinite stolidity, this self-conscientious substantiality. Oh — no no no … no mere Americans would walk like these two. Couldn't attempt it. Would be laughed out of court. No American save maybe some seriously over-constipated

Philadelphian of the middle-class with aspirations to membership
in the Penn Lynn Club (where all the Ozmatic graduated
Peters-of-Philadelphia still play!): Haute Societé Protestante
Amurricaine!

No mind … I love these dear Cubed Canadians …
Angluches!

Cubes have it: earnest, composed substantial … and with
more significance, more mass, more organic matter than
any simple Square, high or low. The Square being finally a
paperweight in comparison with these Canadian-English …
Canadian-Scottish! … not English at all, really.…

And then see them disappear over the top of their compiled
foundation stones, such sullen witness to their discovery … so
full of shit. Small consolation then, for my Canadian citizenship,
if a better body means merely more shit. And as I reel in the
rocking I am babbling to myself in French again … "c'est alors
ça, le Anglo Canadian — le Cul Carré.…"

Hear them firm pounding the ground overhead … they've
closed the culture gap from 18" — for public consumption
that — to 15", for private intimations. Unwatched. Two little
Angluches alone chez une Antiquaire canayenne: bull-calves in
a brothel!

Am I proud or pitying?

A single foot comes down above my head … my calf
twitches: she has pulled up her stocking!

The assistant laughs at me astonished: "You hate them
almost as much as you love them …" and before I can deny my
affirmation they are back down, at the beginning again … afront
the armoire. Still not a flaw in their performance … stance taken
— armoire withheld. Like the Englishman withholds the fire in
his pipe unlike Jew suckling overt on his direct cigar. Armoire
with two doors, diamond panels style Louis Treize, deep cut — I
suspected it … but now I see it! Why? Till now I see his hand
run amok, running down the front of a diamondface, fondling

it in a mutual moan from both of them as they are abruptly
in touch with armoire us and all the shop ignites about them
conjugal. Moan, as if they had been shown a filthy floor show
unwitting and before they could flee, or even call Morality
Squad, found they liked it. Amorous moan — albeit truncated,
reduced to barest essential … quaver in the diaphragm, without
rising to the heights of a full-bodied French nasality.

Bless them — bless you both … blessing all around,
shimmer this shop restoring Body and Blood. …

Sooo … that is it, Body and Blood. That is the reason for
their presence here! Came, disembodied, furtive, as English —
no, as "Scottish" — Canadians, as Protesting Canadians, came
unwitting to restore their bodies … doing it, bien entendu,
under best auspices — to wit a weekend afternoon in Vieux
Montreal. Cubes foraying into this Old Quarter to expose their
stolid bodies proper to this animacy of armoire: ample legacy of
Habitant Baroque. …

What matter the method. Given the results let every
armoire be a Man-Mommy, and every Louis Treize turning a
sodomite's dildo, and every chaise à la capucine a catamite, and
every Ste-Geneviève commode a Venus Callypyge and every
crucifix a phallicity and every. …

"A quoi pensez-vous?" The assistant wonders my frenzied
rocker as I blurt — "this shop isn't an Antique Shop … it's a
Flesh Market for Innocents! Did you see them … pass from
innocence to vulnerability to gloat to purifying lust … it is
Body and Blood."

I sudden realize what I am saying. … She will think me mad.
Turn to eye her. But she understands — completely. I forget: she
is, quand-même, Canadienne. I am talking to the converted!

The couple have already gone. Her stocking was back up.
But as she walked out the door she almost undulated. The Box
had been breached … when his hand touched the armoire!

"What did you think of them?"

Squirm in my rocker — "they're the missing link …
between the Sausage and the Square! … the English Gent and
the Amurrican Guy…."

"They're what?"

"They're Cubes!"

"… they're, English-Canadians!"

"not precisely — they're Scottish-Canadians — corporately
speaking."

"*She* was so unbending!"

"That's it in a nutshell … Cubes — sausage contents, square
form … Square cubed — Sausage squared. Unbending!"

"They're **you**…."

"No — I'm a Celt! … and more English Canadians are
Celts than Cubes!"

"You're a Cubic Celt!"

The rocker squashes my right foot. "OK — I'm a Cubic
Celt … in search of La Place…. And that's all!"

She butts her cigarette: "That's a contradiction in terms!"

"I know."

"And what is La Place?"

"I don't know … I wouldn't be here if I did."

"But you know that this is the Flesh Market."

"It is B & B." Stubborn

　　　"Body and Blood?"

"Yes…."

The shop is limpid … every object incarnate.

She smiles her comprehension — "you are very frightened."

The rocker has stopped in mid-rock. "Yes … until you
smiled, I was afraid."

Silence in our shop. She moves to close armoire door.

Rocker drops … "don't touch that … not now … please —
don't touch!"

She turns slow on me … still smiles — "alors, tu es déjà
dans La Place!" Her blond eyes grasp mine.

B & B abruptly become flesh again ... turn to the window
where a dark blue Jaguar pads to a soft tentative stop while
paleface peers out from under the green sun-vizor: we are
being scouted the way any brothel is scouted by wary McGill
undergraduates prior to entry. Do we pass muster? Pray we do
... I need comic relief.

Four Citizens about to enter — yes, enter exactly as if
entering a public brothel ... but entering from under clinical
and accredited auspices. A tour of inspection only — of course.
Clearly their Excursion for the afternoon. The Cubic Couple
were incredible ... or only too credible! But this foursome is
caricatural ... look like stock figures from a bad bourgeois play
— from good théâtre de boulevarde. Something like *Le Bourgeois
Gentilhomme* — but in English.

Shop assistant retreats to the desk ... as I up quick to close
the armoire door still half-open into me. Diffident.

"May we look around?" asks the chief — Wife #1 ... while
I scuttle back to my rocker. Asks it as though demanding
specific permission to exist. And as though relieved by the
extricated sanction of the shop assistant, they start their round....
Again I watch them watching the furniture ... (when am I
going to have the chance just to see the goddam furniture
myself?) I have the definite impression now that they are
peering at me ... no — not even peering: just peeping.
Hazardously. As though the whole goddam shop were some
kind of peep show. If I hadn't seen the young couple I wouldn't
have believed it — yet there can be no doubt about it — these
people are here as voyeurs! They too are hesitantly in search of
their long-since bartered bodies. Like zombies going to some
body-bank, in search of renewed incorporation. No other
explanation possible — or at least no other honest explanation.
It *is* the Flesh Market ... the Flesh Market for Innocents!

... the women — both in mink coats, naturally. Herding
their mates around like hens their chicks — or rather, like

ducks their "ugly ducklings." One male in blue suit, invested with waistcoating, and black oxfords. As though appearing before a Royal Commission in this Sunday-schooled best. The other is more elastic, in tweedsy sportsiness atop grey flannels. Odd — their accent differs distinctly. Yet both are clearly upper-classified Canadians. They walk with that authority — that is, they follow their wives authoritatively. Can't quite put my finger on the differing accents … yet I know both well. Rock some more, cautiously probing this accent. And abruptly without knowing why it is appallingly clear to me. They are two different cities. Quite instinctively I know it is Toronto Rosedale visiting Montreal Westmount. But why do I know that? By reaction and response. Eye seconding ear. I know it because the gentleman in the blue waistcoating is the Toronto Parliament Buildings, the City Hall (old and new!), the armouries … is a mutation of Premier Robarts and of the Ontario Flag (Red Ensign Canadian) — while the other (the more elegant) resembles those mid-Victorian Canadian engravings of ADC's attendant on Governor-General at viceregal skating parties. One is finally a provincial urban gent, the other is an Imperial Garrison Officer. The Torontonian is a muted version of Australia's Premier Menzies. The Montrealer is a figure from one of Jane Austen's novels. Allowances made, of course.

The Torontonian visits the shop as "a tour of inspection," the Montrealer does it as "sport." At least that is the outward form. But of course both are here for this furtive reason of B & B — Body and Blood; if the wivelihood be set aside. And who knows — maybe those wives still hope that their husbands can produce … a Crucifixion.

And that admitted I must admit another thing (rock harder, Hugh boy!) — namely that the definitive Cube is Torontonese. For a brief moment I flush with pride … then I stop rocking, rigid with hate!

They are upstairs by the time I regain flexibility ... I can trace their step ... that steady foot planted along the left wall is my Toronto Cube (he looks like somebody that Sir William Osler dreamt up!); scarcely a pause. While that straight line along the far wall, broken by occasional ellipses, is the Royal Canadian Westmounted! The wives still precede, in each case ... but that must be the Montreal wife with the Toronto husband ... the taut convolutions of the high heels above my head in piquant halo — while that sterner clump — fox-trot to two-step (Women's Auxiliary tea-dance!) is Toronto-woman. By the time I have them situated they are down again — royally unscathed! I almost want to congratulate them — but they are too busy congratulating the owner (just arrived) on her stock of Canadiana (sure sign they're determined not to fall into the pithfall of purchase).

"It is the first time we've been in the Old Quarter," says RCW, male.

He says it with a certain pride. Proud, that is, to have hazarded the Visit — and to have brought the Torontonese into this self-evident seniority of Vieux Montreal. I am infernally tempted to pin the Fenian Medal lying for sale on the tabouret beside me, to pin that on his left tit. But before the temptation ostracizes me Toronto Wife has discovered the Louis Treize diamond-pointed armoire by the door. The doors like that Greek Goddess ... — whatshername? that multi-titty: Diana of Ephesus. And is ramming hubby's nose at them (if *only* she knew what she was doing!) And again I am tempted. At least he has the sense to look effronted. More probably by the price that he has spotted: two grand for those early Canadian boobs ... Boobs for Cubes! — en diamants (diamonds are forever, honey.)

And then they are safe, out the door, in a final self-gratulatory flourish. Full of a final charm that is undeniable (and why should it be denied them?) — a final dignity that is definitive (the sort of graceful dignity that Vincent Massey worked so professionally at, without, finally, achieving anything more than a certain High Civil Service competence!) — a dignity that is built right in, and which can't be successfully imitated. No doubt of it — that is there. The easy respectabilitarians! And it is just that ease, that dignity that prevents them from being mere WASP (again Tam proud!) — they just *aren't* White Anglo-Saxon Protestants. There *is* something more than that — now that they've gone I can afford this comfort of retroactive charity. No — they are no more merely WASPS than the young couple who preceded them were merely Squares. These people all have that dimension of substance that remains body; that is embodiment — that finally remains flesh, or at least flesh-for-the-waking. And remaining flesh, remaining potentially animate, embodied, remains finally redeemable. Remains human. They may be full of shit ... but that is, in the final analysis, a kind of guarantee of salvation; a guarantee that there is some body there to save. Whereas with the Square one senses a lost cause ... something hopelessly evacuated ... of both flesh and shit. (Sodomy in Amurrica is thus barking up a dead end! Mailer Inc. are all too late!)

No — these Cubes may be constipated: but they are redeemable. They may simply be Squares full of shit ... but it is a Holy Shit then, and thus the Canadian remains a Square-plus-Something which is better than the Amurrican square-root-of-fuck-all.

By the same token this last foursome remains WASP-plus-Something. And that Something is something that was lacking in the first Cubic Couple. It has to do with that charm and dignity ... that steady quality finally of grace. Hell — why hide it: a certain gentility! Ineradicably so. Built in naturally.... The first couple was Cubic WASP ... this foursome was Cubic ... was catholic Cubic — "catholic" with a small "c" that is. There was a certain form to their movement, a certain sense of embodiment ... a kind of implicit understanding of liturgy ... of life as an enactment, and not merely a syllogism. As though

they were Protestants who are also Catholic…. My rocker
stops me — of course idiot … that's what they *are* — culturally
speaking! That's precisely it! They are Anglicans — not English
Anglicans or American Episcopalians. Not Anglican Sausages nor
Square Anglicans … but Cubic Anglicans … Anglicanadians!
Not necessarily "practising Anglicans," preoccupied with the
Nicean niceties — but cultural Anglicans of a specific kind —
Canadian, Cubic … descendants of the British North American
civilization, which is, God knows, along with the French North
American civilization, the one continuous culture in North
America! The senior cultures … by right of presence. Resident
freely in the New World for four centuries…. How the Hell
could one overlook it? Except with malice aforethought! These
are the Complete Cubes! — the catholic North Americans.
Whereas the WASP Cubes were thus but aspirant cubes,
incomplete. These are Anglicanadians … or at the least High
Church Methodists … which is what we're getting (negatively
alas) in this new Church fusion of all Canadian Protestants.
These catholic Cubes have naturally what this new smelting pot
hopes to make by committee…. Oh, well. We've still got the *real*
thing. Still attached, albeit tenuously to their original Adam …
still definitive, and not part of this fake New Canadian Nation …
this Immaculate Conception! So that if

Madame La Propriétaire booms in … "Eh bien …
qu'est-ce que l'on fait maintenant…." Her aide-de-camp grins
malicious … "oh, Monsieur Cube is making silent speeches to
himself …" stopping me short in said silent discourses … and
we are all three quickly lost in contemporary folk-lore.

"Who's buying now?" I ask.

"It's the same … the Westmounters. Few French Canadians
… and when they do it's the French Canadian who is seeking
entry to the Westmount world. The French Canadian still wants
to eradicate his past…."

"And ours … he's succeeded!"

———

Next client — obvious connoisseur … she takes him upstairs,
straight to the prey … a French-Canadian Ste-Geneviève
commode, curly birch, blocked front, rococo-scrolled sides …
six grand. He ascends, silent. Fifteen minutes without a word —
virtually without movement. Then both descend. The look on his
face is specific. The look of the Upper Caste Canadian leaving
the altar rail after Christmas communion. Such a concentration
of pious lust. For him Antique Shop is Flesh Market is B-and-B:
he consummates the Object Incarnate! After he has gone I ask….

"Yes," she laughs: "what you call RCW — he was a famous
athlete at Lower Canada College."

Finale … Mac Clarke arrives, to join our hot-stove league.
He was ahead of me at Upper Canada College … two years I
think. My House Prefect. Liked him … we gurgle delighted in
the warm complicity of known objects. Sharing the wealth. He
always had a joke — still has: "Do you know the one about the
married man, fucking his wife … asks her suddenly 'Hey, you
feeling sick?' 'No, why do you ask,' she retorts. 'You moved!' he
replies." La propriétaire in a paroxysm of laughter — as we both
sudden realize that the joke is on Jack — its why he collects
French Canadiana.

And then they are all gone. I am alone with La Propriétaire,
her bitch-girl and the antiques…. They are magnificent — the
antiques that is! But I scarce see them now. Just sit and rock
me, dumbfoundered. I know that I have to unlearn everything.
Have to relinquish everything that I ever knew…. Must start
over again. The lesson — today's lesson — is self-evident. The
morning tour du monde … la petite place — la grande place —
the church — the boutique, the antique shop. Everything tells
me I've been brought up a deaf-dumb-paralytic … cannot see,
hear, touch, move. Brought up with an implacable and public-
spirited dedication to still-life. Nature-morte!

Yet even as I perceive this I wonder why I must suicide
this way. Because it is suicide I am dealing in with my Novel.
But why now? Why just at the moment of success — when
my career is about to open up completely. I suppose for the
same reason I suicided out of CBC six years ago — because I
knew that to continue was to bury me alive within a framework
that itself meant slow death — slow death because it buried
my sensibility before I ever had the chance to explore it, to
exploit it, to grow into it ... and to grow with it. It meant
death before ever I was born! Or put in another way (thank
God for this rocking chair — I'll buy it as an Ex Voto!) — my
embodiment, my carnal reality, forcefully rejects the negative,
sullen martyrdom of the civil servant, Anglo-American brand.
I must choose between "personal suicide" — self-slaughter —
and mere "social suicide," suicide out of the civil service. Social
suicide is painful — especially to the Canadian — the Cube
— the Loyalist, the Faithful Citizen. But it is nothing compared
with the spiritual suicide that is the direct consequence of
corporal suicide. But bluntly, I can't think with my balls cut off.
There's no substitute for a thoughtful pair of balls. Not even
a Ph.d. — that new knighthood of the emancipated lower-
middle-class: the new closed guild of all geldings....

"You are very thoughtful...." It is the assistant. Young —
maybe 37? Blonde. She hears the furniture singing in me,
vibrant in me. And her eyes catch us both unawares — we both
plunge headlong into their orbit — with the same facility of
presence as there was with Yvon, with Luc, with ... with La
Place d'Armes if ever I dare. "I'll buy the rocker...."

It's all a question of seeing — of eyesight on site.
Swallowing it whole — the way la petite place was in me
this morning (even if it nearly did kill me. Imagine — dying
under a taxi: ultimate degradation! Unpardonable.) I remember
explaining that to Luc yesterday at lunch: "It is a matter of eye
eating site — I call it eyesite: it is carnivorous. Omnivorous.

Sometimes you choke. You're eaten by what you eat." Luc
had eyed me voraciously then.... "C'est comme l' 'inscape' de
Hopkins, alors."

"I suppose — but it's more aggressive than that.... It is
raptor — you become a predator ... insitement. You either eat
or are eaten. No choice. Or else, of course, you're dead. You're
detached from your view ... you become just the surviving
dead end of a vanishing-point."

That had excited Luc — and I realized, with his mop of hair,
his slight tweedsiness, that he is a nineteenth-century English-
French Romantic.... An emancipated version of Little Lord
Fauntleroy. For a moment I envied his latest mistress — but then
I have always enjoyed Luc's mistresses, from a distance, alas.

"You eat the site till it is inside you, then you are inside it,
and your relationship is no longer one of juxtaposition ... but
an unending series of internalities. It's like looking at mirrors in
mirrors ... or rather crystal balls in crystal balls. That's my job
now ... to reinsite the world I've nearly lost."

The assistant's eyes are still on me ... spheres within spheres.
I spit them out, like extruding cherry pips ... I can't stand any
more. Can't give nor take any more. I'm right down to the nub
of me. All that is left is the final gift — and I need that to see La
Place.

Flee the shop ... and in self-defence now, phone George
Carter. "It's Hugh ... do you want an impromptu dinner
guest?" In twenty minutes I'm there — in his modern Pine
Avenue apartment. The "Fraternity Friend" — the only one I
ever had in fact ... an inherited charge of love; our fathers had
been together in the same fraternity. Zeta Psi. I was immensely
proud of it all. So proud of the Montreal Zete House — it
looked like a Tory Canadian's fraternity should: warm Sir Walter
Scott Tudorbethan Gothic. Canadian Ivy League — but better.
Because Ivy Leagues is legitimacy for illegits. And the Canadian
is legitimate. We never called them "Greek Letter Clubs" — or

"frats"; they were really our "clubs." In World War I when the Toronto Chapter enlisted en masse, the evening paper ran a headline "The Zetes Go To War." And then Elder Brother John McCrae had spoken for the whole Empire (remember that thing, the Empire?) when he wrote *In Flanders Fields*.

George was, is, a legacy of fidelity to all that ... a final remaining fealty.

"Hugh" — the friendly bellow of him over the stairwell now. I am up to him ... God, the same George, the same blue eyes, these sad wise eyes of the inward hurt that won't ever say itself. Always the eyes of Edward, the Prince of Wales that was. Those eyes ... I clasp him, and he isn't there. He isn't Luc, he isn't ... isn't what? Why can't I clasp him to me? (oh, odious, to clasp someone to your bosom! Odious! Verboten in our world. Sentimental. Or sick. Or both.) It is what is needed — what we both in fact want. George is five full feet away from me ... backed out of danger of manclasp before I had even sensed it. Before he even had to know that he had evaded us. Yet his eyes condemn his action now (bless him!) — his eyes reproach our distance and belie his retreat.... Ahh — that is it — I see now; how can it be any different: I am the armoire in the Antique Shop — and he, like any of those ... those "voyeurs" (forgive me that, George — but your eyes *do* see — you are voyeur-plus!).

Headspin-tailspin. It's the haemorrhage again ... abrupt bloodloss warns me of instant disembodiment. Stagger into his apartment ... past the scraped French-Canadian pine furniture (I should have guessed!) and the spic-and-spansy kitchenette wherein sounds of wivery — oh yes, I forget all that: George is married now, has a litter ... he's exonerated from living now. I reproach him that. Why? Like that young man on the Rapido — reading "how to run a convention" — he was married, and I was revulsed by the thought, despised him for it. Plummet me into giant armchair that is instant matriarchate before I know it. Must be careful, goddam it ... I know full

well that it is a hell of a lot more serious than "being careful"
— infinitely more evil than that: I'm on the brink again. Why
hide it from me? How **can** I hide it? I verge madness again!
Madness? Madness that is in fact simply a lucidity that appalls
me. The room we are technically "in" stares me out of us …
each object of furniture in utter isolation from its fellow …
each chair, each table, is an autonomy that is incommunicado.
World of windowless monads. Yet this is French-Canadian
furnishing … I know (mentally) that it is warm, flowing,
generous; whereas here it is en huit clos — each item severed.
A closed-ended world. And isolating themselves they isolate
me, from them, from George, from his wife I haven't met
yet. I'm nowhere now. And being nowhere am Noman. In
Noman's land again. Clap my eyes back to George … keep
my eyes on his. Only eyes can rebut this room: the pain, the
soft sweet pain in them rebuts it all, and drives me the madder
with the illicit loneliness his world here has imposed upon us
— willy-nilly.

Wife enters … and is the instant matrix. Everything
hangs upon her. Physically. She is the Madonna of these rocks.
Abruptly George smiles at me, openly — for the first time (they
had been furtive smiles before). So — he is absolved, by her
presence, of his own Real Presence. He exists only as her keep.
Like Bishop Berkeley's man — who exists only in the eye of
his God. Oh — it all makes nonsensical sense in fact: another
man who married everybody's Mommy. Another successful
lawyer. Another dildo. Another man eaten alive lest he dare live.
I mourn us — because thus George manslaughtered I am less.
How could it be otherwise?

I'll have to start my own suffragette movement — for men!
Women accomplished theirs in the last hundred years…. But
they've undone us. Now we'll have to remake our man … we'll
have to unlock the Object … fling open the doors on those
windowless monads….

Sane dinner — sane talk — sane laughter. All inciting me to insanity, in self-protection. Only after I am gone from them do I realize how fundamental it all really is. Not just an incident. The difference in the world of Luc, and of George. Luc's world swarms me. George's world is at least semi-detached. Yet I love both these men. Need them both. Am them both! Whereas if I am but one I am nothing — am neither, am traitor to myself, to my plenitude ... to my responsibility.

George wants to see me for lunch down town next week ... but I know I won't, I can't. So does he. So he drives me home. Tangible affection.

I think of going to La Place ... but I couldn't withstand another change of life — not today. Abed — the respective worlds of George and of Luc, making carnage of me — the world of George gutting me alive, leaving me only his shadow; the world of Luc goring me.

DAY FIVE

Awake just in time for High Mass at Notre Dame. Sunday is still instinctive part of my cultural metabolism. Scrape me from bed. Stumble to the Church — past the amputee at the front door of the hotel … marinating in his own afterbath of beer … down the tunnel of Notre Dame Street that is dark over me, past the tourist buses bringing the faithful, into a pew at the back, to the left, off the central aisle which undulates down a five-degree incline to the communion rail. Watch the Catholics kneeling before entering a pew. But I can't. Can't bring me to kneel — not in public like that; never been given the opportunity. Even an Anglican only kneels within the privacy of his pew — somehow so much more contained, less overt, less exposed. And with this sense at once of deprivation and of superiority, settle down to watch — to take notes for my book. Oversee the whole performance, as it slowly convenes me — exracting my attentions. The Church is the complete detonation … like some giant udder about to burst out in my gut. But there is no danger today. I have it under control. No detonations allowed. Alas! And that the case, safe, can at least use it for Novel now — write it direct into notebook.

"priest's voice over microphone incites the congregation to chant with him — it can't be called singing, much less the splendiferous bellowing of the rural Ontario Methodists. (I'll call him Andrew — Andrew what? Just Andrew for now. Must think up a plausible biography for him.) As the faithful mumble of the people enfold him he realized that

it was an open-ended adventure now.... He had thought he knew when he came how it would unfold ... thought he could control its direction, even its end. At least he knew the target. But now he realized that he didn't really know any of it any more. Except that his very life was at stake — much more than he admitted.

The voice of the chanting priest over the microphone was a broken flute sobbing the entire Church, making the entire service seem one of sorrows. His eyes followed that chant as it fractured against the balcony, and in a mosaic of gold scattered to the very apex of the nave. The entire Church like some interior of a Fabergé jewelled egg, executed by an enthusiastic peasant apprentice. The Church was Gothic Revival — 1830's; that is, Gothic built with a Renaissance mind and perspective ... and there was a vanishing point, a centre of focus, in the altar — at Christ centre crucified. But somehow this sense of three-dimensional perspective was wondrously defeated by the overall effect of the interior. Somewhat in the way that baroque decor took 3-D and blew it up into a celestial mirage. But with the baroque he could never entirely forget that he was finally in 3-D. There was always a point of reference, no matter how heady. Whereas here, the references were multiple. As in a medieval painting ... everywhere he looked, anywhere, it was alive. Everything was central. Baroque still boxed him in — still Cube — trapped him. Whereas here he floated free as over open fields. He thought again of the paintings by Brueghel....

Andrew sat, gazing into the space, as though it were some solid, some opaque body ... some incarnation — his eyes groping their way through it to the ceiling. But by the time his sight reach that height it had been dispersed to the multiple foci, and his brain, too tired to grapple with this splendid dissolution, relinquished the voyage, and left his eyes to wander alone amongst the intricacies of the gilt network, as though lost in the embroidery of some illustrated medieval manuscript. Suddenly the network congealed, became people, converging upon the altar, and he realized that this genesis was the congregation sifting to the communion rail to take the Host. Fortunately he felt sufficiently distant — he was a hundred feet at least from the rail — not to be

*implicated, and could watch with relative detachment this convergence …
like a covey of quail upon grain.…As he watched he realized that his
own Body and Blood were dead … that even had he wished he could
not have taken communion … even in his own Church, even had he
believed. He watched the present convergence as in a dream — happy
to be detached — yet envious of their privilege, their spontaneous
assembly there, called to eat their god. If someone had snapped their
fingers in front of his eyes he might have broken out of his daydream
into their daydream, and sifted forward too. But as it was, he was
utterly incapable of formulating himself. Of intensifying himself to that
point of self-realization which allowed of decision in such a matter. He
remained in his seat, star-gazing. And wondered if he himself might
not be dead now too. But he didn't answer the question. Instead his
mind receded again and he found himself lost in the vaulting of the
nave that suddenly had become four-dimensional … softly become an
open field … he found he could move anywhere at any time in it — up,
sideways, backwards … he could be present anywhere in it, effortlessly.
And then he lost that world and his eyes snapped from one focus into
another. He was back in his Baroque Box again. As he left he stopped
for le feuillet paroissial … and read the news that "la grace qui comble
Marie ne diminue en rien sa liberté" — the Church has liberty on the
brain these days he thought. "But then it uses words in a different way
from my own Protestant society … the Catholic Church uses words to
engage an emotional response. We use words to isolate 'facts.'*

Service done — notes done that are really me become
Novel. Off to lunch at the Restaurant des Gouverneurs.
Place Jacques Cartier. Ideal setting for a sailor's Sunday lunch
in Montreal.…They all look at me now the way those
Westmounters yesterday looked into the Antique Shop — as
though they are espying something untoward, something that
shouldn't be seen. For them I am as much of an obscenity as
the antiques to the Cubes. Curious reversal of roles. It's like

being raped in public. Back to rest awhile. Type novel notes out in full — clarifying them. I must remember to do a detailed description of the interior of the Church. But I haven't seen the details myself yet. I've merely been in the Church.

At 2 p.m. ... out to make another World Tour — this time of the Second Circuit ... the world within the perimeter I settled yesterday. Or was it the day before? Time confounds me. This time I'll go anti-clockwise!

Temperature 4° above zero ... blue sky; wind burns my face. Throw away my tourist guide and my Novel Notes. Must see it for myself ... discover it as it is — for me that first. Down to the bottom of la petite place Jacques Cartier. Turn left. Along the Greyway to the left now ... on either side fine grey stonework — arcaded, pilastered. One of these must be Rasco's Hotel (the guidebook sticks in my mind). Maybe that BCN Building this side of the Bonsecours Market.... It is admirable. Gutworked stone! Cross the street to admire it ... and the view down la rue du Marché Bonsecours ... to the harbour buildings amassed high up and over the market itself. As I turn to cross back again, the building in front of me, in old blackened paint on the stone, asserts with dignity, "Rasco's Hotel" — I was standing right under it. No wonder I didn't notice it ... because this "plush hotel" of the 1830's is now a sequence of tiny shops — rooms to let — deserted restaurants. Alongside Rasco's, la rue Claude Gosford carries my eye through the Notre Dame Street underpass ... curious gap under the squat bulk of the Chateau de Ramezay above it, and above the Chateau, the skypile of the Hotel de Ville.... Turn to the Marché itself. Fortunately the office lights are off. And all I have to see is the magniloquent façade. What a building! The very best in British Rajmanship. The stone singularly white in contrast with the rest of this greystone street. Stop in at L'Auberge du Canada, in front of Le Marché, for coffee and a longer gaze at it. But L'Auberge itself is a site! — with its pot-bellying pillars, dividing the wall-length mirrors into massive arcades topped by lions' heads each with red glass glaring eyes. The bar the same — those pillars with the central bloat — and the painted graining. A period piece still in functioning order. The modern beer ads are simply an accretion: the tone of the place is set by an old reproduction of a picture by Massicotte — showing the habitants "sugaring off": Maria Chapdelaine's Quebec. And not dead by a long shot ... as the habitant-proletariat drinking here now prove. In contrast, the white bulk of the Market seems bland, like some great White Elephant lying there.

On, and into Bonsecours Church. Priest addressing the faithful. No! — addressing a hundred apprentice tourist guides for the City of Montreal. The thought revulses me. All I have to do is follow them for a guide's guided tour of the Vieux Quartier. But I stay ... and somehow my own "tour" loses delight. And they gone, apply my binoculars to the High Altar — a delirious accretion of white marble (or is it plaster, or plastic: no matter, it feels marmoreal from this distance!) With unending biblical activity all over and through it. A kind of celestial merry-go-round (at any moment I expect the tabernacle to open, and the music box start, and the circus....) Behind, the back wall is a glister of mosaics — the most recent 1957, gift of Cardinal Leger. It's in as bad taste as the rest. The whole Church is in bad taste. Yet as I look at it it excites me ... seriously excites me. I feel eyes in the back of my head again ... feel me pried open ... expanded to this wide horizon. I know that this is essential. The "bad taste" of it is irrelevant ... or rather relevant — and to restore the Church to its original eighteenth-century form, still intact under this gaudy aftermyth would be almost as much a loss as the original!

Down to the museum, in the basement ... like being inside a giant historical doll's house. Story of the Church, in a series of "rooms," "period rooms" — miniatures. All the furnishings of course are eternal French Canadian mid-Victorian — for

the period 1650–1720 ... Mère Marguerite Bourgeois —
foundatrice. As I look at these miniature rooms (Catholic pop
art!) I realize that my eyes lock in the same kind of focus as
in the Church proper ... that same kind of distended focus. A
trance effect. And that effect is what is important — trance
in which all my senses are alerted, and my mind free plays
amongst them....

Back outside, the view up Bonsecours Street — the Calvet
House on my right ... now owned by Ogilvies. I thought of
buying it once. The second best address in Montreal. With
Bonsecours Church as private chapel. Marché Bonsecours as
"Folly" (the icicles hanging from the brow of the Marché now
give it an 1880's "Picturesque Canada" air — gingerbread it.)
The Jacques Cartier Bridge over the St. Lawrence at the east
end of la rue St. Paul. And the rue Bonsecours itself ... with
its row of Victorian arcades (now boutiques culminating in
the Maison Papineau (the best address in Canada!) At the top
of the street, appearing to float free against the winter sky, the
Fleurdelysé — what a magnificent flag — the white cross
and fleurs-de-lys on the blue ground. It instantly engages my
response ... as a visual experience, as an event. Although it is
not my flag ... it is theirs. Yet I am they too. So it is my flag by
right. N'importe. It is magnificent. And it excites allegiance.

All this from M. Calvet's front door ... with two restaurants
to choose from — Les Filles du Roi to the east along la rue St.
Paul; Le Fournil to the west. And in behind, if I remember well, a
well-walled courtyard, as there is behind La Maison Papineau....

Up Bonsecours Street — past a pocket theatre. Into the
candle-shop. I don't know why. I'm browsing! The thought
would make me guilty. It's more serious than that (I'm not "just
looking around"): I'm damned well grazing! The candlery: there
is something reminiscent about it. It plucks a string in me ... I
weave amongst them — the knubbly red-and-gold tapers (3'
long — not an inch in diameter): the distending twisting black-

and-red flame tongue of another — "un vrai weapon!" — as
my French-Canadian friends say. I want to handle them ... the
waxen surface catches the flesh of my palm, retains it ... my
fingers explore the body of the rouge-et-noire. I am not even
looking at it ... it is fingerwork. Some others — cast as totem
poles, buddhas, animals ... "cute" — but they lose my attention
... my fingers tap the red-and-black. What is it about all this?
What is being done to me! God — that's it ... something *is*
being *done* to me — that *is* precisely it. I am being done. By
these candles ... am being taken in hand. They are moulding
me, moving me.... Not the "statuettes" — they're just labels —
saying "horse, buddha, totem" — all the work has been done ...
there is nothing more to say — *they* are all a fait accompli. And
being "done" they leave me undone. But these moving, writhing,
mounting, clasping candles ... I know what it is now: it is
what is done to me in the Church ... and what is done to my
condemned Cubes in the Flesh Market — and this candleshop
is a subsidiary Flesh Market ... another Body and Blood Shop!

"I'll take the rouge-et-noire ... $4.00 ... and the taper."

Two pert young girls in ... carrying signs from the theatre
beside. "Ohhh ... look at the totem poles, and the frog!" I
flee.... Carrying with me my loot, and the remembrance of
the Victorian sideboard they used to show their wares ... every
shelf and curlicue and projection lending itself to the display.
Outside my ears clamour, clatter ... and I remember the tourist
guide, in the Church, telling us the streets were still cobbled
under the asphalt. My ears are cobbled by the candleshop!

Past La Maison Papineau — "six generations of the
Papineau Family ..." the historic plaque reads ... and then
reading it, I nearly betray the reality of the house — at least
for the day in me ... I think the house beside it belonged to
Sir George-Etienne Cartier — St. George, ora pro nobis ...
you put Canada together, with Sir John — now it's quietly
dissolving; too many pigs in your trough!

I should go down to la rue du Champ-de-Mars and then across ... but it's so bloody cold. And la rue Notre Dame is si belle. With the Chateau de Ramezay, the Hotel de Ville, the Court. But I force me to scout down the far flank of Hotel de Ville ... to see what it is I would have seen had I followed my route correctly ... from the apron of the City Hall — the Field of Mars, God of Battles — and below, the Armouries couchant. And the whole city rising intransigent above. To the Mountain ... and behind me now the Hotel de Ville ... my hackles coil. I edge further away.... Good God — the candles under my arm, the roar behind the ears ... I look back up, at the Hotel de Ville and I see the altar at Bonsecours Church. (It isn't in the tourist guide book that way — I **knew** they lied. And the thought is a sop to my addled mind). Sooo — the City Hall ... it's no "wedding cake"; it is High Altar. And somewhere inside — Man — the Man of the City of Montreal ... but of course, the Mayor. The B & B of the Big Top. It all makes such inordinately excellent sense. If only I can remember that it *is* good sense. And Drapeau — M. le maire — *is* a Man ... the Montreal Man. The way none of my English-Canadian people are Man, in Ottawa ... or even in Washington, for that matter (even Bobby Kennedy is just an understudy prick, so to speak). Drapeau is the Man-of-the-Town. So was Camillien Houde. (And then the sneaky little realization that in Toronto, No-Man, No-Mayor, nullities.) No one since Tommy Church! And that is fifty years ago! No one of my generation in Toronto has even heard of Tommy Church; yet he was our last Mayor! Last real Mayor-of-all-the-people.

Sneak down Notre Dame (it is the central passage ... doesn't belong on this orbit). Turn north on St. Laurent to regain my proper perimeter ... la rue St. Jacques. The three saints, and Our Lady of Bonsecours — these my street lines. My fortifications. Peer in the window of the modern office building — corner of St. Jacques and St. Laurent ... only a little boy therein ... caretaker's son? And as I peer in the window, I realize that that

interior is an exterior — I am inside outside — RRRRAPIDO
— all over again — and the Tiger has just jumped out of my
tank. The old *Presse* Building. Madame Compresse! Sad, I used
to work for it … back in the days when the French-Canadian
Revolution was an idea, a conspiracy hatched between editorial
meetings. Oh — the guilt I felt as an English Canadian then …
the daily judgment on myself. As I watched the French agonize
under our history. In front of my eyes. And knew that I had
maimed this people … my people had maimed … my maimed
people had maimed this maimed people had maimed.… And
I couldn't forgive me — I tried hard, I fought against the
accusation — but it was I who kept making it.

And had ended by rationalizing: French Canada has to
kill its past, is strangling in its past … it must. But English
Canada has suppressed its past, and its job now is to restore that
past. Our problems are the inverse … and I had fled back to
Toronto to be a history professor, to carry the war, the Holy
War, into my own land. But at that very moment, the final
murder of our English-Canadian past was consummated, and
I died, in the breach and.… So now I have come back to, to
… pay my ransom. (That is it — I am becoming my Novel —
becoming Andrew — living into my alias! Impaled from my
right — a thunder of battlement — the columns rise rampant
— the whole façade is warring for me, over me, in me … I
can save me if I know what this building is … hasten for an
identification, before it sweet overwhelms me … the moose
over the main window, the ram, the snake — deep gutted in the
redstone (who called it "brownstone!" It's hot hot hot … red,
lava, livid.) And at the last moment catch the clustered thistle
over the corner main door.… That's it — the old Scottish Bank
or Building or something — I remember that from the guide.
And clutching this label — I'm saved, saved. Saved from what?
Only from living. But someone else is spying me now … turn
— ahh … I knew it — there is a parking lot atop the rubble

between St. Jacques and Notre Dame ... the backend of some
old stonework in a vestigial buttress, beside it the svelte flank of
the Providence Life Building for twenty-five stories — but the
eyes prying me are those of that clutch of buildings along N.D.
Street ... under which the religious boutiques, all l'Art Sacré.
All eyes into me, wide-spied by their baldaquin. Munificence!
The Baldaquin ... of my Place still site unseen.

Down the side street to La Ruelle des Fortifications — and
along it, eschewing the Place — and up again to rejoin St. Jacques
by the Bank of Montreal ... turning down St. Jacques. Rejoice —
rejoice in these Temples of Commerce. Their cut and thrust and
hew of me. Floral sheath. Hard to choose. All so ardent!

Detail: the doors either side of the building in front of
me, #266 — to the east of Molson Bank — the railings from
sidewalk to door, they tell the tale. One a steep swerve of pliant
brass, embracing the penetrant. Circa 1880? The other a toy —
a ribbon of metal; you would never hang on to it! Circa 1950!
The one commands the hand; the other amputates it, unfelt. Yet
both are handrails. Which is the obscenity? Because one is. Both
are? No — each defines the obscenity of the other, conversely.
Take your choice!

I take Molson's Bank! The man ploughing the street stares
me as I raise my binoculars to salute the lava bodies atop the
bankface. Carved gods ... of Commerce and Plenty. Below, two
red "brownstone" beavers rampage calmly (I can hear their
gnaw). Below again, at street level — the closed newspaper
stand — wire grills over its spread of bosoms and public
flesh. Shadows compared with the beavers that gnaw my root.
Shadows! Shadows, like those who buy presumably because
they can't see those livid beavers above.

Sluice down St. Pierre, still carrying the load of those
Temples ... across Notre Dame and on ... till another exorbitant
bank embodies me. I stand up to it. To the doing. To the
re-investiture. Till gorged with it assault la rue St. Paul with my

reinforcement. Circling La Place d'Youville at the juncture of
Saints Peter and Paul Street. Backend of the fire-station (like
the backside of a Dutch eighteenth-century canvas of a town
hall). The harbour. That same — for me — incognito statue.
And indelibly, a greystone warehouse … a kind of miniature of
the Marché Bonsecours … same militant Georgian, with oeils
de boeuf. Ca. 1810? The whole apparatus of the Seaway Port
beyond, as I back up into la rue St. Paul and along it. No — not
along it — in it … walking down the centre of the street, feet
palming the tire treads tweedy in the snow. Place Royale — that
cameo customs house of the 1840's. Eschew the historic plaques.
Eat the building.

Galerie Ste. Geneviève — oh yes: mustn't forget —
lunching day after tomorrow with Luc's brunette — herself
a Geneviève. She's here — and pass on — … on my left
lombardy poplar withstand the sky that raises above them the
towers of Notre Dame, the pulp of the Providence Building,
all founded upon another excavated building leaving only
the amassed stone and brick works of inner walls behind the
Seminary garden that has unawares sucked me into this skyhigh
site giving me blatant joy….

As I pursue the street it pursues me and I am the same now
as when I returned from my Tour du Monde yesterday … I am
immanent. The world into which I walk walks into me … as
simple as that. A physical fact. My buttocks slither my lathered
ass like a horse that has carted an entire hillside. And my body
cocks the street it probes (bless that building up St. Peter's
Street … the one with the coiled Mannerist columnation that
corkscrewed me to this eau de vie burning my gullet till I gasp
the snowflecks!)

Along this tunnel of love — at one intersection a group of
red-brick offices: how trivial, how diminishing … toys amongst
the greystones. My eye follows the street up: I am closed again.
Decapitated! What happened? Look up again … ahh — that.

NCF — the New Canadian Flag. Of course. But how did it close me ... I didn't even know I was looking at it! What does it? I must analyse it....What *is* its intrinsic power to castrate? As an object, as a site? How does it do it? All intellectual prejudice aside. I glance at it again (the evil eye of it — and I know now: that "maple leaf" ... it is the Crushed Cube. That's it — The All-Canadian Cube, flattened. With its guts bashed splat. It's us all right — but us squashed. A flag for Cubes castrated. Boxed in with red at either end, and set on a virgin field of white. Boxed in, flat. That is the experience. That is what it does with me. And now that I recognize that (recognize the specific nature of the heresy, the unmanning) I can recognize what NCF is "positively." Given the gutting — it remains an idea — an ideograph! A label! It is a telegram. The B & B crushed, there remains the written statement — "I am Canadian." God — how hellish: the very flag that guts us proclaims us. It does both things at the same time. And as "reasonable" animals we accept the one without perceiving the other. We accept the blatant betrayal, because it seems reasonable, on the surface. But even if it weren't for the form, the content of it — that Crushed Cubism — the colour averts me: the "kemglo" of it — inorganic dye. Bloodless. And when they try to thicken it up ... it looks queer: because the organic red clashes with the crushed B & B. Oh Jesus — does NCF ever tell the truth of us! Someday even the academics will use it as an artifact: the Great Canadian Desubstantiation. The new heresy. And then, sociologically, what is it? Easy reply — the flag of the Honest Ontario Yeoman; the Methodist Grit Farmer Squatter — circa 1850! Of course — these stone farmhouse foundations!

Well — at least it isn't mere Square. A Crushed Cube is still a Square-plus! There is still a certain displacement to our body — a surviving tonnage. But the damage is done ... the street has receded from me; I have closed down again — the veil. The site has gone. Sight-sound-touch-smell-taste: all gone.

"I pledge allegiance to my flag...." Fuck that! No — unfuckable.
Unfuckworthy. But at least it locates, situates, defines, the
Canadian Heresy. At least, at last, it allows ground for attack, for
satire, for hate.... Defines the New Canadian Establishment.
And am I going to have a go at the bastards! Am I ever ...
before they get me, get us all, for ever!

All that in an eye's glance. Unwittingly, the truth.

Duck into La Boutique ... but it is too late ... the son et
lumière is all external now. And I have only a memory of the
plenitude of La Rue St. Paul. As a result, that fossilization, the
English-Canadian painting that is inside to the left seems less
offensive ... I have in part been reduced to its dullness. Sullenity.
Only the red child's horse, bright red, with its wrought iron
modern mane, and tail crashing through the horsebuttocks to
ride my cocked-horse revises me somewhat. And I want to run
my toes bare through the hooked rugwork. Still.

On down to Antique Shop ... to restitute me quietly.
Transubstantiation v. Desubstantiation. Slow, laborious
refleshment. Painstaking. Sit and rock me in my bought rocker
back to B & B. And watch the acolytes come and go.

ITEM #1 — a pair of casuals. Different from the Cubes
of last weekend. A kind of considered nonchalance. He dangles
a butt. A soft version of Humphrey Bogart. Puts my nerves on
edge. I've stopped rocking. Instinctively. I watch his tour. He is
Somebody, Something. What? From object to object, prying at
it conscientiously. At once possessive and dispossessive. Easy and
uneasy. Cavalier with the assistant (a man today) — studiously
cavalier. Who's he fooling? Yet he looks at the objects with
abandon ... ahhh — that's it: he doesn't look at the objects —
he bends down and looks at the labels first — price-tag-cum-
provenance, and thus exorcizes the burthen of the object. Only
then does he erect, pert, confronting the object. His possession
of it, like his self-possession, is fictitious, academic. He doesn't

allow the object to do anything with him — but disarms him first. Gutless.

His wife trails him. They have no relationship — other than accidental. They happen to be together.... Her walk — cubicular; her body, thigh to neck boxing in her unsought armoire: untouchable!

As they leave, he congratulates the assistant. He is really congratulating himself for having taken the shop! But he never touched ground here.

ITEM #2. They are on the tail of a "primitive painting" — second floor. It's a Whistler's Mommy trick — old woman sewing, grey; but with a Canadiana kick ... she's in an habitant-type kitchen.

"But it isn't signed. We don't even know who did it...." He is whining. But Whistler's Mommy in the guise of his wife wants — after all it is consecration of her whip. And they go off she armed with the painting, he disarmed by it. Ridiculous. Yet it is what happened. Like so many lines from a bad version of Albee.

ITEM #3, Young collegiate couple from Ottawa. On a spree. Careful spree — i.e. Canadian spree. They buy an old view of Montreal. One of those ones done in 1963 by Johnson. Typical English-Canadian's romantic vision of French Canada, Le Vieux Quartier: as though all these stone houses were rickety wooden cottages. The very opposite of the suave Regency reality of the quarter. And exactly the reason why the French Canadians deliberately desecrate it (as with their new Palais de Justice). What is startling is the relationship of the couple to everything: they have to set up a spoken identification ... "what's what." Like Item #1. Only non-nonchalant. Frightening to watch. They simply don't exist outside of that "what's what." They richochet from pillar to post, quickly establishing identities. Staccato reality.

After, I go around myself, gloomy. French-Canadian wooden capucine type chair on the second floor, thick wooden wings, in copy of the upholstered Queen Anne wing chair … copying impractically in wood the warmth to those wings — the substance of them (chip carved along the edge, ear-muffs!) Sit in it … invited thus. Ears quaver, thrum … warming me. God — it is the chipwork, the vein-red blood of paint, the buttocked wings (no upholstery) — I am as warm, warmer than if there were upholstered wings. Slowly distend, cushion on the chair … its rush-bottom seat … and I am vulnerable again. Opening up! Hawk-eying! And I realize that it is a chaise percé … with central arsehole. Examine it — no, must have had a central segment woven in attached to this outer edging. But in either case it clasps buttocks handily and splays….They were genius, the habitants. The inverse of the Culs Carrés. Even a primitive chair is a rim-job! — around the world … in eighty seconds. I stand … collecting myself — and eye the roomful of us. Jarred withal. Jarred at so suddenly being called back into being. At this unexpected resuscitation. Wary. Watch the room….Yes that is it clearly: every item here commands a human presence, la vraie présence de l'être humain. And with that I slink away — done, undone, redone … all in a day's work. Insubstantiate, consubstantiate, transubstantiate, desubstantiate, resubstantiate….That is the tale of my Tour du Monde. It is precise: Start — insubstantial (clay)

> Marché Bonsecours — consubstantial (at once clay, and B & B)
>
> Eglise Bonsecours and Candle Shop — transubstantial (full B & B)
>
> Flag — desubstantial — (bled white!)
>
> Chaise percé — resubstantial.

Back to Hotel — exhausted. Only enough energy to type out notebook now:

Inner Tour completed. With copious notes between times. And got me a pseudonym — it all grew out of me, alive in the Church and then on the tour — worked at La Presse ... it all grew naturally. The novel is beginning to take on a life of its own, independent of me. Better complete the Biography of its protagonist....

Name — Andrew Harrison. Okay. Make him a few years younger than me (allows for highjinks) — 32. Instead of CBC, worked at La Presse (much more impact) — that's how he got to know the young French-Canadian revolutionaries. Then went back, to U of T — professor in Canadian history and culture. That'll explain his knowledge of Canadian arts etc. Send him to school at TCS instead of Upper Canada ... Cambridge instead of Oxford (everyone goes to Oxford — this'll be different). The rest will work itself out ... will just start coming, as it did in front of La Presse today and started to assume the role, unwitting; that way I'll end with an organic character and, of course, an utterly implausible one. Ideal pseudonymity! No danger of insulting anyone alive. I'll make him quite baroque! High fiction this. Altruistic allegory etc.

Add: three details — those election posters, plastered over the old Hotel Rasco: excellent data — the nice litle Daddy — a Conservative ... offering the new National Film Board Building to his constituency, hands full of proud patronage. The Liberal — beside him ... an administrative type; head cocked competently, listening to "sound ideas," pen in hand. Brush cut (whereas "nice Daddy" looked like something out of a prolonged 1940's film.) And "la revolution tranquille" beside these ... young firebrand, fingerpointing at us, like a pistol ... earnest and vulgate version of the Playboy Executive hipster.

Secondly — in the Auberge du Canada ... the TV — Andrew sits looking at it in the mirror. And therein it is more real than when he looks at it alive. It belongs in a mirror. At once divested of its claim to be real, and at the same time, oddly, more real. TV is the reality of the mirror — but it doesn't mirror reality.

Thirdly — in contrast, looking in the window along St. Paul Street, at the façade of the Victorian building opposite ... it was shadow. In the window-mirror it looked like the world of TV. Disembodied.

Can't get over that joker in the Antique Shop — the cream-puffed Bogartsy type. Eureka (alas) — I know Who he is! He's the man the new flag is made for! He's the Methodist Canadian Emancipee! Of course: ECM — Emancipated Canadian Methodist! Christ — how unhappy! No wonder he was so nervous ... so unsure. Thank heaven it's a novel — no one would believe it in real life — it's all so clear, stares me in the faces.

Better get some data on the buildings of the Inner Circuit.... Some dates etc. Guide book says:

Rasco's — 1835 — held 150 guests. Plans to restore it plush (though 1835 wasn't "plush" in decor — not till 1870).

Bonsecours Market — 1845; Parliament after 1849; then civic building; cost 70,000 pounds sterling.

Bonsecours Church — founded 1657; present Church, 1772, with Victorian façade and interior decor.

Calvet House — belonged to famous traitor during the Amurrican Revolution.

Papineau House — 1748-52. Housed the famous French-Canadian orator and revolutionary.

Hotel de Ville — 1878 ... reminds me of Philadelphia City Hall (1876-86) — but got more guts.

etc.

But why do it? It's not what counts in me ... each time I date one of them, I displace it from me. Detach it. Murder in my Cathedral!

Dinner at Le Fripon, Place Jacques Cartier ... asking the waitress if she can guess where I'm from ... she thinks France. Delights me. I always like to be guessed French by the French Canadians ... and then tell them Toronto. It raises my pride. And then I whip it, by confessing Toronto!

Abed — retracing out my mappemonde. World within a world. Commissioners Street — McGill — Craig — Berri: roughly the old fortifications I discover. And then within — Bonsecours — and Sts. Jacques, Pierre et Paul. Leaves the inmost world — along la rue Notre Dame to La Place d'Armes....

DAY SIX

Awoke to silence ... no flak, no nothing. Test me for broken bone, ruminant palpability (do this in remembrance of me). Dreamt of home — old Toronto Rosedale ... its redbrick converting into clinical whitebrick: it was being remade into a brothel for the state. Lie clasping the silence to me ... till I am rumbled by freightyard and the slow upheaval of the Square. I try to imagine how it looks at this hour — up till now simply too numb to have rendez-voused it really: it has been all I can do to confront it en passant ... surreptitiously passing it through me, always defensive — both I and the Square. Each in large measure closed off, closed down, against our rape.

Outside now the rumbling of carfire is steeper — the race of motors. Alarm bells masquerading as trainbellings. Shrapnel from a backfire to my left. I withstand them all, carefully.

He got up, fragile as though expecting his body to fracture with daybreak, and surprised by his tentative well-being, sat down to write, excavating his nose with the expertise of lover patting a bosom into shape, or a sodomist evacuating assoul for instant action — his nose was an important part of his perceptor set: ears, eyes, nose, anus, cocktit, lips, toes, kneecaps ... all told him the same sort of thing — all conjugated the world around — all were in constant coitus. Only by deliberate effort of will, only by deliberately jamming his perceptor set, could he turn them off ... and then the veil came down over the world again, and he was detached, lost touch — died back. It was at moments like these that he said "I'd make a good professor, or civil servant now ... it's like after orgasm, when I always feel like an apprentice civil servant." But as soon as he recouped, then the civil serviceability went out the window. And now he was beginning to recoup — to regroup himself.

In another twenty-four hours he would be back up to his normal, and his respectability would be shot to hell again, fortunately....

He began to write — a letter to Eric Newman. Eric had been with him in the CBC — had been with him? Had been his boss, #3 man in the whole administration. He too had a brilliant career before him (and behind him!) But at the end — he was forty-eight — he had given it all up — turned down the invitation to write the report for the Royal Commissioners on Canadian Culture (his own poetry had won the Governor-General's Award — sure sign of cultural Canadian competence). And had accepted the presidency of the new university at Brantford. He had, in short, deserted the Canadian Establishment that Mackenzie King had built while the country slept, and celebrated that desertion in a book entitled *The Traitor*. Hugh didn't think the book had gone far enough. But then they were on different sides of the fence: Eric was a sauve Grit-Democrat. It paid! Hugh was a Tory-radical (it didn't pay! — in fact, it cost money: about $5,000 a year over and above his regular incomes which he made up with TV programming for private stations). Now Eric came forcibly to mind ... somehow Hugh felt deeply linked to Eric still ... or more particularly to Eric's book.

In Montreal, Monday. 6(?), Dec. 1965.

Dear Eric --
  You keep haunting me. Or rather your Traitor
does. Because I too have betrayed ... and my betrayal
has become accredited disaster. You remember our
lunch together a few weeks ago, in the Walrus and the
Carpenter, Toronto Yorkville. We discussed your book at
length and the fact that your hero betrayed the betrayal
of his country ... but he never pushed through with it; he
never accepted the implications of his desertion. That
was the problem the book posed me ... the hero deserted
but he never disastered, and came out the other side.
He was a deserter without a disaster. A revolutionary
without balls!

Anyway, that night I sat up alone, with the brandy
(some of that Castillon you recommended to me!) nursing
my flu ... abetted by a couple of cigars, three penicillin pills
and finally a hot bath. Brooding over the thing ... It was
then that it hit me ... head on. I knew that I had to push
through -- or else I would merely be guilty of betrayal. I
had to disaster. It all came to me, what I had to do ... come
to Montreal, confront the Whole Damned Situation ... You
said there was a place, an inner Place in Everyman's
heart, that he never really explored, never really saw
... That was it -- that "inner place." I knew that was true
and as I pondered it I kept seeing the outlines of La Place
d'Armes. But I couldn't see the real body of it ... even
though I had spent four years working in it. I could name
all the buildings, could count the floors ... but I couldn't
see anything beyond the outlines. And then (you won't
laugh, I know) the soap touched the end of my cock and
suddenly La Place was brilliant all over me ... every detail,
every facet -- and above all, the body of it, Eric -- the Body
-- it was all over me, swarming ... I took the soap away and
it all dissolved; I was left, at best with a black and white
picture postcard of La Place. Then I deliberately took my
cockhead between my fingers, and pressed as I might the
button on a slide machine: La Place surged back again
with a piercing clarity and weight -- not an image, but a
Real Presence.

I was confronted with a reality that I could never
again betray. A reality to which I had to bear witness.
And I knew I had to say the thing ... had to say it, write
it down to share with all the others -- had to do my Book,
in guise of a novel. It all came to me, right down to the
goring details ... It was the old brownstone building (-- it's
the Head Office of the Banque Canadienne, till they get
the new one up!) that finally got me -- came straight at

me, from behind, and penetrated. I didn't know it was in till I saw the entrelacs in the Church -- saw that whole incredible interior, painted over my body ... saw it with my own eyes. And then I realized that I had disastered. I was over the brink ... into a world I couldn't control. But I got what I had to say -- ahh, it's an odd experience, reading by the light of one's own auto-da-fe!

I rested a fortnight. Warned my doctor. Even went to see a psychiatrist -- just to check in, so to speak. If anything were lacking, that did it -- that hour with the psychiatrist -- reputed Toronto's best. I knew that he was part of what it was I had to cure ... he wanted to reduce me to a practising member of the Pan-Canadian lower middle-class. And he -- the High Priest for aspirant Squares! That clinched it. I left him and his consolidated philistinism (at $25,000 per annum!) and headed for Montreal.

This time it's for real, Eric. I'll only come back on my own shield ... or else with what has to be said, on paper! Either way it is suicide. If I stay constipated and can't write me out, then I'll blast my way out, bodily. And if I can write it -- and am not exhausted by the very living of it -- then it is equally suicide: social, political, economic. It is odd. But very clear to me. It has all been ominously clear ... all the time.

So here I am ... holed up by that "inner place." Waiting. Waiting for it to happen to me. If it had happened to you ... to your deserter, then perhaps I would have been spared this -- perhaps my generation would have been spared. But it didn't happen ... and no one ever told us about it, never. No one ever told us it had to happen, or else we were but still-born. So I sit and wait.

For the sake of conversation I call it an open-ended existential adventure. But for me it is Life. And the rest is daydream. With any luck I shall have a draft out of me by Christmas ... Certainly I will be drafted by Christmas. I want to be home for Christmas.

I have a splitting headache -- specific result of disastery? -- and the comforting and discountenancing realization that I am at home with the young French Canadians in a way that I never have been with English Canadians. But then there is no English Canadian equivalent to these endlessly articulate "quiet revolutionaries." And never will be: our universities, and Royal Commissionaries and All-Canadian Councils and the rest of them will make sure of that. Hiding their cowardice behind a false disciplinarianism. Their discipline against life.

But pace. I know I love my own people ... my own goddam Toronto Rosedale Toryland, and the Methodist Grits, more than I hate them -- much more; and God knows I hate them. Tell them that, Eric, for me -- tell them that, if I don't manage it ...

Keep your committees clean.

And forgive me my trespasses.

Sincerely,

HUGH

Had lunch with Luc Raymond. His new volume of poetry is excellent. Full of gut, and not mere sheer competence! Oh, the Castillon -- used it finally to douse my auto-da-fe! Bathing in Brandy - Quel eau-de-vie.   H.

He finished it, enveloped it ... and mailed it immediately in the box at the head of the Square. The sort of letter one never sent!

And then returned to his room ... began working through his notes. "The return to normalcy ... the need to recognize that normalcy is a diminution of the human capacity ... that."

151

Suddenly he began to sweat again — to shake all over. The wall lowered sullenly at him, heaving to. No, he would never be back to normal ... never would let that happen to him again. No — never. Sweat salted his left eye. He would go to the hospital right away ... his cock burned. He knew he had claps; must have it ... might as well admit it. Either that or pneumonia. And as he had had neither he could easily imagine both.

Arrived there in ten minutes. But what was he doing ... really? It was as though he wanted to create a guilt and then to confess it ... yet he didn't feel any right yet to either. His guilt was amateur he thought. He didn't know — all he could feel was the necessity to humiliate himself — to destroy himself ... the need to be soiled; the need to utterly destroy his middle-class culture and everything that went with it. The need to be aristocrat or peasant — anything but member of the Canadian middle class. And he was prepared to destroy himself to achieve the rupture. That was why he was here then — arrogating to himself the right to a disease that he didn't have ... consequence of a social disease he couldn't have. Yet he knew that he had no disease. The boys had been clean — he had phoned Yvon last night to see if they felt well ... had a fever? They were well. He had no idea that gonorrhoea mightn't show itself for another week — and syphilis for another two. He wanted it then! A clearcut statement of guilt. And to that end went through all the motions of someone diseased — deliberately and compulsively. And he did also really wonder if he didn't have pneumonia — flu had chased him for too long to be merely flu.

But why is it I want to die? Why do I so energetically destroy myself? There was no answer.

Can't make head nor tail of what I'm doing — yet I have the persistent feeling that it is right — still. Why? The desire to capitulate is strong but I have no choice. I know that too. There is still the Square.

Il y va de ma vie!

spent afternoon writing up novel notes. I can't tell what Andrew is doing — but he keeps doing things without my leave. And all I do is write him up. Mon semblable, mon frère!

at 5 p.m. — intense need for people ... phone Bill Gaunt ... don't know him — safer than someone I do. Eric told me to look him up — said he is a must. Virtually summon Bill to dinner ... fortunately he knows of me — is on night shift with one of the dailies — can squeeze in dinner meeting.... Meet in le Petit Havre — early ... he is there ahead of me: matches his name ... gaunt — dark-eyed, flexible — stands to greet me.... Calves brains (again — but they are too good to bypass) in which he joins me, tentatively. He must be twenty-six. Married — someone I vaguely knew. A good girl. Having commandeered his presence I feel it incumbent on me to engage the conversation.... Instantly serious. And rather surprised hear me saying after a few moments of joint editorializing:

"What I can't understand is why *our* particular English-Canadian culture hasn't produced more ... more of us. More with us." And the Royal We is an entire culture understood between us ... the culture of the private school, the monarchist, the "intégriste Anglo-Canadien" — to use a dangerous term. Yet, all exceptions made, it is right.

"What we are talking about is implicit in that culture, the Tory culture — the Anglican Canadian culture ... Anglicanadianism. It is deep rooted here ... but it has always been silent. All it has done recently is invite Pierre Berton to defecate all over it from his comfortable pew ... I guess I can answer my own question — it is because our culture, which is the particular and distinctive culture that distinguishes this country from the Amurricans is passive ... it is founded on fealty, on high faith, on submission to Authority. We have never stated our case! But now we have to ... because the Authority has betrayed us, all our meanings. We have been usurped — in the name of our own Authority!"

Hitting at this central nerve of us the table united us. The brains and Beaujolais (gourmet's B & B). And I press home, because I know that Bill *is* our case. And our presence here now is our case ... the quality of our presence ... the words are simply vehicles of that presence.

153

"… Edmund Wilson brought it home to me in his big-little book on Canadian literature … when he talked of the literature of La Maison Seigneurial of French Canada … talked of Le Moyne and St. Denys Garneau and Anne Hébert … I realized instantly that this was what we have never produced in English Canada. Yet we have its cultural and communal equivalent. We have a rooted quality culture that has never expressed itself. Our High North American Tory Culture … odious phrase — but never mind the politics of it … anyway much of it is left wing — NDP, in protest. Rosedale — Westmount — the Arm — from St. John's to Victoria, we have never said us. Never sung us. Why? Why? Why?…"

Bill looks as though he is undergoing a public enema … but it is too late to back out of us, and we both know it, and rejoice in the engagement (it isn't an "encounter," nor a "confrontation" — something quite different … can't quite put my finger on it; it'll come.) Bill clutches his wineglass, stares intensely into it, and says slowly —

"I know that … it is that blank sheet of paper … whenever I come to write what I really feel, whenever I set myself in front of a clean sheet of paper, I flee — there is some kind of mental stutter to us. As though it can't be said … I sometimes feel that to say it would kill it, kill us … there they have us — they know once we say us we have done us in … have lost our secret — our private potence. And (here he chewed a mouthful of wine, and spat it into his gullet, closing his eyes, and lurching forward) they are forcing us to say it — all of it — or die!"

An intensity to him now that focuses both of us into the words that project both of us…. Neither of us needs to define the "they" — we both know who "they" are — the enemy is clearly defined in us. Defined by the very way in which Bill is talking … talking from his gut — like some animal wounded in the belly, blowing blood out through his lips. Whereas "they" talk at the tips of their tongues — verbal memos! Always.

I look at him, mesmerized by his inner force ... yet
knowing him as vulnerable now as I ... look at him to make
sure I take in what he is saying — and now I realize that
Bill is already well inside of me now. And I inside him. His
words reverberating me like the organ of the Church. I am
merely trying to isolate the sounds, the syllables. So we are
interlocked.... And I realize that that is what happened in the
first seconds of our meeting — we were instantly immersed
in the truth of each other — in a capacity to feel and know
together — a whole sensibility that bound us in a common
faith about life, its values, its relevance.

Bill continues, between the bubbles of Beaujolais — "we
have never had to live up to the strength of our convictions,
our beliefs." Bullseye. And then Bill blares me in the eyes, soft
trumpet throat ... "we've never had the courage to live up to
our hard-ons...."

And suddenly I see it all, with a lucidity that lowers the
ceiling onto me, but I see it still, and hold the ceiling off with
one eye, while grappling Bill's blare with the other, blurting it
all out as it seethes in me —

"you know that personal failure in front of the blank sheet
of paper, that impasse in our Tory Canadian culture, and in
our national politics, it comes back to that failure to live up to
our hard-ons ... to our failure to feel the other man ... to our
blatant cowardice when confronted with cock — our failure to
touch the next man to the quick."

I am stumbling over my words, falling after them, quick,
before either of us can refute their reality.

"I know that, you know that...." Bill does know — at the
mention of the word "cock" his right hand rises to his nose and
feels along the side of it ... quick check-up on his own facial
phallus — confirmation of my outblurt.

"It is all so obvious — our political impasse, our cultural
impasse, our personal impasse ... our impasse as a people

— they all derive from our gelding! What we must do is find out who is gelding us, and why...."

Bill relinquishes his nose — our conversation is, after all, in no sense a mutual accusation — at least not an accusation of mere carnal indecency. If anything the accusation is the failure to be, by the standards of our society, "carnally indecent"!

He navigates in my right eye (the ceiling still engages my left one — keeping it at bay) — "yes — that blank sheet of paper ... I stare right through it to the end of my ... cock (the word comes slowly to him) — and I don't write and I go back to reporting. Living up to our hard-on ... provided we are allowed to have one! (he says it bitterly but warmly)

"The joke is on all of us! ... our inarticulacy derives from our sentience! Our silence stems precisely from the amount we must needs say to clear our case ... and it is that case that is the key to Canada. The key to our impasse. That is our secret — we are still sentient ... but our sentience is in part tabu. So we are dangerously sentient. That's our strength and our weakness. We still have our balls; that is where we are vulnerable."

Bill laughs — "Bold New Breed" — We passed that billboard coming down to the restaurant, at the corner ... the ad showing the "new male" — the new clean-cut tough-gutster. Exactly the opposite potence to that we discuss. We both laugh — in the warmth of this precise definition by negation. But I can't refrain a bitter cry — "the prick ... god, the prick."

"Well, we still have our balls — but they're trying like hell to cut them off ... at Ottawa. We're hanging by a thread now — a few more cuts and we're done...." Bill fleshes the wine rim with his lips, bites into the Burgundy and then furrows through it — "it has to do with the Crown!"

My sigh of release disposes of the ceiling ... "so you know that too!"

"Yes — our potence is somehow tied to the Crown in Canada. And it is being eroded like everything else in our specific English-Canadian culture. More flesh cut from us.... If that goes we're disabled."

"At the mercy of the All-Canadian Corps of Castratos in Ottawa...."

"We're just second-hand Americans. But how do you explain that to a Royal Commission. After all these commissions just use the authority they really destroy for their own ends. Besides — you can't tell Castratos that the Crown is a question of testicles. They'd be hurt! And anyway, they want our testicles ... can't you see the Centenary Commission ad — 'wanted — old Canadian testicles ... best prices paid. No questions asked. Just send in to Box 1967, Ottawa.'" Bill lowers his eyes.

"I tried to explain that to a French Canadian a few days ago ... Luc Raymond — I think he understood. But now I wonder if I really care anyway."

Bill's eyes catch mine again — "we have to — we can't afford to lose our crown jewels."

There is nothing more to say now ... we've said it all. Or felt it all. It hasn't been syllogized. Hasn't been academicated. No matter. The guts are there — the crazy gutwork of it all. The meaning. The footnotes can be worked out. What counts is the breakthrough. The breakout. Bill's eyes are back on mine ... into mine — like Luc's, like Yvon's, like La Place. Ply this moment sweetly — I knew its truth when I first saw Bill, on arrival — I knew that here was another man with an assoul — with a cocktit, with the whole bloody perceptor set. With B & B. Now our involvement is absolute.... Bill reaches out to his carafon of rouge — fingers touch the neck, ring it ... and I know that his fingers circle my manhood. At any other time I would detonate. But now I don't need to. Because this relationship so completely, honourably, includes embodiment that there is no longer any need to probe carnality. Carnal love is included, without question, and by right. And is thus no longer importunate. God — B & B again ... for the first time in six months, in a year; for the first time (and the truth hits hard for the absurdity of it now) since that abstract new flag was inflicted on Canada — the non-flag. **That** was when I lost my left testicle!

Now, with Bill, I am a complete man again — there is no doubt of it. I believe again — in everything. My country, my people, my love ... I can love again. I love again. Suddenly I am blurting —

"All I want is the right to love my country, my wife, my people, my world. All — all ... the right to love. That is why I have come here ... because I cannot live without that right — I can no longer live without the right to love. And that right has been taken away — conscientiously removed...."

Bill looks as if he is going to crush the carafon to splinters. I remove it from his hand — and as his fingers touch mine cock crows vehement. He looks at me calm — "and you would destroy yourself in revenge at the loss. I know that — you cannot tamper with the inner logic of a people without destroying that people...."

Bill knows all that — he knows everything of it. Because he Knew — it is Biblical that way of knowing ... it is carnal as well as spiritual. Bill Knows me! And with that all is Known. No other way to say it.

I shoot on — "that is why I demissioned ... why I left ... why I destroyed my career.... Only now can I speak out honestly. It's for real now! No dramatics — all the romance is in the eye of the beholder — I assure you! I had to sacrifice the complete Canadian curriculum ... to be what I am, as a Canadian, as a man. The other alternative was to sell out and become Prime Minister — and I couldn't — not another one with no balls! I couldn't perpetuate our national sterility."

Bill's laugh cripples him again ... laugh that is a woman around my manrood. "You demissioned because you believed — that's all."

"Yes, I believe, and the only sacrifice I could make was myself!"

"There are lots of us on the point of demission, Hugh — and if we meet and speak we're the response to the French-Canadian 'silent revolution' — only ours is silent...."

Our conversation flows on around us — country, patriotism, love, lust, eunuchoidality of Canadian Grit Democracy, the number of Tory testicles still hanging in good faith (Hees has one, Roblin 1 ¼, Robarts 1 ½ — but he never uses them....) No difficulty in agreement. Till I realize that our conversation has long since ceased to be the "dialogue" it started out so earnestly Anglo-Canadian — but is become now that hum of commitments, wombtaut mantight conjugation of personalities, that is its own meaning. A communion — with words as music. The area of conversation depending not on intellectual restriction, but on the accepted area of sensibility. And the words are just the counters of the mind, engaging free patterns on that sensitivity. It becomes the same mode of communication as with Luc ... ends up that way.

Silence. And now, my mind alerted, I syllogize — "there is us — what has happened here with us...."

"I know ... I think I can cope with it." And with that Bill gives himself up for found.

"We should end up abed — that is the natural expression."

And with that I take the give and kill it, eating us in the words.

"But hopping into bed won't solve anything."

And I want to say — "no, but it will begin something ... it will let each of us begin." But I don't. None of it is necessary now. Our conversation has consummated us. At last — a consummated conversation. A conversation that in itself achieved our manhood. That embraces our manhood. And it all derives from that first glance that acknowledges life to the quick!

Walk along la rue Notre Dame. La Place behind us. I should take Bill into La Place. But I can't sustain any more — not now. Walk to the Hotel de Ville. I want to share it with Bill — floodlit in its munificent ripple of flesh rising from our flanks. Walk in tandem — in conjugation. Not a word. Any word would kill. Stand at the top of la Petite Place, Nelson Monument behind. I can't withstand any more ... I call the taxi over — abruptly. Sever Bill from me with a handshake ... oh, curse me that — handshake that instantly reasserts our irrelevant autonomy. And then fall down the side of la Petite Place the hundred yards to my hotel. Bereft!

try to sleep ... nightsounds invade me; freightyards never stop in me, shunting me, banging me ... trainbells, clangorous. Voracious after me. Fornication in the freightyards. Can't sleep ... each sound erects a building of La Place in me, into me, batters my portals — each building accusing my failure to penetrate La Place tonight. Why? I came back hoping to preserve both of us intact ... came back so as to see La Place tomorrow ... retaining Bill alive in me for a lustworthy morrow — manned to La Place. But I can't manage it now ... I've been given and taken.... Or was it that Judas-kiss — the handshake at the end that condemns me now?

The bells again ... the goddam bells ... stop those bells ... gut shudders now ... clash or carshunt, lights are on. La Place is vehement in me, unbidden — the Bank of Montreal stentorious, the Providence Building leering, the Church — but before I can even enumerate, the brownstone building has bolted me upright ... and the lights have gone out — my lights. It is 4:19 a.m.... expurgated in abrupt detonation.

Only one consolation now — Bill will still be intact.... He will have to write now — will have to face the blank sheet, cocked! Will have to.... Because of B & B. Take and eat Bill in memory of me who just died for you.

DAY SEVEN

Up late — start straight into the Novel at last, as from my present point.

Andrew awoke about 9 a.m.... and set to immediately on his Diary —

"the railways cars still shunting me up and down my own track, like some accordioned fish backbone.... Am sweating profusely. Last night — rise and fall — still ignited in me. Up to a sunshine that threatens to further consume me, and I pull down the curtain, try to think: but so much energy is involved just in feeling, so much of my being is mobilized to deal with the creative chaos that day is bursting about me — that I can't think. And I know that in any case any ordered pattern presently imposed on what I am experiencing would falsify the experience. My mind must be in abeyance — that is the essence of my first week here; the enforced recognition that any preconceived schema is doomed. I don't know what I am doing. But it is certain that I Know. Or else I couldn't stay. It is, let me say, as certain that I Know, as it is equally clear that I don't know. That is, I don't know factually what I am here for. But I know with the whole force of my being why I am here! And all my discipline is engaged in this second knowledge ... ten times the discipline that I would require merely to know or to record factually what I am here for or what I am doing.

It is all I can do, in other words, to entertain the big factors: staying alive, feeling, hating, loving — without

*obscuring these fundaments by the determined trivia of memo-
ridden efficiency. I can't even keep a date-book now. To keep
dates is to forget them somehow. Whereas now my engagements,
noted within me, candesce my whole week — a week that
is as alive in front of me as the past one is behind me; a
week that is all around me. Like candles in Notre Dame …
flickering live in me. The analogy is the truth … and not
mere analogy. This is the way my world works now — this is
my cosmography, my mode of knowing and of being. Ahh —
this is what I am doing (having Known it, now I can merely
know it!) — I am recreating my cosmos … this adventure is
a cosmogony — a creation of a renewed world for me, within
me. The adventure then is a Copernican Revolution … but
anti-Copernicus, or Counter-Copernicus (that could well be
the title of my novelette). And Notre Dame is — amongst
other things, amongst other roles that it currently plays in my
life — Notre Dame is …"*

As I write I note something very dangerous to my Novel
… that by allowing my protagonist, Andrew, to write directly of
his adventure, into his Diary (which then becomes me! weird,
that), by presenting the rationale of it, his Diary becomes
my Novel, becomes my Adventure, becomes me now — and
my Novel, being merely his Diary is reduced, and what I am
living becomes merely my Novel. Whereas what I am doing
is the totality. And to try to reduce it to Novel, Diary or other,
I acquiesce in the fact that I myself do have some existence
beyond this Adventure into my life, into life. And I thus reduce
the Adventure to an accessory — which, God knows (well!), it
ain't! Take Andrew's Diary just now. By being semi-detached,
by being merely objectively-subjective instead of subjectively-
subjective it kills the Adventure! Dead. It must then cease to
be my Diary — or my Diary of the protagonist of my Novel

... and become the Diary of the Adventure. Because I must submit totally to the Adventure.

And even as I write this I am halfway between the Adventure I am living and Andrew's Diary of his Adventure. If I went out now and embraced La Place, I would be totally in my Adventure — The Adventure — of which my Novel can only be pale reflection. Whereas if I wrote Andrew's Diary, the Adventure would recede out of me, and I would recede, would diminish. I would lose that appalling magnificent immanence of the world — that palpable presence of all sensations goring me now. As it is I'm just half-and-half. Reflecting the semi-detachment of my semi-organic. English-Canadian culture. All High Church Hayseed Ontario roots! In other words Andrew's novel is dangerous to my Novel — to me ... I don't understand!

at 1 o'clock Andrew sortied out again determined to see just what he could see.... Clutching his body around him, he made his way to the bottom of the Petite Place (Jacques Cartier), falling quickly thereto through the thin chilled air, and at the bottom, instead of going overboard, into the harbour embattlements, veered to the right, ducking out from under the pressure to continue falling.... He was safe in the long greycliffed corridor alias la rue St. Paul and on rendezvous ... stopping in only briefly at his first outposting at this near lower side of the Square — the Antique Shop.... There was no further news and he moved on down the corridor. The grey nuns rose stern over him, their cowls bunched from aperture to aperture ... and then reverted to cliffs. He preferred them as cliffs. Some were disguised as shops ... but he paid no heed. He knew this was simply a front. They were cliffs or nuns — shops, never.

The grey walls pressed him on, squeezed him quickly along the bottom of the great Place ... and flitting quickly

across the street he saw that the Great Grey Sphinx
couchant was the right side of the Church flanking
him and sped on ... to another spectral grey building —
architectural exercise in geometricks, old style — it was
plaqued as an historic monument — Place Royal ... he
evaded the plaque, lest it relieve this further sub-square
below the Great Place of its real latent meaning in him
that he didn't yet have time, or energy to confront.... She
was waiting there for him ... for lunch. Looked scarcely
credible — proto-adolescent — the French Canadienne
in the Gallery Geneviève. He wondered what could have
possessed him to seek her out here.... And back then
along the grey corridor. Past the La Boutique, the Antique
Shop (whence the proprietress glared at the adolescent
in mistrust) across the lower part of the Petite Place
without mishap, clinging to the winch alias lingam alias
monument alias Lady Hamilton's Canadian dildo (do this
in remembrance of me) alias Nelson's Monument. And
clinging to the winch thus he swung them both safely
across the bottom of the place, without falling into the
freightyards of the harbour. Great White Elephant on their
right alias Marché Bonsecours alias Parliament Building
(it had been) alias Historic Monumentality.... Its major
purpose only became clear to him as they descended
into the small sanctuary cave which would become their
restaurant. Outward label: Le Fournil. Again deceptive.
But at least he knew the purpose of the GWE (Great
White Elephant) — to stand guard over their subterranean
"restaurant". That was sufficient in itself.

RESTAURANT: glorious disguise — glorious
legerdemain. Like a Kreighoff painting — it all took place in
miniature, through some viewing box (like those Victorian
postcard viewers). Below one's knees. En habitant. Ile
d'Orleans type chairs ... of the simplest variety. Which made

you feel like an overgrown child in a nursing chair. And diamond-point armoires that were soft-cubist mommies nursing the scene ... they sat down. And he looked at her again. Slowly ... looked at her along her line of chatter till he gained her mouth, nose, eyes ... above all her eyes. And then divested her, almost despite himself, of her proto-adolescent disguise. She kept talking — he prompted her — and as she talked she ripened stark before him ... flowered ... was at once Madonna and femme-charnelle. Something impossible in his own English-Canadian Cube Culture ... women were neither madonna nor woman — they were ladies-aspirant, at best — men-manqué, at worst. And as he watched he was wonderstruck at this thing ... the way she was simply occurring, right there in front of him ... almost unaided. Except by the transfixion of his gaze. Rapt. She budded out, enveloped him and the room ... and at the same time he her. It was uncanny. He noticed that her entire body rhythmically vehiculed her words to which he paid little attention. Her body was her logic ... from cave canem to eyeballs. And he was lost in it. Ah, he thought — that logic of the body ... that language of which we know nothing ... and too late, he realized that he was in love of life. She was talking of the English-Canadians on a Montreal weekend paper, while she worked for the French-Canadian counterpart. And he could sense and share her contempt for his fellow Cubes. Her contempt was not expressed ... but sufficient that it implicated his own. He knew, even before coming to the Square, that his own people, were constipated. That there was something significant lacking in them, simply as human beings. But he had never felt it more strongly than now ... as she subtly swayed along her inflorescent syntax across the table from him. Madonna of the Cunt. No — never felt it more strongly as when confronted here again with that "présence Canadienne-

française...." How could he describe it. He couldn't ... it
was all he could do at the moment to both recognize it and
then imbibe it.... It seethed softly around him from her eyes
to her thorax to the body of the armoire back under his
feet and up the low-slung chair that kept him earthbound
happily as in some European sportscar bucket seated....
Présence Canadienne-française. And for a moment he
wanted to weep — something he could never do in Toronto
(except in rage). And he gasped out "oh — chanceuse, vous,
d'être Canadienne française ... chanceux — vous-autres...."
A year ago he would have been startled at himself ... but
now it came merely as a recognized confession. And he
remembered four years ago Luc telling him, half-jokingly,
but also in earnest "to survive as a Canadian, Hugh, you will
have to become French Canadian!" Dreadful earnest that
now he knew.

Présence française.... He drank it up ... eddying in
it ... quenching four years, four decades, two centuries,
of English-Canadian drought — no, more precisely, of
honest Ontario Yeoman drought — emotional aridity. He
wanted simply to immerse himself in it. Before he dried up
completely. Présence française.... Her presence for him. A
presence he had never really known in his life — presence
de la femme. How could he know it. He had been brought
up as a gentleman-aspirant (he, too, had gone to Sunday
school). Présence de la femme féminine ... and not Queen
Victoria (first modern transvestite!) And as he looked
across at her he was haunted again, for the first time in
nearly ten years ... by the love of God. She reposed for him
all those questions that his marriage had first posed. But
love of God first of all.... All those questions that all his
exam questions from high school to university graduation,
had managed so successfully to obscure, evade, override.
Now they all sifted slowly back. So painfully slowly. He

didn't dare move ... lest he arrest the reincarnation. Or at least this proferred possibility of reincarnation.

At last — at thirty-two — the time had come to learn about love.... He had been afraid to love ... all his people had been afraid. So afraid that a book had been published recently proving that they were great lovers. Time to love, now ... when he, they, had been afraid to love anything ... and being afraid, their best bravado was hate.... And now even that was second hand, second class, imported from Amurrica — the latest brutality vogue of the professors and the intellectuals. All he could think of was that to know was to never love ... it said, communicated, better in French: "savoir, c'est de ne jamais connaître."

"Mais si vous autres, vous n'aimez pas, que faites-vous donc?" He heard her voice liquid across from him ... it sprouted over him like a milky way. And as if in some dream his voice returned: "We have friendship ... and politeness. We substitute friendship and politeness."

Elle — "Mais l'amitié, ce n'est pas l'amour."

But he no longer heard. His body was slowly unsheathing, slowly disentangling itself to dance the rhythm of her embodied language....

... after lunch in the cave guarded by the Great White Elephant I returned her to her headquarters ... along the Grey Way (formerly rue St. Paul) and then turned up toward the Great Place. Intuitively turned towards it. Suddenly the greycliff breached to my right, and high above me, quite rampant on the skyface rose the towers of the Church, surmounted by the cumulative pile of the neighbouring office building.... I ducked — for a moment they were but a single beast that drew together even as I ducked, ready to pounce me. I started slowly forward again, from the protection

of the greycliffs, and peered around the edge again, up to
this thundersky of greystone always overtopping itself. It
had subsided. And I continued up to the very entry of the
Square.... I was now on its lower left hand edge. About to
penetrate. And somehow now I was ready to enter — for the
first time. I knew that I could deal with it. Whereas before I
had merely scouted it, shadowed it..., Now I almost calmly
penetrated. Walked along its left flank. Scarcely wary. And
surveyed it slowly ... palping my way along the tops of the
buildings. It all really came down to five buildings ... five
facts. On the left — it was a non-building ... the hole in the
ground being prepared for a new skyliner of glass and metal:
La Banque Canadienne nationale. It was *aptly* represented by
a hole now. And once built, would still be a hole ... or rather
a photo-negative. In contrast with the Bank of Montreal
Buildings in front of me to the upper side of the Square. A
modern respectabilitarian skyslab on the left; and on the
right its pater — as fine a piece of Greek Revival Classic
architecture as there was in the nation. To the east side of the
Place — a brownstone turret of the High Victorian Phallic
mated by an even higher pile of grey 1920's Radio City
Gothic.... Of course, to the south, the Church itself — the
full facade of Ostell's Commissioner's Gothic, and conjoined
to it the administrative building in late Georgian which in
turn congealed into the cobbled stone palpability of the
eighteenth-century presbytery. I looked around ... scarcely
triumphant, but with a certainty of commanding it that I had
not had before.... The Great Square — the Place d'Armes ...
and it enveloped me and I in turn it, as she had done in the
cave of the Great White Elephant. A square within a square
within a square ... or rather a series of celestial spheres ...
three of some seven heavens.... The Place d'Armes within me;
and the Place d'Armes without me ... and I virtually intact
embracing and embraced. I could scarcely believe it. I pressed

on … entering the new Bank of Montreal building — a
Bureau de Postes. But I knew almost instantly that I had been
foolhardy — that I risked to squander all that I had gained
thereby. Because even as I entered, the arid open cubicular
spacings of the modern offices leeched the little blood that had
been intravenously injected at lunchtide, and I felt my own
dissolution, felt my own body vanishing so quickly that it was
only by turning and running out the front door that I saved
any of that resurrection of me at all, I quickly gazed across
the Square at the south side … the Church was indeed still
there, but it no' longer had body but was a façade that mirrored
my depletion, my own reduction so instantly from a tentative
re-embodiment to carte blanche.

I stumbled across the Square. Blued spruce trees, and
candy-flossy pinkies and even arbres au naturel were being
placed around the central part of the square, and in front of
the Church. I made a mental note of them, and sliced into the
Church proper, quickly groping for a pew. For ten minutes
I sat. And for ten minutes the Church interior remained
another exterior, a flat facade — at best a backdrop. And then
slowly it quavered … undulant, like a winded curtain, and
the vaults detached themselves from the nave and I from
them … the thing fleshed out, fleshing me out with it … till
we were fully three dimensional again.… And I could see
the arithmetic progression of the high altar in clear Calvary.
Then it stopped. So did I. I kept watching (pretending that I
wasn't) … till I was aware — but only after the event, not as it
happened — that the nave had become the Place had become
the girl at lunch, Madonne-femme … (what was her name?)
and that once again the world without was a mirror of that
within I could stand no more … any further development
now would be disastrous. And I fled with full battle honours.
Down the left flank of the Sphinx-Church-Couchant …
down to the Greyway and along … stopping, daring to stop,

only when I got to the Flesh Market where the proprietress awaited me for *her* pound of forgotten flesh. I was bushed. And our aperitif served only to remind me that my grasp of reincarnation was slender.

5:35 p.m.

9 p.m. The first week is done. Nothing has gone according to plan. But I've long since given up planning. I feel utterly smashed. Sheer blood loss — haemorrhage. Yet I feel that I'm on the right track. If I failed to take La Place the way I wanted, La Place hasn't taken me, the way it wanted.... We seem to know each other's strength, and are wary. And, given this initial set-back (that's putting it mildly), I can claim certain achievements. For one thing I've scouted the Outer World, and the Second Line. And established these for the novel. Not intimately, but specifically. I've walked the map (in penance — the damned map nearly did me in! That's for certain.) More important, I've identified certain sites with precision. I can call the bluff of the maps and the tourist guides any time I want ... or will be able to soon. There are some more posts to establish — some more identifications, of course. But the thing is in hand now. And if it has been slow I have at least made some direct forays into La Place d'Armes itself, and have begun to suspect some of its identity. I've made three visits, no — four — without decisive loss. Each time with greater success; with an increasing amplification.

The most puzzling thing — and it is the most dangerous weapon out against me — is of course the rapidity with which the dimension changes. Those ferocious, and utterly unpredictable changes in corporeality. I could be slaughtered any moment, caught off guard. Could be dissolved without notice. But I'm more adept now. Quicker at adaptation.

The major step, naturally, has yet to be taken — the inner keep: La Place. But with any luck the next week will take me to the threshold. And I think now that I have the key....

Dinner in La Cave confronting the Great White Elephant. Taking Combat Journal with me for a checkover: the New Guide Book for a Greater Montreal! Joke's on me — on all of us.

I feel sufficiently in command now to circle the Square after ... On leaving La Cave I note, however, that the GWE has changed on me. Don't want to deal with that on the spot ... back up the côte to la rue Notre Dame — watching the GWE all the while, to make sure.... It wasn't trompe-l'oeil. Thence to La Place ... Circle it calmly, with neither side of us pressing our issue. Enter the Church — but it, too, like the GWE has changed — decisively. Taking the necessary defence measures — veiling me from direct assault — I withdraw. Tomorrow will be soon enough to deal with both of these mutations.

11 p.m. go bed down for the night. And safe there the startling and evaded mutations of GWE and La Place seem almost harmless. I sin possessed instead by a vision of the possibilities, the creative possibilities of this new world I enter. If I can ever master it. A world absolutely accessible to the human spirit and body and mind. A world as readily acquired as any other culture. Provided we have the courage to move from one dimension into another. Provided we realize it is not a disaster nor a collapse, but a decisive enhancement — a kind of "conversion," as much in time and place as in heart and soul! An essential for a life of plenitude. Of course there is this crucial moment ... breaking through the sound barrier as it were ... carrying one's body through intact. And initially it is disaster. Utter disaster. Nor can I deny this life risk ... at least in these initial stages I explore now. (Why shouldn't I admit what I know deep down ... that my life is really at stake? Men have staked their life against truth for three millenia now! So must I.) But if I can cling to the positive possibility — to all of these possibilities — then I am homefree. Must just watch for ambushes. And I know the whole quarter is riddled with them ... but I uncap them one by one ... as I discover their

real nature. The thing to remember is that nothing is what it says it is. For example if La Boutique is really a Religious Shop — for High Altarware what then are the "Religious Shops," along la rue Notre Dame? And if the Hotel de Ville is the High Altar what is the Altar in Notre Dame de Bonsecours? Or the High Altar in Notre Dame de la Place d'Armes? And what is La Place d'Armes itself? (there's the nub!) A false step with any of these and I am done! Why hide it? And what is the Bank of Montreal? And what is … anything?

Once my preceptor set is distended to the right range here, then I can explore the logic of this New World, imposing the kind of order necessary to survive it. But that there is a New World, and that it requires a new kind of Man, and new laws and morality and religion and politics and institutions, that is self-evident.

I can only hope the worst is over. But I know it cannot be. I must continue training. I am more adept (and more vulnerable) every day. If only I can control the thing.

DAY EIGHT

He awoke gingerly. What state was he in? Which state? Which of his estates? — it was better to put it that way. The answer was given when, at the same time, he asked himself if he shouldn't get up immediately and go down to the Place. Make immediate reconnaissance tour.

He didn't need to — the Place lurched ominously out of his gut — the place ... the Church, the Greyway, the Great White Elephant ... the whole caboodle in him ... had obviously never left him that night, but remained couchant within him. It wasn't a question of a memory, or a souvenir, of a recollection. Not in the slightest. It was the Place, the entire Quartier — old and new — that staggered forward in him. Plied every organ in his body. It tilted in him, and he rolled with it, over to his left. And then straightened out. He shuddered ... the Place was clearly within his own inmost keep. He had taken the outposts, had even in part taken the Place ... but it had equally taken him. It was tit for tat. He wondered if any victory then would be Pyrrhic. Or a stalemate. Either one was defeat for him.

He rolled over again ... wondering how to extrude this presence in him. How to protect himself from it. He knew that once his lines had been breached this way he was endlessly vulnerable. And he felt vulnerable as he lay there. Utterly. Crunch of bones was railwayshunt was truck loading bottles in nearby alley was the Greyway vertebrate in him was his back cracking under the strain. Fart of carhorn, roar of motors ... a jungle rumbling him. It was all amplified in him — and it all amplified. So that every sound was present in him the way the Place was ... an invasion on all fronts. It all detonated inside him ... and threatened to detonate him. Everything thus was immanent in him ... immanent in the way disaster is immanent — one feels it pervasive, in every pore, every orifice — tickling one's nostril that is one's cunt that is one's assoul that is cocktit is fingercock is toetip is kneedcapcocked is earcunt is — Immanent in the sense that the medieval men must have felt the immanence of God — awesome presence inescapably enveloping them. It was a state of being — it was one of those states, "estates," he was reconnoitering here in the Place now. It was infinitely dangerous — if ever it ran amok in him, he was done for — had no line, no further defined line of desistance. So he clamped down. Asshole tight shut, cock shrunk like a boned aborigine dead head, ears muffled, nose clenched.... He closed the bulkheads.

But that was no solution — it simply achieved the stalemate he feared — the consecrated impasse. He groaned. No he would have to feel his way through (he nearly said "think his way through" — but it was in no sense a question of think-through ... think-through was simply fall-out ... it evaded the issue ... *any* issue by eliminating the problem at the outset. Think-through was merely a proxy death — coward's soft suicide!) — feel his way through. Hubnub now with cocktit he fingered ruminant — cocktit flaccid but candescent. At once perceptor and screen. At once receptive and defensive. Amplifier but not amplified now.

No munificence ... no magnificence ... merely acquiescence in the awesome immanent. But the words were irrelevant. Merely precise labels of the fact — prophets of the fait accompli: archaeological.

Groan. Another car shattered in him. Another driver burning himself out in him through his own exhaust pipe. God — another day. He wondered if he could stand it. Why not give in. His sensibility was ruptured. After all, one could suffer from a sprained sensibility as much as from a sprained ankle. He did. And it was just as explicit. Just as pangful.

Cockglower still flaccid — scared flaccid. When he used to be scared gloriously stiff. And he realized that his potence as a man was linked in some mysterious way with the Place itself, the Greyway, the Churchnave, the whole bag of tricks. Hubnub some more ... burnish the lamp.... His whole relevance lay in the Place ... his capacity to believe, to feel, to think anew, to be.

For a moment he envied his friends who lost themselves in business ... thought of the trio he had seen last night in the Fournil — incredible:

their entire communications system revolved about the politesse and the inner politics of business ... they talked of boilers the way one might of women — if one were boiler-centred.

Or of his acquaintances who had gone on the university — taken their Ph.ds ... what a wonderful solution that was — everything labelled, organized, detached — or rather, in order stood: detached, organized, labelled.... It was such a neat solution to the problem. It offended no one. It touched no one. But it wouldn't do — it was at best nature-morte, still-life ... life absolutely immobilized. Any man who could in earnestness undertake a Ph.d. wasn't a man ... not a man at all — he was simply cataloguing, step by step, his own accredited impotence. He became a civil servant with facts as memos. A new kind of intellectual super-drone. The feat was a simple one ... a coward's martyrdom. Anesthetized martyrdom — painless.

No, the battlefront was right where he was now. In the Place. He dredged himself from bed — his flu had come back ... he knew it was simply part of his vulnerability. He couldn't cure himself by curing his flu. He would only cure his flu if he cured himself ... and La Place d'Armes held the key to that cure.

15 push-ups; 15 toe-touches, palms flat to floor; a dozen knee-bends. Concession to the remnants of his body. And then the Combat Journal:

> ... am still transfixed — in no-man's land ... halfway between one estate and another. Unable to move. I realize now that I am still groping for the best mode of attack. And that up till now I have evaded the central issue. I have been too cautious — frozen flaccid by caution. There is no safe way. I will simply have to abandon caution. Abandon myself. Take the plunge. Realizing that I leave no escape route. Otherwise I risk all my forces in skirmishes. I'll tidy up what is left in these next few days ... and then make the central attack — must, or I am lost before I even have a chance to test my case.
>
> 10:20 a.m.

At noon he prepared to sortie again ... he was to lunch with Norman Jameson, the head of a large Montreal publishing house. An extraordinary man ... in every way. He was one of the few English Canadians, old line English Canadians, Hugh respected; respected infinitely. Norman was one of those bachelors who are devoted to their firm, their work.... Author of innumerable works (four of them) on old Montreal, he was one of the few men to remain faithful to the best values of old Montreal — Old English-Canadian Montreal. Despite the French-Canadian quiet revolution. It took some courage — moral courage. Hugh wondered how Norman would seem now ... would relish him, the new demissionary ... the Hell-bent Heaven-seeker. He wasn't sure. And the uncertainty dazed his momentarily stable world. Down to remove his bowels before leaving — sleek majestic turd — 10" uncircumsized: what came out could always go back in he thought.... It was just a question of putting Humpty Dumpty together again ... of putting the Cube together again, or the man ... a question of circling the Cube.

The taxi took him through the Square ... he had deliberately asked him to do so. "Voilà la Place, Monsieur." ... The Canayen presented it to him like a large patate frite. Hugh saw nothing. One never sees anything from a taxi. Except other taxis, and the backs of buses. It was like driving through a tunnel. He saw only the ankles of the buildings.

Norman was in good form — in his preferred setting, the old Queen's Hotel! — listened to his tale patiently — and then for an hour they talked of Thomas Browne's *Religio Medici*, of the *Urn Burial*, of his phrase "we live by an invisible sun within ..." ... of "the peace of God which passeth all understanding...." And Hugh flowed with the ritual.... He had forgotten all that. Forgotten St. Augustine's two cities. He realized now that Norman was in effect a modern monk and saint. That these men still existed. They were eternal.... And by the time lunch had finished Hugh was, like Thomas Browne, bursting forth with serenity. That serenity he had forgotten. Yet had once known. Was re-armed with it.

He stared back with this renewed weapon, to the Place. And met an old school friend en route — Allan Nisbet ... both products of the same Anglicanadian Cultural Establishment School. Allan nabbed him for coffee ... they had never been friends. Obviously Allan was bored with life, or frightened, or both. Hugh accepted the coffee ... and listened to him intently — watched him start in to talk ... and then, suddenly aware of Hugh's silence, of the fact that Hugh *was* listening intently, Allan stopped, stopped significantly short of himself. And Hugh was then aware of what it was he was really noting ... this lack of the presence that he habitually found with the French Canadians ... presence of body as presence of mind. Allan simply was *not* there ... could not present himself.... It wasn't that he evaded the issue. He simply stepped outside it, beyond it, by talking in terms of political reforms, or committees or renewed administration. He talked earnestly about these ... but the significant thing was that they all fell outside the central question — the question of Allan's very presence, the magnitude of his human fact. It was that which Hugh missed abruptly. And just as abruptly Hugh knew that Allan wouldn't have it ... no matter how long they talked. For another ten minutes he sat listening to this indifferent man talk about indifference ... about the end of English-Canadian apathy — sat watching him limpidly mouth these truths that his own still-life falsified. They talked briefly about Jameson whom Allan had met on various occasions. "He's not the man of the future," said he.... "No," mused Hugh aloud, "He's timeless ... 'men of the future' are all future men of the past." As he left Allan swung out to give him a conscientiously virile handshake — it was like an awkward teenage sideblow in the boxing ring. Hugh caught it on the way past — saving Allan the immanent embarrassment of not having landed it in the right place at the right time (a blind blow meant to prove what it refuted — his vitality). And Hugh was en route back to the Square. He stopped in at the newspaper on the way — long enough to have undermined any superficial glow from Norman's outburst of serenity ... and then walked to the Square.

It was 5:35 p.m. Temp. 35° F. Already dark dusk.... The Square was there beyond any shadow of doubt. It was decisively there. He did not have to reach out to palp it, to feel it out — nor did he have to defend himself from it this time. Neither. It was simply there. Immutably there. It was there with a remarkable overall clarity, And he rejoiced in it. Rejoiced calmly in the lucidity of the buildings themselves — corporate presence in himself ... unquestioned. And then suddenly he realized that there was something strange about it. Because what he was seeing was the complete Square, and seeing it in terms of the buildings — of the substance of the buildings. He couldn't see any details. There were no details upon which his eye rested unbidden. Quite simply the totality of the Square was present. Concretely. All that he saw was everything. Secondly — equally strange — while what he saw was the solid format of the buildings, yet it was just this — just these forms that were least visible when he started to dissect the Square to detail it. In fact the sky was then more visible than the building forms — and in the buildings themselves the visible fact was the bright nightlit windows. Yet he had not seen either of these upon entry this time. He had seen and felt the deep calm substance of the buildings of the Square ... and had seen them whole. Yet by all rights that was not what he ought to have seen. And then he realized what it was he saw ... he had seen Norman there ... it was that "outburst of serenity" — that deep serenity which he saw, which had depicted the Place to him. Which had dictated how and what he saw. "The peace of God which passeth all understanding...." He remembered Norman's phrase in support of the world that he knew in his best moments.

He looked again at the Square — this time he saw the still candescent dusk limning the building tops, and the ignited windows. And at the same time he saw his first impression — the corporate presence of the Square itself in the buildings — the outburst of serenity.

He walked across the Square to the Church and entered. This morning he had phoned down to the hotel desk for some tea. "Pas de service aujourd'hui monsieur ..."

"Comment donc? Pas de service?"

"C'est fête aujourd'hui ..."

"Fête de qui et de quoi," he had asked petulantly ...

"Féte de l'Immaculée Conception ..."

"Ah, oui, j'en avais entendu parlé de ça...." With a phrase he annulled the grenouilles de bénitier. Now he was at the Mass of the Immaculate Conception. And felt the privilege. He went in to the full Church, made his way to the front and sat down. He watched the priest at the altar ... he was raising the Host. Hugh watched not daring to analyse what he was feeling ... lest he lose it. And again it was the same thing ... the complete corporeal presence of the Church.... When the priest moved the Host around the chalice he felt his own flank limned.... He sat — fragile but firm — knowing that so long as he did not think of what was happening to him it would continue to happen ... that so long as he did not molest with words or thought this event, then it would continue to happen to him, and he continue to be an organic part of it. He would be, physically, part of the picture that was being painted. He held his breath.... Once again as on Sunday, the congregation sifted forward to the communion rail. He almost followed. But he didn't want to fracture the porcelain precision of his own participation. People — ordinary people ... with ordinary clothes. Kneeling. And then returning with God in their throats. What a startling, munificent victory it was.... He could feel it for them. And rejoice in it.... After the service he went up to the altar — in his duffle coat, *Le Devoir* tucked under his arm — and kneeled ... the sheer luxury of kneeling, publically and simply, kneeling. Without being in "court dress" of Sunday Best. He eyed the altar that simply occurred in him. And again he realized that it was the "serene outburst" that he had received, intravenously from Norman, As he left, he noted that the forms, the ogival gorgeous gothic, reminded him of San Marco in Venice. While some of the work on the pavilion over the entry ... including the clock, reminded him of Harrods of London. Data, mere data. The important thing was to know that in this building there was all the space, the movement, the munificence, that he needed to live ... that he needed for fulfilment. Here space and time flowed together corporately ... and not excorporately, as in the new buildings. At lunch Norman had said that modern society downgraded death ... here death was upgraded again, because life was upgraded. Here the problem of resurrection was posed, and resolved, in palpable visual terms. The building defined the man it saved.

Outside it was dark. The traffic roared harmlessly by the Church front, shadows on the wall of the vaulted Square.... He turned east down Notre Dame Street following the roaring shadows into the spectral limestone of court house, City Hall and Nelson's Monument.... His sore throat had completely vanished. Till he thought about it.

I'm still flubuggered. It's been chasing me for a month now. Lying in wait for my vulnerabilities. Can't afford to let it get me now. It would completely uprootle my campaign. The danger lies in this fact: the more capable I am of really seeing

La Place ... of really penetrating it, the more I seem vulnerable to everything — including flu: everything penetrates me at the moment I penetrate everything.

— my visit to the Square was successful again today. Thank God — I was beginning to fear that the veil might have descended with permanent results. As it is I seem able to thrust it aside. But it is hard — each time I feel rent ... over-exposed, endangered.

— returned to my hotel after dark (I no longer have anything other than a mechanical knowledge of time ... hours elide) — and tried to rest. Studied the Bartlett print of the Interior of Notre Dame "Cathedral," ca. 1835. I've had it for nearly a week now. My "tourist map" of the innards of the Church. An inner eye available at need. Less a question of looking at it ... or even into it, than of its presence in me ... learning by exposure.

I have known about the print for a long time — at least ten years. But now I realize how bad it is — at least in terms of the Church. (Bartlett's publisher was mistaken — it never was a 'Cathedral') as it is today. I realized this as I entered the picture, oblivious of the preacher in the high pulpit, on the left side, made my way to the altar, turned at right angles across it, and came back down the right side of the nave, to turn again at right angles, now confronting the preacher. I never looked up at the vault. In fact my experience in Bartlett's Notre Dame nave was a cubicular one. A rectilinear one. I was in essence entering an Anglican eighteenth-century Gibbsean church dressed up with cardboard Gothic. Bartlett had failed to insite the Church. The proof, quite aside from any changes in decor that there may have been since, is that the essential experience of the nave insofar as it is cubicular at all, is one of vertical upthrust. But even more important, the experience I feel more and more with it is one of warm liberation. While in Bartlett's church I feel cameo constraint....

Dinner in the Cave again. It is deceptive in its habitant decor. Scraped pine chairs, coal-oil lamps without coal-oil. (I didn't notice that until I went to pee — and standing at the bowl missed, in the lamp beside me, that oily sweat that inevitably gathers on coal-oiled lamps.) Out again to skirt the Great White Elephant ... same effect as last night; but I'm still not prepared to cope with it.

Unable to sleep ... lie enmeshed in the soundscape that blares and bleats around me. Absolutely vulnerable. Increasingly aware of the danger in these sounds. They take place in me ... burgeon unmistakeably from this world around La Place that I eat into me.... So that any noise is knife or bludgeon, or pression in my gut. The noises come from within me — unexpected: any one could hara kiri me. It is terrifying. Yet I see no way to exorcize this reality. It is — after all — at once the reality I seek and against which I defend me. Two-edged sword ... Damoclean!

DAY NINE

By morning he was spent ... his body pooled steep in the perspiration of a night battling the soundscape. Lay marinated in his own sweat. He grasped for his lifebelt, cockworthy — and noted once again that each sound danced on the end of his cock. There was no question of that now — each carfart, busgroan, engineblurt ... each one drummed the end of his cock ... so much so that had he orchestrated the cacophony he would have been blitzed by orgasm. As it was he could scarce withstand this detonation that blasted him from within as from without.

Each outburst was replete with danger — absolute danger. Each one was quite capable of detonating him completely.... Each one implicated an entire response and defence. He had never known before that sound could kill. Not ear-shattering sound that simply blew your head off. But even the slightest sound.

Nor was it a question of void, of some hollow sonority. What he experienced was solid ... palpable. Each noise was a flesh-and-bloody reality. That was what terrified him. The feeling of being buggered by sound ... of being earraped. With his whole body now an ear. Fingers, toes, nostrils, mouth, anus ... and of course cocktit. Everything of him was an ear. Cunting sounds into his gut.

Trainshunt in the nearby yards squandered his last energy ... his cock shrank from the blow of engine against freightcars. He decided to take a day in hiding. Get shots for his flubuggery. Relax if possible. Read some Bozzy if he could ... but he couldn't: the words were either bas-reliefs that hit his eyeballs like braille; or else they simply dropped out of the page. They were negative. He was nonplussed. There was only one remedy then.... Go to the heart of the matter. He dressed quickly and went straight to the Place. No effort to mask his approach. He knew by now that the war was a portable affair. Distance had not only ceased to be a factor … it often simply ceased to exist at all.

As he entered from rue Notre Dame everything was all right. Without thinking his eye ran over the buildings efficiently, outlining each — he noticed with approval the Greek Revival Anthemium detailing on the old Bank of Montreal…. And then he realized with a start that the Square was back in its box again … it was in fact now at a respectable "distance" from him. La Place *was* now a Square — a Cube! Detached from him. But even as he recognized that fact it changed … changed right in front of his eyes (or was it behind his eyes?) — suddenly all the bodies of the buildings slid forwardly from somewhere behind the scene into the sheer façades that he now realized he had been seeing. Suddenly there was immense mass to the façades. And there were the two realities superimposed … the first reality, the one he had been used to, of outlines and three-dimensional perspective. An incredibly safe reality he now realized — in contrast with the second one … which was, if not bestial, at least was decidedly animal … those buildings had moved forward like wild beasts to the kill encircling him — and the Square was La Place d'Armes again! He checked around the Square from his position at the mouth of Notre Dame Street where it debouched upon La Place … they were all there — La Banque Canadienne with its appropriate hole; the Bank of Montreal — new building flanking old — respectable WASP phallus skyrising beside mammary mamoreality of Greek Classic; Brownstone Victorian privy part (uncircumcized), turreting beside Entre-deux-guerres Gothic. Finally the Church itself which he now approached.

It was disarming … frighteningly so. This concurrence of the two worlds. The Place at once immensely immanent — overbearing … immersing him. And at the same time the Square, the Square Cubed detached — or at least semi-detached. With outlines, the old 3-D façades limned on the decisive bulk of the buildings like sgraffito incisions in pottery.

He had never had this happen before … never had these two worlds in balance so equally. Of course the 4-dimensional world had it all over the 3-dimensional one, which now looked like a toy — a game. The 4-D was definitely more serious; endlessly potent. But it was reassuring to have them conjoined.

He entered the Church. Not — it certainly was not Bartlett's Church. Not now. Could it ever have been? He doubted it. And he realized again that pictures were no more a substitute for reality than written words: it was the experience that counted ... the participation in the object. Which then became subject.

Yet if it wasn't Bartlett's Church it was momentarily — that is, as he sat down, he saw Bartlett's Church superimposed upon the present Church — he saw both. (After all, Bartlett's Church had been his last penetration — it was still in him.) And then the imprint dissolved and he was completely swallowed by Notre Dame. But Notre Dame had swallowed the imprint ... and like the Square — Place itself, it was now both dimensions — though with the Bartlett outline completely invisible, engaged in its task of withholding the palpitations of the church immanent.

He returned, reassured, to his hotel. Moved rooms — from the front to the back ... hoping thus to muffle the sound warfare. And dropped gratefully to sleep before a later dinner.

My entire body was suddenly sculpted alive out of solid rockbed. I could feel the fissure incised between myself and the bed itself, as I lay like some revivified fossil wrenched clean of its bedrock. There I was — gifted with wakefulness again. Hell. Then I knew what had happened ... I had been born to daylife by the crash of freighttrain against its shunt of cars in the nearby yards just below Commissioner Street — progeny of the shuntyard. Wretched miscegenation. I crashed from bed and tried to write.... How many lives at once — La Place itself ... my adventure — that the primal reality. The focus. The new life. And then the reality of my demission — my tentative insanity ... and then the novel. I have to live and write a minimum of *three* lives. And I have scarce strength to achieve *one* now ... and after two hours wrestling with words that lurch hazardously from one world to another of me, I carry me and my Combat Journal (pocket talisman) off to Le

Fournil for dinner ... and after, sit musing it over my Marc de
Bourgogne settled in the armchair rocker near the front door
... Marc — it does so much for me. It is all the difference
between Toronto and Montreal ... between the Cube and the
Canayen. Marc — it is gut of good earth ground deep in the
crotch of life ... an uncircumcized cognac!

And, as the Marc confirms the immanence of La Place in
me this afternoon, I more happily recognize that I can never
dismember myself of this new overweening world I have
discovered in me ... this new old circumambience. No — that
is not unhappy (the panelled armoire on the far right wall
now catches that same immanence from me ... and lowers at
me fulsome). If that world presses a little too close for comfort
now, too close for discretion and for politesse à l'Anglaise, tant
pis — because at the same time it is real, it is loaded with
meaning ... a menaceful of meaning. And I can, albeit numbly
now, rejoice at that. I can rejoice at this new inescapable and
entirely prerequisite intimacy with life, with the world — an
intimacy which I have never accepted before — certainly not
publically. It makes my most obscene prior private acts seem
detachable.... Now I have a permanent conjugal involvement
with life, though I am scarce ready for that yet. In fact, it is all I
can do now, to remain where I, perforce, am at....

The Marc was indeed munificent catalyst of realities ... and he lulled
himself there — till he saw with clarity the conclusion to his novel. It
would be very simple ... he started to note it down in his Journal:

"He had seen the Place d'Armes as no one else before had ever seen it
... not in one, two, three, not in four centuries. He had possessed it and
had been possessed by it. And now, as consequence, he was possessed by
life itself ... inescapably — he was condemned for life, to live. He had,
quite simply, *seen* La Place d'Armes."

DAY TEN

I awake — and startle me to note that I am normal ...
neither more nor less than "normal." A curious realization.
Then slowly I follow my change from normalcy ... it is a
specific carnal change — *everything* in me changes ... chemical.
That meadowlark I hear — sharp cutting the ice air ... that is
doorbang; I recognize that now. It is the sounds that change
me ... or I change as I hear the sounds ... now all noises are
angels on the end of my needle. My assoul is a cocked-cunt....
The Place d'Armes is alive in me, abruptly. Not recollected
— but present ... une présence. I regard me, curious, just
this side of fear — the Place ... it is inside me again. How
did that happen? How did it get there again — there now
infinitely more clearly than if I merely saw it. Alive in me
... palpitant ... can see the small newsstand at the corner, in
front of the Mother Bank ... with its barnyard of bosoms, and
flowering phalli — the magazines afloat in space that is their
substance ... it is the "space" that is real ... and the journalese
is the evacuation. The inflorescences spread across the brow
of the kiosk — "Giant," "Fit," "Youth" — a horde of muscled
masculinity.... Ask the vendor "who buys these?"

"Everyone ... lots in the bank ... lots of women ... you?"

"Yes ..." and I am armed with an issue of Pierrot's
Manorama featuring Elfin — male Lolita ... ahh — that will
be the next best-seller; someone will sit down and write of
Elfin. Presumably an immigrant — peddling our lost sensibility
back to us.... After all, we have just had middle-aged women
bodily restored to us by an Ethnic — putting the flavour back

into Canadian life — that's the effective role of these Ethnics ...
more pizzas, more hair-pies....

Yes — La Place pregnant in me.... It is all so inordinate —
yet I know it is necessary now....

I'm still flubuggered ... hounded for weeks by the germ.
But I know for certain now that I won't cure my flu till I cure
me ... my sickness is clinically metaphysical....The Square — it
is involving an entirely new kind of relationship to life, a new
kind of life. I came down to assault it ... the Novel was just the
pretext, the packaging — but now something quite different
is happening.... My assault has backfired. Strange. As though
my open warfare procreates love out of hate. I'm not attacking
the Square ... I'm making love to it — even as I assault
it. Stranger still — what I attack is making love to me ... is
making me. Don't try to understand it. Just be ready — at once
defensive and offensive. But in the meantime I am incapable
of accomplishing anything else at all ... even the simplest
things. My responsibility to the Place — to my relationship
with it — is so absolute that everything else is thrust aside. I
am recreating a new kind of responsibility — based on a new
kind of relationship with the world around me (in me now).
A new kind of responsibility that is a new kind of liberty ... I
don't really see my way clear in it yet — I just sense this. All
I can do for the moment is preserve my sanity — the vestiges
of my male maidenhead — and the need to accede to certain
subtle imperatives in me.... It is sufficient that I am still alive,
unimpaired, and on site, on target....

The fact that he was alive was in fact something of a miracle in itself ...
for the past few days, passing the army reject shop he had been tempted
by a knife — a Scout knife type ... it would be good for his novel ...
to have the knife, as he typed, on his table. But he also knew that it was
for real — knew that he dared not buy that knife ... because he could
no longer tell in any degree what was novel and what was real. He sat

looking at the Bartlett print again — and saw, of course, what it was — the work of a convinced if Romantic Cube — indeed had it not been so fully cubic it would have been merely square.... And then he sat down to read — to finish Jacques Prévost's novel — he was lunching with him today ... was proud of that: how many demissionaries could phone up the head of a Royal Commission on Canada-culture, and be asked to lunch on a few days' notice ... it was a vestigial arrogance: him in his name was still good.

Prévost's book — it read sadly ... confessions of a fellow citizen — confession of a youth rejected ... like Eric's book — *The Traitor* — this is the same exorcism of that rejected youth — exorcism that is belated flowering.... One sentence was the key ... "je haïs la puissance qui est en moi de communiquer la vie ... je haïs plutôt la puissance qui est en moi de saccager un autre corps...." As he read an idea threatened to formulate him ... but he suppressed it — not yet, not yet, he didn't want to know it ... and then he thought of Yvon and Pierre ... of the fact that they had been French Canadians — humans first, but then French Canadians — and he remembered he had not wanted an Angluche.... Suddenly the world was on him again, pervasive presence ... infiltering the darkest convolutions of being. He clamped down. Keep a tight asshole when under fire! — that was good battle tactics....

He glanced up ... his Brief Biography lay on the table beside him.... And he remembered it all again ... he had lost his job, his vocation, his nation, his home, his health ... he was pretty certain that at a given moment he had lost his sanity — and yet, now underneath it all he still had a feeling of rightness! (not of righteousness — but of rightness ... of doing what was necessary....) It was all infinitely confusing. He wouldn't know just where to pinpoint it....

... after finishing Prévost's novel I walk to the Place ... taking refuge, flubound, in Cubeland. The Place is crisply defined ... so long as I don't attempt to look at it, or rather don't attempt to look into it ... so long as I leave it alone it is detached ... so long as I am detached ... God — say that again ... so long as it is detached, I am detached.... That's it — that's the key. So long as I am indifferent it is … so long as I am not in conjugation.…Test this — carefully — on the Bank of Montreal … on its façade: look merely at it … as though it weren't really there … but simply an object to be skirted, a backdrop, with me as the foreground. Like that it is but an outline.… Now — stare at it … God — yes … it shunts forward into me … and I am ominously implicated … I need to do something about the Bank … saved by lunch — Prévost arrives, will-o' the wispy … and in an instant I knew that he was like me … that he too had that inordinate sensibility. That he too was … was a she-man, combining in him the ability to receive, and the necessity to give. I knew that — and I knew him.… He was nervous with me.…We were unable to talk much about his Commission (it was — truly *his* Commission … had been built around him.) The others were In Committee for Prévost — I can no longer believe in committees … prophets of the fait accompli. And in this case it is Jacques who is the fait accompli.… I remember when the commission had been formed … and I realized with a shock what it was — not a commission to fulfill our cultures … but another step in educating a certain kind of English Canadian up to his self-arrogated right to rule … it was a commission to further establish the English Canadian of the Rapido … the Ottawa Civil Serviceable … the ECM — Canadian Methodist Emancipee.

Talk his novel — *it* is the reality here … and as we talk it I realize how real it is for Jacques … his inner truth — the man who rejected his youth — killed his mother in revenge — went sterile — and took his revenge, again … in politics! It is all mad … mad … but at least it *is* again.…And that is why he is at once so grateful and so nervous now with me … as we talk. Either what I say to him, what I ask of him, is outrageous … or true.… Only as we leave and he signs the book for me do I know.…"A mon ami Hugh Anderson … ce livre qu'il a mieux senti que la

189

plupart de mes amis Canadiens-français" And I knew that I had been right ... the allegory had been him.

As we left ... we were in front of the Museum ... I wanted to visit it ... and left him as he walked down the street ... I turned surreptitiously to watch him — that walk, that wonderful walk of Jacques ... toes splayed, nose up, not in arrogance, but sniffing the air, head acock ... it was so sadly, rightly spritely. I remembered his last words ... "suivez vos instincts" ... and his comment on my demission ... "vous avec demissioné pour ne pas demissioner de vous-même...." He was right — and he said it with such concision, such promptitude that I knew he knew what he said ... and I knew that his novel was, in part, his confession of a failure to do the same. He had himself admitted that his political life was a substitute for ... for Life.

The Museum ... that repository of all that is wondrous in the past. God — as I enter it dies in me. It is bleak ... cluttered cavern. I scout the Canadian exhibit — at least it is no longer in the cellar. It is on the main floor. Westmount acknowledges Canadianity ... acknowledges Canada-beyond-the-frontiers ... beyond the frontier of Westmount. But it is all French Canadian — and it is a hodge-podge. Sickly.... And I note that there is no English Canadiana — only French.... It's André Laurendeau's *Théorie du Roi Nègre* again (That was his coup de génie ... that editorial was what we got from him in place of all his unwritten novels, poetry....) — The English-Canadian garrison collecting the works of the indigène. And in the French Canadian exhibits there is no sense of proportion, of order — scraped pine exhibited alongside bombé commodes. Something dies a little in me ... killed by this museum, this exhibit.... As I flee I note that the bombé commodes in tigerstripe maple ... that combination I had thought the apex of Canadian achievement — French-Canadian palpability, English-Canadian concern for visual texture, for play on the eye (something the Americans didn't have) — that combination is wrong ... a contradiction in terms.

My gut sags ...

the modart gallery next door ... exposition Hurtubise —
hard-edge, soft-edge, assoul inside out ... God — he paints
the world I *see* ... I ask him if he sees the world he paints. "No"
— emphatically. But *I* live it. I **do** see the world that way....
And out the big front window look now ... see the cars on
Sherbrooke Street glut the rush hour ... shadows in Plato's cave!

He went back to Le Fournil that night ... a good bombshelter. And
there was always the recuperative Marc de Bourgogne ... at the next
table a young couple — male of course ... decorators from Dupuis
Frères ... one reminded him of George Carter (and instantly he knew
George *was* touched the same — of course ... that same fertile flaw
in them....) They shared a Marc ... and Hugh regaled them with his
afternoon in the Place — returning from lunch, the museum ... the
modart: he had stopped his taxi in La Place.... "I got out and suddenly
they were all over each other ... all over me ... sodomachie. The
Banque Canadienne impaling the Mother Bank with its brownstone
bulk ... the towers of Notre Dame corking up the arcaded entry....
Maisonneuve masturbating the entire Square.... It was magnificent ...
but no one else seemed to notice this orgy.... Suddenly the Brownstone
was after me ... and I ran...." They laughed. But he wanted to cry.
His fever was back. He was violable again. The youth that reminded
him of Carter was interrogating him with that incipient bitterness
born of exile within his own community ... and then they were gone,
to their own sodomachie ... soft sodomachie. He finished the Marc,
walked up to la rue Notre Dame ... was suddenly embraced by the
convoluted Second Empire obscenity of the City Hall ... and fled
to his room, buttocks battened ... "batten down all hatches ... take
up battle stations ... keep your assoul closed." He deliberately closed
cockear thus ... it was a singular trick that he had learnt forcibly that
past week — by clasping closed asshatch he could shut out the sear of
sound.... It was his magic talisman — all he had to do was say, firmly
— "wordkill" — and the world died out of him. "Wordkill" ... killing
with the word ... joykill — manslaughter.

DAY ELEVEN

He awoke at 10 a.m.... His fever had gone — everything had gone — except the deeprooting tail of his flu — the Place had gone — the sounds, the whole insite.... Wordkilled! It was only now by making a conscious recollection of the Square that he had any idea of its existence at all whereas up till then it had been a constant corporate presence (or absence — with the vacuity of the absence as strong in him as much a physical fact, as its presence — either way it was a corporeality).

Now there was simply a souvenir of La Place become merely the Square again: a tourist memory. He could itemize the Square and its approaches — make a mental effort to regroup it — he could systematically recover each fact: and in his mind's eye he walked up past Nelson's Monument with its bas-reliefs, to his right the City Hall and the Chateau de Ramezay — the first with its conscientious echo of every French palace anyone would remember, from Versailles to the mid-nineteenth century, and the second with its stonework that reminded him of the stonework of Ontario yeomen of the nineteenth (and of the twentieth) century. Reminded him that in Ontario the work was at once less organic and less rational (except — of course — the Pennsylvania Dutch Loyalist work in Waterloo Country ... he had owned a small frame house there once — back in his honeymoon days. At the same time the organic quality and the rational quality in the Ontario stonework was more divided.... He chuckled — Eliot would have talked about an incipient dissociation of sensibility and intellect.... He was sure that the modes of structure reflected the two provincial minds and sensibilities ... (again, someday, some no-man would write a doctoral dissertation on the matter — putting back together what no one had ever had a right to sunder ... putting back together that which was still apparent to him, and meaningful to him, at a glance).

Left, down Notre Dame Street — Ostell's Courthouse with that inelegant extra floor added — and the string of delapidated houses converted to drugstores, restaurants and the smallware of daily lives — all habitant run … these, down the left side of the street — till you came to St. Laurent — and the groundhole for the new Palais de Justice on the right. And then a final block of mid-Victorian high-pilastered Mannerisms that housed at ground level, better restaurants etc … and all the quincaillerie religieuse, librairies religieuses — all the art sacré … giving on to the Place d'Armes itself. Again he could make a conscientious enumeration of the buildings — could describe to himself the Square — could even now place all those details such as the ironwork grill over the front door of the brownstone bank building, which details before had been submerged in the thunderous tide of the whole. In fact now he could give himself up to details — that was all there was left to do — go deeper and deeper into details … in some effort to reconstruct the lost whole. It would have made a fascinating study. Each Building was a Style and each Style was an Era: and all of them was a Person — a Real Presence. Thus:

The Sulpician Seminary-Presbytery — Peasant Baroque — New France
                    — High Habitant

Ostell's extension of the Presbytery — Gentleman's Georgian — British Garrison
                    — Regency Beau

Bank of Montreal — Merchantman's Neo-Classic — British North America
                    — Responsible Governor

Brownstone Building — High Methodist Monstrous — Confederal Canada
                    — Man of Substance

Providence Life — Entre Deux Guerres Gutless — Roaring Twenties
                    — International Ivy Leaguer

New Bank of Montreal — The Organization Gentleman — Post-War Prosperity

—The Man in the Double-breasted
Grey Flannel Suit
Banque Canadienne Nationale — Pert Packette — Post-historic —
Noman.

And finally — the Church itself — that amphitheatre that crowned the
Place. He could enter it now, could remember the colours, the gilt, the
myriad arabesques … but in essence he noted, the Church he entered
thus was Bartlett's Church again — the Cubicle — albeit overdecorated
to his taste now.

But that was **all** he could do now — catalogue and index the Place
— none of it impinged upon him — none of it implicated him in any
other way than as a tourist, or as an art historian. If he wanted to probe
any further, why then he could (as he had already noted to himself)
undertake a doctoral dissertation. That way he would be forced to know
the Square more thoroughly — would be forced to be a tourist not
only in breadth, but in depth. Perhaps if he was lucky, he would achieve
something of the awe with which, unwitting, he had begun.

For the moment he had nothing. He was simply quiescent … worse:
important! He was incapable of seeing the Square and the Square could
no longer see him. The reality of both had diminished disastrously. And
for a brief moment he felt utterly capable of an office job….

… dinner again Au Fournil … marinating me in cretons, pigs
feet and Marc. Plowing me under the black earth again — a
rootling process. Till I am rich gourd again, inseminated by the
earth I inseminate. Homefree! The points de diamant of armoire
undulate me … and that constant reel (is it La Bolduc?) that
must be at least a record and not muzak, that reel shudders me,
till I almost uproot to dance my gourded embodiment … almost
greensprout to sunshine. And then They are there — here…. It
can't be that! It is — I watch the incursion….They're back …
in committee — Christmas Committee. Over a dozen — more
like two. Watch them, commandeer their length of table, dividing
the restaurant in two … in two worlds. Watch this amputation of

us — What *is* it about Them? The conscientious cavalier? That's
part of it, alright. The deliberated effort to be gala, to be effortless.
After all, it is Christmas party. Then I see one of the girls — her
movements are marionetted. How? Who pulls her strings? Smiles
— then looks at her smile, swallows it after due time, moves right
arm gracious forward to waterglass — drinks gracious but by
numbers. It is incalculably false ... and touching. She sets the
scene ... for all these marionettes. They are all here in practise
— practising themselves ... practising their role — they're all
on stage here, stage they've bought for the occasion. The girl —
understudy Grande Dame ... understudy First Lady. God — it's
a portable finishing school — and this restaurant in le Vieux
Quartier, is Exercise #17, for advanced students.... The men the
same ... all in their black priesthood — dinner-jacketed — all
preparing their little manhood — their gentlemanhood. Tonight
the exercise is Gentleman-Cavalier ... Gentleman-with-Lady-
on-the-Town.... The Blond Beast across from me, direct over
the shoulder of the First Lady — he is up already, before they are
down, toastmustering the apprentice toastmasters. Fortunately no
one is listening ... they are all practising their own lines, for their
ladies. Blond Beast — Blondebeeste.... Oh how well I know
thee and all thine! Blondebeestie flings arm about shoulder of
second First Lady at his side in attitude #39 — Easy Gallantry
with Public Intimates....

Hate — suddenly I am in hate — like bitch in heat! — I
am floundering steep in it. And come up battling, out of my
pigs feet and cretons — come out ready revolutionary again.
How I hate them — hate their gorgeous enforced gaiety, hate
their apprentice overlordliness, hate ... and my teeth masticate
the Marc till it splinters glass.

Watch the French Canadians at next table watch the
Cavalieros. Like mongrels watching thoroughbreds, wistful in
their whine. Yet accustomed to it ... cowed, comfortable in
their pigs feet. How can they? How can they stand this orgy

of insulting good mannerisms, practised in situ? This entire restaurant turned over as scenario … with live bit players — real nègres, us — the French Canadians … the real inhabitants.…

So that is what I have done — I have completely metamorphosed — have passed completely over, changed B & B, become an inpatriate … an exile within my own land — an In-Canada exile … French Montreal my built-in American's Paris.… So be it! All I know is that suddenly this home, this centre, has been invaded, has been abruptly commandeered — as a launching site — for young Blondebeestes. *Real* red (*not* the red on the new flag!)

Second First Lady is in stride … she moves, albeit only at the table, with all the grace of a thoroughbred. Moves so well that suddenly the tableau she creates about her could be Tatler soirée. Blondebeeste beams approbation. She has carried herself well. And he achieves Exercise #92 — Winestaste … the ladies eye him with gracious, if rather wide-eyed, care … and pronounces it palatable. He *is* magnificent … those big baby-blue eyeballs, the slightly waved kempt blond hair — brushed not combed! — the broad shoulders carrying a torso that is absolutely kouroi, in steep-V down to plaid cumberbund that serves as chastity-belt, for dinner at least. He is almost edible. God — he is God. My head reels now … this is God. This is what we were all brought up to be … this is what Methodist Sunday school boys finally emulate (and I remember the Roundhead Methodist All-Canadian Good-boy from the Rapido ride, whose hair, definitely, was combed not brushed!). This is what I was trained as (like some albino seal) at boarding school. This is the Complete Man. The Gentleman … tonight in his role as Gentleman Adventurer, trading for Prince Rupert's Hudson's Bay Company, from Montreal … and still the coureurs du bois around to salute.… I can grovel now — want to grovel, or stand and salute, or strip naked, and have myself freely gelded, for God's sake. I am immense … in him. He has me … has me. Then I am murder — I nearly fell together for that? For that? Oh no — not now. Hate saves me from that pitfall. They know that hate … they must. Their eyes peer out in furtive glances, beyond their crystal ballroom, out into our hinterland. Who is there? Who are we? Do we see them? Peer out the way those eyes peered from the Jaguar into the Flesh Market, the way the sailors peered at me … at the obscene. And all their noise of gaiety is to keep their courage up.

Marc cocks my known hate.…Yes, I know these gaylords … they are the final outcrop of Boy's Own Annual, and the Just So Stories. I know their schools … Anglicanadian. Or facsimiles. With the cult of sport, and the curse on culture. I know their schools, their homes, their parents. The White Canadian Raj — and he is obscene … because he failed, despite the public sacrifices of his balls.

Stare murderous across at my selected Blondebeeste. Do you have balls, dear? Or is it just bang-and-go-back? Do you fuck? Steeply? Or just fun-fuck as Exercise #63: keeping fit by fiddling?

… ohhh — for brief moment again Anglicanadian Kouroi is lord again. Erect as falcon — all cock. His whole body is lingam. And I want to spreadeagle. And then I see he is untouchable — an Untouchable. Impermeable. Nothing will ever enter there; nothing ever come out. Autonomaniac. He is simply an exhibit.

Walk over to settle me in my rocking chair, just off their end of table. And Marc then. To their discomfit. And then, before going, in contempt, interrogate young assistant proprietor — his lithe body smiles me, but his eyes don't entirely meet mine — the presence of the Canadian Raj has fractured every eyeball in the place: no one sees now. "Oh — it is a fraternity Christmas Party … Delta Upsilon.…" And I remember from my university days that at McGill the DU's were # 1 — the Respectable Drinking Club for Young Westmount. Everything fits. I know who's what as anticlimax … because that very first movement, by

197

the First Lady had defined the whole corpus. That first tentative
movement of her hand ... hand that will never clasp the object
... never, never, never. Her cunt clamped as taut as they my assoul.
The whole world shut out. As I turn to leave I see Blondebeeste
#1. He has erected himself again ... for a moment our eyes meet.
Head on. I breach me open ... blast assoul wide to swallow
him — he looks bewildered, smile shrivels on his façade. I snap
my teeth over the farewell of last Marc, and he dives into his
wineglass. He knows I am prepared to kill.

Outside Blondebeeste is still there ... magnificent. How
did he get there? Afront me. Erect. That great white smile. On
parade. Christ. I did swallow him then, alive.... And then I
see what it is — the Great White Elephant — the Marché
Bonsecours — the one-time Parliament of Canada ... after his
cultural precursors — and mine — had burnt down the old one,
after the Rebellion Losses Bill over a century ago. It is him. But,
Jesus, this has balls! Blondebeeste is but Complete Cube-marqué.
And I, revulsed, am Complete Cube in revolt!

DAY TWELVE

He stirred to the dim realization of daybreak. But he was largely impermeable ... almost completely protected against any incursion of sound or site. The White Raj had closed him down again. In fact he had to feel himself to make sure he was there at all.... It was not an entirely unpleasant sensation, to be impermeable — to be invulnerable and he thought of Blondebeeste. He almost luxuriated in the distant clatter of humanity, cars, buses (they would be going to Church), trains. Luxuriated in their detachment. That must be what those fraternity boys feel like — that is, they don't feel anything at all. Impervious. He had been one once — what *had* he felt then ... all he could remember is that any feeling was untoward — unmanly. Well, now, perforce, he could join the club. With the flu, he heard no evil, saw no evil, felt no evil. He was completely desensitized. (That is what it is like, then, to be a Cube — a condition of undeclared, subterranean flu!) He felt cocktit just to make sure.... It still purred: obviously there was a limit to what flu (and fraternities) could do to a man! Thank God.

He followed the purr — listened to it and as he did, as cocktit purred through to him the sounds of train clarified, and car ... and the din of men — all these clarified ... slowly, and then dangerously. He cut the purr — and the sounds died back.... He subsided into the comfortable anesthesia of his flu. And got up to shave for High Mass. Flu or no flu — there was still the Square. And if anything it was safer with this armament of desensitization.

He slouched down Notre Dame Street — waves of raw cold undulating in his wake. In the Square a demonstration had already started. Several hundred habitants in white berets placarded the central square. "Marie, Reine du Monde, priez pour nous," "Michel Archange, aidez nous," "25$ allocation familiale," "les taxes sont un vol," "Sacré coeur de Jésus ..." ... He watched with rising amazement this congregation of habitants.

They were straight out of a Krieghoff painting, a century out of time....
Well-kempt peasants. Créditistes. They were the rag-tag ends of the old
peasant-Church axis that had sustained Duplessis' dictatorial power for
nearly two decades. Behind them the Bank of Montreal rose significantly.
The Bank had helped Duplessis too. In fact, symbolically enough, the
marriage of English-speaking money and the French Catholic Church
under Duplessis really meant the birth of the new skyscraping Banque
Canadienne Nationale afronting the old Bank of Montreal. All this was
foreshadowed in his mind before he turned away into the Church. He
simply couldn't deal with a pocket peasant revolution at the moment.
There was High Mass to contend with.

As he wended his way down the unimpeded aisle to settle closer to
the alter he was aware that the Church was once again unaccountably
Bartlett. That is it was simply a cubicle, thoroughly overdecorated. A
distanced cubicle. One that conveniently took place outside of him.
Like the habitant demonstration — something he could take or leave.
In fact something that he couldn't "take," but perforce found he had
left. He was outside of this interior. And as in Bartlett's print he could
wander in leisure as though in some public mall. He tried again ... to
see the Church. It was still untouchable. He concentrated his mind on
the finials pendant from the balcony. All he saw was upside-down knobs
from a pinball machine. Could even hear the bells jangling as the ball
careened amongst these obstacles ... it was the bell of High Mass. He
forced himself to look at the High Altar. They were already well on in
their public performance of Resurrection. But all he could see was a
cooking demonstration. He wondered if so many cooks were necessary
... and then presto, it was done — head chef lifted the lid of soufflé pot
... it was ready, and the class went up for a taste ... himself included ...
lined up at the rail — It was a bad batch, clearly, tasteless ... Corpus
Christi ... le corps du Christ ... Corpus Christi ... the assistant chefs
kept chanting. The Body of Christ! It was the Body of Christ ... and as
he returned to his seat he saw that the pinballs were loaded, and so was
he ... the pinballs lowered onto him, swollen into life.... And then the
little man in the greyflannelette suit was on stage for the left-overs of the
Body — caretaker-undertaker ... carting off the corpse.... And Hugh
was out into the Square where the pilgrims were already assembling,
singing, the entire Square singing.... He instinctively assembled beside
them ... as they marched down la rue Notre Dame....

"all these Victorian façades dancing, rippling to their
chant....Vers Demain — Towards Tomorrow. The pilasters
clench and spring in me, greystone coils that Michelangel me
... till City Hall crowns our march, embodying all of us....Vers
Demain ... woman beside me strings her rosary that leaps the
whole musdement of City Hall into our fingers. And then we
are bundling down la rue Bonsecours to the Sailors' Church
... its hulk in fecund convolution under the façade of Victorian
Blondebeeste classicism drawn eclectic from the Marché beside
(Blondebeeste — ah, that is why I couldn't see Notre Dame!
Blondebeeste battered me last night)....I do not know when
we pass from out to in except that suddenly I am pewed as their
chant sculpts me with the hewn precision of the consecrated
woodcarver....Each phrase kneading me....They are all seated
now....Absolute habitants ... across the aisle, and to the front,
a high head, with snood of hair and phallicitous nose is a glory
inciting my counterpoint ... chant: Marie, Reine du monde,
nous vous prions ... Marie, Reine du Monde....Overhead the
suspended ships suspend us, converge on the High Altar that
draws my eye into its body and thus indrawn suffuses my site
back throughout the Church till my eyeballs blaze at me from
the overall corpus of the Church of us and I am inside my own
sight radiant from the altar that is the Church that is the nose of
that giant habitant head across from me that shakes its mane of
hair over all of us qui prions Marie Reine du Monde together
in an act that is patently a celestial public obscenity of worship.
Glory be to God — and to that habitant's nose....A woman
who is mutation of all those early nineteenth century primitive
French-Canadian portraits solos us from the altar-rail ... her
shrill voice laps the entire Church in me, laps all of us, laps the
altar that shifts to the cadence — the habitant blows his nose.
Oh Christ — Mary, keep praying for us ... just the same way!
The bench under me shudders, and I clasp my Holy Turd steep
in me re-embowelled like some Amen....Bell rings — and

pilgrims file past reliquary of Marguerite Bourgeoys at front left ... stoop and kiss ... stoop and kiss. I want to go forward, in them, to stoop and kiss this arsewhole of the world, this rosegilt bone under glass ... kiss this historic Christian cunt ... but I feel that it would either drop my soufflé, or rise my Christ. I don't dare either — not now. I've had enough. Surely it suffices to be reincarnate? ...

Intermission at the restaurant in La Petite Place ... des Gouverneurs ... that sparrowlegged waitress ... who hawks about, infinitesimal predator. Marie, Reine du monde ... pray for her! And then to rendezvous at St. Joseph's Oratory ... 2 p.m. — to follow the pilgrims assembling for the return of their Cardinal from Vatican Deux. Why? Because I can't desist me ... can't rebut the gut of them that has pricked me ... can't turn that inner life off ... not now. Life that is ... that is La Place d'Armes in me.... All this is La Place. The wooing of the Place.... The siteseer.... At 2:05 p.m.... I am whipping the taxidriver to the Oratoire....

Up unending stairs, up into the deep cave ... pressing forward along the left aisle to the Cardinal ... and cocked to all ears hear ... know instantly that that man is more important to me than any other man has ever been.... What he says ... there now — talking publically of love — he dare stand there in front of our crowd and talk love ... "il est plus difficile de se laisser aimer, que d'aimer même...." I stand by the front pillar, leaning against it.... "It is more difficult to let oneself be loved even than to love...." In his virulent red cap and gown.... Talks love, openly — imagine the Prime Minister talking "love," or the president of the University of Toronto (other than of a release into free love for Methodists; too late for him! — thanks be to God.) Imagine any of my people talking love to thousands — talking it, and giving it as they talk! There's the nub.... "We must learn how to love ... learn how to give ourselves in love ... learn anew...." Head reels, and vault thunders ... eardrum split.... Cardinal now making the Host — recreating our

bodies in that of his Christ ... strain to see him ... to see this
Resurrection for us ... if only I can see.... Chalice raised ...
bells again — This will be the Christ. I must get closer ... slide
out to the aisle, eyes strain ... and as I walk forward youth walk
toward me, walk untrammelled into my eyes, walk straight
through and out my cocked hearsay ... will walk away with
me strung between his eyes — batten down hatches ... cock-
kill. And then the veil is down again ... I turn — the Host is
dead, the youth gone. I have just killed the Christ! Kill one, kill
the other, kill all. Manslaughter. And all I see, ominous lurching
forth into me, the giant crucifix freestanding behind the altar,
standing in space, in this space, in the very way that I have felt
all space so often these past days as I stalked my prey in La
Place.... Then they are gone ... Leger is gone.... And gone
that little man-of-God who must have been the representative
of my own Anglicanadian Church mustered here, on deck, to
welcome the Oecumenical Cardinal on his return ... could
tell at a glance — the red of his cloth (Red Ensign red) as
contrasted with that of the Cardinal (the red of the New
Canadian Flag — flag for all us New Canadians — but the
Cardinal's red was for real withal: he put blood in it!) ... and I
am alone, with several thousand others in the thundercave....

Earroarings.... Everywhere I see sound ... I reverberate
endangered. Know my danger — know the signs. And as I turn,
the great Crucifixion threatens to impale me, to engulf me —
both at once ... and I know I must save me from out this place
— this Golgotha — save me at pain of ... of instant (oh God,
must I admit it again) ... of instant life! And of that insanity that
totters me like the crucifix now. At the back of the Basilica turn
once more, to the site ... to the insite, and then eject it from me,
and bundle me down the escalator, only stopping at the distant
bottom where I take respite in their Museum.... Exposition sur
Saint Joseph ... St. Joseph comes to Canada — St. Joseph and
the Indians — St. Joseph everywhere — ad mare usque ad mare.

All I can see is that Sainted Joseph. And — grace à Dieu — I
don't need to read the labels ... because it is in front of my eyes:
to see is to know. The Catholics are still object-centred. The
written word hasn't killed their sensibility — little do they know
that plight of Protestants. Little do the young French Canadian
anti-clerical revolutionaries yet know that it is their Church that
has left them with the fingertits requisite for revolution ... and
then out ... down all those steps, till I stand blinking in the snow,
gazing back at this magniloquent udder clambering white up
the mountainside. Like l'Eglise de Notre Dame de Bonsecours,
it proclaims an external adhesion to arithmetic classicism ... at
the same time its body is rampant legerdemain in refutation of
this. The Church is Christ's body ... incarnate.

    **Andrew returned to the Square ... entered Notre Dame
... and knew instinctively that the Oratoire St. Joseph had
given him the key to the Place, to the Church here ... but
he didn't say it, not even to himself ... not yet. Because
to have said it might destroy him in two ways — it might
absolve him of the experience it described; or it might
impose that experience now ... and that he knew he could
not sustain — not yet. The best he could do was dinner
again Au Fournil. Where he joined up with a single man
he had seen there before ... the painter Michael Arnolid
— they talked of meeting years before ... of that German
mistress he had had ... and then Andrew felt able to broach
his secret.... "I only see things if I hear them ... and if
I hear them they impinge upon me, predators, threaten
to eat me ... as I them. So that if I hear sufficient to see
absolutely I am in danger of my life ... absolute danger —
so that to see is to touch, seeing becomes palpable, and
everything palps me ... the merest sight is insite is incest
is love is threat of death that strikes brains as balls as it**

incites me to that expenditure of me which is fatal.... And
now that I know, I know that not to hear is not to see,
is to go blind, is to die inside me, is to be a living death.
While to see — is to go mad...."

Michael knew what Andrew was saying ... because all
he said was "when I am like that I find a beautiful face,
and I look at it! Otherwise I would go insane." Andrew
pondered that self-evident truth.... He remembered that
night, going to George's for impromptu dinner. And he
knew now he had gone to gaze at a "beautiful face" —
not a pretty face nor a handsome face — but a face that
had beauty within itself.... And he looked at Michael's
face — an effeminate version of Humphrey Bogart — and
knew that Michael's soft, hurt, faceflesh was beautiful too
... and that hurt — because here was someone else who
commandeered his love ... and he couldn't give any more
— not today. He had already been breached — wide-open
— and then had clamped the gap closed when that youth
had penetrated, shutting him out in a false prudence that
abruptly ended his life there and then. Christkiller!

He thought of Michael's art ... of his sempiternal trees,
and palpitant women.... And he knew that Michael had
failed because somehow he had never quite confronted his
cocktree. That failure was his success. His art.

The main thing was that Michael knew the world
Andrew saw — took it for granted. It was a life-preserver
... momentarily. And he remembered again the knife for
his novel that he had never bought — and knew it was
just as well....

"Have you ever had a Marc...?" And Andrew introduced
Michael to his Marc — and felt absolved of the need to
give that was implicit in their encounter. Only days later
did he know that he should have given, more fully — and
then he regretted it, too late....

After dinner he insinuated them into the company of
an improbable couple behind them ... a Lautrecian pair
... d'un certain âge (so much better than merely "middle-
aged") — he hirsute silver hairless.... She like some
aging prizefighter. Etienne Rivard ... living his constant
conspiracy of life ... playwright-ordinary — human-
extraordinary. More Marc ... and converse. The story of
Pierre Blais receiving the Governor-General's award for
literature, in Ottawa, saying that he was happy to receive
this recognition as an accredited writer, from a foreign
country. Of course the English-Canadian papers suppressed
this pertinent lèse-majesté. And the bon-mot about
Madame Vanier ... the "soutient-George" ... and Vanier as
a "nouille." But it was all so right — so hopelessly right;
and once said seen ... and once seen, irrevocable. He
felt another iconospasm. Another God was ailing. Yes —
insofar as Canada had a Crown it was a Queen Mommy ...
Victoria, Alexandra, Queen Mary, Queen Elizabeth, mère
et fille ... Mme. Vanier: all Queen Mommies for the Anglo-
Canadian Blandebeestie. Poor Pooh Bear! No wonder New
Canadians champed at their bit.

... by 10 p.m. his perceptor set was jammed ... he couldn't
receive another site. Photococky out of negatives. Blank.

DAY THIRTEEN

... the fever had abated. He awoke to a muffled daybreach ... the sounds were the same sounds as before — he could recognize trainscreech, carroar, doorslam. They were there — but they were different. He wondered why. Wondered half-apprehensively if this were some new trick, some unknown weapon. The sounds simply didn't penetrate the same way. Oh, they penetrated all right. Cockquiver confirmed that readily enough. But it was a soft penetration — the cutting edges gone, no splinters, no shrapnel; just the great soft sound itself — like a hand wearing a woollen mitten. Each sound muffed. For a moment he enjoyed the muffle — if one was going to be battered, best be battered softly. Then a new sound, one he recognized from the childhood he had been promised but had never had, the sound of a shovel on concrete told him what had happened — reminded him ... because it had already begun to snow last night, late. It must have continued — and this morning everything was snow muzzled. He should have known that — his nose had told him aside from the sound ... that raw tingling at the end of his nose, at once damp and fresh chilled.

Breakfast in the sailors' restaurant across the way ... in the past that early morning array of bosoms and buttocks and bare legs that are the morning nurture on the newsstands of the world. And the backs of the men haunched over their coffee at the counter beside. They had had the buttocks the night before. He watched the waitress (was she one of the available buttocks? Certainly she had fine flying buttresses. His snow-nose glowed at the site) he watched the waitress cutting the French bread — like butter ... and slushed the morning snow down with tea. When he went back out he still didn't dare sight the snow — again veiling his vision ... not sure yet that he could cope with such a decisive change in scene. Another metamorphosis, he thought, and his body would simply succumb.

He crossed the little square, blind — up to write his Combat Journal:

Arranged yesterday to lunch with Alphonse Renaud. It
would be another excursion into St. James Street. Another
reconnaissance from one side of the Place to the other. I slushed
down Notre Dame Street ... even flu-dazed I realized that the
snow rebukes the grizzly façades of the Courthouse and the
buildings beyond. No longer were they sepulchral — great
hollow sculptings of sound that betrayed me centripetally
into their maw; now they were dirty façades only relieved by
the pigeonshit that splattered their greys. Suddenly I realized
that I was already half-way across the Square, without even
noticing it. I was crossing it as I had crossed it so many times
four years ago — crossing it merely out the corner of my eye.
The Square existed only as a traverse. I stopped myself short,
chagrined at once at my ineptitude and at my temerity. Still the
Square was merely something to cross. Its only meaning was
in crossing — in going from one side to the other. I tried to
confront it, firmly. And that is, indeed, all I succeeded in doing
... in confronting it ... placing myself in front of it and looking.
But even then all I saw was the traverse. No use pretending
otherwise. I continued down St. James Street ... to the Royal
Bank Building, at the corner of St. Peter Street ... splendid
corporate body, and entered as one might any mausoleum
and was instantly embalmed in an elevator that dropped me at
the 13th floor. Alphonse worked for an investment firm. He
had originally been a gay blade — then he married, had two
children — joined the investment firm. I hadn't seen him since.
I walked along the hall from the embalming shaft, to the great
panelled doors at the end of the hall — they were energetically
grained teak ... and recalled French-Canadian armoires à
pointes de diamont — a seventeenth-century survival; and they
reminded me that the firm was French-Canadian — part of the
new French-Canadian economic nationalism. A receptionist

prepared to be contemptuous of me (I wasn't in the compulsory stetson and blue overcoat) — and in fact probably looked rather like an affluent habitant — with beret and Hudson's Bay short coat. Alphonse rescued me from the incipient contempt that formed at each corner of her mouth ... and we were floating down the long carpetway to his office. Suddenly I was wary again ... because I was floating ... even protected as I was by the flu, my body had been breached, eviscerated — or could be. I looked at the carpet — that electronic green yellow — the same colour as Alphonse's tie. All the colours were variants of this same experience — each one had the same effect ... as though sending an electric current through my body, and dissolving it into the common field of energy.

"This is the Board Room," he said ... I sat down in the fuzzy blue bottom of the swivel monopod armchair ... but I felt no fuzz — although the fuzz was so palpably there — that is so visually palpably there. Even when I reached down to feel it I didn't feel much. "We can speak direct with any major city in the country from here ... this button" — But what I was asking myself was whether I could speak direct with anyone who might be in this room. Or whether I existed at all.

We proceeded further back, into the lower echelons. Until suddenly the electronic carpet ceased — and the paintings no longer looked like carefully wrought tapestries that you couldn't possibly touch — so palpably impalpable — and we were in the engine room: the main staff office, I never welcomed a civilized dungeon with more gratitude. The framed department store pastoral scenes looked edible. And for the first time I shook Alphonse's hand, and found that I still had one.

We talked family, children, affairs ... Going out he showed me the main rotunda of the building.... It was dazzling — unquestionably a temple. As brilliant and as majestic as Notre Dame — and the Basilica. But absolutely different. Why? For a moment I hesitated. It was all I could do to regroup my body from its dispersal in Alphonse's Board Room. Slowly I pulled myself together and got a perspective on this secular basilica. And that, I realized, was just the difference ... I could "pull myself together" here, and I could "get a perspective." Here there was only me, and the spot I looked at. It was a two-way route. No deviations. No doubts. It was a simple square.... Bang and come back. And while I was aware of the space around me, I could not feel it around me ... as I could at Notre Dame.

I determined to come back ... but for the moment at least I had a perspective on the Square and on what was happening to me in it. There were three worlds, at least ... and each one obeyed different laws. And created different men — created the different men it demanded. The world of Notre Dame itself ... the world of Alphonse's Board Room ... and the world of the rotunda of the bank. Each of these worlds was of an utterly different dimension. At least now I understood that....

We crossed the Place d'Armes again. And it wasn't until we had done so that I realized that I hadn't seen it at all! The thought demoralized me. Drinks at the Vieux St. Gabriel. I had meant to come here for days. It is a curious self-caricature. That is, it revels in being at once a modern decorator's version of French-Canadian Habitant culture — Krieghoff Canadianism — complete with ceintures fléchée, blouses etc. And at the same time it *is* just that ... in the very way it imitates what it believes it has bypassed. The unwitting habitant wittingly nostalgic about the habitant. But my flu closed down on me again — and my perceptor set closed with it.

That afternoon he tried to sleep away his virus. Failed. And at 7 p.m. met the youth from the Gallery Jacobin for dinner at le Vieux St. Gabriel. They were both wary. Andrew too tired to give — the youth wary of being had. But they were both seduced into a total rapport by his fatigue ...

and at the end of dinner had established an open-ended communication that was calmly comfortingly dangerous.... Andrew explained very simply that the problem was a simple one ... he couldn't see a woman if he couldn't see a man if he couldn't see a building if he couldn't see a flower or a tree or a God or a shitpile. They were all one and the same thing.

"Does that necessitate homosexuality?" asked Peter (alias Bill Cunningham).

"Homosexuality if necessary but not necessarily homosexuality," replied Andrew — chuckling at his apt misquotation of an infamous Canadian prime minister ... and noting privately to himself that that seemed about all that he had learnt from his four years of Politics and History at the university. "If I must honour that capacity in myself in order to honour my humane capacity ... that is what I shall do. Quite aside from the fact any human act accomplished with compassion is beautiful in itself ... any human act that contains compassion — even though it is doomed to failure from the start. The only failure really, is to fail to try...."

"So that homosexuality isn't central to your sensibility," noted Peter, staring at Andrew with eyes that threatened to pop into his sockets....

"No," he said, "it isn't central, it is simply presumed; it is implicated as a capacity in the world that I covet. And I have found that by denying it I deny that world ... which I have no right to do. Because I am then the less...." And then he started to laugh almost hysterically. Peter looked frightened because he realized that his own viability as a human was somehow mixed up with this strange man — and then looked relieved when Andrew merely said "what a magnificent revenge on Protestantism — that our denial of a Catholic heritage should finally implicate, as ransom of that lost heritage, an orgy of homosexuality

... the ultimate self-disgrace — the ultimate flagellation, penitence ... imposed by our own pig-headed denial of our own humaneness. God — what a backfire!" And he sat musing over his teapot (vestige of a lost gentility) — We cut off our nose to spite our face, he thought ... and we discovered what Dean Swift always knew — that our nose was our cock and that we had lost all. And now — whether we like it or not — we pay the price of our own arrogance: and we all set out in pursuit of the lost phallus. Ours will be known as the Phallic Generation, perforce. And even as he thought of this he saw, from behind his left ear a face that he hadn't heard in thirteen years ... and without thinking his cock tipped him off — one Loucks — a Cadet Loucks — they had served in the University Naval Training Division — the CUNTS as they were first named — Canadian University Naval Training at Stadacona in Halifax.... And as he turned to make sure that he had seen right he realized that he had never known that cadet; they hadn't been in the same division or watch. He had never to his knowledge spoken to him. They had merely shared the belly of the same destroyer together as trainees — H.M.C.S. *Moncton*. Yet he had known who it was sight unseen. Had he tried to remember who it was he would have failed. Wouldn't even know he had failed, because he wouldn't have known to remember. Somehow he had dredged a forgotten face, voice out of his tired gut — unwittingly — with a disarming lucidity — a disastrous lucidity. As he realized this his head reeled again. And for a moment he thought that he was going to pass out. He saw Peter staring at him from across the table ... eyes open in a kind of controlled terror that knows it cannot escape human nemesis. And he was calm again — those eyes were open, unveiled ... and he realized that he had simply crossed the threshold again into that absolute world where all is humanly possible. With that the evening was exspent.

They stumbled out, dazed. Each heading for his lair. Each overexposed. As he walked along an attractive dark Canadienne passed him — and he suddenly realized that he hadn't dare eye her. That he had veiled his eyes over ... withdrawn. And he realized now that he was as afraid of women as he was of men as he was of La Place itself. He realized that he had been brought up to negate reality — to flee plenitude — to cauterize joy.

It was midnight. He felt released. He disappeared into the sleet of La Petite Place clutching his cubic maidenhead like some last piece of family property of which he still had no right to dispose. He saw nothing. The world had closed down again. He was safe.

And back in his hotel he sat down confidently to his diary — more notes:

"When I am living and writing this way I have absolutely no sense of time. Nor can I detach days, events, people: everything is in an enormous ellision ... Alphonse has become cold, fonctionnaire d'affaires — interested in 'making money and girls'! Something has closed down in him. But what has closed in him is the very thing that remains open in me ... that has opened further in me, dangerously so. Our two paths have criss-crossed. On the surface he is more adult now and I more childish. Yet he himself senses something closing in him. And he resents it. It's the same goddam thing that keeps me homosensual. Once you close that off everything else closes — but everything! There is no half-way house. You cannot look into the eye of the world if you cannot look into the eye of man, woman, or child. And to look into an eye that way is incalculably beautiful and dangerous. The gift of insite.

That is my battle in *La Place*. The right to remain open ... to see ... to have insite. I must incite insite. And if it is necessary to incite homosexation to propitiate my long rejected insite, then it must be done. (*Protestant's propitiation for his denial of Catholicity!*)

That is why I **must** see *La Place d'Armes*. If I cannot, then I am dead. But if I do I risk my sanity!

Alphonse — young, handsome, sensuous, wealthy, gentilhomme....Yet he leaves me out cold now — because he has quelled his very palpability, his voracious charm. Quelled by his community. It didn't need to die. The great man keeps it for life....An inner luminous quality: Berenson, Nehru, Churchill, de Gaulle, John A., Leger (is he the only "great man" in Canada today? maybe!), Derwyn Owen ... Kennedy would have had it. Something as simple as "sex appeal" finally. Try rating the sex appeal of our present leaders! Zero, all the way ... so bad that Lesage finally **seems** sexy!

Alphonse has done all the right things.... In a good investment house (acquiring his "competence" in business!), good club, bought some land outside Montreal.... But he is a victim of that modern office decor of his: he has become, is becoming, a Televictim. So now he has left his wife, gymnasts at the Y, is girl-crazy and jokes about his "potence." He is becoming the reality of his decor. Terrifying — makes my novel more real than romantic. Too real. Because my allegory of the Square **is** odiously real — all "allegories" are — They are only allegories in the eyes of the blind! And I am fighting to acknowledge how real this series of intersecting realities is. Would be much easier to detach myself. Play it cool. But I can't. I must inject blood into this reality even if it means an open haemorrhage for life. Which is what is happening ... I haemorrhage daily. Openly. And only rarely do I take on flesh ... as in Notre Dame, or La Boutique, or the Antique Shop — all B and B depots! With Alphonse I pass *rapidly through three different realities ... two, three, and four dimensions: televisual, cubic, and total. The transitions threaten to destroy me. My language, body, senses, all change absolutely and on the spot.*

Only this Diary keeps me firmly in 3-D ... when I am in flight from the disembodiment of 2-D or in pursuit of 4-D ... 4-D — my unknown birthright, constrained into 3-D, and finally dissolved by 2-D (the proxy plenitude of the positivist priests ... professorial, psychiatrical, professional).

It involves three different men, moralities, societies ... visions. Each in irreparable conflict.

In 4-D body is imbedded ... a world of love.

In 3-D body is detached ... world of common-sense.

In 2-D body is dissolved ... world of non-sense.

And the Canadian is exposed in a unique immediacy to all three at once. His American heritage is 2-D (the American Dream); his British heritage is 3-D (Parliamentarian's Club); his French-Catholic heritage is 4-D (Peasant Baroque!).

Thus, in La Place, when I see the Bank of Montreal next to l'Eglise Notre Dame next to the rising Ban que Canadienne nationale ... I become either Protean, or insane! I either accept an inordinate versatility (Canadian necessity) or am relieved of responsibility for my realities. That is provided I allow me to see these buildings as they really are ... provided I don't merely extrude them — which is a fate worse than death. Thus I am left being either a metaphysical and a physical gymnast (Olympic standards — gods and men); or a flunkie.

Put in another way (I need to ... because then maybe I'll understand it, and live to tell the goddam tale!) — we Cubes (the Complete Cubes, I mean!) we're at once Cavalier, Roundhead, and Square. It's all mixed up in us ... no, not mixed up; all and each intact within us — that's the problem. The wonderful problem. We're all at once Tory Cavalier

Royalist (we read — or used to read — Kipling ... and his
Canadian counterpart of indigenous Northern Empire —
Service); and Methodist Grit Roundhead (Service was a hero
of the Ryerson Press! Just as the new Attic Canadiana —
scraped rockers! — is a hero of the Ryerson Press: morale for
superannuated Methodists ... instant indigenous nostalgics!);
and Amurrican Democratic Square — where scraped pine
Canadiana derives from Log Cabin Davey Crocketry, and
William Lyon Mackenzie is an off spout of Thomas Jefferson
(without his culture!).

Or in another way — I'm all, we're all, you're all at
once Anglican, Presbyterian-Methodist, and Unitarian ... like
that Bank of Montreal building — with its British classicism
(more substance than Amurrican), its Scottish methods, its
American means....

And that isn't just a sleight of hand ... because the
Church is the same — all at once evenly in me: with its
British Box underneath inside — Bartlett caught that well;
and its Amurrican absolute façade outside (find me another
flat-face so well as this in Europe! Or, in — the Yewnited
States find me another such flat-face in full Gothick!... you
can't — too Brrritish! — and too Catholick!) and then
the French Fact ... this Catholic Baroque Habitant fact
(Prince and Peasant ... the fairy tale come true! — despite
us) of the interior of the Church, that upstages Roundhead,
dispells Unitarian....

Which raises that curious truth so clearly now — that
Completed Cube is finally one with Catholic Baroque
Habitant ... in new guise or old — as Separatist or as
Habitant — as French Canadian.... So Completed Cube
is Presbyterian-Methodist-Anglican-Catholic, intact and by
definition — whether he will or no (add the Unitarians for
fun!).... Completed Cube bursts beyond his cubicle — if he
fulfills his heritage, if he but dare!

Somewhere in all that I missed one cog — but the essence is there, the truth — and the truth is … the sexiest thing alive!

Dinner with the assistant from that Gallery … I was too tired to take him. Yet the thing is there. Dined au Vieux St. Gabe. My flu-flood protecting us both, while allowing as much intercourse as we cared. Curious … because this allowed us, by means of the same relinquishment as sleep, an open-ended communication that really implicated homosensation. A world in which specific carnal contact was no longer essential, because already existant and because completely possible. A relationship inside of which one could move anywhere. One could sense, initially the "danger" … and then we crossed beyond it. But once aware of all this I no longer dared eye him — for fear of falling in … caving in. To eye him would have been to expose both of us to that wonderful Evil Eye that is the Eye of God that is the Host … that is the Monstraunce … that is the La Place, the Inner World, the Outer World, the…. We parted untouched because in touch.

Back at hotel, Alphonse phoned me to our rendezvous Au Bistro, for the filles. But the only one I wanted was the male at the bar who wanted me. And I overlooked him — heretical prudence! Then we went to the Discothèque for the career girls … women in search of their daily dildo. The music loomed large in me … and I felt again that same danger as in the Basilica, or when I site the object. I felt the evil of the place … my entire Cube warned me.

Plastered walls — deep rutted for deep rutting. Thunderous.

Fortunately it was sleeting and there were no women. But now I know how much women frighten me. I have never looked one in the eye … because to do so would be to give me — and I can never give me, because I was never permitted to give me as a boy to the boy I wanted who wanted me … self-

gift was tabu the first time around! — the first time it became possible, necessary. I dutiful learnt early never to give, never to give in. So I've never given to a woman, in revenge for my faithful gelding.... Tonight I knew that to take a woman would be to give in in the same way ... would be to fall in headfirst (no wonder they use the phrase "to fall head over heels in love"!).

Watched Alphonse and his copain, the complete Cubic cocks in a state of electronic dissolution — thus open to all contact and capable of none! Televictims!

Abed at midnight — happy to have sustained my "virginity" (after all, I've never utterly given or taken!) — constrained, constipated, congealed. I can't give in, I can't get in, I can't get out, I can't withdraw, nor proceed.... Impasse! Absolute impasse! But I shall — if I have to blast my way....

Postcard from wife — up at her uncle's stud-farm near Guelph ... a picture of the Ontario fall landscape with a doe overlooking a mesh of Queen Anne's Lace. It is herself! — people always choose themselves when they choose pictures, cards, objects, art, anything. And the face of the card was the message of the card. Because that innocent doe kneedeep in the fall flowers is my wife, still. I have no right to change her. Never. Only the right to aid her sustain her miraculous vision of life.

Oh — how difficult to write all this ... each word a brand seering the flesh. Impossible to write it, for we who have never said us.... So much easier to be a Jew, a member of that fraternity of exiles, whose only redemption lives in the magnificent written plaint — in a whole North American literature culminating in Bellow and, in Canada, in Richler and Layton and Cohen. I don't lessen their achievement ... but they were born into a culture of expostulation! They were born with the right to permanent exile. But what of the goddam Legitimist, Establishment, Hereditary, Infeodated,

Loyalist, Christian Canadian Tory? For him to speak his mind ... requires a Counter-Revolution at least. And — worse (or better!) — for him to bespeak his sensibility requires at least a nervous breakdown!

Is there such a thing as a Gentleman-Shit? Because to renege on my culture is to cease to exist: I have been bred, for ten generations in North American soil, to be a gentleman! And even to say it makes me a shit! And I feel shitty.

And then, starting to say it all, there is no structure for expressing it. I was trained to read novels — not to write them! So I start, arrant amateur — to exculpate my culture through the written word — a century behind.

Moreover how can a well-heeled, well-bred, well-educated, pampered Canadian complain?

The answer is that my culture is about to die. Nos morituri, te salutamur! And if we are going to die I might as well say our piece. Get it off my mind — no!, off my sensibility. Exorcize, once and for ever more, our collective Tory Canadian Little Lord Fauntleroyalty! But I know I still hope ... I hope that in the saying someone will see, and that ... and that ... it won't be too late. Except for me! — who am the last veritable Jacobite. (After all, how could I possibly explain to anyone my cult of Charles Martyr?)

Besides — when I am done — I will be exiled both from my Tory Community and from the New Canadian Grit Democratic Establishment. My position is hopelessly ambivalent, I assault the Tories for their failure to think, and thus their final failure to feel. And I assault the Liberals for their failure to feel, and their obvious final incapacity therefore to think.

Of course the easy way to label me will be as a pederast. That will serve both sides. But it will evade the central issue ... which is the capacity to love (much more important even than the capacity to make love!) And better, by far, to be a pédéraste than a "fédéraste" ... trust the French Canadian to find le mot juste for the gelded Canadian who makes a career out of his self-castration in the Ottawa Pork Barrel. All fédérastes are of course pédérastes-manqués....

DAY FOURTEEN

I woke sluggish. The pills had dried my flu ... and me. It
was only with a mental effort that I achieved contact with the
outer world, which otherwise went on unnoticed without
me. Again, just to check the certainty of this I probed my
perceptor set, and the sounds, albeit with some static, trickled
through me. I rolled over — like some deadhead, mechanically
alive. And computed the past week in me ... quite simply it
had been a TKO — a technical knockout. I've been effectively
unconscious — self-defence I presume against a series of worlds
all presuming upon me. It has been an effective defence —
because progressively desensitized by the virus I have been able
to assimilate only what I could, only what I absolutely needed.
The flu has been a screen for my senses. But that is drawing to
an end, and I recognize that the final week of campaign is upon
me — the decisive one in which all that I have already learnt,
and more that I haven't, will be put to the test. And again I
realize — albeit dimly now — that it is still a matter of life and
death. And if I don't realize that, then death is a fait accompli.

As I crossed the Little Place for breakfast I noticed Nelson's
Monument above me ... a dual reality — at once detached
from me, and perched atop the hill, as in any respectable
painting. And at the same time latent in me, like some animal
ready to leap into life if given the slightest encouragement. I
slunk into the restaurant, tail between my legs, just in time.

(11 a.m.)

Lunch with Robert McAlpine ... friend from University days. He was immeasurably gawky then — 6' 4" ... sprawled all over the place. Shy and quiet. Mad about jazz and ballet. And after a few years of business started — of all things — a School of Modern Dance. It has been an enormous success.... But, despite his long-hair calling, when we met I was surprised; he still has the appearance of an elegant Westmounted Executive, or a top level Civil Servant (the suede shoe league with pinstripes!). Still the sophisticated English Public Man. I asked him six times "How are YOU...?" and six times he either evaded the question, or replied in terms of SMD — not conscientiously evading the question, but like Allan Nisbet, quite simply unable to receive, to entertain the question at all. When I did push him to answer and he mentioned a wife and two children ... then he ceased to look at me at all, but looked from side to side, and wouldn't look back at me till the whole problem of a "personal life" to him had been brushed aside and we were back onto his life-love — the School of Modern Dance. Then he could talk freely, openly.... It is to that degree that the English Canadian has achieved a self-detachment ... or rather an extension of himself into his administrations or committees. That is the Anglo-American respectable martyrdom — the unconscious if conscientious elimination of self by translation into committee: secular priesthood. Any effort on my part to presume a personal présence, in the French-Canadian sense is simply unpardonable — embarrassing.

Of course I saw that Bob was another "modern man," in that he is patently homosentient. I could tell — because when I got him talking freely about SMD I perceived that I had him once again on an open line to mutual cocktit. He has that kind of warmth. But he has completely passed into his School (and to say that the Anglican, the Protestant, doesn't believe in "Transubstantiation"! He does ... and it is his own B &

B that passes into his own Monstraunce — his administrative commitment. Thus disembowelling himself.)

Bob toured me the school ... four office floors of it. And as I pounded after his giant strides I was horribly aware of how elephantine I was. How utterly corporally clumsy. As though my legs were in hipwaders. And my torso a congested hulk (albeit not 6' 4" of it). I realized that my body was simply "illiterate" — to use ironic analogy. All that by contrast with the classrooms of students educating their bodies — training their bodies to talk for them. Suddenly I realized that this was Bob's revenge on his own gawkiness — his own body that had always betrayed him in sports or in social gatherings. This School was his rehabilitation. And each student was a further fulfilment of his failure ... at school and at university (they called him "the Gook"!) — fulfilment of his own corporal incompetence. He had an excellent administrative sense, and a real knowledge of music and choreography ... so SMD was born.

Each student for me was a rebuke of my own corporal cowardice, my continued corporal embarrassment. I died watching them rehearse their bodies. Putting words into motion. Their bodies so much more fluent than my typewriter!

*I asked him if there was any general difference between his students ... and he said "basically the English Canadians dance as though they were rooted to the spot ... they dance around that root. The French Canadians dance at their fingertips. What we want is some fusion of the two — of the English Canadian's stability and inner strength, and the French Canadian's vivacity." My mind boggled — of course, a union of English Canadian Cubed-Roots and French Canadian Carnality ... **there** is a solution to the American Dream!*

Asked him what "class" they came from in our society (to call Canadian Society a "vertical mosaic" is to miss the infinitely organic quality of it — is to misjudge the body

*of Cube by the vacuity of the Square!) — largely lower
middle and middle middle class. "Virtually none come
from our background" — his comment reminded me why I
instinctively hate the Canadian Awakening — because it
is a state-subsidized release of the creative energies of that
Methodistical Lower Middle Class at our expense ... we
still "tow the line" while we are eliminated! The Canada
Council, like Massey College, like Parliament, like the CBC
... is simply a Finishing School system for Wesleyans (what
hateful thoughts I have!).*

    *So the Canadian Cultural Renaissance — French
and English — means truly the death of my Nation. Nor
can I join the New Nation.... Their "competence" is the
inverse of my entire culture of instinctive civilization. The
rage for "competence" is a civil service "culture." (And
the French-Canadian Revolution is really become merely
the French-Canadian need to add Cubic Competence to
French-Canadian inspiration.) But God knows that what
the English Canadian really needs is some of the French-
Canadian "inspiration"!*

    *(But who the hell cares about that — better delete it from
the final novel.)*

    *When I left Bob, he so proud showing me "how he
was" — showing me his B & B, I knew that I had to take
the plunge. That I could no longer remain "outside" all of
this. I knew that I was part of this Canadian milieu that I so
much hated as well as loved. That I must finally donate myself
(sweet arrogance! Who wants me? No one dares!) — but I
mean donate myself not "in committee" — we have enough
self-protecting martyrs! — but "in person." There's the rub. My
main civic duty is to be! And the donation must be a personal
commitment. I have to fuck my community and be fucked by
it. I watched me going down those stairs ... out the door onto
the site where Marguerite Bourgeois opened the first school in*

*Montreal three centuries ago ... and followed me up to la rue
Notre Dame ... writing my novel like crazy as I went:*

"He knew now, with tremendous power, that he could
no longer evade the issue ... that he could no longer
see things as he had seen them. Knew quite simply and
forcibly that he was committed now to this new-old
world whose threshold he had barely crossed in fear and
trembling the past few weeks and months. He knew now
that he would have to tear the veil asunder ... that there
was no longer sufficient or even any truth in that merely
Cubic world into which he had been moulded, largely
against his will, as a student. He deliberately went up to
La Place d'Armes. He knew that he wanted to have a last
look at it as it had been. As he had been educated to know
it. Right up to the steps of the Church. It was snowing.
And he saw quite clearly that he didn't see the Square at
all. That what he was so concisely seeing was simply a
précis of the Square ... a reduction of it.... He was seeing
it simply in diminution. He started to skirt it again ...
deliberately ... right around it. And he realized that seeing
the Place that way was simply a method of not seeing
it! Not seeing it at all. It was appallingly clear to him.
Walking around it unwittingly, as he had always walked
everywhere, was just a means of evading the objects, the
buildings ... it was a form of visual shorthand evolved to
eliminate the objects themselves. It was a form of no-see.
Indeed, in that frame-of-mind (which is exactly what it
was — a mind-frame) he realized that he couldn't see
anything. When he stopped to embrace a building visually,
nothing happened: he simply traced the outlines, went
down to details.... Perhaps if he kept at it long enough he
might reconstruct the entire reduced building. But what

an absurd waste of time ... a self-defeating waste. He was
aware as he traced the buildings with his mind's eye that
if he wanted he could stop now and truly see them — he
felt that force in him again for the first time in a week
— really for the first time in many weeks. But it was the
Wednesday preceding that he had felt ready to accost
the Square — and then his body had done the natural
thing ... already weakened by the effort of arrival, it had
protected him by collapsing. Now he had recouped. And
while he was far from chipper, yet he knew that he was
ready. But he didn't want to do it that day ... he would
sleep over it; another night of rest. On the morrow he
would be into his third week. It had — in fact — weirdly,
all gone according to some grim decisive inner schedule
over which he had had no control whatsoever. The most
he had managed was to arrive, to take up his station, and
to establish some points of contact ... and then collapse
in a prerequisite coma whose very anaesthesia underlined
and would increasingly underline the force of what was
about to occur — of that he had no doubts. Now he felt
strong enough. He had to. Because now he had to rend
the veil that while it provided portable protection at the
same time threatened to become his reality. He knew that
he couldn't afford that ... that it was still-life. Now he had
to face up to the fact of life ... look it in the eye ... and
take the consequences. This frightened him. But he was
more frightened at the consequences of not looking life
in the eye ... of not "falling into the picture." He stopped
in front of the Bank of Montreal and looked across the
Place ... to the Church and the Royal Bank ... and again
he confirmed that he saw them as they ought to be
seen, cubicularly speaking. They were there ... external,
irrelevant, detached. They were academic "facts" or
newspaper facts. Again he felt the urge to pierce the veil.

And again he didn't. The certitude that he would do so tomorrow, and in the coming week ... that was enough. And secretly, to himself, he said that if the reality were too much once penetrated, then he could, momentarily recede to this no-man's-land of no-see. Rest his inner eye thus. But that he was committed to penetrate into the inner eye of the Place, of that there was no doubt.

He walked over to the Church, cars passing him like shadows, through him, around him. Untouchable. And into the great nave of Notre Dame. Sat down to breathe awhile. It was just that — breathing space. He noted that the Church was neither here nor there ... like the Square itself. It was, unmolesting, outside of him. But he was also aware of the wallop it packed. And he was cautious.... It was a state of armed truce. It had really been a state of armed truce the entire week. And then he made his way back to the hotel, scared to life. Scared out of death. Tomorrow would be soon enough.

At 7 p.m., chez Albert Streicher, architect of La Place Ville-Marie ... that Other Place that I must visit, out of deference, out of spite, out of hours! And design consultant for La Place des Arts ... where I am going tonight for an evening "out" — need a break. Also joint architect of the Quebec Pavilion at Expo. Met him at lunch today with "Robert McAlpine" (must find aliases for all these people; do it on the rewrite. Roman-à-clef: well there's only one key and it's the keyhole!) — Bob pulled a fast one ... sitting with Streicher as I arrived — asked me what I thought of La Place Ville-Marie ... I riposte it is "an abortion"— and then he introduces "Mr. Streicher ... the architect of La Place" ... with that wry smile of his that simply honours you by sharing his wound. I couldn't be angry. But I have never been in La Place Ville-Marie. So I was grounded

... and Streicher did the only possible thing for a practising gentleman — he invited me in to his apartment for drinks, before the concert tonight. "You can add my place to your novel ... it used to be a brothel ... on la rue St. Paul, just west of La Place Jacques Cartier."

First fine stone house past the Flesh Market — how apt. But he rents the stone house to a telestar. Lives at the end of the arcaded alley ... at the far end, in the warehouse-cum-brothel-cum-skydive that is his town house. Bob says it is the last word in Montreal.... Ring the bell and the door swings open — fortunately with Streicher on the other side of it.

"Come in, come in...." His face gleeful at me shares delight. We are in a long white corridor that is ample urgent conductor up the flying stairs that land me in their vivoir.

"My son lives downstairs" — his limpid eyes answer the formulating question. "Third year McGill ... he's a respectable beatnik." The pride in Streicher's voice is communicative. I too am proud of respectable beats, after all.... My flush of pride is bleeding me to death. Head-throb warns me of instant dissolution ... of brain flowing out earhole; gut bloats, distending me as I stand pop-eyed, pocketed hands hanging on to balls lest I lose me....

"Is that you dear?" — basso profundo from behind the solid wood partition resounds over running kitchen tap.

Streicher pirouettes along the line of roar, disappears into it. The room is sheepish. He forgot to tell his wife I was coming.... Tant pis. Advantage me of his contritional absence — grope me careful to pillar upholding the room. Hand out to clasp its heavy timber ... feel nothing; make mental note that it is there, that I am holding. Withholding.

Fight the detonation rising in me ... another puff and I bloatburst. Christ — what happened? Muster me to account for this treason — muster mind to defend me — slowly repeating to convince me —

"I know what happened ... the same as in the RRRRapido, in the Black Skyscraper, in Alphonse's Board Room, in.... This inversion, of space and time and substance. It is normal ... the modern idiom ... the New Man they're making, for all of us ... it is normal." — like saying my chaplet —

"I know what it is all about ... make mental note of it all, you can use it, for your novel" — My I has become a you and already I am divorced from me ... separated to survive. On with the mental notation — the disciplined demobilization of this room....

Streicher is back — "It excites you? ... look around freely."

I grasp the proferred outlet — "Oh yessss ... it excites me...." (it terrorizes me).

around me the expanse of whited wall, immaculate conception — implacably immaculate contraception. The open-ended room ... that is window wall out onto terrace. At the other an equal open-end skyrising to the third floor....

gut sags again. I hear me saying in my soft underbreath — "and that is a chair, don't walk through it, that is a chair, there, two paces in front ... don't walk through it."

I can walk through that chair ... it is not there. "And you are becoming that chair."

Stare the chair, and outskirt it. Going by the map its boundaries give me.

"Do you like it...?" It could be the chair that is speaking — but I know it is Streicher: I can see his lips moving! And I return to my task of "liking" the room. Once again, call up my mere mind, send telegrams to myself:

"it is a chef d'oeuvre of its kind ... a jewel ... full of sumptuous modern furniture, tapestry, art. It's as good as an ad! Every bit as good and as convincing...." I keep telling me.

Streicher watches me avid — pretending to look the other way, to arrange an immaculate pile of magazines ... but he is espying me ... peeping through his hole into me who am about to jump out of my skins.

"Touch something." It is Streicher — "you can handle anything you want...."

Right — everything here *is* handleable ... is a handle. Everything acclaims absolute palpability. Yet I shrink from it ... shrivel. Absolute chastity in face of absolute carnality. Why?

Polite I reach out to caress multicolour hanging hooked rug canadien. Reach out ... and run fingers over the woolface so aggressively woolly but protect me withholding fingers half inch from the coil, unable to touch, as though under glass.

"It is beautiful, isn't it? Micheline Beauchemin did it...." Streicher is plugging into this wave length. And leaving the rug untouched still, but holding my hand as though plying it, turn to eye his which glows at me abashed as I withdraw insistent both hand and body from Micheline's mantrap baited for us here.

And interrupted Streicher stops talk while I wander the distant objects.

it all says to be touched — all demands it. Each rug, santo, tapestry, object ... says "touch me" — says "I am malleable ... a feely." But it says it only to my eyes that fingertips shy off. Yes — every thing is manhandle.

in the meantime I am being eaten alive. Feel the flesh bereft of me. Why?

and disembodied so float astronautical around this man-eater, dizzy with assertive sumptuosity surrounding me. It is only by specific concentration of mind that I plug outgush of me ... only by clamping assoul that I remain at all intact.

"Have some meat" — the kitchen roar is domiciled into the vivoir — Wife hands me a roastbeef sandwich, rare, as presentation piece. Instant fealty all round, as we land ... I in that absentee chair that beef gorges now with my erstwhile enlightened flesh, abruptly threatening to capsize us both.

"I guess what strikes me most is the preoccupation with space.

"First you create a limitless limited space — mentally frame it and then you place within it all these deliberate treasures.... Sensibility as decor with a framework of intellect. To me that is the opposite of life. I want an open intellect operating within a field of free sensibility. For me content creates form ... and not form content.

"When form imposes content, then content is counterfeit. I suppose it is this that distresses me here. I find that all the senses are mobilized by the mind ... for the mind. There is no thing here that is actually sensual! In fact everything here really warns me to keep hands off ... mesmerizes me like rattlesnake which then buzzes death danger at me breaching the spell in time to save me....

"I know that I mustn't touch. The invitation is urgent, but formal. Nothing here is touchable because it couldn't be otherwise.... It is only your mind that decided to touch here ... the arbitrary Reign of the Mind — at the expense of any meaningful embodiment."

so the beef bolsters me ... and grateful at beef and at re-embodiment I sing for this unexpected supper, saved by the buzz. Perhaps I don't really say all this ... yet I hear you saying me. At least I don't say blatant that it is philistine ... which is what I know: philistine because it is really sensuously illiterate — impotent. Must find a word for this — people who can't read are "illiterate"; people who don't know are ignorant; what about people who can't feel, who can't think with their feelings ... who have no sensibility. There must be a word ... but — and that is our odious truth — there isn't one! Insensitive; insensible; insensate — no, they won't do in any way. None of them conveys the fact of utter ignorance of embodiment. The closest word is ... impotent, which is the end result of the kind of ignorance, wilful ignorance I scathe, bitter because perforce I too am implicated in this creeping disease of us all.

Streicher — wife watches me, attendant upon my

compliments like bulldog glowering its master. Somewhere she seizes upon the fact that my compliments are loaded and with triumphant pity says —

"then you find it overpowering!"

and snaps her jaws shut — another mere male eaten off the spit. But I am currently incomestible ... my remaining meat in cold storage.

Grimly — "no — not overpowering. Not at all. I find it de-powering!"

Wife retracts ... visitor-victim isn't dead yet.

"There is *all* the difference in the world ... (and more gentle) I keep feeling I'm going to fall out."

"Not enough security," wife bellows quietly, still startled by my resistance. Flinches me. No question of that — this vivoir is no marsupial sack. The opposite: it kills Mommy, kills Daddy, kills Sonny ... lethal. And what happens hereafter, the Whole Bloody Family killed, doesn't matter. Everything goes. Absolute amorality.

I'm still fighting. She beefed me up, after all.

"I want to test my virility instantly in here. I worry about it. But I don't think it would do me any good ... I would only disarm what is left of me."

And I want to add — it is the sort of room in which I couldn't get a hard-on, except by recollected lust. Not a real hard-on ... oh, I could work up a counterfeit for fun-fuck — spermatic. But I wouldn't care if I did.

Besides me Streicher lies cowed in his own manslaughter. Looking as though someone had just taken off his childpants ... and found nothing.

And all of this acknowledged, openly admitted to me, I relax, begin to enjoy it ... once I know what I know of it — the Enemy labelled and warned. I feel a little badly....

"We think this room is extremely intimate," wife bellows again to waken her quiet dead. Streicher, resuscitant, nods head energetically. I wonder how anything can be intimate here when everything is overexposed. Like living in a nudist camp ... everything denuded, and under invisible glass. The New Museum of Man; in his own showcase. All that remains is the cataloguing.

And as I cling to my seat, astronaut threatened with orbit, I realize that this living-room is At Home for No-Body.

This vivoir is not architectural revolution. It is Absolute Revolution over our dead body. Absolute Devolution. As architecture it demands different social, political, economic, and moral structures for society. It commandeers a different kind of man: a neuter.

Cuckoo clock strikes me 8 — I can see it strike ... just time to taxi to La Place des Arts. "I'd like to come back ... to be here at leisure — to feel my way through all of this."

Streicher rises with me, glows at this sustaining interest. As we walk to the steps he whispers, "Come back Saturday — at 11...." Wife still seated ... she is Graham Sutherland's predatorial portrait of Winston Churchill ... who else?

At the head of the stairs I see it — suspended inanimate mobile! ... the fish-dried, one of those bloat-fishes that swell in self-defence, burst if surfaced sudden, like bladder turned outside-in.... How utterly right — I remember my sensation upon arrival ... of surfacing to burst me inside out.

Always trust the object ... objects *never* lie — never. And objects always personify the people they master!

Down the stairramp ... over the kennel of Son beneath — Mommy planted overhead; I would make the sign of the Cross if I could — because Sonny will be the New Neuter ... nor can he help it. Flee our nemesis....

Gut clenches, nostrils pinch, eyes focus — shunt of trainbelling — I am rightside in again.... It's the Greyway open arch over and under me.

"Taxi...."

And out through the Greyway rolling into me, up Boulevard

St. Laurent, the "Main," with its jungle of neon — hurdy-gurdy world for the Urban-Habitant ... further up the foot of mountainside to the new world of La Place des Arts. To my right a void centred upon a slick-sleek grey lump eyeing me baleful — Christ, I may well have been wrong about La Place Ville-Marie, but I was dead right, site-unseen, about this new Palace of All-Arts: it is so specifically an abortion — a mommygut sacked, complete with corset to bolster.... But before I can come to grips with it taxi swerves down underground ramp to entry, and the outside pinch of redgables becomes untenable squeeze, taxi halts, depositing me at the entry, pay his ransom, and grasped for breath flee the squeeze into the lobby brandishing my ticket as talisman. Abruptly underground pressure bloats — I am in vacuum ... gut distends to burst ... God — which way *is* in? Or have I been let out. Neckflushes in rising anger of me as I clamp down. Christ — I came to hear a concert, to relax, not to undergo enforced metamorphosis. Want to shout ... "came to listen to a concert" — but no one here could hear me. The appalling truth stops me dead — nobody here would hear me! Why? No — I don't want to know ... not yet. Grope my way to my section, sub-section, seat — and settle just in time for the tune-up.

A few moments to gape around auditorium ... the decor has it, all the way. The same decor as at Streicher's ... and sounds are the same here as in his apartment. I see sound the same way. They are controlled by this decor. Sound all around me, and through me, despite me — not because it penetrates but because I am part of the soundwave ... so that is it; how you hear is what you hear! What you hear is what your body is ... and what is done to your body determines what you will be hearing. No wonder this Art Palace goes after my body ... but why dissolve it, why force me inside out, why?

I won't let them get me ... mustn't ... why let them hear me by dispersing me. Grab for my notebook, in self-defence, in

a state of seige. (The War is portable ... of course). If I am going
to be had at least I'll leave a record.

*the decor again ... I want simply to fall apart into it, to regurgitate
me into it to turn me inside out. Always the same stratagem on their
part ... put pressure on the victim, squeeze, & phttt, you're outside-in
before you can protect your keep. Always that — the finger up your
assoul, the breach, the flick of wrist, & it's done, you're done ... inside
out. RRRRRapido....*

*music starts ... I recognize it yesss.... Not the piece, the mode; it's
Hi-Fi ... Muzak live! Flooding me, all of us, filling the vacuity of the
hall, of us — flooding our evacuations, we are evacuees.... Sure of that
now (beau stratagem!) So the vacuum here must be one of substance that
music is meant to fulfil. Music the new substance fulfiling us evacuated.*

*keep tight assoul ... or I am totally at mercy of this music plying
my inversion that is perversion — that is it, they pervert me to ply me
with live music (it mocks the death they demand first, as mise en scène)*

*either I abandon me to it, gutted, or I close down. That is so clearly
the alternative. Fatal choice. Either way the total insensorium*

*end of the first movement. I am paying no attention to the
orchestra as such ... only to its interply with the setting — because
there is the rub, the crux ... the joust is between sound and site. Can
clearly feel it. With the evacuees as Grand Prix! It is we who are bait,
the victims ... eaten alive if we succumb ...*

*how can I test this (after all, I'm the game! High stakes ... for
little me?)*

*if I keep eyes open — one eye on music one on site ... I'm safe.
Hold each in impasse. But immobilizes me.*

*close my eyes then ... eliminate site! Music hammers at me ...
burnishes re-embodiment. Fleshes me in & out ... fulfills me. Plumps
the gourd.*

*open eyes ... instant security of stalemate ... caught between sight
& sound.*

plug ears.... Ah — caught the wretch — fingering quick my assoul, to breach me ... I clamp on him before he can invert me outside-intake

eyes & ears open — again the security of impasse ... sight & sound annul each other & with that insured security now slow release assoul apringle — & imperceptibly I am disassed ... by the decor ... massages me!

decor slowly has it now — site over sound (That is what I knew upon entering) Site is sound here.... Definitely. The architect has captured the music, for his own ends.... Why? & what? A perceptible treason.

suddenly static ... I stare — static? no — it's the audience clapping. But there's the clue ... to all of this — to the site: it is electric, & we are a TV set — all of us ... and we aren't being played to, but played upon. Reduced to a receptor set which is what it is given. Which plays back only what it is told ... and the key: that initial disembowelling!

Fantastic — but couldn't be anything else. Every sense proves it to me.

static again ... my eye follows the crackle to the ceiling — those biting horns of sound that are our sounding boards. They have stolen my ears.

Intermission — save me out to lobby, regroup me. Watch the denizens swarm out of the hall ... to the bar. It's all like some plush nightspot. Tour this world ... all the arts as handmaids to the auditorium — statuary, ceramics, wrought metal, tapestries (more Micheline, surely). And in the centre — pièce de désistance ... huge gilt bird ... like everything else: inside-out ... and dessicated, fossilized: Pterodactyl! Twenty feet of dried gut and fecality. Everything matches — everything.... It is Streicher's dried hung immobile fish all over again.

"Hello Hugh ... what are you doing in Montreal?" I've walked through the shy smiling form of Rick Appleton. Back up abashed. Yes — Rick. Stooping in dinner jacketed elegance, beneath the great dead bird — Pterodactyl that

Rick — who evaded me in my Montreal years … too much alike. Our truths cut too close to home. And I had the diplomatic immunity of the mere Torontonian then, whereas he lived in his loved Montreal.

"May I introduce you to…?" blonde girl, under glass — both standing separately together — understudy fossils. Pterodactyl is contagious! No wonder he stopped me … to save himself

"Lunch tomorrow?" I accept — why not? Perhaps he can tell me.

Seated

Auditorium sways … like shipboard. It's like liquid vacuum … it is the space that is solid … space the oppressor — as chez Streicher … drowning me in space that absorbs me, blots me up, out … then imperceptible threatens to disperse me again — threatens me with that inversion-perversion….

So I must be solid again — Cubed. Ahh — Rick brought me back to his earth, despite himself.

ceiling lowers the void over me. Walls are void. Auditorium is all photonegative … substance is the negative & space the positive. God — I'm televisor again.…What I see sees me. I only see what sees me. & both are insubstantial. B & B out the window. I'm zomby again.

Clutch one ball … best I can manage.

Dance band starts again … nightclubbable. Music rises … will palp me instantly — but I am already receptively impalpable, & I lurk, watching us all, quizzical in my amoralization. The retained testicle permits my quiz.

but if this music hall is right — if this scenario is sound, then everyone here is museum piece. All this mink-coated cubicularity. Of course it is. But do these people realize that … that the reality is not them … is not the audience? Do they know that this music is being played to them in absentia … at their expense — that they risk their lives … innocent yet complicit martyrs. Fools.

I strain to see them. But can no longer see. Am only seen. All senses are passive now again — mere receptor set.

realizing that the auditorium would be more alive without people … the only live person is Seiji Ozawa, conducting … the animateur

— the Live Object — but he is animating the space, not the people. It is the space that is live.... Space is live? It is cannibal! Living off our dead bodies eaten as we enter....And all Ozawa is doing is animating the site. Architect's dildo!

Stay after concert, deliberately, to see.Yes, the auditorium is itself now ... vibrant with animal life.Voracious.And the music, like the people, but accessories ... to the crime.

What is real are the red plush popartsy seats (remember the people's plush on RRRRapidooo): these seats tolerate the spectators who are not auditors but spectatees....

Exit ... last one out. Everything is in order again, normal. Space space. Body body. How? What happened. Stopped dead I stare ... of course — walking out my eye is caught in the dark glass of window behind the balcony ... looking in this window-mirror the reversion occurs — substance recurs. So — my response is not accidental here ... there has been an inversion, deliberately. People gutted, turned inside out. Raped in front of their own noses. & space is the Prima Donna ... the new Mommy eating all, everyone — thousands sacrificed to this new smotherlove. And I remember the wife.

This auditorium is a lie ... sound isn't here. Sound merely gilds this lily. Not an auditorium at all — but a sightsea — a sitesee. And if sound truly defines sight, then here we are both blind and deaf — worse ... we have been deliberately blinded and deafened.We are deliberately immersed in the absolute insensibility ... in the name of the sense.This auditorium is an Insensorium!

Someone is lying, about everything!

& this auditorium is not only a gilded lie ... it is mass murder! The evidence is overwhelming.

Why why why why?

ahhh ... because Object has been made Subject; & Subject, relegated to Object, is dying....The perversion-inversion....

Why — still why?

Wrong question....Who?

Outside I threaten to burst — again — the sitesee lifted from me ...

the surfaced fish again; burst inside back from outside in ... always the
moment of detonation. This time rightside out — burst into fleshment.

*   Taxi drops me at the discothèque ... it is 11:30 p.m....Already*
the young divorced wives gather to catch their nightly dildo. And the
men gather to service them.... Dance with one demoiselle who wants to
eat me — I know why: I am herself gone male — same features, same
facial vitality. She doesn't realize that. Watch the dancers ... instant
courtshipments. And again my body betrays me by its ineptitude. I
cannot move with these dances — my torso frozen — hips to shoulder
... frozen in perpetrated propriety. A young CBC scriptwriter joins me at
the bar.... His first sentence — "est-ce que vous aimez?" — and I oh so
envy these young with their immeasurably "sophisticated" bodies ... and
their innocent hearts! And leave the maneatress ... once again satisfied by
a rapport that knowing includes the flesh ... and the flesh thus honoured,
no longer importunes! — no longer imposes consumation....

Back at the hotel Andrew started to write some lines
again for the novel — "It had been, curiously, a good
day ... his body has been restored — by the Discothèque
which had all the guts that the Place des Arts so patently
lacked ... and then he remembered this, the architect had
told him he should see the Discothèque ... obviously it
had meant something to him; but there Streicher had failed.
Because now it was clear to Andrew that the Discothèque
achieved what the auditorium *wanted* to achieve — some
kind of need for the flesh — some kind of imposed need
for the flesh that was imperatively satisfied within the
terms of the building, the site itself. The Discotheque was
its own morality ... the auditorium was that same morality
manqué.... The Discotheque implied evil as a joy ... the
evil of the auditorium was in its utter absence of evil —
and thus of good....

And then a few notes in his Diary:

"that auditorium kept trying to spit me out! It actually despised me — abhorred me. I could feel its contempt for my being. It is lèse-majesté. The hall itself kept glaring at me, staring me out. It was voyeur ... eyes at me. Ah — feu le spectateur. We are no longer spectators ... in some way we have been commandeered to a performance from which we are deliberately banished. The whole place is pulpit. I'm on the outside in ... exvertebrate! (as against invertebrate). Makes me the permanent outsider....

Again the feeling of being seen through a peephole ... peepholiness! C'est magnifique, mais c'est la guerre! It's all a revenge on us ... it is full of vengefulness.... The constant extrusion.... All the visual equivalent of legerdemain ... legerd'oeil! We are literally in outer space.

God — I feel like some netted, dried, and mounted butterfly, in the collection of some infamous etymologist ... I presume it is no accident that the man whose sensibility pinpointed the world with Lolita was himself a butterflier. .

I am not expansive ... simply diffused. It's the New Leviathan. Oh — the ardour with which it hates me, the fervour.... And then, afterwards, back outside, the feeling that they've just sacked Mommy, outside in. To what end? (in contrast with the interior of Notre Dame ... I can grow therein; it is spacious — the only real cathedral in North America)

... just reread these lines: they don't make sense ... but that is what I felt in La Place des Arts.

Sauve qui peut!"

Exhausted, Andrew dropped to sleep, resentful of the inordinate inefficacity of art ... the enormous carnage he wrought in himself to achieve these few lines.

DAY FIFTEEN

awoke at 10 a.m. ... the sounds already prickling against
my aural maidenheads ... I closed over them to sort me out.
Tired from the incursions last night made on my slight preserve
of energy. Nose and throat guttering lightly. Not the day for
optimum apprehension. Phoned Rick Appleton to confirm
lunch and slumped back to the maternal sac ... wheeling me
full circle hands clenched to cocktail.... Ruminant. Operating
en huit clos ... two ideas wheedling my belated brain. First —
that any plenitude must incorporate carnal joy and not extrude
it ... must presume it as part of fulfilment. And if any way of
life finally extrude it, deny it, then that way of life is endangered.
Second: that the phallic frenzy of our generation is indeed a
belated pump priming! It endeavours to rectify the extrusion of
corporeality by forcible carnage. And it is doomed to failure ...
it simply consumes our last remaining point of contact with an
incarnate world....

... at 1 p.m. I thrust me into la petite place, bent for belated
lunch ... happily Rick's office is in the bank building on
the corner of the Place d'Armes. My luncheon appointment
was also penetration of another of the temples of the Place. I
wheeled through the doorspin that shuttled the denizens of the
building out onto me ... they bounced off me harmlessly ...
none of them saw me. Not one. And of course not one saw my
Place. That pleased me. I could see no reason sharing this inner
square with the deliberately defunct. Had they been able to see
it while in their condition of life I would have felt sullied ... as
though sleeping with second-hand goods unnecessarily....

Hugh chose a gap in this expectoration of proxy people, and shot
through the door into a marbled and tiled hallway that clearly carried
the twenty stories of skyscrape … clearly a subterranean chamber. Once
again into the embalmment of elevator and found himself outside a
door decorated with a cluster of Q.C.s and Q.C.s-acolyte. The names
were suggestive — in order they read Goodison, McTavish, Robichaud,
O'Donahue … these were the big names … all Councillors of Her
Majesty, the Enforced absentee Canadian Queen. And underneath —
the acolytes — Portakis, Guité, McBain…. A magnificent statement
of national caste … Goodison — Anglicanadian, McTavish, Scottish
Presbyterian, Robichaud, French Canadian, O'Donahue, Irish Mic …
and then with the understudies, Portakis as a New Canadian, Guité for
a further French Canadian…. That was about right, in the Canadian
power structure. He entered. Dismayed. The office was an amalgam
of the names. Mahogany bank-directors' desks, some rather austere
bookcases, two pieces of scraped French-Canadian pine habitant
furniture, some maudlin orchard greenscapes, and a weak modern daub.
What was magnificent was the view over the Place itself … down below
the central square was a white garden gridded with a propriety of paths
that showed no single member of this business area ever merely doodle-
dawled across … all the paths were straight lines direct to one exit or
entry of the Place itself. They were slender runway strips. In the centre
the statue of Maisonneuve, and the candy-floss Christmas trees…. The
Church angled directly up at him on the left, while the old Bank of
Montreal squatted smugly on his right. Out the far window the Jacques
Cartier Bridge was a junior toybuilder's kit … and the new bridge to
Expo 67 looked like a simple causeway. A few trees below the Hotel de
Ville could only be depicted as primitives….

Rick's office betrayed his own betrayal. Law casebooks barricading
and buttressing a severe mahoganized desk, and on the walls, his own
gouache drawings for stage-sets.

I watched Rick angling up to me like some puppy about
to grow out of his better judgment, his feet still splayed, like
those of Prévost, the feet of a ballet dancer slightly inebriate …
complete refutation of his cubicular bureau…. He met me on
that angle and dragged my right flank by implication off to the

various views.... His blue pinstripe suit happily simple did not relate in any way to his still sweet gawkwardness. He was simply carrying the suit around with him, the way a dog might a bone he didn't really want, but required for prestige purposes.

Suddenly I felt simply belligerent. Why had Rick collapsed ... why had he given in to all this.... I knew he didn't believe in it. His walk, his manner, his personal decor, his own devious self-presentation to me as I arrived — all of this specifically annulled his own participation here. And I felt angry.... At lunch I assaulted him brutally ... unable to await his own subtle self-revelation.... He had only gotten as far as saying ... "but I am going to be changing jobs soon ... going to Ottawa as personal assistant to the Minister of Finance...." He said it with an evident air of apology for himself as though he realized that both his law practice and his posting to the capital were inadequate.

I pounced.... "You say that with such embarrassment ... I can only understand it is a deliberate act of expiation. That is the way you say it. And that raises my fundamental concern ... why didn't our culture produce ... our Anglo-Canadian 'culture seigneuriale'? What happened to us.... None of us has broken through, has enunciated himself. You came as close as any of us ... your one-act plays, your critiques, your wit, and vitality.... What happened? Why did you stop? Why did you balk? That is the question.... Why did all of us balk ... so many of us. We got to a certain point and then stopped. There are dozens like us. We had the best education in the New World ... the most complete ... the best homes ... the most rooted of North American cultures, barring French Canada. And when we reached a certain point we shied off ... we stopped. Something went dead in us.... Oh, no, it is worse than that, we all killed something in ourselves, stifled it ... denied it deliberately and in so doing cut ourselves off from all self-expression, all flowering. We took out some weird hidebound life-insurance policy against living."

Across the table from me Rick twitched, gnarled his slender fingers, eyed me evasively. What I was saying was so much a breach of confidence and decorum that he either had to leave, or confirm the truth of my accusation by staying to hear it out. He stayed. And he stayed not because of the truth of my accusation ... but because what I was saying was not accusation so much as concern with the *consequences* which derived from the truth of the accusation. What I was saying presumed that accusation as a fait accompli. I had betrayed him into an acknowledgement of its truth by touching on the sore spots that resulted from its truth. I was onto the marrow of us ... and we both knew it.

Rick squirmed and finally defensively (his very defence again accredited my accusation!) said, "I simply decided at a certain point that I did not have the talents to continue."

"But that is the equivalent to capitulation ... it is an acknowledgement finally of impotence ..." I said ... and I thought to myself that the real truth was not that he had decided that he did not have it, but that he was genuinely afraid that he did ... genuinely afraid that his sensibility implied a cockiness, a cocksurety that his society rigidly condemned with all the force of its being. A man, creative man, procreative man, sees with the end of his cock ... and our society doesn't like cockseers.

"No English Canadian, no Anglicanadian, can face up to his own cock. We flee from it....You have fled it....You have made that denial, not positively but negatively ... you have evaded the confrontation. And in maiming yourself that way, in failing to honour your sensibility, in doing that deliberate craven injustice to yourself, you have assumed a guilt that corrodes you. And you now expiate the crime, you now flagellate yourself by becoming the perfect upper caste Canadian Civil Servant. Your "martyrdom" is a negative expiation of your crime. It means you become a member of our eunuchoidal Canada Corps at Ottawa ... and that you too will impose on our nation a gutless culture in your own self-defaced image." Rick writhed, and I apologized for my brutality, but I was out for blood ... out for what was left of our blood. His failure implicated my own ... and I hated him for defaulting.

"Either what I am saying is an enormity ... or it is truth." His eyes blundered across mine as he said ... "it has truth ... we *are* all hurt this way, we carry this hurt...." And I watched his eyes carelessly. They bounced around my own, floundered, and fled. I turned the knife further ... into both of us: "But the worst of it all is that a man who has desecrated his own manhood this way is a man who will never achieve consummation with a woman. He has amputated with a two-faced sword ... will never establish a full relationship with *anyone*, of either sex, ever again! The initial denial of self-presence is decisive. He is nonsensical for life."

Rick looked drained.... "Yes, my posting at Ottawa *is* an expiation. I know that.... And if it gives you any satisfaction I have wondered if I could ever achieve a satisfactory relationship with a woman...." And as he said it I realized that I had penetrated to the very heart of the Canadian quandary ... the endemic gelded quality of our current nationalism. That it was the product, the mechanical product, of craven self-geldings. No wonder the nation flounders. There isn't a convincing hard-on in Ottawa, and if there were, it would be Tory and not Liberal, that is certain!

"I can tell you in one sentence then, why you have not produced." He looked stricken ... and I said, only to myself, "because it implied homosentience."

"I was in a bar last night ... a young French Canadian from Radio Canada talked with me at the bar ... I didn't know his name nor he mine. But his whole being shone as he asked me outright, nothing else mattering ... 'est-ce que vous aimez....' He didn't ask me do I love someone now. Or do I make love. Nor did he make jokes about lustlove. But quite simply asked me 'do you love?' And I knew that that was the heart of the matter. That I was member of a society that specifically forbids love."

We stumbled out ... Rick had stayed twenty minutes beyond his office appointment. And then he was gone ... in his blue overcoating, his Afghan cap, and his air of Canadian Commisar Royal. I went on to the Square ... over and over in my battered mind the phrase rolled — "presence of sensibility" ... we need "presence of sensibility" — as against mere presence of mind. Oh, the sheer humane luxury of self-presence ... of presence of sensibility.

The Square was a glory. It rose immense around me, luminous, the buildings incorporating me....The dizziness no longer frightened me ... it was effervescent. I entered the Church and sat briefly. There was only one satisfactory way to say what I knew — "the peace of God that passeth all understanding be in your hearts and minds...."There was no other way to say it. No other possible way to say it. And why indeed need there be? Rick had said he was atheist. But then he had bartered his balls against respectability. No wonder he had lost capacity for faith.

I didn't try to site the Church. It simply occurred around me. I neither pressed it, nor it me....As I left, however, I noted that the flicker of candles around the nave thundered in my ears ... I could hear them — and the sight of their sound was heaven.

Outside I carefully closed me down preserving my insite intact ... and returned to the hotel to display it on paper. I remembered Appleton's closing words...."Your thesis is interesting ... I'd like to think more about it...."Thesis, I thought — thesis — Christ ... I haven't got any thesis ... I don't know half the time what I'm doing. But I do know that I'm doing it — and I rarely dispute the logic it imposes upon me. What I am doing is rehabilitating my sensibility, and reconstructing a mind that was founded on bad faith. I'm busting out of my box — Cube's revolt!

At 6 p.m. Bill Gaunt phoned him ... just as he was settling in for an evening of ruminant writing. At last. The call disrupted him. It intruded on his whole slowly growing inner logic ... it had been painful, inordinately painful these past weeks and days, re-establishing that inner timetable, that internal sense of timing; a timetable in which things grew, had a natural place of their own, occurred because it couldn't and shouldn't be otherwise. And now, just as he was writing again, in command of his assault on La Place d'Armes, here was this eruption of Bill back into his life. He couldn't discount it, because it had happened ... it too had a place by the very fact. Yet it threatened to topple his entire laborious insite just at that very moment he seemed to finally possess it. It was a serious menace. He asked Bill if he could phone back in an hour ... stammered something about the timing of his novel on the Place. But of course the novel was him ... it was no novel. It was for real.

He could hear Bill stammering back ... he had known perhaps he shouldn't call. And yet he had called. And they were committed by the fact of his call. Moreover Hugh knew that Bill knew ... that he was someone who understood all these internal verities. And as he listened he could sense Bill's entire metabolism shifting, probing, wondering. They could not withdraw now. They had no right to. That was clear. It was equally clear that the best night to meet was that very night.... Again the stammering over the phone ... not verbal stammering — the words came out alright ... but a spiritual stammer — a persistent uncertainty about the logic of the spirit. Yet they both knew they best meet.

For an hour Hugh lay on his bed ... drained of his capacity to write; drained that is of his capacity to be. He knew that if Bill came then they were engaged — his very arrival demanded fundamental acknowledgement. And if this was so, there was the danger, the two-edged danger that on the one hand they would fail to acknowledge that engagement, fail to enact it; which would he a disaster for Hugh at this time ... it would undermine his entire capacity again to undertake such an exposure, such a self-exposure. It would destroy the small reserve of Body & Blood he had rebuilt these past days. Drain it to no good. Other than decisive refutation of everything that he was trying to affirm, recreate.

Yet if they did acknowledge their humane immersion, then there would be the glorious carnal outrage which their community denied, and which his new logic commanded. And if that occurred, then he undermined his capacity to capture La Place d'Armes ... because he knew now that the two things were intimately linked. They were a part of the same conjugation. He did the only thing possible ... he lay down and meditated at cocktit. For the hour. And it became absolutely clear what must happen. Bill must come ... directly to his room — before they dined. And he must ask him to lie with him. Beyond that he could not see. All he knew was that he himself could not balk at this point ... could not shy away from their fact.

... At 7 p.m. he telephoned Bill to come ... and when he arrived Hugh was in his dressing gown abed.... But even as he did arrive Hugh wondered if it was right ... whether he should not wait till they dined. No — they were both drained already.... It had to be now. Bill entered and they talked around themselves for twenty minutes ... both aware of the core. Hugh felt a pudeur, sitting in his dressing gown ... felt the boniness of his legs, afronting both of them. But there was no evasion of their presence. None at all. Except at risk of death ... at risk of a self-negation that was suicide. And they both knew that. As they rose to go ... Bill said "I'll wait for you downstairs" knowing that Hugh must say "I want to lie with you first...." Bill replied "alright ... yes." Calmly ... knowing that was the truth of them.... And then they both stammered again — the spiritual stutter. But they made it ... and were enlaced together in a community of flesh that was immeasurably peaceful ... but not before Hugh had deprived Bill of the cigarette he threatened to ply as carnal contraceptive. Bill started to talk.... But it wasn't a time for talking. It was a time for corporate meditation — Bill balked, yet his presence was pliant, warm, distended. They must just lie and unfurl. For five, ten, fifteen minutes ... simply conjugate unmoving, untouching but in absolute touch. It was an incalculable enrichment.

When Hugh at last touched Bill at his quick Bill flinched his denial. And Hugh knew that they would not consummate. For a fearful moment once again the world seemed to close down on him again ... the veil seemed to drop as a steel mesh. He couldn't understand it. Their presence here implicated consummation.... Yet he knew Bill was right. Deeply right. Any consummation now for him would be local ... would merely shatter the tabu. It would not derive from that potent field of joy that he had yet to rehabilitate in the Place.

He lay astride Bill, looking into him ... his hand softly on his cock ... neither of them erect. What they were doing was much too important for that. And as he looked into him ... as they looked into each other, even sustaining this local denial that needed despatching, he felt a tide of love for this man, through this man, that swept everything else aside. It flowed through them like a soft refreshing current ... palping every ounce of fleshment. It distended their entire being, without rupture. It returned to them everything that their community had denied to them ... the right to be in touch. For a moment Hugh congested with tears ... his whole body shook with the congestion. Again he looked at Bill's eyes — they were limpid ... and like a Chinese landscape painting, one could walk into them for a thousand miles.... They kissed lightly on the lips. And it was done. All accomplished.... There was nothing more to be done there. They had come together; they had honoured their presence in each other. And by some narrow margin had escaped that mere sexual devastation which would not have enhanced them at that moment. The inner logic had been honoured in the full.

At the restaurant their conversation was slight. It had already been accomplished ... enacted. Bill said simply that he knew that this encounter was essential, that he had feared it as much as Hugh, had hesitated as much.... "What was important," he said, "was that we reach that point of no return! So that we couldn't turn back from each other." And Hugh realized then that this was that point of balk about which he had talked to Rick that afternoon. They had had to go beyond that to begin anything. And they had. Now they both felt an elevation that towered over them ... and it showed each time they looked at each other — it was an immeasurable, implacable love. An open-ended love that they both felt at cocktit....

Bill added something that was also evident ... "lying with you that way has added to my virility ... I will be infinitely more capable of my love, my relationship, with a woman now." It was incomprehensible. But Hugh felt the truth of his comment.

At 10 o'clock Bill left ... to meet an incoming friend at the airport. It wasn't till the next day that Hugh realized that the "friend" at the airport might well in fact be the girl he had talked of ... in which case she would receive fair fruit of their virilization. The thought then invoked a pang of jealousy ... and then a wave of delight ... if Bill's cock carried the imprint of their meeting ... the impact of their immersion ... then he was redeemed. And he lived in their conjugation. And was the larger for it.

As Bill rose to go, they shook hands, firmly.... And as they did so Hugh remembered with sudden revulsion, what an inadequate shorthand for their immense intimacy this handshake was. The handshake in fact was not even a shorthand, in his community it had become an evasion ... a self-evasion, a looking away — it was like walking across La Place without seeing anything, in a state of no-see, vision serving merely to evade insite of objects.... Vision serving merely to extrude the surrounding world. Just as this vision was anti-vision, so handshake was an antibody ... a rebuttal of what it proclaimed — corporate acknowledgement. It would have been much better not to have shaken hands. Merely to have entangled themselves again on each other's eyeballs. But already Bill had gone ... and he was left pondering the reality of their love — and the fact that it had evaded carnal consummation. Because he still believed that such consummation could and should be beautiful; and he was mystified by Bill's statement that such consummation in the past with men had brutalized him, the while he instinctively understood the fact. Somewhere there was a path that used this capacity for joy without debasement. Somewhere. And somehow his capacity to love women was linked to his ability to accept his love for men — as Bill himself had said. And both — and this mystified him most — both were related to the Place and his capacity to see the Place.

He sat there stunned by love. By recrudescent love. Love that at once drained him ... and revived him. For one thing he could now see the restaurant for the first time ... it did not yet make a whole ... but he was at least able so piece it together....

... when Bill had gone, I realized that he had left me as immediate legacy some insite of the restaurant ... he had left me with partially restored eyes. And I advantaged myself to restitute Le Vieux St. Gabriel that I had known in past years ... but which I had in fact evaded these past days out of deference to my own inability to see.... Again I see its curious

combination of the real and the bogus ... with the bogus as
a confirmation of what is real in it — a confirmation of the
paysannerie that it claims to have grown beyond.... Again
my eyes light on those grotesque reproduction chairs, with
backslats in mutation of the magnificent Chaise à la capucine
— the real chairs had slats that looked like cherubs wings
conjoined; these looked more like svelte-pelted batwings. Or
the ceintures fléchées worn by the bartenders ... presuming
an eternal winter — surely, I thought, these were outdoor
wear most of the time. And the waitresses dressed in costumes
that reminded me of American advertisements for Fromage
suisse. There were other details that smacked of conscientious
culture — the spinning wheel set in the window. The bad
reproduction of Beaucourt's famous eighteenth-century
painting of his Negro servant ... the scraped pine Twiss
grandfather clock boldly labelled "300 years old" — whereas
the grandfather clock had not been born by 1666 ... and
the Twiss clockmakers, American itinerants, had to wait
another one hundred years to be conceived.... There was all
this paraphernalia of cute Canadienism ... exactly the sort
of souvenir that the French-Canadian Revolution sought
assiduously to destroy.

And then there were details like the repro repoussé
brassware over the fireplace ... trinkets beneath the sonorous
copper pots above — but pillars of veracity in contrast with
the magniloquent coat of arms between that could only be
some bloated cigarette ad piece ... something taken from the
American cigarette machine vendor with its neoclassic broken
pediment (utterly alien to French Canadian culture) standing
by the door ... the rhetorical gilt plasterwork around all the
doors, coils of nuts and leaves and berries — including the door
to the toilet — while above this latter gilt orgy stood a simple
white bright light TOILET, stark as the porcelain within. Or the
sentimental sketches of Vieux Montreal (by an English Canadian,

of course!), along with some oil paintings by a French Canadian, full of garrulous energies, almost bad enough to be primitives, and certainly avid of that life in the Flesh, which the funereal competence of the English-Canadian sketches eschewed. The English Canadian painted a "nature morte" — the French Canadian painted a life of voracious credulity.

I strolled out to the bar ... past the private dining rooms with their combination of knurled Victorian mantlepieces, reproduction American captain's chairs, and bargain basement trestle tables (plastic and metal). The bar is a Victorian High Altar remarkably similar to those side altars in Notre Dame ... only in place of a glister of candles there is that of bottles and glass reminding one further of an old Chemist's Shop. And in place of a painted reredos ... a topographer's view of old Montreal — again, nearly bad enough to be good. At a table just in front a French-Canadian foursome shouted at each other intimately. I walked to the front lobby ... wound the music box ... and settled in a rocker. Overhead a compulsory stag's head looked like one of those prim lady's at presbyterian teaparties (no habitant stuffed **that** head — and again, unwittingly I found me criticizing my own "maudits Anglais," and withdrew the comment about the stuffed head). Beside me an incalculable variety of visceral sounds gurgled around the edges of a newspaper. I could not see the face behind — but the feet were marking time, presumably to the metre of the reader, the hands traced the page like a chaplet, and when the paper finally did drop and an eternally elderly man appeared, still bubbling, humming, groaning, gurgling, and criticizing his own running commentary on the reading, I was looking again at Kreighoff's habitant and I regretted some of my intellectually fashionable contempt for the paintings.

The whole restaurant was simply too much for me at the moment ... I couldn't make head or tail of the place.... It was a gorgeous infamous orgy of High Church Victorian, Catholic plaster of Paris, reproduction habitant and coureur de bois, modern claptrapping, and interior decorators' chi-chi. All the baggage of the modern Urban Habitant! Plus ça change, plus c'est la même chose.

Then I went back into the dining room again, to look … to try to sort it all out … the large Church candles on the tables, the photo of the Famille Brossard duly autographed … thirteen children — all dressed in white and that folk red, that is also pop-artsy red, that is the new Canadian flag, the imitation wrought iron chandeliers that looked trivial beside the old B.C. fir beams rising nearly twenty feet from the floor.… I stood and listened to the clatter that reminded me of a pub or European tavern … like some flock of feeding fowl. Beside me I heard a travelogue.… "We're going to catch the morning plane arriving in Vancouver for dinner. That way we'll be on time for…." And I dimly realized that this voice was completely at odds with everything I was seeing … it cut across the voice of the room itself … sliced dismally through it. I went out … wound up the music box with the lion's paw feet on casters! and settled again. Someone rang the ship's bell at the entrance for a taxi … the music box wheedled my delight and as I listened suddenly the entire restaurant focused for me … everything fell into its place.… No longer did it all seem a delinquent gather of unrelated objects … exactly the opposite: all the objects were spontaneously and subtly part of the same soundscape. Everything I saw sounded the same. I rubbed my eyes … and it still sounded the same. The objects were part of the clatter on the parquet floors, the chant of the French tongue, the clamour of the dishes and of the cash register.… Only if I heard what I saw did I see the infinite harmony of the place … and when I did I knew why I had been deflated by the travelogue in English beside me … it fell ominously flat in this magnificent hall, which was in effect a "music hall" — it deflated that harmony, made it mere batter and clash … and as it did so it threatened my carefully reconstituted B & B. I could not *see* this Vieux St. Gabe, and *hear* that conversation ... the one was at absolute war with the other. But what I could do was note that conversation in the context of the restaurant, note that it was a separate note — a flat note — and containing it thus, pass beyond. My choice was made. I could only live relevantly, fully in this apparent din which, once seen, was a resplendent harmony — and which, I now realized, had to be heard to be seen. He who has ears to hear, let him see.... And as I saw all this I felt Bill's body rich around me, and I was deeply in love with my wife.

    I staggered out ... punchdrunk, my eyeballs pounding — and furrowed my way through the pursuant din to La Place.... It was munificently present. Simply there ... the way the restaurant had been there when finally I had sited it ... only now, imbedded in that din, and now in the Square, I felt myself in a vaulting sonorous silence — the din was utterly peaceful. I strolled around the Square ... and then suddenly found me deviate ... I wasn't going around the perimeter of the Square ... I was meandering out into the centre, off the paths beaten in the snow, I was simply adrift in this garden of white. And only then afterwards did I realize that I, like all these people I had seen traversing the Square from the skyscraper heights, I too had always skirted, crossed, or traversed the Place. I had never dared or cared to wander it.... Around the statue to Maisonneuve ... that statue that so often seemed to my common sensical English-speaking eye merely a florid Victorian baroque outburst, that was now only sufficient to the glory it created ... only just sufficient. The green-tarnished Iroquois squat at the base, scattered with snow was vivid with flesh ... and these sickly candy-floss Christmas trees now illuminated from within, these were now the natural complement to all that I seeing heard. But it was still too much ... I felt inundated — fled the Place ... stopping only to espy the façade of the

Church … long enough to recognize to what degree it was truly a "façade" — a rhetorical façade … but one that could only be truly fleshed at the expense of one's own B & B. Ostell, the architect, had been an Irish Protestant … converting only at his death to the Catholic faith of his grandparents. His Church was a half-way house. Only inside … and with the complete redecoration of the second half of the nineteenth century had the French Canadians recreated it entirely in their own image. All this was very clear to me as I fled. Fled, groping my way down Notre Dame Street, past the Royal Bank building that loomed immense with flexed black buttresses above me … down past the grey sepulchral limestone fact of the street that scrutinized me … past the Hotel de Ville … to the neutral ground of my room.

It was midnight. The beginning of the 16th day … and still, I knew, I had not seen the Place d'Armes. But I had been ready to on at least one occasion. And I was beginning to know what it might be like … and what might be required of me. And each time I made the right advance I secured my ground. Whereas each time I attacked "blind" I was cut down.

DAY SIXTEEN

He awoke slowly as day slowly carved him out of sleep ... as each carroar, and trainclash, and buscough, kneaded him free of night. Slowly he was felt out. And lying thus, half-born, his mind strolled freely as he about the centre of the Place the night before.... Unformulated ideas jostled freely — his persistent need for chastity, the simple urge to get fucked which seemed some sort of prerequisite to it all, the incarnate love of his fellow man, and the preoccupation with knowing how to love his wife ... with knowing how to love at all. All these things occurred simultaneously ... and all these things seemed to grow simultaneously in him ... each one apparently contradictory, but each one as evidently now conjoined — all conjugated in the simple quest for joy. For a joy that was humanly possible ... that was what defined the human experience and potential. Joy ... it seemed crazy as he stood knee-deep now in sheer shit. His whole life upside down ... or more truly, like La Place des Arts, inside out.

None of it was explicable. All of it was suicidal ... in terms of his society — which he deeply loved — oh, so much more than he hated! so much more. And yet he still felt he was doing rightly ... maybe doing rightly in the wrong way ... but doing rightly. In any case for the first time in his life, he staked his life one hundred percent against his beliefs ... at the very moment when his beliefs seemed least clear ... For the first time in his life, while sore with fear, he was not craven. He shone with the faith that he sought. Borrowing deeply against it.... Perhaps committing himself thus by the very nature of his mortgage. He hadn't clarified much yet ... but he vaguely knew that without faith he could not love, without love he could neither give nor know joy, without joy he was dead.

... I know now why sexual frenzy is depletion in our generation — why it sterilizes ... because it is an act of despair.

An act born of despair. It despairingly seeks joy, knowing full well it cannot be achieved, and that "sex" is but the last tattered vestige of some original condition now lost to our century. That is why I could not consummate with Bill last night — because the enactment as such cannot recreate the joy it remembers. All of us was exspent in procreating that joy in lying together! Beyond that we were literally, physically, incapable of going. To have consummated would simply have depleted that total stock of joy we had just laid in.... Carnal consummation must be a rejoicing at joy — a Te Deum laudamus ... or a Magnificat. Mancock is not God the Father but God the Son ... is Holyrood. Quest for the Grail. Kill one and you kill the other ... all the others.

... last night ... that magnificent moment of no return with a fellow. The moment of le grand dépouillement ... the great undressing! Henry James with his clothes off! Ghastly prerequisite achievement.

I know, more and more, that this attack is a quest, has become a quest ... for the beauty of holiness ... made flesh ... in man.... And that this means a new sort of man ... post-square, post-cube, post-beatlenik, post Sick Set, post-everything. If only I can see more clearly, can focus finally on it ... just once, please!

... (12:20 p.m.)

3 p.m.... just back from a completed reconnaissance of the waterfront — that is, of the warehouse backs.... Down the Greyway to lunch at the Neptune — this time deliberately in jeans, unshaven — looking so delicately unkempt, alas. And again, therein, that instant uprootling of me. The recognition of being at the mercy of a world that is not mine ... and with only one slender tendril deeprooting me still to an age-old culture back through Vimy, Confederation, the War of 1812 v. the damned Yankees, the Amurrican Devolution of 1776, the Boyne, the Restoration, Charles Martyr, Henry's harem,

257

the Field of the Cloth of Gold ... right back to Adam ...
tiny tendril, unable to withstand completely this deliberate
disorientation now....

sitting with the St. Lawrence seawaymen ... on tolerance,
testing my validity — theirs. Another grotesque miscegenation
this place ... with its Victorian tin repousse wall scrollings, its
urinoire floor, its fishnet decorated ceiling like some marine
bar (again, the self-parody of these places), the romantic pictures
of the Great Eastern, of galleons, and overwheening all, the
frightening absurdity of half-a-dozen neonescent "eyes" ...
clocks, beer ad TVs, plain TVs, colour TV nickolodeon ...
all illuminated — all selling the good life ... as shown in a
cigarette ad featuring a golden green golfcourse: so strange
in this tavern — the "good life"; so ironic. On the one hand
the men in the ads — the "bold new breed" are so specifically
devoid of anything other than the most banal and irrelevant
masculinity ... standing like fruits-manqué over the moose they
had just manslaughtered with portable howitzer. On the other
hand ... these "eyes" — clockeyes, telev-eyes — blaring coldly
into our corpus here ... dissolving what they contemplate —
till sitting I become the televizor, become the machine itself
... my body dispersed as the screen itself, and only preserved
in fact by my hardclosed arsehole protected against the world
that disorients me again here. Sit and watch the remnants of
Western manhood, the workman, in his trough, unawares of
his own immanent dissolution into this world that I flee.... Six
different beer companies competing on this open fleshmarket.
Six different eyes ... blind eyes, blinding us. Back to the men,
who sit in judgment over my obesity again. I can understand
Hemingway now — playing at becoming a he-man again ...
but that way is even less open today.... Nor is it my way. Poor
Hemingway: half-ass he-man. Now we're just half-ass she-
men. The men around scent my obscenity ... feel it in the air.
Hackling. But they can't pinpoint it. One of them eyes me for

a quite different reason ... and I chuckle. Tough titty, mack —
I'm closed down today ... battens screwed tight. Cook wallows
in his shepherd's pie for some inconceivable reason called
Chinese ... and tells me he is from Hamilton. He remembered
my last visit — no wonder.

I sit — and writhe in my Canadian bourgeois cripplement
... can't I rise above it or sink out of it ... is there no escape?

on to Joe Beef's, past the Place Royal with its architectural
Georgian garrison jewel, past that statue commemorating the
Anglo-Canadian prophet of Montreal Harbour whose name
was still unknown to me ... into Joe Beef's ... mutation of the
Neptune — with the same Beery Televizors interrogating us
... stealing men's eyes, and minds, away ... a beer I can't stand,
pisse froide; and more of those Good Life he-men slaughtering
wildlife on the walls while at the tables workmen pick up
workmen for private manslaughter.

And then on back across the front that arches along to
my left — a line of nineteenth-century stonework as fine as
anything in North America ... culminating in Le Marché
Bonsecours.... On my right the St. Lawrence — or rather its
grain elevations — great grey satanic mills with intermittent
warehouses arcaded in Victorian Tuscan style.... The trucks
slosh past me — but for an hour I see what every one arriving
in Montreal saw a century ago — that splendid crescent across
the front ... crowned by Notre Dame ... and of course, today,
by the banks. A drunk accosts my distempered respectability ...
and I hate his poverty, hate him for it. And impervious thrust on
... to the Marché with its new dome, its guardsman greystone,
its firm garrison lines ... surely the finest of its kind in North
America ... the British North American Georgian officer. Stand
and let my eye follow its assured lineage. Standing at attention
in admiration ... behind me the grand dungeons disappear, and
that yellowbrick gothic control centre ... I am on parade ... my
eye marching with precision down the long files of windows,

up the command centre to the saluting base ... the front door,
pediment, and finally crowned by the dome, now restored. I
walk slowly on ... and suddenly I am under attack again ...
my solidity is threatened, distended, becomes grotesque, bursts
dishonourably into great convulsed fleshments, I gout and heave
... my eyes blind and I am all ear again ... the train bells ringing
me out and back in ... the Marché Bonsecours is become
the Great White Elephant again in a Euclidean theorem is the
Complete Cubicle is everything I recognize I instinctively hate.
I rub my ears again....What has happened? It is simple ... I
have seen the rear end of Bonsecours Church neighbouring le
Marché — seen it with its baroque convulsions, its upheavals,
its curvetted cupolas, its arched angels ... unwittingly I have
passed from one reality to another — and have been completely
swallowed, digested, remade ... complete metamorphosis. And
I realize what had happened to me ... visiting the taverns I
had closed down — closed me off in self-protection (for good
reason): assoul barred ... so that when I reached the Marché I
saluted myself, my solidity, my cubicularity ... and only when
I skated visually thence to the Church, with its rough stone
walls, its eerie undulations, did I open up again, only then
was I perforated ... and only when the trainbells clamoured
the Church into my ears did the Marché devolve into the
Complete Cubicularity which I suddenly saw as such.

around the end ... past a floating Victorian house tower
that seems an outposting of l'Eglise .. and back along the
Greyway — this time alerted to the situation ... aware of the
dangerous confrontation here ... yes — it is decisive ... there
they are again ... inversions, one of the other: the Church,
with its resonant reticulated stonework ... pocked with lunar
cavities ... and convulsing me with outcrops of momentous
flesh — over which is imposed a cleanscraped delineated
façade of pilasters and pedimenta ... a lipservice to the
geometricity of the Marché beside the which I now realize

is an intellectual exercise for subalterns. Enter the Church —
and again I suddenly hear the trainbells with clarity, with force
… which I did not hear as I eyed le Marché originally on
the waterfront. My earing was silenced by its stern sequence.
And then the trainbells are the Church candles are the ships
suspended from the vault are the nun ministering to the altar
that explodes into me, and I am again inside what I am. And
nothing is merely outside me. I am what I see … and what
I see is me … and any effort to detach some given item is
merely an intellectual exercise tentatively touching some
chosen part of us. And all the pretence at perspective in the
Church is fortunately mere affectation … because there is in
fact no real constraint of that kind.

my body tenses … and then releases … my assoul opens,
and I am free again … and I remember that I had not kissed the
reliquary last time and go up and kiss this openfaced cunt of the
world that is a gilt rose that is Marguerite Bourgeois bone that
is my own deliberate accepted self-defamation into love.

drained, instantly, I shadow me out … and into a boutique
… with its gather of energetically palpable textilities … it is the
same as architect Streicher's apartment … the conscientious
acquisition of sensual touch … the acquisition of what is
natural to the interior of the Eglise Bonsecours. Intellectually
acquired … and thus self-defeating. Or — in some of the
French Canadian textiles whose form is not "designed" but set
by custom — as in a tie, a placemat, a natural vitality governed
by the material itself …

back to hotel — drained again by this response …

and at 4:30 p.m. subside into an apero with Géneviève au
Vieux St. Gabe — noting that our open-ended relationship,
cock-tingled, is in fact the natural state incurred by the sound
of the decor itself. A fact I confirm by fingertitting us — tip
to tip. So that I know that the sound of the sight, which is the
same as the sensation invoked at Holy Communion, is the same

as an open relationship with another person. And each of these things is the thing implicitly denied in my background. That is, my Anglo-American upbringing is by definition, "senseless." Deliberately sense-lessened!

And as if to confirm that, I sense with her that our relationship is dangerous in the way that sounds have become dangerous ... they could take me anywhere ... to insanity, love, murder, suicide, creativity. Yes, le Vieux St. Gabe is sound-sited — whereas la Place des Arts is sight-sounded!

The apero with Génevieve had in a sense been an escape from La Place — from facing up to La Place ... but she had finally closed down on him. And her open failure to give, when he knew she wanted to and hadn't, that drained him again. He could not withstand many more such suicidal human self-negations....The result was direct — as he made his way back in to Le Vieux St. Gabe for dinner after she left ... he didn't conjugate the place ... he didn't insite it.... And all he saw were the Cubes — the little Cubes — la petite bourgeoisie canadienne-française. All those mamans, and pères de families ... all those daughters with the sweat weaseled faces ... the withdrawn chins, narrow lips, spindly legs (he didn't need to see them to know it), the towsled coiffure, the more or less fine aquiline noses.... In a sense it made him nostalgic — here were momas, and popas, and families ... still extant. Still operative. Still la vieille poullailerie ... he saw it every day at his hotel. Perhaps that was a reason, too, why he evaded his hotel somewhat. He could watch it nostalgically — but he couldn't possibly any longer be part of it.

In any case — once again he was cut off. And as he saw cette petite bourgeoisie canayenne, he asked himself if what he had seen precedently at le Vieux St. Gabe was true ... or had it all merely been a by-product of his own enthusiasm. Because now he saw only the great cubed dining room and its occupants ... He didn't hear anything at all.

Behind him a birthday cake arrived ... he heard three voices sing thinly ... he turned as the flashbulb shot — it was the proprietor. The four girls huddled in intimate public embarrassment over the birthday cake, and the birthday girl herself tittered behind her napkin.... He knew without

waiting for their talk they must be his own ... Anglaises. Around him
the Canadiens clapped — and the proprietor rang the ship's bell....
The contrast appalled him. Why had they come, parading their eternal
virginity to life here? He was dead again — veiled over; and his heart
sank. He wondered if he would ever see La Place. Up till now he had
never entirely doubted his capacity to see it — but now he doubted ...
his mind sank to his heart level — he began to flounder — he groped:
and again he knew it was a question of joy — of the capacity to give joy
— to create joy. And he wondered if he ever could. If only he could....
Or was it too late — had he simply come too late — had he given
himself too late. Was it too late to say himself any more? He foresaw
one end to his attack very clearly..... It would last at least till Sunday.
And then if he couldn't see ... then all said, all in his notebooks, there
was only one honourable course — only one convincing conclusion —
to prove what he had lived, to prove what he believed ... a knife, that
knife in the army surplus shop, in the guts — in the Church itself, after
impotence. It no longer even really frightened him now. The alternatives
at least were clear. It was no use trying to pretend he didn't know, he did,
with paralytic lucidity. It was do or die — die into life by doing, or die
out of life, by failing. He wasn't going to fail!

After dinner he convened again by the music box ... some English
Canadians were about to leave, and his friends of the previous evening
were there, tiddled, mocking the Anglais gently in that kind of banter
the Anglo-American doesn't really understand.... Anglais like those at
the Antique Shop.... Suddenly he hated again — and he started to
imitate his own people, their walk, their talk, cruelly ... frozen, shoulder
to hips.... The Canadiens laughed as he donned their citizenship. No
one stopped to think that he was himself ... Anglais. And then a young
English lad came in ... still feline, still alive, toe to head ... with that
natural willowy quality of the unspent English public schooled boy —
still avidly fertile ... and Hugh opened up again. Came alive despite
himself.... He went quickly to La Place, forced himself — and it was
incredibly beautiful now ... luminous in him (bless that English boy!).
He was alone there — alone with this incredible beauty of the Square
... and then someone was photographing the centre of the place ...
someone else had come to rejoice and he was happy.... They talked
briefly ... and then from discretion he left the Square to him ... and
walked down la rue St. Jacques ... past the magnificent Cubes ... a

street as unique in his country as was la rue Notre Dame or la rue St. Paul or la rue des Commissaires ... as unique as La Place ... the old Molson's Bank, for one — this splendid "Club" that had strayed from Florence to Rome, to Paris, to Amsterdam to London to Montreal over four centuries slow certain evolution.... And then on down the street to the massive Royal Bank Building.... It was open, and he entered — God, it was a splendour ... with its huge high vaults, its coffered ceiling, its multicolouration ... at night it glowed over him in a patina that in daytime had seemed merely feeble.... A night policeman accosted him — "hey mister, that's closed...." He tried to explain that he was admiring the beauty of it ... that he was deliberately there to see it. Only by leaving his wallet with sufficient credentials to convince a bank clerk did he obtain leave to sit perched on a bench at the head of the stairs, lost in the soft munificence of this temple. God — how many people know this is here...? And then the nightwatchman's suspicion deepened and he had to leave — but he promised himself that tomorrow....

He stopped in at a floor show in a hotel in the Petite Place ... watched it briefly through a window by the bar — and after disentangling himself from the hail of bosoms, saw the audience ... impaled on those bosoms: it was like watching TV — all of them were televisees!

Asleep he dreamt ... there was a tremendous explosion in his ear — his head had been shot off while trespassing on a neighbour's farm. He had never heard such a sound before. Awake — he thought at first that his brain had been blown out ... it was as though he had been fatally violated ... through the ear — as though the world had been thrust suddenly manful through the maidenhood of eardrum, and now was probing unrestrained deep in him, procreating at each thrust an entire new universe — drawing the world into him.... He was thoroughly awake now, sitting up — and felt the top of his skull — expecting it to be brainsplatter ... and then, his aural chastity belt ruptured, and resigned to this fact, he slumped hopefully back to sleep. It was just after 1 a.m. and fortunately nightsounds were few ... this initial aural haemorrhage would be small....

DAY SEVENTEEN

I awoke with dreams still tailing me ... take them as notes
for novel:

> "he was back in Rosedale, walking along that central
> undulant penetration of it ... walking to school — daily
> walk. Each house he passed was a clearing house for
> rememorable events. Each house a process of anamnesis ... of
> creative recollection. At the first, the redbrick (it happened to
> be one architected by his paternal grandfather) Tudorbethan
> Gothick the figures were all from his College days ... an age
> of fleshpottering. The Georgian house with the trim lineage
> was an insite of his army days ... with the reserve officers....
> The third home (it was massive — the home of that elegant
> little shit, English war refugee, David) gave him his only
> lifetime friend, Arthur Nelson, just back from journalese
> in Moscow.... The next was an exposé of his friendship-
> raté with his high-school roommate ... bumsucklers both,
> bumsucklers-raté! Hadn't had the guts of their guts. Lastly
> — in the only duplex on Crescent Road ... his mother,
> aged, one month to live.... He awoke, startled by that lucid
> simultaneity of life, of vision (the details had been so precise
> ... architecturally and personally ... there was nothing vague,
> nothing Romantic). — simultaneity which exactly parallels
> my experience with La Place...."

notes taken I realize that I am resounding again. Richly
ominous ... and I am relieved: my ear escape has been opened

up for certain ... aural maidenhead rent in permanence. No
going back on it — that was what happened last night.... My
aural virginity shattered. Thank God. Lie still abed, while the
vibrant world occurs constantly around me, honing me.... The
freightbelling again ... and with five fingers my right hand
plies the sound arriving on me ... fingers up like a face into
the sun for light — No question of it, I can feel that sound, at
fingertits! Feel it as it arrives in me. And as I palp this surge of
soundscape ... cock crows. God — yes ... as the bells bound
at fingertips my cocktit glows. Explicity — because each
finger that perceives the pouncing sound — each finger out
to greet the bell is imprint on cockhead. So that now, if bell
continues to ring my fingers I will detonate. Hold my fingers
up to the light and stare them ... suddenly cock threatens
outblurt ... and withdraw bitten fingers. What happened?
Bell hasn't changed ... still finger-pounding. Hold them out
again ... again I am bitten, and cocktit careens.... It is the
light ... the sunbright on them.... As I immerse hand in the
sunstroke ear thunders me.... "Thinking at the end of one's
fingertips" — that is how Eliot defined sensibility. But it
isn't merely thinking, then ... it is seeing, hearing, talking....
Fingertits cock me, man me, resurrect me.... Wriggle fingers
... in the sunshaft ... and then it is toes, kneecap, nose — all
wriggle. I must be explicit. Put forefinger into the sunshaft
now — God — it is utterly explicit ... as I enter, millimeter
by millimeter it is big toe that penetrates sunstroke.... It is
only the same big toe, right big toe — Pierrot's toe! ... and,
patently, cock makes same penetration. Test it again ... run left
forefinger into the sunbright. Nothing happens — nothing at
all. Sit me bolt upright at the betrayal ... I can't have lost it
already ... and then I know what happened, I ran fingers over
sunbright on the covers, but finger itself wasn't in the sun, was
still shadowed, and it recorded that fact precisely, as did cock
and big toe....

Carnal joy, joy incarnate, then, isn't joy made by carnal manipulation, by mere phallacy ... it is a rejoicing at the world I already know ... it is quite simply the perception of that world, at any moment, eternally. Eternity intersects time at the moment, that ... the moment that you see — really see. And makejoy is killjoy. Phallicity is fallen....

Fingers still pull the bell ... and the Place is squarely insite ... placidly, substantially ... the curious double dentellation of the Church façade, the statures in the triple arcade (I have never, to my knowledge, yet looked at those statues before ... yet they are clear in me now ... particularly the left arm thrust up in gesticulation by the right hand figure ... no, it is his left hand, he is facing me now ...), and then the Royal Bank of last night.... But it isn't so much a question of "seeing" these, not in outline, as of feeling in them ... that upthrust left hand gives that away in me....

The Place is in me now ... I rejoice....

And that done he could relax, could doodle with his mere mind — his sensibility had been largely secured, and he now felt a need to relapse into the world of intellectual byplay ... now he could afford to build mental card castles, write books, learned treatises; he would even require this relaxation as sport ... because not to retreat from time out of this absolute world of insite, of soundsite, would be ruinous.

He might even do a Ph.d. — It would be diverting now that this real discipline had been pre-established.... After all, a Ph.d. would accredit him with the new educated philistia of the petite bourgeoisie — the ECM: Emancipated Canadian Methodist ... whereas this sensibility of his would simply horrorize their pointed roundheads. Yes — now he felt ready to let his mind ply within the open-ended sensescape. After all, no holds were barred now. And that understood, he felt capable of visiting the Square again — the first morning in a fortnight!

Out to the Palace ... but even as I set out, I am nagged — that meeting with Rick ... it was so brutal. I should give him his comeback. And as I walk down la rue Notre Dame I am strung between open eyes and directional eyes ... between eyes that derive meaning utterly from where I site me, and eyes that peer down a long tunnel to some pre-ordained rendezvous. So that is it — a rendezvous, a meeting, kills sight, by focusing it beyond the environment. And a life founded on meetings, that life is deliberately blinded — deliberately defaces site.... All the difference between an open and a closed rendezvous.... My rendezvous with the Place is open, but with Rick it would be closed ... timed. Oh yes, what you see is the way you do; and how you do, is *what* you see ... change sight and you change all — siteseer is not visionary, he is resolution! By the time I reach the convulsion of Victorian Mannerist that is the tight delta opening onto the Square I realize that already I am feeding on the buildings — or rather the buildings simply feed me ... as I walk them, they reach out, and feed me — exculpating me from worry of Rick. And then I am left alone again, with my open-ended rendezvous, with La Place. It opens up around me — and as I go to swallow it I recognize the truth of it — that I had never really wanted to see — that I too balked — that I too closed my eyes to what had seemed the cursus dishonorum ... I am no better than Rick: no wonder I attacked him who is me. His balk has been mine, ours ... I too have constructed an elaborate defence against seeing, against being — it consisted of several university degrees, a published book (on "Taste," of all ironies!), a wife and two children, a potential company presidency ... and then, surely that is the crowning

— somewhere in the distance — Minister of Canadian
Cultural Affairs ... Weird — I who have thus so thoroughly, so
conscientiously, vitiated myself, would end up there ... taking
my posthumous revenge on creativity, by Ministering to it.
Like those Englit profs who, twice deviate, become university
presidents. As Englit professors they are in fact refugees from
their own capacity to create — and as refugees, disgusted with
their meekness, they fail again — haven't even the courage of
their own deficiency, nor the humanity of it, and flee again, to
the administration of their own defeat, as university presidents:
doubly dammed! And damning us doubly in sad revenge.

Mind reels ... and Square is cul-de-sacked and I duck into
the old brownstone building housing the Banque Canadienne
Nationale.... In the front lobby "Le Grand Projet" — scale
model of the new head office ... "il y aura un certain retrait
de la ligne des trottoirs ... conçu selon les données techniques
modernes offrant les meilleurs garanties de confort et
d'efficacité ... 32 étages.... Cet important edifice ... s'élèvera
à 432' au dessus du niveau de l'historique Place d'Armes. Son
style harmonisera avec celui de ce coin qui demeure le centre
des affaires de Montréal...." God — the sheer GLOAT of the
blurb. The chairman or president of whoever blenderized those
words must be insensate.... Or drunk with the spectacle of
this new French-Canadian phallic tower dominating a square
that the Maudits Anglais have deserted in any case for la rue
Dorchester.... Pillaging the Square of its sun, its real harmony
... (how **can** he say that the new BCN will harmonize with La
Place? Unless he is specifically **blind**, or lying?) There is nothing
in La Place remotely like it in touch, feel, or sound.... In fact
this new building will invert **all** the senses of La Place.

Stumble out from this gloat ... I can still see, but I know
that I have been closed down somehow ... on down Notre
Dame St., to reconnoitre Delmos for Oyster Bar lunch ...
as I walk a young buck prongs me and I distend again, my

ears thunder, rent open, and I can see again … and I realize now what happened when I came out of the Banque … I couldn't hear … I remember the sudden silence of La Place that I hadn't noticed when I came out of La Banque … the absence of sound. And thus site went unnoticed because I was concentrating so on seeing, thus making the cardinal mistake of the Squared Cube — le Cul Carré: the heresy of the renewable aural maidenhead!

Once again this absolute predicament … if I want to see I am open to manslaughter … nor do I want to explain that to myself … thus explaining it away. I must live it — not safely — but I want to live through it.… And I know it is all tied up with sighting La Place.…

Over to the Royal Bank, as promised … enter without seeing, although once again (bless that pronghorn) I am open … yet I do not see — not until I mentally note it, and then recognizing this suddenly see it all. (Does the Cube-squared, then, literally divest of any need to see … is all its architecture merely a map, in three-dimensions, a guide taking you to your destination? I don't know — all I know is that I was open and I saw nothing on entry but went straight to the end of the hall, as though conducted … and when I arrived I felt cheated.…)

— the Main Hall … locates me, confirms me, and then permits me a soft glow while declaiming a munificence of decor that is yet withheld from me. I watch me … I am wonderfully smug now … I have found me (no one ever got lost in here!) … I am a mere man. I have been remade as a civil serviceable. Right in front of my own eyes … I can take notes, and do — elsewise I never dare! I stroll the hall — every step leads me to a wicket … again I don't need to see — and I realize that I hear nothing (although there is quite a buzz of business … it is muffled … I am muffled). I see all this modesty of munificence … so discreetly — and at each step again, I am located, situated defined. I feel diffident, if sure. Then I make an effort to hear ... no, it is virtually impossible to hear, except by deliberate masturbation of the senses. Everything is quiet ... the tables, the chairs — nothing moves, nothing noises, nothing ... touches. It is all so unobtrusively "hands off." It defines the man that creates it! And I am asleep awake ... lulled into such a respectable security. I send a deliberate memo to me: "carry this manmade world now down to La Place — see what you see ..." — and as I do I recognize that this Bank is the Thermal Bath of my Toronto Union train station, before the Respectable Hicks captured it by billboarding.

I carry me obliging to La Place. It all consecrates me in a silent sweet effacement ... nothing obtrudes upon me ("it couldn't be nicer") — I hear the phrase from a bank vice-president I know too well). The modern Bank of Montreal skyscraper *does* harmonize with the old ... they are both the same to my eye now. And the old brownstone skyscraper does meld happily with the Providence skyscraper. The whole Square is mellifluent....

I begin to comprehend that the head of the BCN may be right when he says the new skyscraper will "harmonize" in La Place.... Because the BCN will set the eyesite of La Place — and all eyes will focus from it.... Abruptly there is a throb of noise ... and the Place I have been seeing is suddenly stripped of all meaning ... its melliloquence reduced to a soft irrelevant purr that belies the great buildings that sudden tower again into me ... I have been looking on a hoarding by the site of the new BCN at an old view of the Place, in 1875 ... and as I look my eyes are telegraphing to my ears all the relentless brogue of this brownstone Place with its rich writhe of muscled and crowned and crenellated and creeping embodiments ... high keep around the iron-grilled garden that green keeps Maisonneuve lush in his place. The mere sight of this makes of me a sounding board.... And I am metamorphosed once again. Force me now to enter the

Church, quizzical. What will *it* do to me at this moment? …
the Communion bells me — priest is raising the Host — I
glide me forward on broadloom feet … seeing only the altar
— le Corps du Christ … le Corps du Christ … le Corps du
Christ. The communicants intensify my bland body … and
I am congested with B & B. My throat tightens — I am not
worthy … I am not worthy … I am not worthy … efface me
discreet from out the Church to lunch pre-reconnoitred at
Delmos. Seat me stooled at the oyster bar — still distending.
Till my eyes are caught in the face of a young man along the
bar-line — eyes caught as they skim down the mirror that
friezes the clientele as part of the restaurant decor.…That face
grasps my eyefloat. Familiar to me. I know that man …

   that sweet blondebeeste
   that listless hair with soft necknape
   that flesh sits passive on me … awaiting,
    soft-sodomite he — but where? Where do I know him?
"I'll have a Boston Clam Chowder and"
    "pour dessert monsieur?"
     "a Maine Clam Chowder!"
      "Oui, monsieur"
and chowdered I hie back to that blond face, probing it
uncomfortably deeply in us … till I Know … till I know I
know — because as I look I am walking into the muted colours
that are the plasterpainted tapesty from wall to wall around of
the Royal Bank I married this morning.

  it is Him — his face that mates that marriage now.… He is
progeny of

   that interior I penetrated this soft morning
    the sort of face that peers out from the vine
entwinement of

    superannuated Art Nouveau … from the friezes of
which we, in this mirror now, are one, beneath the painted sweet
Rabelaisan frieze above our mirrored heads.

There — there ... my lass — I have you: you are the Boy
that the Bank Built

You are the she-male of that building ...

"I'll have a white wine please ..."

"en verre?"

Oui ..."

And then back to my Bank Incarnate.... Ever meet a
Bank Boy? Espy him closely ... and know he is gutted, could
only get a hard-on in a broadloom masturbolator ... and that
not at his own behest.

and turn away from this offspring of my visitation ... but not
before his eyes clasp mine unexpectant in the mirror — his eyes
cling to mine, in a sudden wound that betrays the gutting — tells
me all I can dare know ... and I want to walk over and touch him
and say "I know — you are the Boy the Bank Built," but I would
only deepen his wound and hide the other half of my truth —
that he is the man the Bank fecundated in me this morning so
that when I sortied forth I had only to recognize our Son.

"Votre vin, monsieur"

"merci"

and turn, released from
such incriminating Knowledge, to the pile on my left ... we
talk — Delmos is clubbable, and those therein are members....
One, M. Giroux, head engineer of the Port of Montreal, as he
discovers himself for me. Complete C2 — massive, walrussed
mustache. Looks like Sherlock Holmes's Watson — and blushes
satisfaction at my thought blurted out — confesses that he is,
instead, Québecois pure laine.... "I served in the Royal 22nd
for twelve years."

Ah — I muse — an habitant become garrison-seigneur.
And after our lunch we stroll on Commissioner Street because
he wants me to see their Board Room for my book.

Never in my life have I strolled ten blocks with someone
to view a Board Room. Such hard work now, just to stroll.

273

Along Notre Dame ... down McGill Street to the tip-toe
of the mountainside by the river — wander, like E.V. Lucas
reincarnate — "A Wanderer in Montreal." And looking back
up the incline, back to La Place, there, worlds away, stand
the antlers of the Church, and above, the soft bulk of the
Providence Building (first cousin to that Boy I sired this
morning but one Bank-brothel away).

as I look up, still astroll with us, a liner veers upon my right
flank: Grain Elevator #1, rising high on the harbour of land just
beyond me; its vast prow caught my cornered eye as I looked up,
exposed thus.

and above us all, the Mountain Royal, with its great cross —
not yet neonized, thank God.

"We took these glass doors off during the harbour
strike...." And Walrus Watson shows me with demure pride
the frosted plate-glass front doors with cut coat of arms
thereon which deserved indeed to be taken off during the
strike I didn't know about.

"Ah — you took these off during that strike."

"Yes and put them away."

"Of course ... well done."

and Walrus flushes satisfaction and parades us (without
trumpets but full of glory) to the Harbour Board Room that he
proffers in a coup de grace that musters all my manhood.

"This is the map that gave Montreal the idea of Expo on
the Island."

The map hangs modest framed on the mahoganized walling,
unaware of its achievement, while I engage instant battle with
this Board Room.

"Can I be alone here ... just be alone."

"Of course — I'll arrange it with the secretary...." And he
arranges my meeting with the Board Room while I stand at
attention awaiting its bidding.

Exit Walrus.

I am massively alone … to take my place with the
Board.…Where to begin? With the Board Members … the
chairs around the great table — every chair is Chair — sculpts,
defines, ordains me — infinity of legitimation — Order
amassed upon Order. Till one enthrones me diffident … and
settled am sudden Heart of Empire —

the great harbour boats, the port of Montreal, the
freightyards shunting full of Canada

the greatest meccano set, the greatest toy railroad kit in the
world. Real Empire of Boy Builders.

Awe and instant penitent. "Forgive me — I thought
it was all a Romantic Fake — I have been weaned of this
dream … not my fault, it was all done imperceptibly — by
public writ. I can see you now … I know you were no
dream — you had your dream, but it was real — it is true.
Now I understand Kipling and you, Masefield. I understand.
And *Chums*, and the *Boy's Own Annual* … and I know that
Robert Service was real. Because I hear you here … your
voices, your rhythm, your vision — all come true out of the
gut of this room onto the Empire of Canada. Dominion from
Sea to Sea. And **only** Kipling, and **only** Service **can** say what
is felt here.

So — the "romance" was, is, truth. No one lied. We have
lied defacing your truth. The truth of this incalculable empire
of engine and ship. Oh, more truth in their driving rhythms
than in all the conscientiously acquired brutalities of our career
artists today.…

Saint Rudyard, ora pro nobis;

Saint Robert, ora pro nobis …

Chums bums pummel me penitent!

I am Chaired … and outside my office window all is simply
extension, intension, of this Board Room … in this room
enough of the stuff, enough of the lodestones, to grow the
entire transport network from itself.

stare at the hearth — hearthside Empire this. Armchair
Empire. Yes. You understand once you've seen the Chairs! They
are the crux — magnificently impervious. You don't sit in
them, but upon them.... Hands filch the carved woodworking
— stolid to the clasp — woodwork that feels cast iron. Yet
everything grows sensibly out of anything else in it!

world of cast-iron organic. This is the Ironheart ... no —
Ironsides! Out of whose flank spins transcontinental track, with
mettle to spare.

Chairman Chair accosts me — and I face it — face up to
it; sight its face, its Man — beard, sharp eyes implacable — I
remember those drawings, for his children, of elephants on a
vacation, sent as postcards from anywhere — pre-Pooh-Bear.
And I know who He is ... Sir William Van Horne — dynamo
run by dynamite. That is the Man of this Room — That species
of us — like my own grandfather — who train-tripped more
than once with Van Horne. These mighty men. How else say it?
Why say it otherwise?

The Chair, the Room, the thousand-mile view up, and
down, the River of Canada, **these** commandeer the presence of
this kind of Man....

Weight compresses me, condenses me — to renewed
density of purpose ... the opposite experience, I remember it,
to the RRRapido. Even as I feel my own flimsiness.

Butterflight ... is the secretary flitting through. Paperweight.
Petite Canadienne, stabs me with my sudden lust that startles me.
This unexpected capacity. It is the Board Room reconstituting
that in me.

Ask her to sit down ... "would you stop a moment ... and
sit in that chair — the Chairman Chair." Sits ... and grows
an instantaneous cubit — is abruptly Grande Demoiselle
Canadienne ... despite herself — Chaired!

She is an early portrait by Paul Peel — 1880's — Hamilton aristocracy.

A heroine from Henry James, first phase … Apprentice "portrait of a lady": our variant, de facto, of Whistler's grandmummy!

… with that abrupt sufficiency of flesh that leaves me all unwitting endowed again. She is gone … and the chairs stare me in sheer flush of wickedness, plump my gourds, making my petite Canadienne first into demi-mondaine and then, once lapped on their luxury, converting her into understudy Queen — Lady of the Day.

Van Horne is back — and I ride my envy at their legitimated lustworthyness, at their sin-bidden flesh.

"You may go now" … I am dismissed … and as Van Horne closes our business, I see his colleagues all around the panelled wall — all Harbour Chairmen, since the beginning … all the same Man — progeny of marriage between Sam Johnson and Queen Victoria….

"Dismissed!" — and I retreat from the Board Room, carrying with difficulty my resubstantiation — brawn. And only in the hall, the door closing after me, do I know that it is the Confederation Canadian who has just accosted me — the Complete Canadian Cube, as he was when he first flourished.

Climb the stair — to the dome of the building — the whole harbour spreads out, the Lachine Canal from which Canada grew like some voracious creeping transcontinental vine; l'Ile Ste-Hélène — Champlain's own island, and now site of the Canadian "change of life," Expo 67; and the elevators huge harboured, the crescent of la rue des Commissioners extending down to the Great White Elephant, and the Little Sphinx rampant beside (together fused in the near distance they resemble Castle Howard — English Georgian plus French Canadian Victorian Baroque!); the massive crane that for all its meccano lifted a 150-ton boat onto drydock yesterday….

Oh, yes, Montreal … our only city — an impossible city, inconceivable, but magnificent.…As I leave, the young secretary is at the door … in a modern plywooded office — and there she is become substantively irrelevant! What is relevant is the elevator shaft … the old caged elevator shaft that I descend … and I realize now what it is I feel when I am in modern office buildings, when I enter them … it is like being dropped up this shaft. I can't explain that — but I know it clearly.…

Outside I am aware of a sudden that I am no longer afraid — the huge presence of fear has dissolved … and all I can think of is the phrase "in my Father's house there are many mansions." Place Youville — the Flemish Baroqued fire station.… Up McGill Street, to la rue St Jacques … to la Place Victoria (they haven't bombed the dear old bitch yet? It's a wonder some **English** Canadians don't do it …). On my left that huge black phallic skyrise office.… It has the same svelte-pelted menace of masculinity to it that the new styled outboard motors have — the new "black knight" of modern manhoodsiness. Emasculate conception.…Armed with the Harbour Commission Building, I enter it … a mutation of La Place des Arts … all these modern buildings are the same thing … the same progressive insubstantiation … my body strings out now so fine that it scarce subsists … like the thread of candy floss.…All that remains in my mind as I leave is the gift shop, with its Ookpik — the Eskimo-handicraftsy owl-cum-shmoo-cum-poohbear-cum-beatlenik that is so exactly our Canadian smugliness … the Canadian half-beat smugly cuddly … with, to cap it all, a statement on the card — "by appointment to Her Majesty …" that the salesgirl, of course, cannot explain to me. Out — virtually unscathed. No — there is no tiger in any of those tanks! No wonder it is desirable to acquire tigers nowadays.… Down la Rue St. Jacques (I remember the story I heard a day or so ago, of one of our bicultural Royal Commissars, who arrived ebullient at

a Montreal cocktail party bearing a placard — "à bas la rue
St. Jacques; à bas les castes ..." — and I grimly realize that
his is the new Canadian caste I fight ... the half-castes! The
half-asses ...). And I recall his photo on *Maclean's Magazine*
cover with his French-Canadian co-chairman ... and now
I know what it is I saw — faces from the new counterfeit
Canadian coinage — Our Beloved-King-'n-Queenie. Into
the Royal Bank again ... for a double check ... the pallor
of it, the cosmetician's hue ... and then the Mother Bank
of Montreal, in La Place ... *it* is for real! — with its black
marble pillars ... it is the perfect Cube — infinitely more
stern than its Amurrican counterparts I know in Philadelphia
or Washington. B of M — complete Canadian Cubicle ...
and then sneak up to the executive floor — the third ... a
complete open maze of high cosmetic powdered panelled
walls — part of the Closed Cubë ... sit and browse a
magazine till uniformed guard informs me "this isn't a waiting
room" — his voice hard, full of shock at my very presence ...
the very presence of someone doing nothing ... of someone
"loitering" (ultimate Anglo-Canadian sin! — to loiter). And I
stayed thereafter, only longer enough to salve my dignity —
and to scout the pictures — Waterloo, Trafalgar ... and then I
left, I was in fear again.

Into the Square ... wondering, did I **hear** the Harbour
Building? I can't tell now. But the Square now is within
me — it is placed — it is La Place again. I take it for granted
within me now. That is why, sometimes, I **can't** merely see it
... because it is within. Into the Church — slowly expand ...
open — and then know that I did not hear the Port Building
(**I** was what was heard!), because here, under the side-aisle, my
eardrums breach as when descending in an airplane, and I am
again spread-eagled to the thrust of soundscape.

To the hotel....And then lie down, drained by this, the first
day that I have even dared commit me to the Square....Armed

with the knowledge (it has taken so long to sink in) that the problem is not to see the Square, but to hear it! That is, the problem of seeing the Square, of insiting it, is to hear it.

Lie — drained — in impasse ... caught now formidably between the two logics — that of the memo-pad — and that of the rememory, of the assoul ... (after all, anamnesis is just a big word for the recollecting assoul). These two logics are simply incompatible ... stalemate each other. Must learn to use my new logic to cap my assoul ... there's the rub. A new anal-ytic logic.

Thinking of the memo-padders ... the thought that for the English Canadian everything must be "cut and dried" — wonderful phrase for it! ... and then the feeling that, nevertheless, I come close to some truth now — truth that relates to a sequence of potences ... to the world we make around us.

Thought: Bill said — "I can't make love to you now...." It is over this making love that the Anglo-Canadian Cube fails ... he can't make love because he can't love, and he can't love because he can't hear ... and he can't hear (oh, God, the syllogism is wicked) because he's constipated — assoul plugged — is earsoul plugged.... So I am left advocating a paroxysm of transcontinental deconstipation ... by any means. Well ... b-b-b-b-but.

Lie and burnish my cocktit ... as a prayer, my chaplet, to restore my soul. And so doing I know that the Complete Canadian Cube is a square with an earwhole, an assoul, a point of penetration, a centre of density, of intensity ... a Cube is a square with a full circle still in his gut! A Cube *is* a redeemable square. And my Square, my Place d'Armes, then is the Canadian Cube that I circle for point of entry, to release the constipated.... And then it's gone again.

For dinner — to Le Vieux St. Gabe, by default. Don't want to eat. Force me to, drained. Enter — and find that I can't hear myself think ... therefore I'm merely Cube again ... it means I'm coming to my senses — that is coming out of my senses. All sound now molests me — exacerbates me. But even as I realize this my ears open — and the common-sensicality of cubicularity is qualified … is charged now, perceptibly with a palpable immanence … the chairs close in upon me — the whole room takes on flesh with me….And then there is that balance, between detachment and immanence … that hazardous equilibrium that is my mitigated sanity.

I suppose I have closed down in effect for self-protection — to repose my sensibility…. It is odd but I think I can only write when I am Cubic…. I don't want to write when I am in full form and force — It is lèse-majesté to write me then — it is all I can manage simply to live the plenitude. While when I am desubstantiated in the two-dimensional world of modernity, I am simply universally impotent — I don't need to do anything at all … passivity is all-embracing. Writing, then, is a 3-D affair! And there I'm trapped — because the essence of my siting La Place is 4-D. And the very medium I use to convey that insite, the written word, betrays my quest … or at least betrays its success. The moment I put pen to paper I'm a deserter…. Even thinking this now, noting it, while awaiting my carafe of rouge and the côte de boeuf saignant, assures me that I am completely, dispassionately secure … I am absolutely out of touch again — alive only in a mentally constructed box: framed! And in this condition, the more I look, the less I feel I see…. It is at this level of sanity, of course, that I fail … that I become the Civil Serviceable. And when I am like this — sane and sound, better say saved from sound — only Holyrood knocks me inside right, only eyeball mans me again. Only direct injection of sensibility revives me…. Quick suckle on manroot recrudesces desire for life in me.

The Complete Canadian Cube *is* a deep sleep of all sensibility … 3-D *is* death in life … and cocksuckle is the lifesaver. In 3-D I need to put a tiger in my tank — no, that's the square. In 3-D I need to revive the tiger in my tank.... but for the moment I don't want to know — I **want** to remain 3-D — nature morte.

Listening now to the music here ... I note now that I "follow the tune" — the experience, as a Cube, is directional ... whereas in immanence, in 4-D, I *am* the tune ... I am attuned....

So I sit — with a foot, legitimately, in both camps ... with one ear and one eye, half-cocked, lazily — lazy-manned. C'est pourquoi, en tant qu'Anglo Canadien, j'incarne un énorme besoin du Canada français ... French Canada resurrects me ... adds the requisite dimension to my Anglo-Cubicularity. Though tonight the restaurant leaves me cold because tonight I am cold ... and passive.... No wonder there is no expression in English like "c'est passionant" — literally, it is empassioning!

Out, untouched and unscathed by Le Vieux St. Gabe ... to La Place — and placidly note that intellect and sensibility fuse now in a palpable delineation of the Square. My hazardous equilibrium, compounded of insite and fatigue, provides me now with a Place of Substance....

A later cognac chez Jean-Jacques Garant — ancien copain de Radio Canada. Jean with his 19-year-old "neveu" — presumably his latest accouchement. And with him, and later Georges Pelteau, talk — for the first time, really, since I arrived two weeks ago — talk the old French-English Canadian chestnut ... note their new hardness on the subject ... their separation from us, from the rest of Canada, is now a spiritual fait accompli. I know that because they don't talk about it ... instead they talk the constructive measures they are now taking to consolidate the state that is now, de facto, separated — l'Etat du Quebec: a state of mind founded upon a state of sensibility! And I am startled now to note with them something that I have unconsciously noted these past days — the new "fonctionnairisme" of the French Canadian ... the new preoccupation with being a Civil Serviceable. Georges is ferocious on the subject. Ironic — that the French Canadians seek that English-Canadian nemesis, just at the moment that we English Canadians, conversely, are in search (insofar as any of us are seeking anything at all beyond the down payment on our new swimming pool — fair fruit of a career at the expense of Canada!) of a renewed sensibility.... And then:

— Expo as an open market, buying off French-Canadian talent and trouble for 1967; the White Market for Separatists.

"le triomphalisme du Cardinal Leger" which bores them and revives me.

— the eunuchs at Ottawa (here we all agree; no balls in the national belfry).

— my revolution against the Anglo-Canadian devolution....

and we separate, after I have admired the phallic symbolatry of Jean-Jacques' collection of French-Canadian primitive crucifixes (they always carved their Christs with barrel chests, small legs — en habitant!) ...

stop in Au Bistro ... the officer cadet from Le College Militaire Royale de St. Jean who proffers himself ... the two American bearded beats — something different about Amurrican flesh, I can spot it ... somehow less convincing and less convinced than Canadian fleshment ... the young lawyer from the East Block in Ottawa, preoccupied with the Crown in Canada, and with my ringed little finger — "It is an invariable sign" he notes ... I should have replied "your perspicacity accredits your own guilt of sensibility" ... but I was in 4-D.... And at 1 a.m., left, unscathed. Leaving the CNR cadet intact. Why? A certain fidelity to La Place! — although it is quiescent in me now, and as I visit it, en route to the hotel....

DAY EIGHTEEN

flute-throating at the end of my cock, first sparrow song dredges me from three hours of sleep — and leaves me at the mercy of the intestinal horn of seaway ship that is steep in my fundament. I ply my cornucopia in prayer ... wonder how much more of this I can withstand ... how many more hours ... can I wait till tomorrow? Or will I exspend me today ... evacuate me? I am tempted to try my fortune this morning ... the early service. No use trying to sleep now. Too congested. And if I succeeded this morning ... why then I would be free....

... my fear is to disperse me before I have sited the Place. To evade the larger issue there.

The whole thing, while still clear in broad terms, has become immeasurably confused in specific terms. Which step then? Which releases the others? Which kills?

... last night as I fell asleep I thought of my Fall, upon arrival, over two weeks ago ... and I realized that it wasn't an end to virginity merely to smugness. The virginity somehow remains ... the male maidenhead.

it is after 7 a.m.... I'll go straight to the Place now. That is the best ... admit vulnerability. And accept the conseqences. Odd — I came to assault the Place. Now it is, to say the least, give and take. I no longer know who is assaulting what. Merely that there is a War. More — it is a Holy War. Between whom? For what? And what is for the winning?

But still I *do* know — the right to love, the right to rejoice, the right to give, the right to die and thus the right to live.

trainbells me, dazzles my earscape, thrusts deep ... massages back of my neck.

how will today fall...? If only I knew. But if I did — I wouldn't be here. I wouldn't need to be.

it no longer seems mad — simply incredibly difficult.

Get me gone to La Place! Now 7:51 a.m.

En route ... "ça saute aux yeux" ... again, I find me, as so often, living in French ... and what I am seeing, living, says itself so much better in French. How can I say as well what I experience now than to say "ça saute aux yeux...." Everything along la rue Notre Dame "jumps into my eyes ..." — the convolutions of pilaster, of capital, of pediment, of acanthus, of rustication in stone, of scroll in wood ... the sybils, the lintels, the grotesques, everything — all the way along, is an amassed spread of the Hôtel de Ville ... all those architectural idioms that in books are but ideas, but assembled are fact, and insited are flesh and blood.... How could I say it in English at all? It doesn't "hit me in the eye" (suggesting I am hurt, struck, offended)....The fact of the matter is that I am living me in French, **being** lived in French, and writing me in English!

Reached La Place ... and I realize that it is now ... now is the moment.... Now — not tomorrow — but now. Look at the Place. It is palpably lucid in me ... mount the steps ... the Bank of Montreal bows across the Square at me. A bell tolls 8 a.m.... I resound the Square ... and then I am silenced ... the bell doesn't sound me right ... and I realize of course that it is some sort of hi-fi apparatus atop the Bank and not a bell at all. On further, and stand me afront the old presbytery ... its stonework does resound me. Return to enter the Church. And as I do, I realize that I am afraid to give, and afraid to be taken ... I am afraid to love, and to be loved. It is simple.

Enter — realizing specifically that I am here now because of last night. It is the same as last night — the same thing entirely. I am not here to expiate nor to obviate last night. But for the same reason ... to give and take.... Circle me up to the altar — seeking my situation ... to the left side, near front. No — that looks me the wrong way — I read from right to left — still. Move to right side ... and settle ... and realize that I have instinctively sat just afront the episcopal pew. Natural High Tory! Sit — and wait.... Est-ce que ça va prendre ou non? That is always the question of eyesite ... of eyes seeking out other eyes. Will it take? This time? The priest enters — totes his Host around.... and I realize that my very consciousness of what we do prevents it occurring ... I think of last night again — of all the lost nights ... when I failed to follow my eyesite. Yet eyesite is the only way to revive the sleeping tiger in my tank — in this church — and I know that my withdrawal last night is my withdrawal now ... withdrawal that I realize as the communion bell urgently remembers me the Mass, and at the same time informs me thus that I have not transubstantiated ... have not resuscitated my B & B. I have been dormant. And then it is gone ... done ... the dais is empty of everything except my own immeasurable regret.... From behind, in la Chapelle du Sacré Coeur, the organ reminds me that marriage is being consecrated ... that flesh is being bound (and that bound in this way, despite what anyone may say, it can never be totally severed — no, never ... not if all the world became Las Vegas).

Immeasurable sadness in me ... fulfilling that great reredos. Now — only now that it is done and gone, am I focused to its fact. And I slowly know ... oh, odious ... that to achieve this communion in Body and Blood ... to transubstantiate, that I must give myself by defilement into beauty ... must do so by giving myself to a man I take. This, then, is our Protestant curse ... our Reformation "penitence." It is hideous (on reflection) — but simply, and lovely, in the recognition. It is not a question of further protestation. I have no choice but to absolve me of the arrogance of autonomy, of asserted independence, in this way ...

by umbilinking me from cock to cock back to Adam. To pass into this plenitude, the Kingdom of God, of love ... I must reinvest me, I must incur the consequences of Protestant hell.... That means that tonight I must, must ... I have no choice. Yet I had thought it was the other way around — that it had to be the other way ... that first I had to incur the Kingdom of God, to incur the wrath of Holy Love before I could consecrate it in the holiness of that carnal love which is man's Te Deum laudamus ... his finite metaphor for heaven.

... I have to expiate the arrogance of our cult of civil serviceables. Have to expiate our negative priesthood of non-believers, rendered unto efficacity by sterilization and self-gelding.... Ah, bittersweet madness.

back down Notre Dame street ... and for the first time feel able to cope with these religious boutiques.... Enter the first that is open — it detonates around me like the Church itself ... wide-eyes me in thundering ears. The shop clamours the Mass around me still.... My eye touches all that it hears. So that, as I wrap eyeballs around Virgin, cock threatens resurrection ... and I know that I can here have that consummation that I denied me at Mass.

... a new Canadian Flag stands here ... another of the banners — the colours are right for the shop — but not the form ... the form is still crushed Cubic.

into Palais de Justice — same thing ... the torchères resound me, I drum me out ... the world is not inside-out, it is outside-in again. And I can rejoice somewhat at this partial restitution.

...

At 11 a.m. rendezvous me back to Streicher's fiat in Greyway. **Must** understand what is going on there ... if I can grasp that I can grasp what is done to us at La Place des Arts ... and in all these modern erections ... must.

Enter, past Son-kennel, up flight-ramp to vivoir, look for
the fish-float ... quick — phooom: too late — I'm inside-out
again, before I could find that fish.... Inside-out even after
warning me ...

around the flat — Streicher leaving me in peace. These
objects — all of them ... are the dried innards of me ... and
all this vivoir furnished with my involuntary evisceration upon
entry: that instant involuntary martyrdom by disembowelment
... as on entry of La Place des Arts

can feel me flying apart ... can hear this room trepanning
my headtop.

if I can get a word for it ... words kill by definition ...
might kill my killer ...

flying apart — Anthropocentripetal! Magic-Wordkill ... and
I am released to spectate my own dissolution! Self-dissolution
spectated in tranquillity.... But laugh, or cry, as you will ... I
can observe now — for example: these assertively voluptuous
textiles — I know what they are — they are merely condensed
flesh, with water added. Powdered Flesh, Instant Flesh. Instant
B & B (the very opposite to the Flesh Market next door ... oh,
Greyway, if you could see me now — pray for me Greyway!)

Instant B & B — the Protestant Communion: it merely
Commemorates the fact of resurrected B & B ... lip-service

but of course — Instant B & B — the Total Insensorium
all over again. Like the Artsy Place.... And these green potted
plants (poor souls) give it that final touch of living death — a
living monument as conservationists say ... to the dead!

All the intensification of this morning drains from me. What
is this thing? Is it the Hollow Square — or, indigenously, the
Excavated Cube? Square, Place, Cube — in a self-perpetrated
vacuum — the very opposite of "spaciousness": an onerous
vacuity that we all fulfill at risk of death — Instant Death.

these puffed cushions ... these are my own tripe. No
wonder dried flowers look well here as decorettes.

I'm draining again … despite all precautions. "Anthropocentripetal" be damned …

quick — before I embrace this doom … what *is* being done to me — quick … tell them what is being done to us — before you are extinct.

what is it?

Everything is given here — but it is really nothing … because before it is given I am bereft of life — everything sucked from me — instant blow-job with no climax!

Are you sure?

Yes — positive. This Hollow Cube absolves me instantly of life, love, death, joy, despair.… Life merely a dispensable game herein … vile mutation of belles lettres.

Force me to ask me — "what do I ear?": nothing. Because earing is asswhole, and I, dispersed here, am scarce permeable. Yet to the eye there is the same effect as the Total Sensorium … as 4-D … but the danger signal is clear: no reverberation … no Revertebration. Outside-in exvertebrated again … like pterodactyl in La Place des Arts. Farewell assoul! Now everything goes in one ear and out the other … or the same ear.

Spurious — all of it … this apparent transfixion here — apparent exaltation: it is merely transfiction. Mock Magnificat.

Streicher leaves clucking wife. Simpers: "can I give you a noise?" and self-accredited Impresario of the Insensorium winds the cuckoo clock with its giant pendulum.… It tocks hollow — I can see that.

Ironic — the horror vacui of the Renaissance Mannerists now become a horror of B & B: and at the moment of proclaimed release modern man is simply annulled. In every way a hollow victory over environment.

Husband-and-Wife tiptoeing their Hollow Cube … so that I can better hear clock-tock. And I turn with social gratitude to assure us that it is indeed clocking.…

Can't stand any more … Streicher, assured of his conquest seats me. Sucks me up … feeding on me…. This whole place is man-eating. Mantrap. All my enforced radiation engulfed by him … he embraces my dispersal: piecemeal seduction.

"You must abandon yourself to modern architecture … you must plunge," leers Streicher, confident of his triumph.

And it is truly abandonment … and truly a plunge: one drowns in this space. Yet have I any choice? Between Cube and this square root of Cube? Between Complete Constipated Cube and Gutted Cube? And as Streicher eats on I place Toronto so readily: Toronto — the Complete Canadian Cube … with its City Hall — the last of the static monuments: more static, more grounded, in fact, than the old Romanesque pile it displaces. Or our Performing Centre of All-Arts — O'Keefe Centre. Looks like a beer case beside the Montreal Abortion. Or Massey Hall where those Mendelssohnian Methodist Valkyries rant. All are the same: the Complete Cube. Nothing changes. Impenetrable!

Streicher: "What did you think of La Place des Arts?"

Me: "It is the space you hear!" — in sorrowful recognition.

Streicher gleems — "of course"

Me: "and the people are self-evidently ephemera…."

Wife-&-Husband concur beatifically.

Wife: "you don't really believe … in **those** people?" Incredulous.

Me: "They are my people…."

raucous panther laugh — Wife: "you are insane…."

Streicher — with personal satisfaction: "There is no such thing as insanity any more…."

And snug in Cube Hollow here, he is self-evidently right.

…

back to hotel to recollect me. To remanipulate me. And lying down I feel immense need to flower, to blossom, to bear fruit … le besoin de m'épanouir. The urge in me is implacable

now ... and for the first time I have open rendezvous in my
soul with le quartier, with La Place ... with life.

...

down to Antique Shop ... where the Objects are people
who lie in wait for people that are Objects ... people who are
objects in need of animation. While these objects here are les
animateurs ... les metteurs en scène.

outside snow rumbles down in light flakes ... a Royal Mail
truck flushes past the red coq in the window ... nothing, of
course, is Royal any more in my country ... yet now, for me,
quite despite the fédérastes, everything has become firmly regal.

a young cubic couple stalk past ... look at the window
tentatively tantalized ... and dare not commit themselves to
their glance: coitus interruptus, always....

the top of my head tingles. I am on tap again. Thank God.

... quit the Cube-trap, and on to La Boutique. Down the
Greyway all whitely. Enter into it and know immediately that
this *is* the Religious Objects Shop *is* Notre Dame ... all one
and the same thing. If I blur my gaze to the blare I am in all
three. The sensibility is identical. The placing of the objects. Ces
tapis ramassent les couleurs ... they amass colour! And as I blare
to this colour crash warm into me, I understand the importance
of "scraped pine" pionera furniture for the Canadian Cubes
— it softens the blow — it makes accession to the object soft
as against hard sodomation. It does the ungenteel so gently ...
rescues that whole bland generation of the Sons of the Royal
Bank, the washed out mannekins, rescues them ... resculs them
— to pun biculturally!

again, near the door — the single Anglo-Canadian painting
... I find me looking at it ... whereas I look **into** everything else
here ... and everything else here looks into me.

young couple enter ... touch, talk, enter into complete
conjugation with the objects ... and are implicated in the
objects. And as soon as this is done I am conjugating, and I

no longer require that persistent phallicity that pursues my
Protestant corporealization. Oh, God — that ferocious phallicity
is only Protestant backlashing! So obvious.

brief visit to the Museum of All Arts again … the defunct
Cube. With its irreverent collection of French Canadianity
all given in memory of Anglicanadians. And quick flee the
mausoleum. My case confirmed.

rescue me at Le Bistro … and sitting in this fleshpot, know
that I married to embrace impotence — civil impotence
… and that I'm impotent because I married. My marriage
by definition my own emasculation. My failure to confront
cocktail. My failure to create.

watch this new generation of fuzzy-wuzzies…. They
have everything we lacked … and they got it for free … and
the clue is in the consecrated neck nape — no longer shorn
Roundheads, they are all felinity … natural Cavaliers.

sit, and ponder this belated self-confrontation. My body
sagging here on this open hunters' market — the spirit is
willing, but already the flesh acclaims its own betrayal.

…

back to La Place … it is the black leather coating of the
boy at the bar who rejected me as I lined up like any other dog
to nuzzle. And inside the Church all I can contemplate is the
prerequisitioned demission of tonight.
(7 p.m.)
… the real trouble is that I don't want an open-ended adventure.
I want neither security nor freedom. That leaves me with what?
It's easy to answer "responsibility."

at 9 p.m. Au Petit Havre. My legs directing my nose.
And seated alone watch them watching me in paisley black
and gold shirt and red ascot: my closest approximation to
beatnickelery. Truly at best a half-beat! And a half-cube (at
least I'm not yet merely a square root!). Can feel that impasse
in me again … that self-blockade that annuls everything

— the old stalemate. Table across from me is a party of eight
French Canadian petite bourgeoisie respectable … equivalent
to our United Churchies — but so entirely different (Thanx
be to God!) ces grenouilles de bénitier are at least graceful
… there is a certain felicity to their social presence. If they
are cubic, they are also undulatory … like the walls of
Bonsecours Church. They aren't Roundheads. Beyond them
a young regimental couple. That is a couple regimented
around his regimental tie and her état major. He looks like
any one of several hundred of my acquaintances (lifelong
"friends" I was vested with before I could do anything about
it). Anglicanadians. Their love is forever … with a warranty
by Birks. Beside them a group of non-clubbables … the man
nearest me has that narrow neck, the close cut hair, the shock
of cropped hair that would wave if it weren't carefully combed
with water. Methodist — with a strong Mommy somewhere.
His partner is that healthy Canadian girl who would figure in
a Better Housekeeping kitchen ad were she pertlier.…The
whole room is a study in the vertical Canadian mosaic. Except
that I don't fit in — I've deliberately opted out … and I am
in no-man's-land again. Neither flesh nor foul. Constipated —
full of shit — corporately if not anally speaking. My assoul is
congested. I'll have to ramrod it out! Yet I feel over-distended
… my goddam sensibility is ruptured again.… Result: my
asswhole is battened in self-defence.

    my waitress is the earnest energetic blonde of that lunch
fifteen light years ago with Luc.… So diligent. She belabours
me with the problem of redemption.… Isn't there anything
that can be done? Must it always be like this — this repetitive
provisional Hell of day-to-day. Le petit train-train de la
vie. Surely she merited something better than this and the
impending Canadian social welfare security kit against living.
Well, thank God — at least the welfare state reimposes the
problem of redemption … by default.

A pair of lesbiens-manqués straddle by ... English Canadian
Authors' Association types ... or secretaries of the local
historical Society. They have that fascinated eyes-off look of
all Cubes ... when confronted with the presence of the flesh.
When confronted with the steep carnal pit of life, in any form.
They eye me furtive as though they want to eat me, spank
me, fuck me, jail me, in that order.... Instead they clutch their
costume jewelry necklaces — secular chaplets, talisman against
the evil eye.

Au Bistro — for a stint. Item: one English-Canadian journalist
... who shifts his furtive eye through me, accusing as he goes,
his own imprecision. That look I find increasingly with Anglo-
Canadians now — a self-evasion, that is in fact a self-accusation —
an acknowledgement by default of the failure to confront oneself.
This boy is an instinctive homosentient. But he is condemned to
jail for life — jail within himself. Self-imprisoned.

listen to him talk — he is with a Montreal weekend
magazine. Age 27 ... indelibly seedy.... Just as well — dirt, like
overweight, is a good protection against self. Too much dirt, or
too much cleansing — either one efface!

I stare his eye ... watch the intermittent glaze of it, the
hesitant veil. Watch the rising impotence in this eye till it
threatens to rob me of mine.

"Il faut que je me sauve ... faut me sauver" — and I am
backing out the front door of Bistro ... backing out, parrying
all eyes on me.

"Where am I going?" ... I don't stop till I am there, till I
am settled into the carnage, the supple healing carnage of it ...
seethe of sounding into me, convulse my body, undulant that
Cube constipating in me thigh to chest — my whole chest-
of-drawers bulging rampant into that bombé commode in the
Flesh Market, in the Church, into me.

Brueghelian flesh in Baroque peasant stomp: Yvon's Eden
Rock! That's where!

Ahh ... Bistro is counterfeit of this ... weak imitation for faint-hearts. Bistro acclaims corporeality that motivates this, animates it. Bistro covets this, this animation of the Object, even in its grotesquerie. But Bistro is way behind ... hallmark of half-beats: so clearly that. All beatniks are half-beats ... all Bistro-beats are but aspirant habitant-beats! — trying so conscientiously to be what these superannuated habitant peasant goons of Eden Rock still are by birth ...

seat me in centre sector, to watch to watch, to make me mental

notes ...

head resounding, stunned

I'm not watching no not watching at all. Impossible to "watch." I am. I'm in it ... seethed in instant immersion

everything here is me again.

On the stage dancers in red flare of tights straining buttocks that rampage bigger than American bosom ads (when bigger and better bosoms are built Bistro will build them! — but this ain't Bistro ... this is the Real Body)

gouts of buttock

and bosoms to second these buttresses.

Real Presence Real Presence Real

women hurl their she-men from pillar to posting

men glide with grace of woman and felicity of boys.

The pause that refleshes: around the walls, siteseeing sightseeking eye the wall postered rumple of nudifications as large as these larger-than-life battlements still rampant to the dance of us

across from me a plump little immense man gurgles delights

ogles entire hall as fused fleshpot, evading simultaneous with me the misplaced English-Canadian Cubic creep opposite who assaults us visually

and even as I defend us my hackles rise unbidden behind and I turn to hackle back into the blond eyes of the

unseen youth whose gaze peeps out my assoul unbidden....
Bless you bless you bless and nurture from his gift carries
me honourbound back to the dance raging aroundalay as I
steep cock-eyes in this exhumation of all dead flesh risen in
insurrection that dares exhort resurrection

Resurrection of the Body, which was promised to You and
to all Mankind

the woman in the red tights eats her mannekin unprotesting
(neither she nor he, both catholic in their taste) and then
descends to her table farting him out our communal arsewhole.

another replaces her on the dancefloor — platinum
Madonna with her small proletarian habitant Christ that would
be excellent for home use for only $4.75 monsieur, plus tax,
and dancing on my floorface beside Platinummy are sixteen
crucifixions of rising size, from clear pine traditional (Habitant
tourist trade, government subsidized — winter works projects
— don't laugh, **you** are paying!), to indigenous hardwoods
stained to look imported

to mahoganized Christs with kemglo cleargloss finish is
eternally yours

to ironized Christ stricken fresh from the crafty forge

to clubbable Christs in Distressed Pine with knotholes
where they should and shouldn't

to that five-foot high pottery nibbley-nubbly in charnel
house grey

oh Christ Christ for sale, a Christ for every garage for every
nook and closet for everybody (you meet the **nicest** people)

"Je peux vous aider, monsieur?"

"Non, merci … je ne veux qu'admirer vos Christs."

"Ils sont jolis, n'est-ce pas?"

"Ah oui — très joli!"

I recognize clearly that I am in the Art Sacré on Notre
Dame Street and the drummer boy on stage is the big Christ —
nibbly-nubbly … pot for my pottery and that (clasp the table

now to steady and pray that that blondboy's eye still nurtures my hackle because I would oh so will to sitesee now if ever I am to be allowed to see)

and that all these Crucifixes are the red ride-a-cock horse and distraught iron of Chessmen straddling my floorboards (and only that one bone dry picture is Misplaced Person) ...

yes, unquestionably, if I focus clearly, focus not mere brain but entire being, pumping my presence into the placement, I am in La Boutique which **is** the Religious Objects Shop that **is** l'Art Sacré on Notre Dame that is here and now immersed in this homosentient nightclub, Eden Rockbound. Same colours thunder same sound to make same people in me.... Eyeballs still popping I follow the focus of me one further, beyond the drummer boy the Christ,

beyond the Christ the Red Ride-a-cock-horse,

beyond the Ride-a-cock-horse the white marble rump that is the Red Tight Girl's buttress riding high in me now, white pliant, moving up to the coiled columniation thrust to capital that carries the High Spangled Heaven ... the door of the tabernacle batters wildly open and Hosts surge out candles stamping claw-and-balled footwork and attendant Sister wide-eyed battens down black robe from outrage of convoluted flesh that is the Sternum of Sphinx whose High Altared White Marble Rump I have just ridden with Red Horse over the assment of redpanting lesbian ... and the candles are suddenly merely beer ads, luminescent on the walls of Eden Rock, and over the high altar Christ has been replaced by a little brother watching us who is beerworthy on a lifesize ad like the rest.

... singer grasps my microphone and outblurts in open sodomation of the hallwomb that soars high, burst into a heaven of stars set against a French bleu ciel ... descending only slowly to define corruscating Gothic of reredos and altar and clerestory and pulpit and I am aware that Notre Dame has imposed upon us, that all of this has taken place as I sit in the

Church after dinner, and that the nightclub is only a figment of
the imagination of my Church ...

everything is open. Everything. I can move walk soar ...
anywhere, in a series of intermarried worlds — everything
flows into everything. No holds barred. Never before ... enter
this plenitude, diffident ... as promised, always promised (Eden
Rock is become Garden! — ah ... my Canada Shield, goddam
Granite Shield — 3,000,000 squaremiles of Canadacube — is
become a flowerbed ... always promised, as was written)

try to walk into this land, each step absolute, body
skyflying (I was told that, too, that the body would rise, with
the rest) as my hawkeye spreads the world around me ... there
remains only the voice of my father that I know is behind the
next cloud. How could I have ever doubted that.... It is self-
evident now.

The Word was to be made Flesh ... ecce homo.

So — they didn't make a single mistake ... not one; they
merely said what they saw, what was revealed thus to them
for Holy Writ. They didn't use imagination, or metaphor, or
allegory — they simply told what was all around them. And
they couldn't have told it in any other way.... It is we who have
made the metaphors ... reduced their reality, reduced reality, to
a metaphor!

It is we who have made irony, in our own reduced
image ...

And mindful of all that

it has gone it has gone gone.... Start up to catch back the
last site.

Gone

I am alone

in the carnage of the nightclub.

Pyrrhic victory

The blondboy — he **can** restitute

turn round to clasp his eyesite in us

He is gone ... gone, sometime when I was walking out from
the White Marble Rump within the rumblegut of the lesser
Sphinx of our Lady of Good Help, even as I walked out, and
down past the Great White Elephant into the Greyway, curving
archly past the Flesh Market, to the greyhead couchant of the
Great Sphinx de Notre Dame de la Paroisse — gone right out
from under my blooded nose.

    Blondboy, oh blondboy — your hackling eye opened
everything up in me, smashed all barriers

      absolved me instantly of twenty years of still life
purged my penitence in the flash of eye

      and all the world surged wide back into me, over
me, through me, and even as you gave and I took you were
expropriated ... and I am alone, again.

    Sit for another age. Piece the world back together over
my now dead risen body. Watch the communicants. Waiting
for a resurrection. Opposite me a pair of dumpling she-men
keep up running comedy that verifies Shakespeare's finest farce
— only they are for real ... these people that are People, here
... these ignorant, uneducated habitants, now, mounting a self-
parody that our theatre will never touch. At once themselves
and mocking their selves, plying nonexistent bosoms that are
instantly real, imitating the rural accent Canayen, which they
normally speak ... imitating what they are, what they have
always been, defining themselves in me for ever. They merit
instant Canada Council grants ... I don't see how it would
be possible, however, to convince the Advisory Committee
on Grants at this time, given that the next sitting of the said
Committee isn't

    Just let the matter drop! (Petulant)

    Out to pee me, prostrate. And scout the bar where the
young queen of the male harem chez Yvon-Pierrot sits with
the singer — queen bee with her portable stinger. In Hudson's
Bay coat gone wuzzy. While around them the entire court of

us … in a natural heirarchy, from top to bottom, from bottom to bottom.

returning to my seat young boy jostling past cradles my cock friendly as he conjoins sextet beside. Eye the group that nuzzles me: they are, to a man, graduate photographs of some Roman Catholic Collège classique (except that in real life their teeth are as rotten as thrice-cooked patates frites!). All dressed with propriety, in suits and respectful smiles. Tous fils à maman. Neat. All the dirt pushed into the cracks. Something about Catholic kids … some quality of flesh, of deportment. Something non-cubicular … or, rather, cubicular-plus. C'est coulant. That's it — there is a flow in them, a certain kind of animacy that is a flowing … always mass in motion — always: this habitant Baroque — of course … fool, you are out of your mind, to forget the fact. But I didn't forget the reality … merely the phrase to label it, to dispense with the Knowing, to…. And don't forget that it is mass in motion. Flesh, whereas in Rapidomotion we are disembodied.

A queen drifts by on air … leaves me cold. I realize with uncharitable clarity that this is not what I want … it is not the homosexual that I want — no, not at all: because there is something decisive missing in these men, some final reality. Some … some what? — out with it, what is it? Some capacity to give. Some capacity for compassion. Something to give that has been gutted from them. It is the opposite of the man who lost his soul to gain the whole world: these men lost the whole world to gain their assoul … something like that. Somewhere, somehow, they are saints-manqué! Every one of them — I nearly said Every Mother's Son of Them … but even in that evaded ply of words there is a truth, a hidden Pietà — a son-slaughter.

Saints-manqué … there is the truth of it? But why? Why? Because they had to touch? Doubting Thomases all!? And every time they touch, they prove lost faith.

but they come so *close* to sainthood ... sooooo close: I feel it all around me. So close to a Communion of Saints. And then, falling short, they fall all the way ... they Fall. Leaving only the husk behind ... Real Presence bled white. Then White Mass become Black Mass.

Saints-manqué ... sainthood of the child lost, forever lost. Conscientiously children, forever — and in the conscience of it, a trickery, a failure to acknowledge, an evasion ... of the rest of life.

and in a world where there are no Saints, these become they ... the best we have. Saints-manqué who become Saints because ... because — because the Object died! Their life dedicated to proving the virulence of the Object proves only that it must be dying. Their faith asserted is the face of wizening Faith.

A Saint-manqué is better than a Cube-constipate
and a Cube better than a Square
and a Square better than
No-Man.
Amen.

No — it is not the homosexual I want ... it is the sentient man.

A new **kind** of man. The man who thinks at the end of his fingertips. Like the homos. And to this end I am prepared to take some cue from them ... just as I am prepared to admire and respect them for their dedication. Their dedication to Heaven, and their witness of Hell. And take some cue from them the way I take some cue from the heteros; or from the neuters — the professors, priests, psychiatrists. But I no more want to be mere homosexual than mere heterosexual.

thinking at the end of his fingertips: Word made Flesh — of course ... the kind of Man I want, must have ...

the Saint.

Nothing else matters.

The youth beside me works at CPR — a cleansed
Canadian Cube. Instinctively I look down on him. He reminds
me of my elder brother: mitigated Roundhead.
    The thought sins against him … I turn to make honourable
amends, to give…. But he has gone.

    slowly reconstruct the hall around me — conclude
with the tempestuous filth of the place. Oozes filth. But it is
accredited filth. Beatified filth. And the reconstruction achieved
I realize that I gained my vision … the missing vision — but I
lost my man, by default
    left to do only one thing — to La Place d'Armes. My
Place…. There in six minutes, walking, brisk down the Greyway,
up to Notre Dame Street, and in. Temperature: 21°. Instinctively
out to warm me, to the centre court of the Square — my rose
garden … that garden which descends in my eye's mind from
that site I had of it from twenty stories up, in the bank building
down upon it, when the snow was pathed across the court in
diagonals and skirted around Maisonneuve bold in the centre
    garden that descends direct from that rose garden devised
upon the sketch by Samuel de Champlain of his own garden,
at Port Royal, in 1604, and then, in 1608, at l'Habitation at
Québec, and which surely must have been the first planned
garden of which there is visual record in North America!
Rosegarden on granite, on Canadian Shield. Bitter beauty
    out then, into my rose garden now — snowgarden —
alone. To pluck the fruit … the roses, ignited upon those trees
that surround
    the central court, within the walls, the high walls of this
Christmas close here

out and breathe their fragrance that thunders into me
thunders, these little roses with thunder under their breath

reach out and pluck a red one rife to hand that burns burns
my hand open to its quick beauty burns

and I realize then that these roses are bright lights electric
on the candy-floss Christmas trees that circle the court and the
thunder is the bells tolling

I had not heard those bells. Only my roses that burn in
Canadian winter

bells are tolling

bells are tolling me
and the whole Place dances, convolutionary around my rose
garden still masquerading as Christmas trees this merry season
and bright

tolling while I watch the toll

of bellpull in me

till the Providence Life shuffles perceptibly

and the Brownstone Building bulges and rumbles beside, and

Brooom ... brooom ... brooom toll the bell
toll the bell in me, toll my bell

brooom ... brooom ... brooom — it is you Gros
Bourdon ... oh, all eight feet of your bellbottom brrooooms
... all twenty-four thousand seven hundred and forty pounds
of you pounding within me ... I wouldn't have believed it,
wouldn't have believed the guide book — but every inch of me
proves your weight

brooom ... brooom

Brownstone stomps, rippling now with a flush of brawn

while old Mommy Bank of Montreal broods complicit
chaperone over this impending rite

my Place dances, embracing me

oh, toll the bell, toll me ... Gros Bourdon
brooom

Brownstone lunges forward past the Leda neck of

Providence Life that snakes down into my Maisonneuve sneaks
into my rosegarden
    past all that candescent Christmas
    but only breaks its beak against the Ironsides of Brownstone
brawn flexed hard to breach my
    brooom brooom brooom goes Gros Bourdon
    Mommy Bank shifts uneasy at her site
    while Brownstone turns stern flush into me retreating
now in full flight of dignity into the Church, into the sound
sanctuary of Gros Bourdon Brownstone only held at the portals,
tumescent in desire
    while Mommy Bank remains implacably complicit …
        I've been had I've been had I've been had I start to hue
and cry, but stop in full halleluia — the Church, the Church …
I've just penetrated my Church and it is
    La Place d'Armes!
    and being in La Place I have been in the Church all the
time. In the Church in La Place in the Rosegarden of Eden
Rock in New-Old Montreal. Holy Mary Mother of God!
    roses still trumpet.
    Brownstone still broooms
    Gros Bourdon still thunders

    St. Maisonneuve — pray for me now and at my brownstoned
berth
    Order! I must get some order into this plenitude.
    Where is here? Peer out between my fingers still
roseburnt…. It is the Church — I can see that now. Definitely
the Church. And the Church is candescent, everywhere. No
part of it is quiescent now. Every inch of my flesh is bright with
it. From reredos to clerestory — ignited. Every inch sears light
along gilt of entrelac and finial….
    Find a cranny, a ledge, a shelf, to shadow me
        find shelter

Nowhere. The entire Church is bright as a Saint. No sanctuary
from Sainthood. No sanctuary and no quarter. None expected
… alas. Sit and burn in afterose … the whole Church-Place
gorging on my proffered credulity

     pray for the blondboy I lost
who somewhere now is imbedding   in thanksgiving

       Brownstone strumpets at the triple portal (beast … Holy
Bugger! — and the Mommy Bank sits vile on its strongbox!)

     I can withstand no more … must sortie — Sanctuary is as
rife as Sodomy

     Holy is Thy Name …

     out — skirting La Place, quickly … no one moves. Mommy
Bank, Brownstone, Providence Life, Presbytery, Maisonneuve,
rosetrees…. Everyone is in his annointed place.

     It is a trap.

     No — the Gros Bourdon has desisted. All is clear.
Thank God. I walk free down la rue Notre Dame, past l'Art
Sacré, past the Courthouses becalmed in the quick snowbright
night. It is 1:26 a.m. And all's well.

     … down past Lady Hamilton's Canadian Dildo … and Civic
High Altar, fall down La Petite Place, past my Hotel Nelson,
that I don't enter yet. Instinctively heading for the Greyway …
homefree, into it, plunging left along it, past Rasco's-where-
Dickens-slept — down to the Great White Elephant

     oh, you great ruminant beast — Leviathan … White
Whale … ahhh, that is it that is it. Moby! I knew it … I knew
that I only knew the part of it, that I had only grasped one half
of your person … Great White "Elephant" … that "eyed" me
as I descended the gut of the street to feed: eye of the White
Whale, of course, by the harbour, by the ships, where the sea
comes steep into my land.

     and Marché-Elephant-Leviathan is magnificent in me now.
And named, identified … I am safe with it — and can press on

walk along its façade, realize that I am somewhere else ...
that somewhere else is here. That feeling I had, several nights,
here. Stop, glance up — nightstars are all blue ciel ... Sainte
Chapel: the nave of Notre Dame de la Place d'Armes. Of
course — how could it be otherwise. Why have it any other
way, when I can have it this way?
when it is this way ... till rejected.

It is what I have always sensed, never dared merely know, till
now, thrust upon me under the very Eye of the White Whale —
sensed when I walked here, walked the Greyway, walked in the
Place, anywhere, that I have always been inside the Church that
was inside of me

and knowing this, know now that the Great White
Whale is but a reduction of this, a splendid one-sided
presentation of it — one wall of this greater reality ... and
that was what I realized in looking through that wall into
the bright nightlights of its offices, those nights ago. A
reduction of reality.... And all these reductions (always in the
name of reality), splendid in their own right, are simply the
munificence of the nave of the Church, spun out and spun out,
like the iron of the flank of the chairs in the board room of
the Harbour Building ... to infinity.

Walk on. Cock of this Walk. Whistling ... loud and louder.
Whistling as I never did before. (Gentlemen don't whistle!) And
singing. Who never sang. Sing, because I cannot now prevent
me. "When you are in love, it's the loveliest night of the year...."

my whistle, my song sprout out from my startled mouth
limning the Calvet House straight ahead of me, limning each
sash and ledge, limning them fleshing in this outline of lintel
and edge till the house stands full-formed afront my song that
ricochets from this rebirth up Bonsecours Street, along the
Greyway, front and back, giving birth to line and form to the
entire quarter in me, till with twenty bars of whistle and shout it
all stands Body and Blood in me.... Object Incarnate

306

rampant thigh of the Lesser Sphinx lunges up my flank
and is the bawdy baroque of Eden Rock of happy memory ...
plunge down between its dark bulk and the cleancut stoneware
of the Market, to the front ... where Elevator #1 (or is it #11)
rides high galleon in me.

The port is asleep.

The Church is asleep.

The Market is asleep ... with its blinded neoneyes blaring
silent at us all

But the entire Place is alive in me, living in me, avid in me ...

the flesh of my whistle-and-song falls over the Church and
Market, Sphinx and Whale ... marrying Catholic and Protestant,
High Incarnation and Low Chastity

watch the infusion ... the Baroque bawdy of Church
immersing Lord Burlington's disembodied Palladianism: a site
for sore eyes ...

then scramble back up the cliffthighs of this fusion into the
Greyway now all white in snowfleck, back into this embodied
echo of my outblurt ... back down the Whiteway — back into
the Body and Blood of my song.

Oh — I need all of you ... all of you, to love.

I need Great White Elephant and Bonsecours Sphinx
and Greyway-gone-White, and High Altar de Ville, and Low
Chateau de Ramezay and La Banque mère (vile two-timing
bitch that you are, in court dress)

and la rue St. Jacques, entire, unmolested,

and Delmos and le Vieux St. Gabe

and Lady Hamilton's Dildo and La Plaçe des Arts
(everybody's artistic anti-body)

I need Habitant and Half-beat

and Cube and Square-Root of Cube and Civil Servant
(many are interchangeable)

and Revolutionary and Presbyterian and Methodist and
Catholic

and Homosexual and Heterosexual and Asexual
Priest, Citizen, Brother and Sister
Notre Dame
Place d'Armes
All of this is only just enough
only just enough
to love in my land.

Back in my room. Fold carefully away into me the Ancients
and the Moderns. And collapse abed. The Place taken, and lost,
and taken again. I have consummated, withal ...

2:30 a.m. And still no novel ... I must begin again ... must
go on in it. I am ready now.

DAY NINETEEN

The self-absorption of the Anglo-Canadian ... this black (or is it white) narcissism ... this process of imbibing oneself by suppressing oneself. In any case, it is compounded narcissism and inverted narcissism combined ...

and then he was wide awake. And dressing ... as though for his first communion. Which is what it was. Surely. Dress carefully, clean white shirt, black oxfords, suit, gold and blue handkerchief ...

and out to the Church — confronted by a hobo of the quarter as he left the very hotel: his Anglo-Canadian heart hardened appropriately, his eyes closed, and he brushed by — but the request of the drunk followed him all the way to the Church, hounded him ... and he knew even that he couldn't buy off his conscience with a little welfare any more. It nearly spoiled his morning. But by the time he reached that final Mannerist limestoned canyon of Notre Dame St., the Baldaquin just before the Place, he had been thawed by the bells ... he no longer felt the fact that it was 20°F ... he resounded warmly ... as last night — Gros Bourdonned. Yes — it was going to happen despite him. He ducked quickly into the Church — it was already on 11 a.m. A few minutes before High Mass. And worked his way dazed down the right-hand aisle, to his position just in front of the episcopal box. And awaited. Nervous. Uncertain. Changed seats ... went back further ... he was too close. He didn't want to see details, he wanted to imbibe the whole.... He dropped back ten rows. And sat expectantly, on the edge of his seat.

Already the processional had occurred without him....And already now the priest was sermonizing ... "l'amour sans l'exigence me diminue" ... these were the only words, only specific words he heard. They homed into him like bullets...."Love without any demands diminishes me...." It summarized his three weeks in La Place. It defined them. He remembered vaguely the priest talking of the necessity of penitence ... but in fact what he really heard listening to the sermon was not the priest but the Church. The priest was really voicing the Church ... the body of the Church ... was corporally its mouthpiece. He bespoke the Church. And in so doing he had the ear of the Church ... he was the ear.... It was confusing — but clear. And in listening to the sermon and thus earing the Church, he saw the Church with decisive clarity. Each phrase of the priest's body clarified the body of the Church and his own body. What the priest said was how he said it. It would have been foolish merely to follow the words with his brain ... a completely ignorant act. A deliberate act of falsification — of evasion, of self-evasion.... It would have been a total flight from truth. And yet — and this was only vaguely in him now — he knew that his whole university education, his whole high-school education ... had been this flight. He couldn't go into that now ... his mind was elsewhere. It was on the realization that last night had been his first communion. Last night had reconstituted and consecrated communion in him ... already.... This was suddenly terribly clear in him ... perhaps it was that bell signalling the Body and Blood of Christ, that was suddenly the drum last night in a bodyblurt when he had not known it was the communion bell, just as he knew with implacable certitude now.

the Church imperceptibly and quickly, like a movie camera moving in and out and back into a new focus, the Church suddenly shifted focus — moved both in and beyond him.... All around him soft beautiful menacing eruptions were people sifting forward through him to the communion rail ... it was that medieval landscape again, wherein everything moves and has intense being, and is infinitely potent. They were sifting him forward into themselves. He sat still ... his mind sent him a comparative message: these people were moving in the same kind of way, with the same kind of immeasurable easy order as they had danced in the nightclub. With the same kind of irrational implacable logic as the montage in the Catholic Religious Shop.... It was an infinitely complex, rich, harmony — and accomplished so spontaneously. Whereas in an Anglican Church it was all done row by row, people were on parade ... they lined up ... a trooping of their colours.

his eyes followed the refocusing of the Church in him ... it was, at first, as though his eyes were glazing over. As though the objects were disappearing, blurring ... he was losing the Object again ... And then he realized it was no longer in objective relationship with it ... it had penetrated him, and at the same time, it projected him from him, infinitely. It was not confusion ... it had become profusion — again, he was married to what he saw....And his mind sent another little message through to this new world ... "your eyes are simply out of focus." But he knew that this glazing was a new focus ... and that it was both real, and permanent.

his eyes handled the altar, the high altar, the reredos ... down the thigh of Christ Crucified, down the back of the Madonna ... down to the door of the Tabernacle, and he found himself walking into the door through ... and found himself in the Place d'Armes — specifically in the Place ... and looking up, skyward it was no longer day, but night, starstuttered, and he saw that it was the nave of the Church that overvaulted La Place ... and that he was astride them all, and that they were indissolubly in his entrails.

there was no use trying to explain that to himself. It was all he could do to live it and know it. All he could do to acknowledge the fait accompli.

it was like a world of interwoven concentricities. Spheres in spheres.

he saw the altarbox again ... he was coming back out the door to join himself, and he realized that he would meet himself halfway at the communion rail as he knelt and stared at the high altar and saw that that landscape into which he had walked from a hundred feet away, that corruscation of rocks and hillocks up which he had clambered, straight and always up high hill to tower over the acceding land, which recalled Pierrot's body, he saw that this was a cluster of angels winged around the Host. But he didn't have any further time ... Corpus Christi, le corps du Christ ... le corps du Christ ... was thrust into his open mouth and clung to the nave of his mouth, as he stumbled back to his seat, the corpus still there ... still bread, still infinitely finite bread, tasteless, sullen swelling into disintegration on the roof of his mouth.... He sat disappointed in himself ... disgusted almost ... realizing what he had done. What he was doing. Pillaging someone else's cookies.... He wanted to spit the bread out, but it kept disintegrating despite him ... and he swallowed it to dispose of it. And looked up to see if he had been noticed ... and as he looked up the nave was on him again, was immense around and over and in him ... was illuminated in him again as it had been illuminated last night.... It all rubbed his eyes ... and he found himself exploring the space about him, mounting the gilt entrelacs of the pillars, jumping from finial to finial upside under the balcony, flowing from bay to bay, falling up the path of sunbright, impaled on the Gothic turretings of the reredos (just to the left of the Passion ... that saint he didn't know) — impaled ... and then back out through the tabernacle door again.... He kept roving, intact, and absolutely omnipotent through the body of his Church.

and then he knew that it had all happened despite himself. Against himself. Despite the fact that he thought he knew it. And he remembered that he had swallowed the bread — to dispose of it. Swallowed the swollen bread ... because it hadn't been B & B — and now, quite simply it was B & B — had given him back B & B at the very moment when he denied it. He remembered at the altar now ... that he had renounced any hope of taking it by assault ... had renounced that, and giving up, his body had relented, and there had been that inept decongestion attendant upon his submission, decongestion that had been tumescent in his throat ... so that he had been had, had given himself by giving himself up for lost. And then, that occurring, he was transubstantiated — had been given back B & B ... given back everything ...

he couldn't take too much of this realization ... and he pressed himself to talk to Père Amyot ... they sat together in the Baptistry painted by Ozias Leduc — Holy Art Nouveau and seeing this work by a French Canadian he remembered the huge Plamondon Stations of the Cross, also done for this Church, in the 1830's — but they had been too powerful for the Church fathers who had commissioned Italians ... so now the flaming Plamondons graced the English Canadians' museum which he regretted ... the père was listening, trying to situate this young man! "But we no longer think in terms of heretics, and schismatics ... all that is over ... we are brothers, that was the genius of Pope Jean XXIII...." And Hugh was confronted again with the fact of a new Christendom, a new brotherhood of men, a new love ... and somehow he felt betrayed from his hate: just at the moment when he was prepared to renounce his hate, that renunciation was taken from him. And he knew that wouldn't do — he couldn't get away with that.

He was stammering now.... "I can't explain it ... it is the Protestant Hell — we have inverted Heaven and Hell ... we have worshipped Hell as our Heaven ... our guarantee of Heaven. And now, because of that, we have to live it out ... have to pay our way with flesh out of the Hell we smugly established as our guarantee of purity...."

The père was talking again ... "did you come to the 12:30 Mass last night ... it is our most beautiful service ... 2,500 people ... perhaps the most beautiful in North America...." Hugh listened incredulous, his head reeling ... that was what he had missed ... that was why the Church had been so completely illuminated.... So he *had* had his first communion last night ... he had lived it, and missed it.... He couldn't withstand any more.... He was out in the Place now ... it was there only cursorily — that Place which this morning of all mornings was to have been triumphant, was merely a shadow in him ... merely shadowed him.... Once again, then, he had fallen into impasse — had achieved neither the one thing nor the other.... He stopped at Le Restaurant des Gouverneurs, shaking with cold. It was 18°. He was depressed enough to take notes ... minor penance.

radio organs ad for new Montreal housing development ... the voice barrelling straight from the testicles ... that deep diaphragmatic surge of voice that sounds some gelder's sermonizing — sermon from the fount. But it is blenderized sperm! And then muzak (which *is* blenderized sperm) — Muzak: really a music of consolation for the lost testicles, the lost life — a music of mourning ... singing not for joy but at joy lost. Singing, if the truth were known, at once to forget and to commiserate. All the satisfaction of a middle-class funeral parlour on vacation. (Muzak will put those parlours out of business because it obviates the fact of death). Muzak — the proxy plenitude. But it cannot, alas, fool me now — it merely beats my vacuum into synthetic whipped cream. "The world's best loved music" mourns cheersomely on....

I keep trying to see out the window that gapes blankly at me ... to see the panorama — Hotel de Ville, Nelson

Monument, Chateau de Ramezay, dome of the Great White
Elephant....And as I look I understand why I don't know
whether I see anything or not outside — because while the
Place still tolls in me, yet in here I hear nothing ... the muzak
merely gives me the impression of earing. And that known ...
the outer denizens are deep in me ... back in their wonted
place. And they thus deep in their place, I suddenly shift into
mine ... I am back in my Cubicle! My box. Identified by what
I see and the way I see it. The muzak is meaningfulfilling now ...
and for a moment I share this posthumous dream of a return to
normalcy. I wonder if my wife is well ... if my daughter passed
her music exam ... if ... Peg O' My Heart — muzak pumps
more spermicide. I remember playing that piece at parties ...
and as I remember I also realize that I had learnt the music to
such pieces as an annotation of the words, as an accompaniment
to the words. The words came first — the music was an
afterthought. Whereas in La Place — that Place which I have
sought and disastrously won, and lost — in La Place the music,
the belltoll, sited the Square....

Looking out the window again ... looking in my
window ... the buildings have again seceded from their proper
placement ... seceded? — or acceded to that no-man's-land
again. The very echo of the bell of La Place in me suffices to
collapse my 3-Dimensional card-castlement....

The pudgy eyes of the proprietor take on a look of enforced
"benevolence." And I see that a poor habitant elder has entered
... looking for warmth. There is the same "oversite" in those
proprietorial eyes, as in English Canadians' eyes when confronted
with the obscene ... the same evasive evasion of the obscene....

Look again out into the windowscape. Is it out, or in, or
both, or neither? I am nowhere!

... phone Rick — make a return engagement. My desire
to crush him is my own desire to free me from that of which I
accuse him.... Foul play.

At 7 p.m. Pierre Godin is at the hotel ... not many minutes
after I finish his novel, *La Foire aux Puces* ... Luc was right —
it is a startling complement to my own "novelette," my own
demission, adventure. Pierre's free flight from the irrelevance
of day-to-day, into homicide, into the reacquired right to
kill — rather than to be dead alive, rather than to die living....
His personal uprising, insurrection. And most weird, yet most
understandable, his enemy, his target and victim, and vanquisher
— alias John Troyer — it is me ... my kind of English Canadian,
that Pierre so patently loves as much as hates. It strikes me three-
quarters of the way through the book.... Pierre is pursuing Troyer
to kill him because he loves him — because he covets him body
and soul. And because he oh so wants to be loved, body and soul,
by Troyer ... quite specifically Pierre veut se faire enculer par
Troyer. Oh — weird weird — because I am here to proffer myself
to the French Canadian. In belated expiation and release. Here
of my own accord, freely ... and not sent by Order-in Council
nor by Parliamentary Committee nor sub-committee nor ad hoc
committee-in-permanence, I am here because I must be, because
I love my people and my land. And because nothing can prevent
my love nor replace it. Nothing (much less the Canada Council
for All-Canadian cultivation)! I am here despite all concerted
effort to kill my love, to kill all love in my people, to kill all care
of joy, I am here, despite ... despite the buggering of us all by
craven Parliamentary default — ah, what can be worse than
buggery by default, by abdication in the name of power? Am
here to return Pierre's need, each unknown to the other. Because
what Pierre doesn't realize is that his Troyer needs to be taken, in
his turn, by the French Canadian. Needs to proffer himself of his
own will — needs to give ... and then take, compassionately. But
which is it, precisely: am I here to bugger or be buggered — here
because I have been buggered or because I have buggered? Think
man! No! — feel! Your assoul will tell you. Ahh ... the answer is
so clearly both. Thanx be to God.

So, Pierre will be here in minutes. I will make him come up ... be his Troyer ... because that is who I am — I, the proffered Anglo-Canadian Cube ... here to deconstipate my Cube-squared ... my C2 — Cul carré. Pierre up ... enter; I want to kiss him on the forehead. But we are both abruptly wary, shy because suddenly aware, each and both of us, without a word said, that it is for real — that I am Troyer, and Pierre is ... is La Place d'Armes ... so it is true ... we **are** chers ennemis. And a worthy enemy is my best friend. My only hope for resurrection ... for that incitation to redemption. We talk, surrounding us with a warm belt of words that is the converse of a chastity belt ... it envelopes us in an embodiment — a corporeality that obviates instant need to reach out and touch us ... it obviates phallicity by imbedding us absolutely in each other ... talking up a wordwomb that conjugates us.... And then save us from the Hotel — to Les Filles du Roi ... and settle in to Chablis and seafruit (how much more lush — "fruits de mer" than "seafood" — the difference of a people, a culture, a sensibility ... I'm seafruity!) ... Pierre opposite me ... the real confrontation — le très cher ennemi ... le très cher! — ten times better than le très honorable! This, the man who would kill me, who tried to kill me his months past, his generations past ... Pierre — $10,000 and one sanity mortgaged ... his price paid so that he can see: that's what his novel cost him in dollars and sense; that lucidity of insanity. "He whom the Gods love they first drive mad...." Oh that they had loved me a little more deeply ... would that they had insanitized me, my assoul, more profoundly.... But as it is. Pierre has already eaten.... He is simply feeding me ... and Chablissing.... My God, he is there — so absolutely there.... There the way those early saints are there, in the Byzantine mosaics, in the twelfth and thirteenth century illuminations ... in those first insites of Giotto.... Incalculably there — candescent. The first man I have ever met who is utterly present in me, with me.... And I know his secret — because it is my own....And I know that I can talk with him....

"What gives me courage is what I call my life insurance...." Pierre looks at me — he knows what I am going to say — "the fact that I am at any moment prepared now to kill ... and to kill myself, to suicide — citizen's suicide! This gives me absolute control — permits absolute **présence**. No one can prevent me from giving what I need to give ... no one can prevent me from loving." Pierre laughs — divinely ... because we both know: "Absolument, mon cher ... j'ai cette assurance vie, chez un ami, en bouteille — assez pour tuer vingt hommes ... en vingt minutes...." Our life insurance ... mon assurance vie ... assuring me of life! That is the guarantee I hold against all the cripplement of my society ... I stake my life against my right to love ... the way I need to love. The security of suicide. And now, with Pierre, the security of suicide in common!

And as I talk to him, I know why I have not suicided weeks ago — why I did not, that first time, after lunch with Eric, when my Cul carré was penetrated by the brownstone building — and I saw the world as it is ... as the saints, and all those oh so holy sinners saw it in the brilliance of the Dark Ages. I did not suicide then because it would be negative suicide — flight, and fear. Whereas now, this assurance-vie is a positive suicidality — it is affirmation, for joy: truly Citizen's Charter!

Pierre — "no man who does not hold his own life, daily, in his hands, is free, is a man...."

Over Pierre's shoulder the bartender cocks my ear ... and I see. And the Chablis sings. God bless habitant cretons that I savour now steep in our truthsomeness.

I blurt us on ... "and holding my own life in my hands, I hold the life of whomsoever I talk in my hands ... I hold the eternal capacity to kill — the right to kill, which alone permits the right to love. People sense that now when I meet them ... it may be the last sense that they have — this sense that their life is in question."

And then, this common ground known, we are free to foray into the outer world that we share inside us....

"It all comes down to the courage to confront your own cock.... If you don't, you are dead ... that is where René has failed...."

Pierre's body is high undulance approving my words now.... His whole being tidal in acquiescence ... like some modern danceman accompanying our shared verity. "Bien entendu — René's new novel shows it mercilessly — he comes so close, so terrifyingly close — terrifying for him — and for me reading it, because somehow he evades it, shies clear of life. He is afraid of his own cock...." And as Pierre talks I discover the unstated fact — and outblurt it — "René — c'est une Reine-manquée ... no, worse! Because he could have succeeded. He's a Reine-ratée!" Pierre gurgles in his wineglass ... "C'est vrai...."

"I will put it to him ... I lunch with him Tuesday ... if he denies his own cockiness, he dies. He becomes impotent...."

Pierre — "I wouldn't dare ... but you can — you are from outside in now. Il te redoute...."

"I sense that — he avoids me. I know that he is afraid of me ... I sense that with many people now...."

"once you have assurance-vie people fear you. They know you are dangerous. That you menace their still-life."

"but all you quiet revolutionnaires ... it is the same ... you are all homosexuals-ratés ... men half-cocked. René is a supreme case. You are the only one who knows your sentience, honours its livelihood. The crime is to be half-cocked. To have gone off on half-cock; as escape from the deeper truth.... And afraid of homosexuality they kill their homosentience, and killing their homosentience, they kill their capacity to love ... and leave us adrift to tabulate the implications of this incomplete revolution."

We go down the names ... René, Luc, Louis ... all the same. Their art is their evasion. And their evasion kills their art.

"they become fonctionnaires des arts! — Civil Servants of the arts ... cinéastes, televizors, radiophonies....All Fédérastes!"

"that is the potence of you démissionaire....Your demission is your puissance."

"you're right ... what was at stake was my manhood. They were after my balls ... had already forced a mortgage on them."

And then we are gone....As we walk back along the Greyway I remonstrate us ... "if we are to make our case we cannot suicide ... not yet ... or else we can be passed off as merely crazy. Each day is a day gained. For us."

"that is why I undertake future commitments ... that I want to honour...."

Pierre has left. We had come as close as humans can come — and lived ... lived because of it. We had hit the rockbottom, the fundament of the new logic in us. The right to live founds upon the right to die the right to die — for joy.

It was cold. Hugh walked along to the Square, and then, at the last moment, sidestepped it. In five minutes he was at Eden Rock.... He was "on duty" again. Assholy. The blond boy of Saturday night was not there, of course (he had thought he might be. Truth is so persistently stranger than fiction). Sat, and watched the kept queens ... he was getting to know the harems, the ménages. At closing he had picked up another $5 investment, from Ste. Agathe ... André Germain. Age 18. Blond beatlenik. Fed him. Three others joined them....All the intimacy of their illicitude. A Portuguese clasped Hugh's hand to his cock, under the table, in the restaurant. And then he took André back to his hotel.... Gave him his $5, and said he could go if he wished ... André stayed. For an hour they talked. He was an orphan. Had been in Montreal for a month. Couldn't get work ... got men. English Canadians, lawyers — picked them up Au Nouveau Monde. Young lawyers. Some were OK. The last one — two nights before — had been maniacal.... Had sucked him five times dry in the night.... And then they were abed. André's lean body was benediction. It was all Hugh really needed. The human body, alive, accessible. Ecce homo. The rest, once again, was accessory, once the embodied human had been restituted thus. But there was the obeisance to make. And he knew that he had to make it. Had to honour that need to stoop, to carnal fealty, to humility, to be humiliated, and to crown himself a kingdom again. André's phallicity was understandably tired. But it responded to his lips ... Hugh balked as he mouthed it. Was it really necessary to do this? And then he knew again it was, and thrust himself wholehog onto the cock, foreskin unravelled to flower the cocktree till André was risen and the rood deep into Hugh's high humiliation. It was life, a life, given and taken. Carnivoracious charity. Till André took Hugh's head like a buttock and thrust steep onto him his life haemorrhaging against Hugh's gullet like the rich farewell of a Côte de Nuits....Then it was his turn to die into life, as André squatted over his forbidden flower — that was it ... flowering the forbidden phallus. André clearly enjoyed it ... did it with gust. Head down into the rood ... and then up, till his lips cupped the cockhead and tongue haloed them ... Hugh watched this livewireness on him till abruptly André's suction steepened, and with one hand he cupped Hugh's balls, drew up with his mouth in a single stroke that decapitated ... Hugh lay cleansed again — the sensation was one of deconstipation ... of purification. And as he lay he realized that he had been hearing the bells of La Place deep inside him....Le Gros Bourdon!

They talked awhile longer ... André unravelled the life of the Main to him ... explained the heirarchy of clubs....At the top the meeting place for white English lawyers ... and CBC. Then, two blocks east, the middle-class mixed bar ... it sounded like Irish Catholic plus well-heeled New Canadians. Then the French-Canadian nightspot, for salesmen, and clerks. And Eden Rock — très peuple (the best flesh, said André). The same "vertical mosaic" as on the entry door to Rick's office. It held true ... save that here the pecking order was inverted: best flesh was bottom of the legal list, and top in fact.

"But where do you fit in?" André asked, quizzical. Hugh laughed, uneasily — "oh — I'm a Métis ... Methodist-Presbyterian—Anglican Celt!"

"Are you Canadian?" André pursued with kind concern.

"By definition!" Hugh laughed.

"English-Canadian?" said André hopefully.

"There is no such thing ... there are French Canadians and there are Scottish Canadians ... the rest are in the melding pot. Canada is Scotland's revenge!"

André sat up and gazed into Hugh's eyes: "You are running away from the Scottish Canadians! ... I can understand you now. My grandmother was Scotch."

"That is why you speak English so well."

"Oui!" — and they both laughed.

"But why are you here?" André was disastrously persistent.

"Because you have the key ... the key we lost...." Hugh didn't entirely understand the reply he was making. But he had the sensation, at once disturbing and satisfying, that André did ... and he eyed this overgrown gamin who held the key to his kingdom. Could he trust him....

"We quite often have visitors from Toronto ... they go to the white English lawyers' bar ... in bed they are different. They just go through the motions, but there is nothing in them. They do it so seriously for fun...." André was appallingly pertinent.

And then they were asleep, easily, back to bareback.

The world was alive again in Hugh.

DAY TWENTY

traingrunt shunts me awake ... a clock tower knocks four
a.m. into me ... André is up, at the dresser ... at my wallet!
What a fool I am ... no — I deliberately emptied wallet before
imbedding with him; all my money hidden in waistcoat, in
the cupboard. Not a dollar in wallet. Let him be ... he's only
digging for another bone. Has no morality.... None of the
goddam Canayens do — not deep down.

Watch him, curious ... watch this man balked for pilfer. His
lean back to me limned by moonbright cusping his buttock —
clean bite of flesh. Can see the goose pimplery on him, rippling
taut skin. My nose tells me it's cold.

André turning ... glimpse him through shy closed eye slyly.

As he turns ... moon beaming his crisp fleshment turning
slowly in the cold toward me, catches his cocknose high
up right-thigh. Christ — he's risen ... hard on rood — in
that cold,

while he pilfers my empty purse.

walks calm, pursued by moonwhite, around bed-end
— noble thief ... so calm, to bedside and inserts himself —
indelible chastity — beside me, his cold flesh reeking heat rolls
against me cupping my upright back ... cups my back while
cock finds easy placement nuzzling in thighs to undersack,
tipping my own insurrection, then slowly withdrawing back
till cocknose kisses my assoul ... Judas kiss! — as I clench to
smite the Philistine ... and clenching tight to strike sense the
sin in the blow not yet thrown, stop me short.

Why hit him?

Why? — because this man's taken your money and now wants to bugger you....

I roll over, playing for insight...."Et puis, tu te réveille, André?"

"Oui — je sens bien maintenant ... et toé?" His hand finds me risen and takes mine to him soft along the firm flesh he proffers so easily. Mind reels ... as I seek solution to this. What is being done? Who is being done? ... What has to be done? Something seethes me steep ... if only I can wait to know — to be sure of it. Moon catches André eye on me instantly in as I open, turn over onto him, and ply his proffer

eye still in me unbending ... the eye will tell me, tell us — follow the eye, by ear ... follow

André's cock brushes my assmouth as eyeballs startle

"J'ai jamais fait ça ... tu veux?" Broom brrroooom brooom ... "tu veux?"

cock bright at assoul

tu veux

too bright, room is too bright. But lights are out. Brownstone shunts forward.... La Place, present, implacable concision.... Mommy Bank purse-lipped watching

clench shut. Tight. Cockthrust

prangs.

No.... Non, pas ça. And roll me over on my stomach to rest ... to withdraw as La Place eludes my sight.

Dark all around me dark. Save at the bottom of La Petite Place, where it is light.... Elevator #11; turn right — LORRANGER ET FILS, MARCHANDISES (I don't remember that sign!).

frill of cast-iron balconies on rusticated façade of house beside — Sydney lace it's called in Australia whence it was shipped as ballast to adorn the homes of Sydney Merchants already made, and in New Orleans de même.... And this then is Montreal lace!

At the far end of the Front the fire station, straight out of a Dutch still-life, on the site of the Old Parliament Building

that we burnt in derision at impending democracy (I am the
last Tory!)

as I turn to look back up Commissioners Street my man
comes toward me from far end ... comes toward that National
Harbour Building, for police I think ... at last, my man — but
does he know? That Harbour Building.... Shouts me out to
him — "watch out"

yellow brick iron-clasped by black lintels and dentilation
"Watch out!" — and my shout identifies that Building
that I knew was lethal...."Watch out ... it's Seaton Delaval....
Seeeeatttonnn Deeellaaavaaaalll ... de Laval"

of course. That is who that building is. Thank God I know
in time ... to warn him ... unmasked in time. SeatonDelaval
—Vanbrugh's own Folly — most dangerous home ever built in
England — puts mass into motion ... emotivates substance —
rampant flesh. Utterly Un-English!

and this is a Canadian mutation of Seaton D. — Methodist
variant, High Methodist ... Well, they **couldn't** have known
what they were doing

but that man, coming at me, flouting Seaton Delaval to its
face is

Me ... and I am scouting round the end of Grain Elevation
to the Harbourside (I never dared that before ... always intended
only) — looking me out over the Saint Lawrence to l'Ile St.
Hélène — where those building for our Centennial Expose arise

two worlds in the palm of my hand — Expo and (I turn to
look at Great White Elephant ...) — but that Other World isn't
in site — the Grain Elevation obtrudes

someday we must remove it, turn it on its side, bury it ...
bomb it

so that we have our River of Canada back in view, mediator
between these two worlds afronting each the other

shouting "give us back our River sight" — shouting
as I listen to me from La Pointe de Callières where we first

inhabited Montreal under Louis XIV and hear me at this
intersection of the two worlds of us —

"Give us back our River site!"

And then I am retreating back around Grain Elevation,
stumble, half-fall — turn my binoculars from La Pointe de C.
onto this event of me and instantly perceive who is predator as
amassed body of Notre Damned Sphinx de Bonsecours shifts
forward formidable into my harbour — her sternum abruptly
forward bringing the mountain down to the seaside in ships
that her new front now is rising high in me with Our Lady
of All Help skywise above holding the world of this circuit in
homage while the sullen face of Great White Elephant remains
untouched unmoved unwitting beside … its Egyptian portals
always correctly impenetrable!

But I am running now, for the river wall, jumping over
greywall witholding the Old River of Canada when the
Harbour once rode right into the Sphinx Sternum of My
Lady of Bonsecours, once lapped right up to the gaiters of
Marché Militant

running till I am at the Quai Jacques Cartier climbing up
into his Little Place climbing climbing to the very root of Lady
Hamilton's Canadian Dildo

"Stop stop stop" I shout at me

as André tongues down my backbone down the spinal
column as the Front quakes along my shudder of life from neck
to backnape praise be to God

hot lipped along this Outer World that holds the Inner
Circuit in place around La Place around the Nave of Notre
Dame de La Paroisse de tout le peuple canadien

tongue outlining building and harbour and road and sign
and monument … concrete tongue procreating the reality of
this Outer World that I thought I never saw and never would
but must have despite me all André's tongue down my body's
bone I flinch

"Tu n'aime pas ça?" — André is incredulous hurt

"Oui j'aime … il faut aimer…. il faut …" as Greyway
follows on our heels….

"il faut aimer … aimeraimeraimer" — André hot lickety-
splitting into siteseethe of the Inner Circuit

ITEM — Chagouamigon Lane … all the beauty in that
name

ITEM — the first building to the east of the High Altar,
on rue Notre Dame … it is so clearly obeisance to the
high altar itself … counterpointing Mansard Roof, high
pilastering, French Chateau facing

ITEM — thunder along the Greyway is stonerumble of
rough face rustication — conscientious vermiculations
— nothing to do with nostalgia but much ado with
thunder of stone wrought as cast-iron should —
Lambert et Fils, propriétaires….

ITEM — the blackbirds shimmering treetips afront
Ostell's scandalized Courthouse (imagine a choir of
lawyer … in tree loft!)

ITEM — the large FOR RENT sign plaqued over the
main door of the Scottish Life Building … memento
more! Someday it will be over the still unbuilt new
Banque Canadienne Nationale

ITEM — item — item beads along my vertebrate
rosary — simultaneous halo this Inner World rim
around me rosy … all warm in the circuit.

around and around my world, tailspin, headspin in halo
of room that suntingles my fingers on our pillow as André's
hands clasp each buttress of my street and tongue high-tailing
inner circuit thrusts into La Place of me deep in to mate the
underside of Lady Hamilton's Canadian Dildo …

silent in the night, silent in the Quarter, silent at the port of
entry to my nation, silent in all my land

and silence as I turn and am thrust unthinking down the

gut of the Street of Our Lady of the Greater Sphinx, past
Ostell's choralled Courthouse and its Palais-in-the-making,
      past the neoneyeballs of Boulevard St. Laurent
      deep past the convulsing groin of Baldaquin
      past the bas-relief of Providence Building whose
buttocks pry in me ... thrust steep into the unwitting Place
where Brownstone Banque Canadienne Nationale is heinously
alive in me larger than life, its coil of floral high relief at portal
deep gutting me in florid incarnation

    God those Victorians were buggers! All of them ... that had
any Man in them.

    Floral recoil faces me....

    Yes buggers you were!

    and more precise — the accolade can be given in full —
you were soft sodomites! and not hard ... you liked the
    floral relief founders in La Place again,
        coil and recoil
    you liked the Object in La Place ... but you didn't like to
place the Object — froward that would be. Ungenteel!

    Don't ask me to explain ... it is all I can do to Know —
one day I'll explain, condemning me thus to forget. But let me
Know for now

    Brownstone floral release ... and I meander me around
the garden of La Place ... the garden of the 1880s, from the
hoarding of the new gutless rising Banque Canadienne (no
floral relief, low or high — a mere hip slickster it — stick and
run: no art to the Object ... no roses and no Eden Garden
to implant)

    meander that earlier garden with its sheathe of trees around
Maisonneuve

    and the iron fence around both. The Brownstone verity of
us all: the Object in Place ... in La Place, ironclad but in ... in
La Place in the Garden

    whereas now pauvre Maisonneuve, denuded stands all stark

in this garden of stone with appliqué underbrush that
no-man could ever implant.

It takes brownsoil to push up rosebeds!

this cold garden of contemporary stone — horrendous
infertility: thus Eden lost and then refound and lost again under
my very nose ... miniature ossification

(like the painting in La Boutique that was ... ahhh — that
was what it was: that tableau d'Angluche — a rendering of the
stonegarden of my lost Place ... garden of stone for a Square. I
have but to wait and everything comes home in my roost!)

Of a sudden cool snow in La Place ... flowing, snow
eddying gusts in La Place ... cool snow melting in my nostrils,
seeping into me ... snow everywhere repoussé, rehaussé by
snow ... every edge and ledge and lintel. Snow seared. Winter
thunderstorm. And the rich furrowed earth of Brownstone
covered in the smelt of snowseed is my Ontario land out the
window of the Rapido as I left my Other City a chastity ago
... is my Ontario garden given and received in La Place ... is
the voice of La Bolduc rampant Au Fournil, singing Le Petit
Bonhomme au Nez Pointu.

I always had a weakness for M. Duplessis! Or at least since
his successors proved themselves Hommes-sans-nez, sans flair,
sans-tu-sais-quoi-Monsieur. M. Duplessis's great nose ... son
suivez-moi-mesdames-messieurs ... and I reach up and pull
André's nose handsome deep into me....

"Follow your instincts," said the Royal Canadian Commissar,
with that sweet lisp of his body that proved only that he hadn't
and still wishes he had....

"Pull that fucking nose"

And I pull it deep

deep into La Place where I am pulled ... surging into the
core of it, dancing on the point of Maisonneuve's baton ...

brooom brooom brooom ... goes Gros Bourdon

shunkshunkshunk the trainshunt

"Pull that fucking...."

soft snow along my face, down my nostrils ... slush at my feet

"Maudit Angluche ... maudit angluche ... je t'aime enfin."
Brownstone recedes ... snow vanishes ... La Place remains
aglow in me. André lies beside me, exspent, recoiling along
my perimeter.

"Maudit Angluche"

"Yes."

"You gave it back to me...."

"Yes ... I gave it back to you ... to all of you."

"... my land ... you gave it back to us then, didn't you?"

"Yes — the land, the garden ... I had to; I needed to...."

silence in the rosegarden, in La Place, in their City

silence ... and still La Place glows — and within La Place
the nave of Church, and therein high altar, and on high altar,
the monstrance holds my Host ... B & B — Body and Blood
there, that I haven't yet taken ... there to be eaten — Word
made Flesh....

André reaching for my Host in hand ... implants me deep
over into him ... my Host touching his Body ... touches
Blood ... blood down the body, red, and I lunge for the give
and taking

cockthrusting into his cocksack, sear in the coil of hair
under and filches asshole, cockthrusting André lifts his legs up
wide open to Notre Dame ... open widening as my Holyrood
takes his cup

thrust into the open way — assrim bites my hothead, bites,
to thrust cock lost deep in the nave now....Yes they were all
buggers ... all of them, us, cockthrusting

André's eyes wide on me, ripping us open as his Host rises
on my bellying rises Cockrobin stiff to mate my rood in him

processional in his nave, bearing the cross

his cock flushes my navel that I avid stoop to kiss and I
am out of his nave (can't have your Host and eat it too!) —
smell of Marc de Bourgogne, furrow of land, plowed black in
springburst.

André recoils over to stomach … cocks left leg up to take
my sperm-slick cock against his portal, slither through the sharp
mesh of hairy sitessee and implant the rosebed again

thrustworthy till his buttresses pillow my balls that groan us
in counterpoint — diaphonal

thrust and counterthrust … fresh odour of Marc (I always
knew Marc was manmusk) — sweet distillation of dregs (all the
wine squeezed before — just the body left)

André winch sideways, snubbed cocknosing out from
under his acquiescing belly — Holy Hermaphrodisiac … and
I manhandle his gift … right hand on his bedded shoulder for
leverage, left hand plying him as I steepen into nave

fuck — fuck this little bugger … fuck back the money he
stole … fuck this Canadien — fuck the French and Catholic
out of him … and into me (oh, pray to God I can!)

André thrusts assoul onto my rootle, generous bequest as I
ride acceptance down into his shunt

trainbelling outside in, shunting freight to feed
our nation

shunt my freight André
rolls his eyes into mine spying deep in us my cockflare bright
with colour

woad flesh

with gold and red on blue
can see in us my cocktree flowering

roses in La Place d'Armes

roses in his Nave
can see with such precision in his eye on me the gilt
lineage of choirstalls (I don't remember that before. Yet there it
is clearset in our very eyes)

the entrelacs up pilaster to clerestory, finials bobbing
bobolinking us

Oh, no image, no analogy this site — but what is seen now,
in La Place in the nave where we are processional
   carrying my Cross to the Chalice and both
   to the Host of us replaced whole in the nave

André moans Magnificat as assoul clutches steep on rood
   Cocked chalice
   (more freight shunts alongside Lachine Canal, beyond
Wedding Cake, where Van Horne still seats)
   whole world reborn in our Host that quivers me André
sensing withdraws me out to the rim of his world, plies my
quaver, secures my Holyrood at arsedge and as I bore back steep
raises his nave off our bed to capture my Man thrusting homage
into our sunburst monstrance as I reach out reach out in
   to the Host in the Nave on the Altar in the Church in our
Place d'Armes, reach in for that Body and Blood now reborn in
the flesh, made sheer flesh ... Man reborn, made whole in me
... donnant donnant, for my Land given back to André gave me
the Host
   bloodworthy, gave that back to me as key to our kingdom
gave it back to me as I reach out to the bloodspurt of the
Object resurrected in me, Manned once again
   and as André cups the blood of my new life I kiss the Mona
Lisa smile of his quiet face
   trainshunt farewell of Marc along our Greyway
   Bugger buggered and damned: what more can a man
want? ...
   André gone to shit out my sperm ... roll me to bed-
edge, and up. I'm done then ... demolished. Damned to High

Heaven ... and rolled in the bargain — my money?! ... only
$29 left till Christ's-mass

over to waistcoat, arsehole shimmering sleek in its renewed
chassis (can a man ever walk the same who has been quimmed?
— back broken ... no, that box broken inside me ... Cube
cracked ... not snapped outside in, but breached, encircled
— the Square circled.... La Place d'Armes alive: Cube's revolt
successful

that girl, in the Flesh Market, my first Cube site, walked
with that Box, unbreached: never been fucked, no never been
fucked ... impervious)

fart splatter spermshit in a farewell of Marc out recoil of
assoul

the money, in waistcoat. Still there ... enough for six
more days

but it was wallet André filched, that I left empty

(sperm treacles my rosegarden)

checking wallet

$5

Oh no that's wrong it was empty there
wasn't any money in it all removed none at all $ 5 $

nonono mustn't be there, must not be

brooom brooom brooom ... tears smart the spermslip as
my mouth belches silent laughter wracking my Place with roses

André — our land — the man ... donnant donnant

Thank God.

After André was asleep Hugh lay ruminant. His mind kept coming
back to the phrase — "the rebirth of the object" and he knew, but he
couldn't explain why, that the object had been reborn for him with
André ... had become the Object again. And he therefore had his Faith
again. As a Man and as a Christian (he didn't seem able to avoid the
Christian part of it ... he kept trying!) So that it seemed that when the
Faith died it was necessary to restitute the Object ... by resuscitating

the object. And when the object died, disappeared, was disembowelled ... then Faith, Hope, Charity died.

And when he had the Faith he was puissant again.

It was very strange — and very clear.

The Christ part of it — that was disturbing. No cock no Christ ... and no Christ, no cock! No Hell no Heaven. No Heaven no Hell. With mere fun as substitute. Well, he couldn't trade Heaven for fun ... so he embraced Hell. The result was joy ... and insanity. And he couldn't even distinguish clearly between these! Particularly when other people obviously considered joy a madness ... an uncivic act. Which pitted the Citizen, the complete Citizen, against the Man, the complete Man. And he was left opting for the Man ... against the mere citizen ... the Citizen was Man-without-Salvation ... was mere man, man reduced, diminished ... in the name of what? — of public convenience?

The logic of it kept surging ruthlessly out of him onto him. Binding him to life ... to a life he had never wanted (it was so much easier to be a citizen than a man, a human! And immeasurably more respectable). Binding him to Life — he hated it, feared it ... but insofar as he was honest with himself, there was no escape. All the Civic Righteousness in the World couldn't finally evade the entirely personal, private, internal, intimate fact of life given in birth and each day a battle for, or against, that gift which was implacably Grace.

"The Rebirth of the Object!"

He remembered speaking to Père Amyot about the young Séminairiens ... the new priesthood. "Ils ont tous le problème du sujetivisme ... ils ne voient pas comment Dieu peut exister en dehors d'eux-mêmes. Ils sont tous fermés." Hugh had laughed and said "je sais bien ... cette fermeture-éclaire — il nous manque un moyen de la faire rouvrir ... nous n'avons aucun moyen liturgique ... il va falloir vraiment les violer...." The loss of the Object was the loss of God was the loss of Faith was the loss of Love was the loss of Life was the loss of Man was the Loss ... was the Fall! (He'd have to rewrite the Bible, that was all.)

And André had given him back the Object — the Man in him.... It was all upside right — Insane!

And then he recalled the arrival of John Alexson in his hotel room ... had heard of Hugh's stay in Montreal, and traced him down to see him these five years later.... Hugh had loved John — innocently. And he still loved him when he saw him again ... and again there was that crisis: what to do about love for another. You can't shake a hand! You can't kiss à la française, you can't sleep with Everyman. Yet something has to be done ... some form of dance, or mode of showing that love. "You go and write and I go and act." (John was an actor) But that wasn't enough either — it was indirect, an evasion. No — something had to be done about it.... And then Hugh was lying in André again — each probe a prayer ... "this is for Peter Lawrence, and this for Janet, and this is for you, Mary ... we never dared. And another for Home...." Sodomite's chaplet. Retroactive Sex — Retrosex! And it worked!

Then he thought of the evening again ... madness. He wouldn't use it for his book. Obscene, they'd say. Not that his book would be banned ... it was Hugh who would be banned. Banned because he had declared his love ... had had to find some mode of declaring it, had to, when everything else was closed in a closed community.... Banned because he had dared name himself. Dared look his life in the face. Dared see. Banned because he knew Who he was. He remembered his panic at giving his name to Père Amyot ... writing it down for him and giving it to him with address: panic at "naming" himself ... that feeling of absolute vulnerability again — and had Père Amyot then taken a pin and stuck it into that name, an hour later, Hugh knew he would have died! And he had waited for that hour ... but Père Amyot hadn't stuck in the pin. Names were sacred. Like words. Hugh was accused of playing with words often enough. But what others didn't realize was that for him words were sacred: he really didn't dare *play* with them, because they were him. They did things to him. If he said "in three days I shall die ..." then in three days he would die, unless he managed to break those words somehow; that was one of the difficulties with his Novel — he didn't dare write it in full because it would eat him alive, in front of his own eyes, and he would be powerless to stop the carnage. Words were never words, they were always "Words." He had to honour them ... or risk reprisal. And when Words became merely wordage, he died back to nullity. Life became academic. And when people forced him to "play with Words" they risked his life for him, for their own bemusement.

He thought of his novel again — of course, it wasn't a novel — it was Life. Much of it was down now … in notes, in diary, in full. He had read over parts of it — and he knew that the real book — his book — his Testament, was in fact all of it … he knew that he would never get it all reduced to a novel. He couldn't. Or if he did, it might be a good novel — but it wouldn't be the book he had to have. It would be less than life…. He thought of his Combat Journal, his notes, the diary: which of these was the reality? He no longer knew … or even cared: they were all real — and all prerequisite … all part of his revolt, his Holy War. He didn't dare delete any of them — nor anything from them — at pain of death; nor did he dare stop living any of them. He knew that some of it didn't make sense … particularly in the past few days — when people and places blurred, became shadows, or else pounced omnipotent upon him. All he could do was tell what happened … tell it to save his own skin, to ward off the evil eye opening into him. So it didn't make sense — but the fact was (and in his deep gut he knew it) it all made sense, inordinate sense, because when he couldn't understand what he wrote he would read it aloud, lean his whole body into the words … and if the words made off with his body he knew it made sense, he knew that it made sense because it remade all his senses. And he left it at that.

Diary, notes, Combat Journal, novel — he knew they were full of beauty and of magnificence. Which is what he had wanted … what he had staked his life against, willingly. It was only when he staked his life to the full that he could write at all — only when death was immanent in him … when he heard that thunder behind the ears and knew that he was exposed again, knew that he had intersected with Eternity and that he was willing to prove it by giving his life — only then could he write. Then the Flesh was made Word. Let those laugh who would. They would laugh once too much … and he would have to pay the proof in full: the privilege of Anyman. That was alright with Hugh. He set but one condition: that he die for joy, in joy … as a gift.

And the realization had come during a newspaper interview for *La Patrie* … when he hadn't dare say the gut of the thing, that his deepest concern was that of sainthood. Not to be a saint — but to bind to himself that reality of which the harvest was the saint. Nothing else mattered. He had known that since he was a little boy ... had asked himself when he would be like David of Bethlehem and had kept putting it off. Fortunately twenty years of education had put it off for him ... had talked him out of the truth of it....

It sounded maudlin ... but he knew what the answer to that was: to prove that it was for real. He had to act upon his faith. There was a moment when he had had to act on that faith — a moment when daily life had intersected with that final option ... and he had told his president that he had no balls. And then his whole life was out the windows. Which was prerequisite. And now his whole book was a battle for faith ... it was written on the sternum of Notre Dame de Bonsecours — "Foi, Espérance, Charité." Same goddam thing. It would never change. That was what he needed to write. To use Words. To love. To life. For even one moment.

To write ... he had to be in that state in which he forgave all, beginning with himself. That state of Grace. (What the Hell else **could** he call it? There was no word for it in his particular constipated culture — so he would borrow it, because the word defined what he felt.)

So they would call him a Christian Humanist ... and miss the point completely. Well they could stick his Christian Humanism up their arse ... (which apparently was what was needed!). And then he thought of an important distinction to make in Canadian Cubes. Both were impenetrable. But the one kind was full of slit and had balls: that was the Tory. The other was scared shitless and had no balls: that was the Liberal.

None of it mattered ... if a hundred people heard him he was blessed. If fifty ... if ten. If one. Otherwise he remained damned. André stirred beside him. Oh, yes, Hugh could count on the damnation! And that was the Protestant half of his bargain with life honoured in full!

...

He awoke to the world of the body beside him — a certitude. A certification. And then slowly he realized what he had done.... The ordure. This slut beside him in bed ... with those reeking Canayen

336

teeth ... patates frites ... and the same flesh. Hugh had fallen again. Why had he done it? He couldn't for the life of him understand. Till he heard the trainbells freighting again ... and he remembered: he had been opened up, awakened wide in himself. Au naturel! That was why!

André borrowed his shaving kit, standing naked over the foot of their bed, at the sink (Good French European custom that, he mused — sinks in the bedroom ... for peeing). Hugh watched the lean convolutions of André's musculature. It reminded him of something, that body. The lines of it. They were scarcely Grecian classic, nor American Good Toughguy, nor Anglicanadian. Then he remembered the wire-wrought lines of cartoons by La Palme ... that particular embodied rococo wiriness of line, compenetrating everything. That was it ... that corporal Habitant Baroque again. It was in everything ... their bodylines, their furniture, their iron stairwells rising from streetlevel to second or third floor, their dance, their altars, their churchbodies — specifically so: André, the bombé commodes in Flesh Market, the Quevillon altar in Notre Dame de la Paroisse, the Lesser Sphinx.... Hugh relished his recognition ... and followed his eye over André's body-baroque again ... plying the line of embodiment with his eye.... And as he did he realized that he was going to outblast ... that simply by following this embodied line he could consummate — merely at the sight, untouched. Eyesite was palpable now. And he knew it.

Nor was it a question of hard-on ... Hugh was not erect ... it was a question of his entire body, his entire being: head to toe — as though all of him were cocked, all of him open — he became Host and Holyrood ... and to sight any incarnation — man, woman, house, tree, flower ... object — was to sight Object, and then to marry it, conjugating, body and soul....

André finished shaving ... and turned to dress — then stopped, looked over at Hugh lying free on the bedtop, relaxed. He dropped his undershorts, and walked over to bed-end ... put out a finger, forefinger, and without thinking Hugh touched with his ... they were risen again!

Flexed to their passion. Hugh felt an urgent but gentle need to be blown again. He couldn't explain that ... other than mere lust. And something infinitely more important than sheer lust (which was important enough

in itself) was in play. But what? Again he could only entrust themselves
to that set of inner rules that he had first encountered that lifetime ago
with Yvon.

With generous grace André bent over Hugh's rood ... raised it to his lips.
Hugh watched as his whole being focused in André's clasp ... and then
he saw (Holy Mary Mother of God) that André did it instinctively, with
the same concern, the same kind of concern as the Anglican pratiquant
raising the chalice to his Communion lips.... And as he realized that
Hugh saw, coming down those stairs of the Flesh Market, the man who
had been up to sight the bombé commode, and had returned ... "silent,
on a peak ..." (it couldn't be clearer ... Antique Shop was Flesh Market
was Body and Blood Shop ...).

There was nothing flippant, nothing cavalier to it. André's attention
was absolutely on the cock ... entirely engaged on it. So that was it:
cock was something André honoured, instinctively; not something
to be played with nor rejected. André looked cock in the face and it
became Holyrood ... Hugh became Holyrood. His whole presence
vibrant, bursting to share summonsed B & B, as André's eyes swallowed
Hughrood. And then Hugh realized that his own eyes had that sudden
profundity which came if man eyed him steep.... He remembered the
unexpected gaze of the youth in the Oratoire, that had penetrated his
eyeballs as Hugheyes sought the Host ... penetrated and come clean
out the end of his stunned cockface. Now the inverse was proving true:
André eyesite Hughcock, and his sight, entering cockface, followed
through to come out Hugh's eyeballs. It was a startling but self-evident
continuity ... and he remembered again the medieval scarecock ...
the depiction of the Devil with manface as scrotum.... Yes, that was it
alright: except that they had it all wrong. They advertized the evil of
eying Man ... and, from thereon in, man was blinded, deafened, finally
put in his Renaissance Box in a false liberation....

As the ideas and images convened in him, running free Hugh recognized
that André was about to consummate this flow ... that his free-flowing
body was this free-flowering mind of him.... And he wanted to retain
this flow ... to detain dispersal of mindful body. He knew now exactly
how to achieve this detainment. All he had to do was mentally run
the printed word in front of his eyes ... and that would do it ... sheer

wordkill! Killing with the printed word that reduced life to little black letters that were inquisitorial little black priests censorial.... Easy to kill that way, to disembowel, to gut.... Kill with words, written wordage ... life all labelled, footnoted, in cold storage.

And even as he mustered his magic wordkill, spraying his B & B with the black ink, all feeling ebbed ... and he was left leaden from mental linotype.... Disastrous control — lethal — allowing mere Mind to un-Man ... inverting the classic verity, mens sana in corpore sano, to something like "a healthy body tolerated within a healthy mind." And he knew that that was unhealthy ... and that it was the ingrate verdict of men who were frightened of incarnation, and abused their mind to cow that fright of living....

... André drew his head up from Hugh's calmed cock, cradling it in his right palm ... eyes quizzical on Hugh who lay in the comfortable security of wordkill, unsuspecting, as André's eyes caught him smug thus ... killing wordkill with a glance. Eyes twined, and Hugh could hear trainbell again. André smiled and cupping Hugh's conjugating glance slowly brought his face to the chalice, mouth to the lip and drank in deep slow to the base, pausing softly before surfacing firmly drawing Hugh's eyes out through the end of rod that he burst into Holyrood. André sat up ... caught Hugh's eyes still in his ... smiled, and deliberately swallowed the Host.

Wordkill had been killed ... there always was that margin, that specific margin of indelible Manhood ... words, written words, could only kill if you allowed their treason out of hand.

He watched André.... It had all been so simple, finally, this final enactment. But there had been so much in it.... Part of it was in fact a gratuitous expenditure — simply a dispersal of self; a kind of rebuttal of his enforced Protestant corporal avarice over the years. And it had been confirmation that a man's entire body is cocked. As well as a test of wordkill ... wordkill pass with flying honours, because it could fail! Finally — there had been the metamorphosis ... the fact that André had taken this prerequisite corporal expenditure, this sheer need of lust, and made it into a gift, into a redemptive gift ... made it into B & B, as he swallowed the Host of the Man he had resurrected in Hugh.

It was definitive. And Hugh felt an immense sense of release. He got up … dressed — and as they left, gave André his sweater and his scarf. They were only army surplus, from the shop on rue Notre Dame. A small gift. But huge, because it was a gift, unasked. Hugh had felt André's parka — it was derisively thin — and the temperature had dropped to 16° yesterday.

He dropped André near the Eden Rock. And as the cab pulled away Hugh looked back out the window at him. Where was André going? He had thought maybe to a film. Where would he be tonight? André hadn't known. On February 1 he was to be taken on as a painter's apprentice. At first Hugh thought that André had artistic hopes … but he found that it meant a sign-painter's apprentice. He pondered all of this as the cab dropped him for lunch with Lisette Roland. Lisette — executive secretary to the head of Expo 67 for Quebec. And André … it was André who had the courage, who was immersed daily in life. It was André who was the unconscious hero. He accepted life — no holds barred. He was a hero and he was holy … except that be was unaware of both, and therefore perhaps neither. But was André unaware? André had known, had Known, what was being done between them … even more clearly than Hugh. Hugh had known that something needed doing … André had known how … and, uncanny, apparently why! Had known it was a question of Land and the Man … of the lost Land and the Lost Man … had known that it was French Canadian Land and English Canadian Man … knew that, Hugh suspected, as Canadien … and, more, had known that the loss was somehow universal — that Man and the Land had been lost for all … and that somehow they must be restituted. As Catholic André had known of the Host. Yet André wouldn't have known had he been asked, and wouldn't have understood had it been said … all the while he Knew.

The whole thing was simply inconceivable. It couldn't make sense — yet implacably it did … kept on making sense. This inner logic kept on, quite simply, bearing fruit. For example, last year, that young English Literature professor from Harvard … Proper Bostannais — their relationship had been the same — although they had both remained shut in their box as Untouchables. Had been the same, but the other way around. Because it was Hugh who was the Man, and the Bostonian who was the Land.... It was Hugh who was the Loyalist, whose people had escaped north with the Crown Jewels, already two centuries ago. And it was the New Englander who had stolen the land, stolen All-America out from under Hugh's Crown Jewels. And they had sensed that when they met ... had talked of it. And it had been understood between them....What needed doing between them — but they hadn't enacted the restitution — only acknowledged the need.

Hugh laughed ... he was enmeshed in a series of pan-continental sodomations ... territorial reprisals for the sake of Absolution and Blessing. Laughed — because his truth hurt.

"... c'est un piastre quatre-vingt ... tout hyuste!" His taximan pulled up....

"Vous êtes Beauceron," Hugh said ... the husky "H" in place of "J" in "tout juste" caught his ear happily....

"Ouai ... de Saint Hyeorges de Beauce, m'sieur."

Hugh opened his wallet ... André's $5 lay on top ... he took it. Handed it to the driver — "La Beauce est tellement belle. J'en ai une girouette." and left the startled driver holding André.

As he walked to Lisette's office he missed André already. Yet he knew he would never see him again. That he better not see him again. Because it couldn't be the same. Their enactment was complete ... their liturgy. A Liturgy of Life. Their acts become enactment, were definite liturgy ... Hugh knew that now. To view them in any other way was foolish ... was sacrilegious!

Odd, he thought, as he met Lisette ... from Heaven to Hell, or Hell to Heaven. What would this woman think if she knew I had just dropped my $5 bugger ... Lisette, who epitomized the French-Canadian Britannic Haute Bourgeoisie ... who lived in the Château ... that curious marriage of Georgian Garrison and Seigneury Canadien....As they met Hugh felt an immeasurable potence surge in him. And he blessed André.

Hugh rejoiced in the company of Lisette then. He needed her ... and they were quick accomplied in gigglery that mated them for life: it was a holy moment — and he knew it, but he didn't know why. They

ate baby squid with gusto — Lisette with a muffled cutlery action that
accredited her gentility; Hugh with a guzzlement that was effortless
"son et lumière" — it was an Action of Grace. He explained the novel
to her — "an existential adventure in La Place d'Armes ... the hero is
La Place; but all the action takes place in the sensibility...." Of course
he was delighted by Lisette's single-minded admiration. "I'll send you
a copy — provided you only read it in bed ... with all your eyes open
— four-eyes ... bosoms out — the book as your candle." He plied the
book as candle as dildo. They laughed deliriously.... High innocence
all round. Hugh thought how weird it was that his Jekyl and Hyde
apparently each manned the other. No — obviously he couldn't have
Heaven without Hell or vice versa. So he had plumped firmly for Hell
... and here was a little Heaven sent ... and he gouged a little more
squid. Lisette said "it is so romantic." Hugh flinched — they all thought
it was "romantic" ... and so it must have seemed for everyone else. He
wondered if he dared tell her ... il y va de ma vie. But she wouldn't
understand — she couldn't allow herself to understand; he knew that.
How could he explain that to her ... or his immeasurable desire to
capitulate, and thus acknowledge his impotence as a human, as a man,
for life? No — it was no use ... so he sank deeper into the squids and
their laughter: laughter that he created even then at the expense of his
life — laughter that was a freshet of arterial blood ... bleeding himself,
deliberately, as in the old times, to lower the pressure, pressure of life. It
was just that he had to remind himself when to apply the tourniquet!
Laughter that was love of life. She took his pint of proffered blood, and
never knew. Save that she was radiant in their exchange ... allowed
him to say things that were otherwise outrageous ... because they were
bathed in the love-bath that she didn't comprehend. Words floated on
B & B (to use his own terminology) ... Masturbatory! Suicide — for
safe-keeping and for joy.

Then they talked Georges Pelteau, an old escort of hers, and now head
of Expo's Art Pavilion. Pierre Godin had astonished him by telling
him that Georges was a firm homosexual ... that Richard Goodfellow
was his wife, but that no one ever dared acknowledge it. Georges was
too dangerous. The idea had shaken Hugh. Georges was so very much
Grand Seigneur in the best sense. And so inalterably Grand Inquisitor
— Man of Iron. Quite so, Pierre had said ... "Georges simply set out to
show that being a homosexual made him more and not less the man...."

People quail in front of him." That was certain — Hugh did ... and he
wondered if Lisette knew. He eyed her as she recalled their ski-weekend
together — à quatre. Yes — she must know without ever having said it
to herself. Because she had given up her vie de salon, and had become
a thoroughly efficient secretary in a very meaningful post. She would
be excellent at it. Just as good as Georges at his.... He remembered
having asked Georges that night at Jean-Jacques Garant's apartment,
how Richard was ... quite innocently. Pierre had been staggered when
he told him that: "no one, absolutely no one in Quebec would dare
do that...." Well, he had been innocent ... or had he? — because even
after those five years, Richard's eyes crotched him, and he felt alive....
He looked at Lisette — his vitality now, thanks to Richard's five-year
foresight, was her tragedy. At least she had immense dignity. But their
lunch was done. Over in that flash of a second that brought all that back
to him ... he could no longer laugh. He knew he might cry. Lisette
must have felt the sudden breach.... Moments later she was gone, taking
all those forgotten remembered names with her and abjuring him to
visit La Place Ville-Marie — it had been built since his departure from
Montreal those centuries ago....

... first visit to La Place Ville-Marie ... along Dorchester
Street to the central entrance on this new broadway of English-
speaking finance. Enter under the sign of the Big Maple Leaf,
an eye into my brow, huge, encircled ... the sign of Air Canada
... eye glaring at me enter under its brow ... eye into me ...
and I balk ... no — not **into** — not at all — eye **at** me. Why?
Why that? I walk hesitant in and try to locate me ... in to the
central shaft — elevators ascending in marble ... squeezing me
into their ascension that I evade, backing down the corridor
to meet me entering an open place that changes my pace to
conscientious stroll — till I stand afront a suspended   marble
slab green serpentine, massive, leaning on it ... and survey
the site. My eyes are halted at a warm mahogany segment,
mounted over my entry, mating the Maple Leaf I thought I had
left ... lion rampant on the mahogonizing ... The Royal Bank
of Canada. I am standing at a cheque-table ... how many tons

of serpentine thrust up to my bankrupt signature? Guilty, back away, around to the far end ... to the people ... assembled — in sharkskin, tigerskin, pythonskin ... sharp knives tossed at me by each of these fellow-citizens. Knives of damascene, with champlevé multicolore.... And beyond them, a photo-display of Canadians-at-play, in black-and-white. Sign reassures me that there are FIFTY SHOPS WITHOUT SETTING A FOOT OUTSIDE inside here, down the escalation I accept as release from my pointless banking ... down to les boutiques that echo my flanks as I escalate me now along between them ... there I am the new sealskin boots I want to buy against Montreal snow ... here I am the bottle of Marc that I do buy from La Commission des Liqueurs de la Province — where I see the diamond-point armoire of the Antique Shop that is now reproduced in the counters of La Commission des Liqueurs, modern homage to la Nouvelle France, and the Marc, my liquiflame (tiger for my tank) ... Classic Bookshop — "do you have *Eros Denied*?" — "no — were sold out!" (I had intended to buy it in Toronto — at Britnell's, before leaving — but the woman who came to serve me had taught my little brother at Rosedale School — and disgruntled I gracefully asked for Bellow's *Herzog* instead) ... Giftshop — full of Eskimo carving ... magnificent narwhale in serpentine ... the heft of it to the handling. $100. Too much ... "Didn't I see you on television," the countergirl asks. I say yes — it saves time. Besides she is right.

And out, to the Théâtre de la Place to watch Albee.... Headspins — I shoot out ... to the lunch counter ... for a moment's release — till I am all eyed again ... TV, in the corner ... "ici Radio-Canada" — that Big Maple Leaf again. I must get out of here ... get out. One ball suddenly gone....

Hang on to my remaining testicle ... and shoot 30-odd floors up the shafted marble to Expo '67 ... to see our Pan-Canadian Nemesis. Enter as though I know where I'm going (if not where I am). Nobody sees me, happily.... Then

I doublecheck — no! nobody sees me. I'm invisible....As I
walk past no one sees....And I look — no one sees anyone
here! My head reels me and I stop, regroup me, and look
again. I don't see anyone ... no one need see anyone here ...
till gliding down a hall, peering a board room, I do see Alain
Valéry ... deep in a 14-ounce suiting of English tweedery and
suede shoemanship — English cloth, with a French cut, or is it
French tweed looking English cut ... or both. In either case it
is Alain, with his genteel crush on English guardsmen and Lady
Molson and the arts. Divine parody of everybody. He turns his
deep brown spaniel eyes and his clubman manners into me and
I have arrived at Expo planning offices. Sorties out and finds
me someone to tour me around. A draughtsman? A beardie.
An accredited sensitive. We stand shortly afront the models of
Expo, at the end of the hall — appropriately cul de sacked. An
upjut of huts is patently Everychild's image of African tribal
compound, reworked as an architectural geometric theorem.
Clever abstraction of the body, but even I can tell it is but
disembowelled huttery. And mourn the body if not the huts.
And all around it variations on this geometricity ... the whole
thing a formulation. One, despite this post-graduated Euclid,
has about it a prickly palpability that reminds me of Spanish
Colonial Santos ... it is the Mexican pavilion. And another —
my heart sinks ... it is blanched, blandiloquent, indelibly cubicle
... reminds me of the new Toronto City Hall, the new Toronto
Airport ... the New Toronto ... part of Creeping Parkin's
Disease — oh, yes, that must be an Ontario building. My guide
who had discovered himself as a fellow Trinity student with my
eldest brother, says — "that is by John Parkin ..." "I couldn't
have guessed," I said, in false irony ... because it still hurts. What
is there about it? What gave it, and us, away? I look again. It is
geometricity like the rest ... but there is a squatness, a stolidity,
a certain enforced concern for monumentality — an echo of
solid stoneslab walls. It looks like the new University of Toronto

(the administration and its pronunciamentos) feels. Call it
enforced concrete — preflab!

Overtopping it all, the theme of Expo — Terre des
Hommes ... Man and His World. Gasp. What hideous irony!
Man and His World.... And savage, turn on my guide, mocking
Expo through him ... "there is no need for man here, no
need to be present in this Expo at all ... no one need attend
it. One might call it World Without Man." And instantly I
know I need never visit Expo — it will show better, be seen
to advantage even, on TV! It is a world that is simply an
extension of the complete TV kit. People are incidental here.
"Man and his World" — oh, what a brutal jest! All so heinously
ironic ... Canadian Centennial — defining the All-Canadian
at the moment of his vaunted new, true birth, at the very
moment when human identity as such ceases ... and this World
Exhibition on Canadian soil.... Oh, cruel profligate irony!

And I cannot help thinking of The Great White City, the
Chicago World's Fair of 1897, where my own grandfather had
taken his honeymoon (I still have a cup from it ... a massive
Victorian Rococco-Renaissance Revival cup, painted by my
grandmother ... and suddenly it takes on new value for me ...)
... The Great White City that "set architecture back seventy-five
years" according to the professors. And so it may have ... but
at least it didn't set Man back seventy-five years ... it didn't
abolish man, didn't disembowel him on the spot! As this does
... with its theme pavilion — "man interrogates the universe"
... again, viciously ironic, because if anything it is the universe
here that interrogates man.... Not bad in itself ... in fact
good; but what is bad, what is insistently evil, is the implacable
inversion of man and his environment here ... the implacable
nonentity of it, of which the meaningless heiroglyph that is
the symbol of the fair, is excellent example! Crown of thorns
for electronic Cubes! It is like La Place des Arts, it abolishes
the people it claims to serve; it is a revolution-devolution. It

acclaims a man it will create at the very moment it merely
destroys a man it renders obsolete with comforting reassurances.
But the truth is that Expo, like La Place des Arts, needs No man.

My weirdie-beardie who is a court eunuch here, escorts
me with a bland attentiveness that accredits him ... Oustide
the south-east corner of the building, a skytop view ... down
to the St. Lawrence, the site of Expo, and La Place d'Armes....
How implacably opposed the two are — Expo and La Place
d'Armes....And I remember that the British played The World
Upside Down when they left Yorktown in 1783 ... they should
have played The World Inside Out, Cut up and Dried! The
resentment congests in me, tumescent ... till my eyes mist with
the heat of it, and I know I am killer again ... if looks could kill.
I eye my guide ... who knows what is going on within me ...
after all, he is from the same Anglicanadian culture as me ... I see
him, bland in his comforted capitulation here, acquiescing easily
in my statement that no human need desecrate Expo ... that it
accredits the Complete Canadian Zombie ... and I wonder if it
wouldn't be better to capitulate....No — my left ball won't let
me. I have to fight, I have to hate ... because I have to love....

Suddenly I recall that Eleanor Bazin is here ... is in fact super
PR for the executive office ... a Rovergirl ... who can handle
everyone from the Queen to the Mayor of Montreal ... and
has, indeed, manhandled many of them. How can I forget that....
Five minutes to extricate me from my bearded wonder and I am
at her office. No — Mrs. Bazin is absent ... in South America
... till January. The secretary raps out the reply...."May I see the
view from her office ... she told me it was spectacular"....And
I wander the office ... the same electrific office as the Board
Room of Alphonse Renaud's company. The same spermwhip!
Muzak with a short-circuit blenderized in....Around the wall
the depictions of Eleanor ... and her manpower....Eleanor
with the Prime Minister at a cornerstoning; Eleanor with HRH
Prince Philip; Eleanor with the Mayor of Toronto ... Eleanor and

our Big Men. It is staggering ... so patent that it is no question of their eating out of her hand ... Eleanor eats them! Alive, in front of my eyes. Mona Lisa with the mask off....

"Some coffee?" the secretary feels it her duty, at least.... And I sit. Blunderstruck. Secretary sits down, in Eleanor's chair ... interrogates me. I answer, without thinking ... as though it be Eleanor. Of course! It *is* Eleanor — this secretary is the same thing ... I turn slowly and accost her steep with my eyes ... plunge our foursome down down down ... till we have conjugated at cunted cocktit. Of course ... Eleanor has her own kind as secretary ... proxy-Eleanor.

Admire this she-male ... can't help it ... with her virtuoso torso, her manned hips, that torsion of the body — ahh, that is it ... it is the body of a nude by Pontormo ... a male nude! Mannerist Man. She watches my appraisal astonished ... because she Knows that she has been penetrated.... Knows the same way as my cock Knows ... I pounce me into our breach, before the curtain descends in either of us, before we are unwilling to acknowledge the redemptive mutual violation ... pounce while our Conversation has thus been saved ten years of preliminary discussion. "You hate men, don't you ... despise them?"

"Yes" — her eyes narrow measurably, but mine are still in, hard in her body, and she cannot expel them and her pride won't let her retract ... "Yes — I despise them."

"So do I ... I despise us...."

"Why?"

"Because they have no balls...."

I should have gone over and assaulted her on the spot — fucked the balls off her ... but I need to say me — now....

She bears down on my imbedded eyeballs....

"How many do you have?"

"Three," I reply ... "three ... that's the trouble. And it's only just enough, for example, to carry me intact through a Visit of Expo ... to fecundate it for me."

She eyes me quizzical — nowise frightened — but implicated in us. My mind matching hers easily, my body speaks her language, at fingertit, my cock outprobes her. Her eyes still probe mine, clenching her ... as long as I have her eyes, she is conjugal. "You can't speak to me like this...."

"I can — I do ... and you're still here. Anytime you want me to leave you can ask me ... I'm a shit ... but a gentleman-shit. You want me here. You want to hear what I have to say. You don't believe me ... but you want to."

"Of course ... my husband had no balls ... I could have run his store better than he did ... art supplies...."

"So now you hate us all."

"Yes."

And I know that my possession of her is complete. I could consummate us at twenty feet. I tell her that.... She doesn't look surprised ... we are talking along our inner track. And what we say is self-evident....

"I suppose that what I say is a revenge...."

"On whom?"

"On my fellowmen ... because they are gelded. I have to make up for their defection.... On both sides of the fence ... but it is self-immolation."

"Why?"

Every time I beat her mind my body holds her ... it is simple. She is a mindeater. I'll feed her a little, and leave me in to soak while she nibbles.... That's a fair deal.

"Self-immolation because every time I take revenge for the defection of the man, for man's failure to honour himself and thus women, I lose my chance to possess the woman specifically — I expend the consummation I pillage from her in wordage ... in flagellating her in front of her own eyes.... As now...."

Her eyes suddenly break from mine, too late....

"... I have just lost you by turning your own whip over your own back.... Your cunt just closed again, taut tight."

Her eyes are dry-ice. But she has been had and she knows I know it.

"A moment ago your cunt was open, and wet. Admit it!"

"Yes — if you must.... But how did you know so specifically?"

"Because I could hear your cunt opening ... I could hear it the way I hear candles in a Church — rumbles my ear, and then roars. I can hear wet cunt at thirty yards. Suddenly the whole world is in heat! And I'm in rut."

I'm standing in front of her at the desk — her eyes still slitted.

"Here ..." — I hold out my right forefinger tip and without thinking she touches it with hers, as though simply accepting a routine office request. Stares at our fingers ... and I am laughing — "you're open again...." And even as I say it she has suddenly realized that vulnerability and has withdrawn her finger from the candle.

"It's a dangerous little game you play. Do you always win?"

"You know the answer to that — whenever I contact that way I am bound to lose ... it's like grounding lightning."

"Don't you ever lose control ... after all, I've never really been accosted in my office before...." She is bitter-sweet. But I am serious — "I never try to keep control ... not of all of me. That's the whole point of the thing. There is always a ten percent margin of improbability. That's what makes me and life dangerous. I will never allow me to control it. The moment I do I'll cease to be a man ... The most I will do is guide it. And then it bursts out, like now, unexpected."

I change our conversation ... to Eleanor...."Look at this woman ... sitting in her tower, astride Montreal ... predator. She's the best man in Montreal...."

"Yes...."

"But she won't find joy that way. All she can do is find the biggest cock in town ... and use it as a portable dildo....What a magnificent novel there is in her. Her tower. Her eyrie. Her

350

raptor's post. Sitting on the city ... whip in hand. Beating the big ones on the head with their own soft cocks!"

Watch the woman ... the natural conclusion now is to take her, on the spot ... what she needs, wants, won't believe. But I have shot my bolt, word-killed. And I lie victim of my own Pyrrhic victory in defence of men's honour. Victim because I still do want a woman ... still do need to give, in love. Victim because I haemorrhage now in my need to give ... blood gouting at every orifice.... And then I am on the street ... walking to La Place d'Armes ... immeasurably puissant ... armed again with that vast security of suicide. Ability to give life, to take it, to bless it ... all one in me.

As I walk to La Place I realize what La Place Ville-Marie is.... *Who* it is — and turn around just to make sure — yes, there it is: the huge Maple Leaf. Eying me. Big Brother at my back ... inescapable — everywhere ... on the Hotel Reine Elizabeth afront me Big Bloody Brother — Big Bloodless Brother (Orwell was right ... bless his damnation!). Yes — that's it ... the whole damn works of it — infernal: the new Monstraunce — the eye of the World. And the Maple Leaf as the Host ... whether I will or no — and I wouldn't, but I couldn't stop me, because once inside La Ville-Marie it took me, huge marble shaft up my ass and whipped me inside out ... gutted, backasswards, and there I was, in the Mommy Bank, or cousin-once-removed, standing at the altar to write my name, absentee, against my overdraught on life, that green-marble serpentine, looking at the Mahogany God — piece of the True Cross in this place of absentee landlords, watching those sharp tigerskins stab me — and only now realizing that they were a colour-photo display of mannekin styles, and what I thought was the black-and-white display of Canadians-at-play was in truth the customers up with their written names to cash in at the tabernacle for some of the Host ... then down to les boutiques, I was around the circle of shops of La Place d'Armes, around the nave of the Church of

Our Lady, with each boutique a side-chapel, and each article of
sale, more Host, and the narwhale of the giftshop, the lost Object
— the Holy Dildo … and only standing there on the street now,
out into the open air, do I know how counterfeit that object
is … while I remember, in the small antique shop … along the
Greyway, Charles de Chartres, for sale, at $20, the real "object,"
that I couldn't afford, burl maple pestle for pounding the meat of
man … of the Man who made this country only a century ago.
Honest Yeoman. There his bit.

And the Théâtre … the new Morality Players. And the
TV — with the Maple Leaf always within … the Eye of the
New Leviathan … Moby's Dick. And the new body within….
Which is why I felt that I was on stage as I strolled around those
boutiques. Because I was truly merely a figure on a television
screen … processed through the screen I screen. Televizee!
Always the same in these modarch buildings … the new Temple.
The same desubstantiation. All suffering, all pain, all fear and all
hope end here. Because I end here. No need to resurrect the
body. No body to resurrect! Thanx be to the New God! No
wonder I kept trying to find me there … no one ever there
… sought me throughout the bank. No one. Shadows in the
Platonic Cave. And that same consumptive space as at La Place
des Arts … space that literally blots you up … dries you out:
unwitting, unsatisfying … unholy blow-job!

While upstairs, the workshop for the New Faith — Expo
67 itself … "Man and His World!" And therein the New Priests
(always eunuchs, the priesthood, since the world began!). And
in place of Maisonneuve, the central statue in La Place, in his
place … Eleanor Bazin … Maneater-At-Large! While the Place
Ville-Marie itself so aptly in form of a Cross — "the largest
cruciform building in the world!"

Oh — it has everything. "Fifty shops without setting a foot
outside…." Absolutely everything. Narwhales in serpentine
(dildo's for appreciative citizens). Everything except the Man

... except B & B. Except the True Object. And it so blatantly lacks that! While La Place d'Armes so blatantly has just that. No — there's simply no choice in the matter ... between La Ville-Marie (the New-Non-Mommy-Mommy) and La Place d'Armes (Holyrood) ... between La Place Désarmé and La Place d'Armes. The choice is simple: it is die in comfort, or live and be damned. May God in his mercy damn me ... or I am as good as dead!

Cross the street ... a beatlenik pries me wide-eyed and I die alive again — ahh ... object, object, who has the object. Answer: this new generation that regenerates the Object — is in full pursuit of the Object — the "male suffragettes" ... no wonder they pursue the Object: it has been so utterly eliminated. And now they must insurrect it. Or we all die. Search for the lost Grail ("the cock and the chalice" — still). Bless them. The long and the short and the tall! Because without that we are done for. So they pursue the Object — because they know they must. And they **are** the Object ... the only possible denizens of this new deep. All the others were gelded in giving birth to the New World of us. Amurrican nemesis ... nemesis that my people were born to resolve, and have now, all witting, accepted as their Identity. Oh, Christ. How to say it? And worse — How not to say it?

The New Flag splotches my eye ... Crushed Cubes: and I recall with consternation the cubes in the station on arrival ... over the entrance to the Rapido ... crushed cubes ... great illuminated toy-blocks, hollowed (of course) stacked with higgledy-piggledy precision atop each other ... advertising the RRRRRAPIDO ... (roar, tiger, roar! — else you might pee in your panties.)

Walk on ... past the Italian restaurant ... the squid — the squid: and hideous now. I know why I holy haemorrhaged at lunch with Lisette ... because of the squid ... because it was remembrance, eaten in remembrance — the last time I ate squid, was in Venice, in 1956 ... Summer, off the Grand Canal, with the Provost of Trinity College ... we had met, from 4,000 miles apart, coming around the smile of one of those trecento Uffizi madonnas that are still miracles, had met, and had arranged to lunch together ... and had squid. He was on sabbatical ... and I at Oxford (his old college, John's) — we talked universities ... he laughed when I said that the University of Toronto was the biggest single centre for philistinism in Canada ... barring the Civil Service — and asked what I was going to do about it.... We never met again — he was killed in a plane crash. So I ate squid, with Lisette ... in remembrance, without even remembering — and had haemorrhaged.

Walk on, incredibly potent now (bless you, André!) away from this Counterfeit Place to La Place — La Vraie Place ... d'Armes! And I remember Jack Macdonald's invitation to drop in, at the Mother Bank ... great-grandson of Sir John A. — the man who made Canada ... Jack — who sits wounded in his law-office, wondering, about us....

Around his office, portraits of Canadian prime ministers ... the full accusation of them on me.... God — that Rembrandt face of John A. — was he the only full man we ever produced ... the only soul in Canada? Is that it then? Is it given to a people to become carnate but once? And on around, past Laurier (bland version of John A.) ... to Arthur Meighen ... the PM-manqué. Look at that face — the Complete Cube ... The last of the British Square. And I reject him like the electorate did — so often. And then suddenly I relent ... why? It is those eyes ... I want now to stab mine out — because his eyes have just stabbed mine back in again ... way, way in ... too deep to retract now. Those eyes. Complete Cube — but with eyesite ... I realize abruptly what happened. Intellect and sensibility still fused in that face, in those eyes. Meighen — that's it — that's where we went awry ... Meighen — the Canadian we never allowed....The greatest prime minister we never had ... because beside it, to confirm me, the paunchy piglet face of Mackenzie King. The man without a face: the "unknown Canadian" … the man who effaced us … I want to cry now: because all we are today in my country is, at the very best, a splinter from Meighen's Cube — we are the result of some fracture there. And all I can do now is confront Jack with me … with my eyes … and know that the accusation must bear fruit. Provided he and his get off their little pink assholes.

At 7 p.m…. meet Rick in his office, across La Place…. Reeking with my potence, lost and found … and from his high window see again La Place and its radii … see how the whole city grows from this heart — see how it grows organic, quite despite the meeting of English and French — a graft, and not in fact a clash … "deux présences" … hopelessly intertwined. Wondrously. Then we are at Le Vieux St. Gabe … deliberately I choose this spot … immersing Rick in it … confounding mere dialogue — rebutting mere confrontation — and imposing instead the French-Canadian verity … la présence … présence totale. Présence all around us … a maw … battering eyes into the back of my head again. Enormity of this présence humaine. Rick makes a first step … and withdraws, dizzy in the whirligig. His line of words overwhelmed … I watch, fascinated, horrified at this truth — this fact that dialogue dies within full presence. Real Presence kills mere words — demands that words be Flesh. Watch Rick strangling over this verity. While I entangle us in the wine-list, my eyes circle round and round in it … focussing abruptly on a Loupiac … a Loupiac — haven't had one since Bordeaux … those magnificent hills across the river from Sauternes … Loupiac — with the lushness of Sauternes but not so sugarred — rainwashed sunshine — whereas Sauternes always threatens me with sunstroke. Loupiac I shout to Rick … it'll levitate the Coq au vin … manage de sensibilité sinon de raison!

Loupiac levitates me … in an afterflush of my meeting with Eleanor-Proxy — I hone my accusation of us … both of us …

while Rick sweats and says, "I know what you're going to say, but you don't need to say it...."

"Ah, but I do," I shout above the mêlée ... "I know — even if selfishly, for me ... we have both defected, both failed, because we didn't honour our cocks ... we aren't homosexuals: We aren't even homosexuals-manqués. We're the worst. We are homosexuals-ratés. You know it and I know it."

Adjoining tables are a party of French Canadians from Radio-Canada ... fulminating in mirth ... their din careens us.... And I laugh at this blockade of mere dialogue ... laugh at this prerequisite static on the vanishing point of our brains. "You don't answer me, Rick...."

His eyes now are dilate ... deep — confirming my accusation of us. He is trembling and the sweat blurts out on his brow.

"You came looking for an argument, Hugh." I am stunned, and only after we are gone, only after Rick has literally fled, phoning his fiancée for sanctuary while I am in the men's room, evading thus any further penetration, only then, alone, and as I walk around La Place, do I know my answer...."No — I wasn't looking for an argument ... I tried to eliminate argument. I was looking for a man ... a human being." I looked up at La Place — it had vanished — with Rick. I stumble back to Le Vieux St. Gabe ... take a Calvados ... the restaurant is clearing.... Over the stairwell, a French-Canadian farm scene ... family home of Rosaire de Pelteau, propriétaire. For an hour we talk together ... Rosaire directing the fugue ... abetted by Irish Coffee. "Mais c'était qui avec vous ce soir?" he asks....

"Rick Appleton ... a lawyer from La Place d'Armes."

"Il avait l'air tellement sensible...."

"Oui.... Do you have a Marc Rosaire?"

"Quoi?"

"I didn't think so — it's all that's missing here. Let me bring you a bottle next time."

DAY TWENTY-ONE

He awoke to a phone call from René Lalonde ... who explained that he couldn't come into the centre of town today. It was an open invitation for Hugh to suggest they drop the meeting. But he wouldn't ... René wasn't going to get away with it again: he would have to face up to Hugh. Godin was right — René feared for his life ... his presence. Feared Hugh. Just as René's wife sensed him out ... had understood him at that last bitter-sweet dining together two years ago. Now they would meet. Man to man ... and he would palpably present René with his failure.... Failure which founded upon René's rejection of what Hugh was ... upon his rejection of the capacity to love and be loved. That was it — surely. Hugh systematically returned to haunt those who had rejected life, had rejected his surge to life ... returned gutted into life, bound up into it, and implanted in the zombies a recognition of their failure — implanted ... he specifically fertilized in them this budding self-recognition.... That is what he had done yesterday with Jack Macdonald — palped the failure till it hummed aloud in him.

Hugh sat grilling himself:

"Still why do I do it? Is it revenge? Merely? Revenging myself on the zombies. Going back and flinging my rejected potence in their still lingering cockface, expunging their final twinge in this ultimate self-recognition I impose upon them — is that it? Raping them of their last capacity to Know, to be, in this deliberate accusation.... Not allowing them to pass into limbo unaware of their disaster! Is that it?

"It is a madness ... each time I do it ... I bereave me of their love. In enforcing the confrontation I commit mutual manslaughter ... I use my own puissance, exspend it, in focusing them upon their self-secession. As I did again yesterday ... once, twice, thrice....

"And each time I do it — I evade the Place d'Armes ... I rendezvous me away ... I betray it. The while yet carry it pregnant in us."

And then ruminant awhile on Eleanor's surrogate ... "I need oh so to penetrate — And I know that my triumph yesterday was again a failure.... Pyrrhic victory consuming the flesh I preferred untouched."
...

He sat thus saying his rosary, half-cocked ... snuffed the manmusk of the aureole, and as he did so be heard the roar of the traffic outside unwittingly, and he remembered the trainbells plumbing him at waketide, and the roar of the candles in the Church that were the roar of the woman's cocked cunt yesterday that he could hear at thirty yards....

— — — (10:30 a.m.)

At noon he rendezvoused at La Grange — a large nineteenth century barn remade as a restaurant ... half-way out of town. Enforcing his presence upon René who arrived even later than he did ... and promptly evaded their self-presence by whisking them both off for a drink with the propriétaire, to whom he would present his latest book.

"I watched René — so as not to frighten him openly. Watched him dazzle the propriétaire with his footwork.... And I realized that all of this was evasion ... all this inordinately able footwork. It was an effort to seduce me into an acceptance of the genius of René ... into the genius René should have had, and still vestigially could mobilize, but for some reason would not.... In the propriétaire's private office — a snugglery — full of Canadiana ... with a Gothic revival tabernacle as liquor cabinet ... and everywhere on the walls, sculptoral sketches of driftwood that palped me. Propriétaire appropriates us ... eats from our flesh.... Something is happening — I don't quite see what yet. Propriétaire recognizes my "nom prestigieux," distending me by flattery. René ripostes by telling him how to improve his restaurant Xmas card by colour. Blatantly tells him ... over my deadened body that he kills en passant — The converse dallies … and I watch René intermittently watching to see if I watch him…. Incredible performance his — he seduces those around him into instant intercourse with him … and then cuts them off at the moment of penetration…. Requisitions sodomy and then rejects it. Sleight of hand. Legerdemain! He extracts your carnal homage and then withdraws in renewed assertion of self-virginity … smug saying with his darting eyes — "écoute m'sieur pas moi …" He engulfs you in his own endlessly elegant intellectual impasse. It is an incalculably brilliant performance … draining René of the very consummation it requisitions.

watch him autograph his book for propriétaire…. He does it with a flair, an empanachement that is a suivez-moi m'sieur for the rest of his … his little assoul coquetting us … and suddenly he is a woman … a full bitch, in heat

watch the eyes of propriétaire — watch him watching René sign — same look on his face as on face of a communicant … watching Renéhand voraciously … each stroke of pen patently touches him….And I realize again I watch a B & B process … another transubstantiation! The book is the Host — the flesh passed in redemption to communicant. René plays God in witting disbelief. Wondering if I know he disbelieves himself….

I am uncomfortable in the recognition … because in it I recognize the fact that René is dead. Or that he is dying. And knows it.

the incredible "style Lalande." It is almost sufficient expiation of his defection.

lunch … in a setting of phallic incitement that is only surpassed by the home of a respectable Headmaster I know … everywhere objects … outils du passé … all the past implements of man's mastery of his world … the tools of his mastery. Skates, hammers, planes, adze…. And burl ware, wooden ware … over the bar coqs gaulois … while by the door,

a piece of treen that is only exculpated from blatant phallicity
by the self-evident fact that if the proprietor knew why he had
it there, he wouldn't place it there!

sit in the back room ... I militant now ... eliciting from
René his gradual avowal of a "long-term death ...," of a slow
agony.

René — "I've been put in formaldehyde" ... and as I listen
to his avowal ... his eyes flee ... and then, accomplished, they
slowly seek mine out again, no longer hiding his acceptation of
an imperceptible impotence. And I know that his is another of
these incredible cases — of a man who flees the implications
of his procreativity as an artist, and so doing, subsides into that
bitterness that is the fruit of his self-imposed barrenness.

"It is egotism ... to pursue my creativity," says René —
"egotism ... besides, I'm cornered — I have a family. It is too late."

And I realize that I am listening to the excuses of a man
who finally doubts his own genius. Who finally doesn't believe
in himself! It is tragic. Because he was — only four years ago
— a contender, and a conscientious contender, for the title of
French Canada's Brilliant Young Man. And all his brilliance was,
was a smokescreen for his own encroaching self-indulged failure.
All that brilliance merely to mask the inner fright ... the fear to
confront himself ... to hold up the mirror — to cockface. And
the result, now, is not mature "responsibility" — but an end
to love and thus, inevitably, an incapacitated responsibility. It is
that that undermines me now ... this willingness to kill love ...
to corrode it, in the name of falsified responsibility. An end to
love.... My head reels at his reality ... reels at this rejection of
life ... reels as I listen to all his reasons, his "right reasons" for
his slow death — ending with his lucid recognition that there
is nothing more to say in the novel, little more to be said in
films, nothing in theatre ... René is the dedicated non-man. "I
am a zombie" — and his truth hurts me ... as it is meant to —
because I am one of the slender final chances he has that he is

not right. If he is right — then we are all dead. If I am right, he has betrayed himself. He cannot afford, for his own self-respect, to let me be right.... But I am his last chance — I hold a last grasp on the necessity to love. If I can love more than he hates — then we are both saved I watch him watch me ... watch me stagger — the jacksaws on the wall are sharks whose teeth roar me, and again the objects are militant, are lethal — I hang on, hang on, while René watches me — and then by an ace I have withstood his betrayal — have withstood it by watching him ... and remembering my inalienable right to love him — I shout over the din of lunchers and saw teeth — "Mais je vous aime bien, René. Je vous aime ... tu ne peux pas m'arracher ce droit!..." and so saying, I have overcome that total solitude his tentative hate imposed.... That solitude that is death — for us both. And as I do — I note that his eyes are back into me again ... he is open, if incredulous ... as he leaves he gives me his new novel — and so doing confutes everything he has said ... I sit, half an hour, ruminant.... Men only exist through love — and love has never been so important as now ... art is love — even an art of hate is love — the optimism of despair — creating despair in hope of hope.... back into town by bus, basking in the armpitted air searing us all.

Into the Château de Ramezay museum — as relief — haven't had the energy to insite it before now — need it for the novel — All these tawdry coins and mementos leave me cold — there is something obscene to them — like collecting offal ... some perverse secular iconolatry. This whole museum a reliquary for those who have not the courage to avow eternity, but revel in secular sainthood ... I want to brush my teeth. It tells me nothing about us ... only impedes us. And then I realize how wrong I am. I realize that this museum is not important now for what it tells us about who we were ... but for what it tells us about who we thought we were (just like academic texts ... but with better, more spontaneous evidence)

— Here is absolute, convincing, delightful, despairing evidence
of the Romantic Vision of Canada: the image of the Cavaliers
as against the Roundheads. Image of flying canoes, and eternal
Brueghelian habitants, and grand seigneurs, and Princes of the
Church, and Soldiers of the Queen, and Loyalists whose fidelity
is to the Grail, no matter how many times changed in outer
form. Everywhere I turn, the evidences of this high hopefulness:
and suddenly, as I recognize this reality ... as I recognize that
this museum is not what it purports — a witness of some
distant past, but rather the faith of a past still upon us as to what
that past was ... then I can enter in to it, and partake of the
faith, and rejoice in it. This is the equivalent of the *Heroes* by
Kingsley or *Westward Ho* ... it is a great-grandson of Waverley:
and it is legitimate. What an oaf I would be not to rejoice in it.
Its very language defines my feeling about me as I contemplate
the defection: I would be a "churl." And suddenly the clucking
hen by the door, who sells tickets as a nun might a piece of
the true cross, is no longer a hopeless impediment to serious
museology — but an essential counterpart to what this Chateau
has to say to me. Suddenly she **is** (and no one can take it from
her) a Mother Superior ... and her gabbling over the phone,
the sale to me of a *History of Old Montreal*, this triumphant
report to headquarters of another infidel centre breached, this
all makes sense.

I look at the Church rooster ... "seventeenth century, from
the Church at...." Its style is indefatigably mid-nineteenth
century: its full prosaic embodiment, its man-of-substance
stance, its eyes that deal with one thing at a time ... no — it is
not Baroque, let alone peasant Baroque, or anything like. But
who cares — the imagination of this museum **is** Victorian
Baroque. So be it. Somebody it will change — probably soon. It
will become a residence for the City, for distinguished visitors.
Or a home for the Mayor. Or an official reception centre. It will
be restored to clinical exactitude. The false nineteenth-century

tower should be removed. The false pointing of the stonework
rectified. It will be magnificent ... like the White House. It
will be finer in every way — except one: it will be a fake! A
requisite, efficient, fake. Give me the secular reliquary. The
academic stage-setting is a false verity.

down to the Flesh Market ... for a last visitation — struck
by the noise of the furniture — even scraped as it is — it is
full of rumble and hum. And as I unwitting recognize this
— unwitting admit this sound, I realize that modern noise is
merely visual! Things say they are noisy, with colour, but they
in fact aren't noisy at all ... they merely assert stridence, by
telegram. As in op and pop art: art for a society of voyeurs ...
out of touch.

and then to La Place ... muzak Xmas carols which deafen
my earing ... muffle my earscape, pulling a sound barrier over
it. And I duck into the Church, blinded by the muzak ... and
within I hear again despite the whipcreme of muzak without....
Watch the Church grow me — and wonder if it is not in
truth for me English Gothic revival to which has been added
the Catholic folk earscape we all lost when Henry VIII went
cuntcrazy, and cut the Church. Is that not it? This is the absolute
restitution? Not of a dogma — but of a reality that we lost ...
the restitution of sound and light?

out again, the muzak plops over my head blurring the Square
again, blinds my earing ... and I wade my way through to the B
of M.... It is performing for me ... a songfest, of carols, for the
entire Bank caste, in the main hall. A command performance
for me ... mobilizing it as absolute testing site. Too good to be
true. "Good King Wenceslas" ... and I watch the room carefully
— yes, this is all the music this temple could permit ... the crème
caramel of Xmas carols in modern guise. It occurs harmlessly
within the flanking black marble pillars, leaving them absolutely
untouched. I watch the people tiptoe in and out between carols.
Tiptoe because earing is absent — that's why they tiptoe. Because

no one can really hear the music. Whereas in the Church, people struggle in and out, scuffle the aisles, stand or sit as may, mumble, talk, move. And they can do this, because their local noise doesn't affect the fundament of earing ... doesn't in any way obscure the thunder of site, is in fact part of it. Tiptoe music is music for deaf mutes. It proves impotence.

the choir. Forty zombies and a mistress. Watch her. In front of her grand piano — in green dress for merry, caught between choir and the careful ranks of the caste ... beginning with the King Cubes in the front row. I watch embarrassed ... by her. By her aggressive corporal innocence. Her hands berate the air, fingers twitching as though marionetted ... as though finger and arms and body were run by plucked strings. No body movement as such — but a remote-controlled ferocious grace militant. She is the vicarious annual felicity of the entire staff. Their optimum formal abandon. Fuck by numbers! Her accredited greensleeves ass bounces and bumps, jabs the clean-brownnoses of the King Cubes (who religiously blow these noses after every second number) ... the choir mouths the Infant Birth. Such an earnest wholiness. Those eyes that drool goodness (take home a package today, you owe it to yourself) ... in the backrows, those balding men, from twenty-two to sixty-two ... all on a careful ladder of irrelevance.

they carol the Ukrainian bells ... and for a brief moment the sound barrier is threatened. For a brief moment there is multiplicity of sound ... and the hall threatens complicity ... but finally it is just muzak, live. Even the negro spirituals are harmless. And then everyone is cordially trooped around the Xmas tree for a final song.... It is a remarkable achievement. No one breaks ranks — although there is no formal ordering. Quite simply everyone keeps his station ... King Cubes first ... I don't know them ... but they are easy to spot in their dark blued suits firmly tailored to their square root. A certain elegance — rather like prize steer. Groomed for show. Their shoes have thinner soles. They wear a coloured silk handkerchief (no one under a general manager does so). Their flesh is well kept, full ... they look immeasurably benign. They are convincing. Surprisingly convincing. Without much trouble I spot #s 1 and 2. Perhaps two of the most powerful men in the nation. They are self-effacing Big Daddys. They sound (when they talk) as if they were walking on unending broadloom — it is a kind of deep purr that their entire body exhales (like a deepseated aftershave lotion). And I remember now there was beige broadloom in their executive suite whence I was ejected for "loitering." One of them imitates the style Grand Seigneur ... bends to shake little boys hands ... genuinely wants the part of Big Lord Fauntleroyalty. He is the less convincing. The other remains immutably erect. With just the slightest concession to humanity in a certain stoop to his shoulders that his tailor has carefully matched.

A son with one of them. Junior version. Age seventeen? He has the felinity of youth — but already over that imposes the same kind of jerked electronically controlled order that entirely governed the body of the choirmistress. His brain keeps sending out messages to his body. Do this. Do that. Don't do that. And his body conforms correctly, but always a split second after the order, so that there is that accusative slight divergence.... Mind over matter it is called. Or intellect over sensibility. The beginning of the long slow death. Yet the boy is still alive ... his eye catches mine. Out of 400 in the hall ... he catches mine ... and follows, the way a dog follows its food ... follows instinctively. Rightly. Why? How does it happen that way? How do we know where life is ... and where death has been self-imposed? I don't know. But that boy's eyes are still gazing into mine, down through my gut, and out the end of my cock that sees the thunder of the Church candles again ... and I know that he will always carry my eyes with him — whether he knows or not — my eyes will always be a warm wound feeding him.

I slip around behind the tree, through between some wreaths to the evident disgust of one of the choir zombies, a self-assured elder of the Mother Bank. He glares in disbelief at my deviation. And at my green corduroy suit. And when a child passes the same way moments later gives to the unfortunate the chastisement he wanted to give me. It is not lost on me. He is obviously distressed by my presence, my reality. Outraged in a way he doesn't understand. But at least he has the sense to realize that he is outraged. And five minutes later, armed with his Veteran's badge, his blue waistcoat, and the immense moral superiority of his participation in choir he accosts me with a rigid politeness that is deathful — "Are you looking for anyone?" — meaning "How dare you be No one, and be here!" And with a hate that more than matches his, and drawing on nine generations of Canadian Loyalist blood, the fact that my family fought at Lundy's Lane, Batoche, Vimy, and Dieppe, and that I still use my great-grandmother's crown Derby dinner service, I square him off … "no, I am not, thank you" — and my eyes warn him that he has encountered something more solid even than his own cubicle … because for that moment I am at once utterly opaque, and absolutely lethal….And he withdraws. It is only then that I recollect that the Chief Cube here is in fact a relation of mine … is In the Family … the Mother Bank is in sorts a pocket borough of mine, metasocially speaking. And it is that subterranean reality that has quailed that Senior Citizen and Choirboy: and again I knew it is not what you say, it is the way you say it … and the way that you say draws from B & B … always. Blood is thicker than heavy water.

A brief visit to the Bank Museum … in the corridor beside. In contrast with the Museum in the Church this is simply an illustrated text! In the Church the display incidentally adds a text to the reality displayed. Slight distinction — but it is all the difference in the world between the two civilizations: French-Catholic, and Anglo-Protestant: the one is still immersed in reality, the other is detached from it. The Catholic display doesn't need the text, the label. The Protestant one doesn't need the display. One is B & B; the other is skeletal. The one invokes reality ... drowns you in it; the other merely recollects it, at one remove. In the Church I don't know which is real after I have made my visit ... the Church or its miniature museum? Both are deeper than life. In the Bank now I know that neither is real ... each is less than life.

Peruse the brochure on the new Mommy Bank Building ... entitled (Believe it or Not?) "Historic Home-coming...!" First page (happily) presents a message of Faith, Hope, and Charity-that-pays from the President, along with his photo (looks like a shorn beaver!).... A list of those who built the new office — "To These Belongs the Credit...." Including the Beaver Demolition Company!

... the new post office included in the Bank Building ... and I recall now that picture of the old Place, on the hoarding of the site of the new BCN Building ... showing the Post Office built in 1876 ... splendiferous! Of course in this brochure a bad-angle photo is shown of it in demolition. But it didn't need "son et lumiere!" It was a Thunderer ... and its thunder ignited! I know! (all I need to do is look at its contemporaries still erect — the Life Association of Scotland building for one — Côte Place d'Armes). Now it is displaced by this "man in the grey flannel suit!" — double-breasted of course. And above it, the Canadian Ensign of the day ... equivalent to a regimental tie. A section entitled "Statistically speaking." Great — dig this — it weighs 80,000 tons! As much as the Queen Mommy — (I mean the Ship, the Q.E.). Vital statistic ...

... modern comfort and convenience for the staff ... an architect's rendering of the lounges ... in the "modern idiom." Christ — have these people no sense of irony! Those hollow figures (style Bernard de Buffet) they show shadowing their way through the cafeteria **are** the reality the modern idiom has

created (no wonder they all want and need Tigers put back in
their tanks!)

I need an injection ... back up to Jack Macdonald's office.
He has gone. But the picture of his great-grandfather is what I
wanted. And beside it — that of Arthur Meighen ... those eyes
are what I am after: of a wounded deer, wide, deep ... infinitely
sensitive. The eyes that we lost in Canada for two generations
— eyes that were veiled over in deference to Mackenzie King's
mommyfuckering, and his single crystalline ball! Meighen —
the last King Cube. "Unrevised and Unrepented": he was a man
... and a human. And he was defeated — and Canada with him
— by $ from this Mommy Bank!

Back through the Place — still muzacked ... stop in
at Religious Boutique sur la rue Notre Dame, to gorge on
chalices and monstraunces and chasubles (Meighen's eyes
opened me back up again). And now, as my ears drum, I know
why I came in ... opened up, I wanted to hear. Pick up a
medium chalice ... it freights my hand, reverberant as I lift —
and I understand the meaning of the phrase "en or massif." I
can hear again. The rest is irrelevant. As I go out the door I find
my hands instinctively plying my mittens ... kneading them
into a sculpting of the madonna by the chalice. Hearing makes
a sculptor of me!

Return to hotel ... puissant (no wonder the French
Canadians at one time liked to use the formal title — "La
Puissance du Canada," for the Dominion of Canada ... and
how typical, that our inferiority has even frightened us away
from the magnificent meaning of "Dominion!" — because that
is what Canada is about ... dominion over four million square
miles of land, by a resolute handful of peoples).

I realize that what has been restored to me these past days
is my self-respect. I have gone through Hell for Heaven's sake
... and found my human dignity. Bless Meighen's eyes, bless the
chalice, bless the Mother Bank and the Great White Elephant

and the Flesh Market and the Sphinxes Large and Lesser and the Wedding Cake, and the Greyway and the Front and Holyrood.

...

at 8 p.m.... en route to the Church, for a mass in the Chapelle du Sacré Coeur ... I still can't get over how appropriate it is, how insanely right, that it is a copy of Raphael's "Disputa" that is over the entry! — the Renaissance Dispute over Transubstantiation.... Of course Transubstantiation won ... but the irony is that Raphael's depiction of this victory of B & B over the forces of disembodiment was painted in 3-D, complete with vanishing point ... his very mode of depiction was the Anti-Christ that killed King Cock! (Should have called my Novel *The Chalice and the Cock* ... last of the Henty books!)

After, talking to Père Amyot again ... talk the dualism of body and soul. The way he says things is the way I need. But what he says can scarce absolve me of my particular Protestant Penitence for the Body Despised and Rejected. Canadian Jansenism. Boys bathing in private at college, and wearing a bathing suit. How can I tell him (darling eunuch!) that phallus is flower. Why bother?

He on the "mystic origins of Montreal." He is right. There is a mystery to the origins of Montreal — a movement of the spirit. Why deny it? And it lingers. And after — tour the presbytery ... the poverty of it accuses me again as Angluche. Like the poverty of Canada's best paper — *Le Devoir*. I understand these wounds of French Canada now that I understand my own so much better ... and I hate me, us, for causing their wound. The *imitation* French Canadiana, with which the presbytery is largely furnished. Reproduction chaises à la capucine beside sensitive eighteenth-century Canadian Régence chairs in butternut, with a modern bargain basement refinish!

The père persuades me to stay for the Christmas Eve Mass ... He is right: I should — if only for the novel.

...

After the service and the tour Hugh went to dine at Paul Marie's ... chef-martyr. He felt alone ... tried to phone another prey for his novel. But it was masturbation pure and simple. He didn't quite know why, but it clearly was. A penitence again. And the fear of being alone to confront himself.

Afterwards walked down la rue Bonsecours ... Papineau House (there had been something magnificent about Papineau — and he thought of Toronto's equivalent — Wm. Lyon Mackenzie ... "that runt" — the words spat loud out of him. The distinction between the two men was, alas, symptomatic of the two cities. After all his book was by implication a *Tale of Two Cities*, Montreal was his Mona Lisa ... and Toronto "the Second City." And he knew that he would have to write one of his Toronto, finally — second half of this diptych). Around him Le vieux Quartier droned slightly in the snow-scurries. The St. Lawrence Seaway was dead under ice. He dropped into Le Fournil for a nightcap of Marc. Talked to a young couple performing at the Saltimbinques, the theatre at the corner ... they belonged to the new generation of dedicated androgynes ... the new "neuters" — promised to sterility for the sake of the arts ... such a creative sterility. But they were suspicious of Hugh's interest in French-Canadian arts, and remained impermeable to his vulnerability.... He returned to his hotel — the Old Hen of La Petite Place. He was beginning to forgive himself for staying there — every man needs a lair in Mother Earth, For the first time in days he sat down relaxed to make notes direct for his novel.

After his lunch with René, Andrew stopped in at the Château de Ramezay — he had been in Le Vieux Quartier for three weeks, but still had not visited it, it was unfinished business. On his right as he entered, a plaque listed "Those Who Have Occupied the Château":

La famille de Ramezay — 1705–1745 (with 16 children!)

La Compagnie des Indes — 1745–1764

Les Gouverneurs du Canada — 1764–1849

The American Army of Invasion (under General Montgomery) 1775–1776

and the Comissioners of Congress, Benjamin Franklin, Samuel Chase and Charles Carroll

The Special Administrative Council (Replacing Parliament after the Rebellion) 1838–1841

The Ministry of Public Education — 1856–1867

The First Normal School of Montreal — 1856–1878

Laval University of Montreal (Law and Medicine) — 1884–1889

The Magistrate's Court — 1889–1893

The Antiquarian and Numismatic Society of Montreal — 1895–

It was an astonishing list, reflecting the entire history of Canada ... and a large portion of the western world ... a Governor from the days of Louis XIV; the great trading companies of the days of the gentleman-adventurers; the pro-consuls of the British Empire; the American revolutionaries ... and Bennie Franklin himself, bringing the first printing press to Montreal, and installing it in the Château itself!; the surge of public education in the

Victorian world; the courts of law ... and then, lastly, the museum — a world under glass like TV!

On the far side of this another plaque ... "Les Premiers Colons de Quebec ... ils ont été à la peine, qu'ils soient à l'honneur." And he remembered being told that the French Canadians supported the project of restoring the Vieux Quartier as a monument to their own history, whereas, in fact, the architecture dated mainly from the English regime. C'est la vie!

He entered the Council Room — first on the right — the Hervey Smythe views of Quebec in 1759 ... an aide-de-camp to Wolfe — magnificent scenes: the interior of the Jesuit Church, of course, perhaps the finest ever built in North America ... certainly the most voluptuous. The Intendant's Palace. Part of world that was described in its day as civilized as anything in France outside of Paris itself. The series of scenes by Richard Short — a lunar Canadian landscape. And then, but fifty years later, the watercolours by Colonel Cockburn showing a pastoral Canada, at once Gainsborough and Regency Gent and Habitant.

And fifty years after Cockburn — the High Romance scene by Henri Julien of Dollard des Ormeaux au Long Sault, Mai 1860. ("notre histoire est une épopée" — how the modern French Canadians hate *that* — but then they haven't yet got to the stage where they have no history left; we're way ahead of them in our uprootedness! — thanks to the search for the All-Canadian Identity — careful, don't rock the boat there ...).

And after Julien, some illustrations from "The Habitant," by "Dr. Drummond." More of Maria Chapdelaine's habitant Canada. Yet Andrew wondered if the picture of that society had ever been better shown. All evidence was that that was what French-Canadian life was indeed like. And in any case the new Quiet Revolution was as Romantic as the rest

— it drew heavily on a Romantic Vision of life ... although that was beginning to run dry (his lunch with René proved that decisively!)

He went around jotting his notes ... "the uniforms ... these were the Man ... the Cocked Hats! ... The Flag of the Rebels at St.-Eustache ... a *real* Flag ... I can honour that!"

Outside in the hall a couple of tourists were talking to la vieille poule about the seige of Khartoum, as though it were yesterday ... and as though it belonged in and with the Château. He listened incredulously ... and then he realized that of course it *did* — that was part of the reality of this place ... a live tradition, albeit going dead. And then he finished his circuit ... admired the room itself ... its proportions, high ceiling, neo-classic mantlepiece ... and passed into the Church Room — full of "the white and the gold" (Costain's Canadianism) and on into the stairhall where a lithograph of Toronto, Canada West, hung cruelly over the door in contrast with the Church carvings behind ... Toronto — ca. 1850 — so flat and so sullen. So grey ... blur of black-and-white. He realized that he always saw Toronto in black-and-white — felt it in black-and-white ... even though this lithograph was in colour. Whereas Montreal so grey, was always colour. He mused: colour TV in the long run would probably have more impact on Toronto than on any other city in North America.

"The French Salon ... that Louis XV armoire from the presbytère at Trois Rivières ... unique example of French-Canadian Baroque (what was the name of that Bishop from Three Rivers who brought in Belgian craftsmen in the eighteenth century? ... *that* must explain this piece) — strong in black and gold....

"The Indian Room — 21 cradle boards! Idiotic ... but God — they are splendid. Curl the hair on my ass! The painting of Indian Chiefs, 1841, in full regalia ... fantastic

composite: part habitant, with their ceintures flèchées; part
Soldier of the Queen, with their silver medals, their guns;
part Indian, with their moccasins, beadwork; part Civilian
Gents, with their stove-pipe top-hats; part Black Trash.... A
hideous parody of the Canadian "melding pot"!

The beadwork on the clothes in the cases ... rings my
ears — Our artists have never achieved what these Indians
did ... their beading is abstract, yet it concentrates colours
of the land — I keep smelling, hearing, feeling that land
that the Garrison Officers painted, that Paul Kane painted,
that the Group of Seven painted (though their paintings
are *so* silenced!) No — we have never achieved that entire
harmony with our environment that these people did.
That full-dress for example, in the case to the left of the
door.... It is Wild Turkey and Great Horned Owl, and
granite and doe and Cardinal Flower and blueberry and ...
I suppose that the closest the white man came was with
the French-Canadian Parish Church ... the eighteenth-
century stone rubble church, its walls scraped from the
land, and its guts an improbable Glory! Baroque Habitant!
And after that, the next best, the Honest Ontario
Yeoman's red-and-white brick home, squatting over the
earth it masters but disclaims. I suppose that Expo 67 will
be our endeavour at synthesis. I must remember to force
me to see it!

Still the noise raucous in my ears ... sweetly raucous
(these Indians had rings on their fingers and bells on
their toes ... and music from coast to coast. *Real* music,
of the inner ear.)

And with this, a curious filth — a sheer brute dirtiness
to it all. The relics of the life, of the barbarity (they didn't
use toilet paper, or Ipana! I'm soiled that way I guess).
Combination of filth (I shrivel) and sheer beauty (I
distend). At least there is nothing mediocre to it.

Drawings by Zachary Vincent ... last of "the pure blood Huron Chiefs" (sounds like a line from Hiawatha ... or Pauline Johnson) — alias Telari-o-lin. Depictions of himself — habitant-cum-Indian-cum-American primitive.

... one Eskimo soapstone carving — how bogus it looks here, amongst the blood and slush. It *looks* like a civil service memorandum on Eskimo Art; like a white man seeing with Eskimo eyes. Overfed Eskimos, pensioners-in-the-making. Affluent Eskimos, making Archetypes for Suburban Living! (stop, stop, you fool — it's the only art that English Canadians have produced in two centuries that has drawn international attention!)

— photos of the western paintings by Paul Kane. 1840s. Indanecdotes for the eternal Women's Auxiliary. Superb — dammit.

... can't get over the squalor of the room: yet magniloquent. It's like being in Notre Dame ... these colours are windows out into my world.

He went on into the Reception Room — admired the flexed flesh of la chaise os du mouton (*those* bones weren't dry!), and then turned to the walls which were covered with prints, paintings and drawings of Montreal. Montreal everywhere.... Again, the windows, in, and out, of him. Window-pictures.... For insites, as against picture-windows, detached views. Beginning with the series by R. A. Sproule, 1830 ... Andrew knew the series well — had almost bought a set once; now they were too expensive. The "View of the Champs de Mars" ... with the British fifers parading, the habitant audaciously antedating quite firmly Kreighoff! View of Montreal from the St. Lawrence — pillbox in the Ile Ste-Hélène foreground (toy soldiery) — and the hulk of Notre Dame Church domineering the town as it was intended, matching even the bulk of the mountain-couchant, the Greatest Sphinx. St. James Street

with the first of the Mommy Banks and those Flaxman
bas-reliefs over its lower windows. View of the Harbour
— the ships parked where now the grain elevators heave
to ... Notre Dame Street — so largely the same in feeling,
from Nelson's Monument (that Nile crocodile *is* immense)
— with Nelson looking like some sad Napoleon, his back
facing the river; while at the end of the street the body of
old Notre Dame stops the street so happily — interrupting
the vanishing point before it can vanish with the observer
— in Toronto one so often vanished thus. Finally — La
Place d'Armes itself ... a view of the original Church still
flanking the wide-eyed façade of the new Gothic building.
And as he felt his way through the window-picture around
that original body he knew that it did to him as an
exterior view what the interior of the new Church did to
him now ... both bellied him. And he felt about the old
Church as he did still about Notre Dame de Bonsecours
when he circled it ... "l'animal!" The new Church was
preconceived; the original Church had been conceived, and
still conceived him ... made him divinely animal rampant!

Patten's "View of the City" ... 1760 ... showing it as
an Eternal City. Making him realize that Quebec was not
Canada's — was not North America's — ONLY *Eternal*
City ... Montreal was a good seconder. Patten's engraving
had the thunder of the waters in it, and the mountain
was congested with cloud.... He carried on around the
room ... a print of the Jacques Cartier map of Montreal
as Hochelaga, 1535 ... the palisaded Indian town ... and
another by Whitefield of the city in the mid-nineteenth
century — a prosperous print, an "American View," bird's-
eye.... The Protestant Episcopal Parish Church — 1822
... ahh — the complete Cube ... a final Lower Canadian
Adamesque variant of Gibb's St. Martin's-in-the-Fields
(Parish Churches for Englishmen Everywhere — from

Sydney to Bombay to Philadelphia to Quebec to Toronto!)
And another stern's-eye view of Notre Dame de la Place
... showing how much it also was cubicular. The French
Canadian had really only captured its personality by doing
the interior over again ... and underneath Bouchette's
description of it "as a chaste specimen of the perpendicular
style of Gothic architecture of the middle ages." Well,
externally, it was indeed "chaste" — positively falsetto!
But that interior! — that made up for the chastity.... And
Bouchette going on to write (1832) "the embattlement
parapets at the eaves of the flanks, which are peculiar in
the crowning of Gothic edifices, are omitted on account
of the great quantity of snow that falls in this country in
winter. The severity of the frost, also, prevents considerably
the decoration of buildings in cold climates."

James Duncan's "Panoramic View of Montreal," with
the Marché Bonsecours giving a St. Petersburg air to what
might otherwise be some medieval European port ... the
Marché in that setting so clearly a descendant of Palladio,
Inigo Jones, Gibbs, and Adam. With that peculiarly English
Trinity — central portico and clear balancing units at the
end of each wing (he knew perfectly well, though he
couldn't demonstrate it and wouldn't have if he could
have, that this architectural Trinitarianism, the Anglican
theological emphasis on the Trinity and, for that matter,
the English political Trinitarianism — Crown — Lords
and Commons — were all one and the same — and thus
to call an Englishman a Cube, much less a Square, was
essentially wrong!)

Kreighoff's magnificent scene of La Place d'Armes in
winter ... with the Mother Bank as backdrop ... (the one
he had an old postcard of).

a view of skating on the river, along the Front....

Montreal eying him thus from all sides.... He slid out

of his view, into the Numismatic Room, and for a moment
was lost, couldn't see at all … till he finally focused on
a single coin … and stopped short as he realized that to
look that coin in the eye was to look his own eye in the
face and he felt suddenly molested by the fact. Decidedly
numismats, like philatelists, were peeping toms!

A glance at the Canadian silver in the portrait gallery
(more bad portraits of general interest in this room than
anywhere else in Canada!) … but he was tired, and there
was no response till the large Amyot Monstraunce caught
his eye, and he peered through its pale crystal eye and
fell and saw despite himself a series of views of Le Vieux
Quartier … saw Whitefield's aerial map superimposed
upon Kreighoff's Place upon Sproule's Old Notre Dame
(if *only* they had left its tower as Campanile in La Place)
upon Patten's Thames-side view upon Hochelaga upon La
Place that he knew all through the eye of the Monstraunce.
Suddenly he realized that he had an importunate hard-on …
and he retreated into the next room, stopping haphazard to
die slowly in front of a piece of oak from Jacques Cartier's
ship, *La Petite Hermine* … behind him the stonework gate
from the Champlain family garden in France.

At 10 p.m. that night Andrew was back in his room and
started to write his diary, which was really his novelette.
He was quite aware of that now.

> "… *after the visit to the Museum and the Christmas Folly
> at the Mommy Bank, a brief rest, and then dredged me from
> bed to attend a Mass at the Church of Notre Dame … Père
> Amyot had invited me — une Messe des Adorateurs Nocturnes,
> dans la Chapelle du Sacré Coeur. As I stumped along rue
> Notre Dame on the raw of my knees I wondered what the
> hell I was doing.… Why this? Heaven knows I've 'done' the*

Church — and I don't need la Chapelle du Sacré Coeur. One tid-bit, anyway; going past the Providence Life Building, the bas-relief on the walls … I could laugh — 'that's it … la vie anglaise, toujours en bas relief.' But the joke was tired.

Into the side of the Church and down to the Chapel. It looks worse than ever. Bloated with bad taste. Slump into my seat — bored. Les Adorateurs Nocturnes … and I look around at them … all that little world of Gabrielle Roy's Tin Flute … these distortions — the remnants of a people! Not one of them looks "right" — each one is a maimed man … too short, or too long, or tuberous, bulbous, almost leprous — the people that the Quiet Revolution left behind. And I remember talking, at La Presse, a couple of days ago about these "Adorateurs Nocturnes" — God, we laughed at the very phrase … as I had those ages ago laughed with Jack Greg, about Audubon's great auk. The very phrase somehow defined the laugh — said everything.… Les Adorateurs Nocturnes! Well there they are — with their Monstraunce-medals pinned on their lapels.…Adoring the Nocturnity! The weak, the disabled, the ill-born, the poor-of-head … and above them, the giant religious murals — including Dollard des Ormeaux and his band at the altar before setting out to save the world for New France. It is pathetic. I revel in my dismay — no wonder French Canada needed a revolution.

And then Père Amyot has sent someone to accompany me in their service … and the kindness disarms me completely — it is the kindness here, the complete sincerity of these blockheads. The Père processing now, with his acolytes in white gown … and they are mobilizing all the apparatus of a Mass. I watch, detached — alas — and then, faute de mieux, up to take Communion insubstantially, out of courtesy to the Père because I had asked him the other day what he would do had I presented myself at the rail, when I had truly wanted to, and he had said "you are in communion with us in the spirit … I would give you the Host." So I went up — and ate that bad bread. And then back in my seat, made patient again.

An acolyte brings in a silken white and gilt-shot umbrella
... and Père Amyot is kneeling by the altar in a complete new
outfit (this is a Liberace Program!) ... I have been thinking
that while the Mass apparently makes these people submissive,
it makes me militant — or should ... though tonight I am
too tired. Only the acolytes focus me desultory.

Then they are sifting again ... the Adorateurs Nocturnes
are sifting some from themselves up to the altar and taking the
great candles and Père Amyot is still dressing ... I am excited
— and revulsed. More incense — it's worse (and better) than the
old-time train shuntyards. There is something obscene to it all —
something disgusting ... this man up there swathing himself in
raiments. Bathing himself and us in incense. Something filthy to
it ... the White Mass — of white, blanched flesh. Something
incorporeal.... Why do I revulse? Why suddenly want the
Mass Black? Why do my nuts shrivel.... Is it a moment of
gelding? Is that it? Something is awry. It's all upside down
here.... Our whole religion is inside out then — our expulsion
from Eden occurred when we lost our nuts! Is that it? Yes it is.
And these people are consecrating the lost nuts ... consecrating
the loss — with these same nuts ... Yet all these men here are
fertile — hideously fertile (it is so evident — fertile in the way
the wild boar is, sullen with unspent vehemence). No — I don't
understand anything any more. And then it is too late to try ...
the whole apparatus has turned on me, is moving down the aisle
on me and we are all down the aisle with that machine behind
me and the Father under his umbrella, with that indescribably
vulgar Monstraunce peering at me ...

(and as I type this diary now I realize that my novelette
is in fact some deeper assault on reality than I cared to admit.
It is war ... between reality and me — I'll call this diary
a Combat Journal: That's it — my Combat Journal — I'll
stick a label on the front cover ...

I want to laugh ... but I fear I may cry ... still that
apparatus eying me behind ... and in front the Adorateurs
Nocturnes with the Christ Candles parading me and the Holy
Float out of La Chapelle du Sacré Coeur, under the Disputa
whose perspective now our procession confutes, around the
sternum of the High Altar of the Church proper, into the right-
hand aisle that clusters candles along my flanking past altar and
altar and altar, up to the end — still dodging the steps to the
pulpit and writhe us left, turning the whole world left into the
body of the Church, into the body of the nave that blinks at
me with the lidded eyes that are the dormers of the old Eglise
Notre Dame that they destroyed but which is now the interior
of this Church that they thought they could make into mere
Cubicle ... but the reality is all other as we plunge down the
central aisle ... past the original high altar of the Ecole de
Quevillon, with its bulgeous habitant baroque body blessing
my embonpoint and proving the true sensibility of this interior
of us now (the Gothic is a fake, a front ... this Church isn't
Gothic — ahhh — there I have it now ... I knew there was a
reality inside it). This Church, this nave, this *is* the Body of the
Habitant ... of the Habitant-Seigneur-Cardinal-Canadien ...
Baroque Habitant ... Ecce Homo ... they couldn't finally hide
that, even under the Cubicularity. This Church is the Canadien
... my missing Man. My other Présence ... Moi-même. Ah, voilà,
que je te prends, mamour ... te voici enfin ... en dépit de tout
ce que l'on peut nous dire du contraire ... te voilà, corps et
âme! I take and I eat you now, in memory of us ...

as we navigate the turn I want to drop behind, to see the
sight ... that Monstraunce, the Machine but I can only glimpse
... the Père under his panoply of seraglio-silk carrying the Host
high ... I am sucked back into the body of our processing till
we pass the high altar now with its gross of saints and are back
in la Chapelle ... the Père divesting himself of the Host, atop a
ladder that scales the Tabernacle. We are chanting the victory ...

hands outstretched, wide open to the massacre (and I thank God that His Machine is no longer following me behind) — hands outstretched, disarmed ... and as we stand the procession is still in me, still flowing around the nave and into me till I penetrate La Petite Place and on the instance know that this Tour du Monde was the Tour du Monde that I made those days ago around the Outer Walls and then around the Inner ... this is that same procession around that I accompanied unwitting for precisely the same reasons (acolyte Adorateur then!) ... and that being so, then Amyot is André and that Machine is ... and the knowledge of this is sweat on the palms of my outstretched hands now.

Then they are all gone save those who keep the Adoration all night. Watching over the altar, the Church, La Place ... the city (and as I watch the altar I remember that the city hall is the Tabernacle and the Mayor our Man and ...)

Sit now in this night silence that is thunderment — so different from the silence in which you can hear a pin drop.... This is no soundless silence ... no silence from which sound has been banished ... no silence in which nothing is expected ... nothing untoward. This is a silence in which everything is expected, everything is possible — immense anticipation of potence, omnipotence....

Then I am gone ... I can't stand any more ... not now. And when I stop running I am in the restaurant, sitting with my back glued to the wall — trying to hold the world at bay....

Back abed ... I am shattered ... every body in my bone broken ... every muscle aches ... I've been pummelled till the nerve-ends bleed. Ache all over ... body and soul — the body of my soul aches. Outside the train bells that I heard during the Mass.... No no no no. No man can see God and live!

Suddenly I have it ... have it all — the novelette — the story ... absurdly clear — even the name of the man: Hugh Anderson!

DAY TWENTY-TWO

... thunder behind the ears again! Thunder ... that I always
expected but never did hear at La Place Ville-Marie! that's
it — I remember that now — I never **did** hear anything at La
Place Ville-Marie ... it was always a cheat — opened me up, but
never came! Silence. Dead silence, always. I hadn't noticed, not
there, not then. But now with the thunder-ear again blasting
eyes into the back of my head ... owl eyes for me to see my
encirclement. Circumambience. Now I ear that deathful silence
of the Counterfeit Place.

    Up, bareback on this thunderment, to write direct into
novel while I am still impaled by life.... Light the great
convolution of red-candle from la rue Bonsecours, and then
ignite me from it in cigarillo. ("the moment of truth" — sui
generis!) And sit to my desk ... to write my truth, at last — at
last, goddam it ... still I am hesitant ... to "write," at any time,
demands faith, is self absolutely vulnerable, absolutely exposed
to the pry of words ... to think it any other is ignorance. I can
only write at all when I am absolutely given.... It is like naming
me ... the horror I have of giving my name when I am opened
up this way ... for fear. As with Père Amyot! To write — to
recreate the world from one's own gut. Not to comment upon
it, not to footnote it, but to procreate it.

    ... last night — les Adorateurs Nocturnes! And as I ran
ran ran away home slushed in the car-crushed street snow,
the sight of the Hotel de Ville ... great hollow hulk in the
velveteen dark ... absentee Object that was all familiarity
to me ... familiar not in form, but in presence, but which I

only recognize now in the fierce lucidity of this renewed day, presence as in a photonegative ... with the Object void and the day as night eating out the Object. The Object a white sepulchre, for only the bones left barren of flesh ... as in La Place des Arts at the concert, when I felt dispersed along with every other thing or person. As in modern pop art: death of the Object! Ahh — modern version this then of those Adorateurs Nocturnes — then Modernists are Night Adorers ... their Object lost in a night-tide — last of the Romantics! Theirs is the Black Mass ... mass lost in night-black ... mass hiding its void in a new crepuscularity. Poor things.

Must write the novel.... Dare I? Still? The mystery of propitiation — of placating the Protestant Gods in me ... so that I can allow me to write, to rejoice, to procreate ... to achieve the commanded Grace of the Catholic God in me. Forcing me to grovel in sullen practical details before I permit me to write ... each time, the last person I met must be placated, must accord his forgiveness of my deviation from Protestant parsimony of the inner word. I must enact the Holy Grovel before I am allowed ... Holy Impasse — Holy Constipation ... steep me in it ... till the outburst! Now, now, **NOW!**

"... so that now for the first day, he felt capable of entering La Place, and filching it of both essence and detail. He was at once too tired to be dangerous, and yet too dangerous, too much in command, to be taken. It was like that now. When he awoke he heard the freightbells in him, avid within, yet withstood — voracious and accepted while withheld. It was a kind of procreative impasse. Both were there, if not in conjugation, certainly most conjugable, which was the new basis of responsibility ... founded upon responsibility. It was a real presence ... the Real Presence. He thought again of the Communion. That was

the verity ... of Body and Blood. It was inevitable. If not
yet completely achieved. The bells vibrated again in him
... dringtingdingingating ... strummed in him ... till he felt
their danger ... requisitioning him again.... He sat down to
his Combat Journal....

"It is the first day. I know that ... I have never dared to face
La Place. Have always withheld me, withheld something of
me. Now I must see it. Am incredibly lucid now ... my body
reassembled after these days of carnage ... recreating the world
around me. The First Day. Genesis!"

— he descended to the lobby ... his entire being
focusing upon La Place d'Armes ... the manager stopped
him, had seen him on television, was happy to have him at
the hotel ... Hugh squirmed, tried desperately to pay his
past week's bill for the room ... and then realized what
he was doing — he was trying to save himself from the
man by reducing their relationship to business ... trying to
absolve himself of acknowledging this man — and thus
was killing him. Doing what those visitants did so often
in the Antique Shop — turning proferred flesh into blood.
The realization broke over him in a cold sweat — guilty of
murder that way, failing to see the Man who invoked them.
And he knew that he could no longer do that. He stopped
and talked, trying desperately to resuscitate the manager
... accepting him as flesh and blood. Accepted his presence.
Nothing else to be done. And as he talked the fierce
presence of La Place in him ebbed ... his joy was absolved
... he was left with the manager, draining into him ... his
small reserve of blood siphoned off that way. Yet he had
to.... Then the manager was called to the phone, and Hugh

was out the door ... applying a tourniquet to what was left
of his B & B.

Temperature 11° above zero — an ice-blue day ...
crackling against the palms of his feet; snow bunched into
the foot-crotch hackled his nape. Into La Petite Place ...
cars already parked around the central core. Odd — he
had never paid much attention to La Petite Place ... had
almost kept away from describing it ... a certain pudeur
— never preyed upon it. Like a hawk that won't touch the
small birds that nest in its nesting-tree ... home-ground
is sacred ... and they are all in sanctuary. Hugh walked
to the top of this small Place now ... to where Nelson's
Monument stood atop the hillflank in him. The monument
firmly clenched in the skyline that was the reredos of
which the Hotel de Ville was Altar and all the Front the
Frontal outspreading from the foot of the monument....
Walked up slowly ... past the imbedded guns that snorted
up from the piled snow — pop-guns that helped build
the Greatest Empire the World Has Ever Seen (God —
Churchill was only buried a year ago! And He had charged
at Omdurman ... had fought the Mahdi! He chuckled to
himself — at John's he had met the Mahdi's grandson, at
tea, during the Suez crisis ... the Mahdi's grandson — at
Oxford, of course *that*, after all, was England — England of
the heart, still.) Hugh clambered over the railing around
the monument ... patted the sternum of Nelson's toyboats
that had consolidated that Great Empire The bas-reliefs
that squared the base were magnificent ... perhaps some of
the best stonework on the continent. Not "bas-reliefs" at
all ... not like the work on the Providence Life Building
no, deep-carved reliefs that thrust straight into the base of
the column. Above him, that improbable Nile crocodile
swallowing la rue Notre Dame. Yes — some of the best
stonework ... no one thought of that, of course; so he had

to think of it for his fellow citizens. Had to palp precisely
each thrust and gut of stone ... and each time his eyeball
touched a stone the bells of the freightyard carilloned him,
and La Petite Place was the Governor's Garden with its
rose-bed thrusting blossoms up into seventeenth-century
suns ... and the Petite Place backed up into him, thrusting
him right onto the frontal of the Tabernacle that was
the Hôtel de Ville — call it la Versaillaise! — that was
endlessly undulatory.... He was whole again. And without
turning his head he saw, refracted from that frontal that
was the frontal which Jean Le Ber had worked over two
centuries ago for Notre Dame under those same rose-
bitten suns (and which he was determined he could see
today), the entire perimeter of La Petite Place. The Château
de Ramezay behind him ... precursor of this same bête
couchant in front of him, Hotel de Ville ... the same
animal. The dome of the Great White Elephant ... bland
grandeur of Washington Capitol — but set pure atop
British North American stone. Beyond, to the left, Our
Lady of Everlasting Help above Notre Dame ... Statue
of Liberty, but with warmth in her womb. And the
angels around her (all echoes of the Great White City at
Chicago's World Fair, 1897) ... sweated green with the
grime of steamers. Out-topping both, the Grain Elevation,
that was a magnificence only diminished by the fact that
it blockaded the St. Lawrence to all but the inner eye.
While at the base of the Little Square, the viscera of that
same grain elevator, shafting whole-wheat and workers
from one Tuscan warehouse to the next. On the east
side of the Square ... his own hotel, Nelson — that was
a French provincial dame of dignity ... where everyone
had known him simply as "le petit Français en 313 ..." his
room number. And opposite, other hotels, a nightclub, and
two habitual restaurants ... his greasy spoon for breakfast,

and le Restaurant des Gouverneurs, where he drank fresh
squeezed orange juice and surveyed La Petite Place — did
its customers know the world that was theirs from out
its windows? ... He had sat there one afternoon reading
excerpts from the *Montreal Herald* of 1814 —

Item: "March 26th - Under the heading of
          Matrimony, an advertisement:
          A Gentleman in possession of a
          handsome income concerned in a
          house of respectability, of good
          disposition and agreeable manners,
          but from the tedium and ennui of a
          single life rather attached to his
          bottle, wishes to Connect himself
          to a Lady not exceeding twenty
          years, of a handsome person, elegant
          accomplishments, and pleasant
          temper. It is hoped that none will
          answer this, but those of undoubted
          respectability ... N.B. The connection
          will be rather of a platonic nature."

Item: "December 24 - Wanted, a Female
          Servant of good character, who
          understands Cooking and the Drudgery
          of the House. A woman having a child
          will not answer."

and in 1815 —

Item: "April 29 - The Drama. The Play of
          JOHN BULL was performed on Thursday
          evening by the officers of the
          Garrison, with great ability and

success. From the proceeds of the
play the Amateurs have been enabled
to make two donations of 50 pounds
each, to families in great distress."

Item: "August 12 - On Thursday when the
great news from Europe (the defeat of
Bonaparte) was known to be authentic
Mr. Dilmon planted his Patereroes on
the Place d'Armes and fired a salute."

... La Place d'Armes ... he still wasn't there. He turned
to the left ... down la rue Notre Dame.... Every detail
seared in him. He was implacably lucid ... and incredibly
vulnerable. Everything touched him.... Vulnerable ... was
it always necessary to be this vulnerable, just to see, to
hear, to know? Did it have to be that way? And then
he knew that it did. That that was what was marvellous
about man ... his vulnerability. That was the adventure
in life. The adventure of life. To close it off was to close
off life. So he had to embrace that vulnerability ... or live
dead. That vulnerability defined him ... as a man. It was
desirable, essential, inevitable.... The trees in front of the
old Courthouse, imbedding it in deep space ... alive with
blackbirds ... those trees, erect in him, every branch veined
in him ... disastrously present — gloriously. As he ran his
eye over each branch he threatened explosion ... and had
he raised a finger to trace his eyesight, he would have
detonated ... instead he passed his right hand back and
forth across his sight ... as his hand passed in front of his
face, his whole body snuffed out, and then, once passed, he
was ignited again.... His right foot stamped the pavement ...
till he stopped it. On past la rue St. Gabriel ... and le Vieux
St. Gabe ... he reinstated that picture over the bar ... that

picture that toured the world around him it sighted in him
... giving him always eyes in the back of his head. A bad
painting, that restored his sight! — what more could a man
ask, of a painting.

And with these eyes back into his head he realized
that the urns atop the Hotel de Ville were trailing him....
He turned to remonstrate — disengaged them from his
groin — and replaced them fastidiously atop the Hotel.
Admired the confrontation of Old and New Courthouses ...
and then continued down towards La Place d'Armes. Past
Paul's Tavern, with its stain-glass windows in a dignified
ribaldry. Opposite the gigantic hole-in-the-ground that
was the new Palais de Justice. Now at its most beautiful,
its most impressive ... a hole. Another ziggurat. Streicher
had explained to him that this new Palais didn't need to
tower at all — it didn't need to overshadow this street.
But its proponents wanted a tower. Eh bien — soit: it was
an empty phallicity, like all the rest. A hollow erection!
And the street would always have its revenge — because
one day men would realize that this tower was symbol of
accruing impotence. Whereas the smallest of the limestone
shops here with its garish painted pilasters, Victorian
accretions, bound more potence to itself than the entire
tower would. He turned from the hole-in-the-ground, to
the calm effrontery of these greystone shops ... his eyes
fingering each arcade and lintel. Yes — they held the
potence all right.... Odd, but a fact. Of course he was
nostalgic — for puissance.... He was opposite the surplus
store where he had bought a pair of khaki scarves, for
touring this world in the December sear, and where he
hadn't bought the knife ... the surplus store was a typical
case, with its warm agglutination of paint and dirt over,
and the improbable outburst of carving up the centre
of the pilasters, proving that the pillars themselves were

secondary to the convolutions of the flesh that the entire street acclaimed.

On, past the Main ... the newsstand with its convocation of All Bodies. Into that final canyon ... giving freely his obeisance to the amassed stone office face on his left ... surmounted by its date — 1886. It was doing something to him ... and he didn't know what — till he found himself backing across the street oblivious of the traffic that lurched around him cursing — backing across the street to confront it. Ahh — that was it: the building demanded that he square off afront it, stand easily at attention at thirty paces distance.... He had already done so before he realized it ... and they stood dialoguing for several moments. A distinct exchange of ideas — no nonsense: syllogistical. And then he was dismissed (the presentation had been polite, perfunctory, firm) ... behind him l'edifice Cadillac ... le sieur de Cadillac (was he a vrai Sieur? Qui sait?) had once lived on that site ... but had gone on to found Detroit, and infamy in the car that vulgarized him. He passed on down to that final cluster of shops selling the vestments and objects and books of the Faith: the Baldaquin. On his right une librairie ... in, to scout it briefly. Always that same quality, that same feeling, to these Catholic books — the figures on their dustjackets were always at once fluent and substantial. Never static. Never. They flowed. In him. Habitant Baroque: this time he remembered.

He gazed out the window of the librairie ... across to the Baldaquin ... threatening to riot him. His eyes embodied the mounting pillars that clenched and then sprung upthrusting three stories, four, above his headiness. He felt his calves gather and tense ... light on his feet.... And then plunged across the street to preclude pole-vault. Into the main shop selling Christ. Looking at all those statues ... the whole store blatant around him — a gross of Christs for the purchase. He knew, objectively, of course, that they were all in the worst possible taste — but now he knew as well that "good taste" was contraceptual — merely a protection against life and against love. He stood watching the statuary ... till he was again aware that they were watching him ... every one of them had a life of its own — independent of him. Every one of them stood erect in him ... insistent, indelible. He didn't know what to do about it. Then he remembered that of course this is what they should do ... and he knew how it had happened ... he had run his eye around the base of the first processional cross ... and as his eye circled the base the base circled his head, and he was again all eyes. And ears. For several moments he felt compelled to sculpt them, or at the least, to paint them ... to depict them; then he realized that he really wouldn't dare do that — because painting any one of them would expose him to absolute possession by it. He would literally have become possessed ... he could feel that — and his hackles writhed in warning. No — he would never be able to depict these ... only to propitiate them with words ... by describing them they acknowledged his adoration by releasing him momentarily. But if he failed to worship, then they canniballed him. There was little choice. But then he didn't want any alternative ... because when they commanded his worship they were the entire world restored into him ... his whole being distended, grew. Till he could withstand it no more — then he offered up his peace-offering, in thanksgiving. Magnificat. "My soul is magnified in the Lord...." And that was that. There wasn't any other way out of it, nor into it. He watched them ... and began to take notes, hastily ... and then they receded, placated. And his heart rejoiced in them ...

I know what you are ... you are all the missing people
from the new interior of the Great White Elephant. You are the
absentees ... the lost objects. Here you swarm me ... each one of
you like the figures on the dustjackets, across the street ... you flow,
and you are substantiated. Each of you is the Host. I won't try to
escape that. Never ... I know it won't change. Will always be the
same. I must give and love....

And as he wrote these words, the figures ceased to
swarm, but stood firm with him amongst them like trees
erect in snow-swept fields.

"I know — I must share this joy. If I don't share it with
others, they will kill it in me ... and kill me. I must share
Heaven.... And Heaven, then, is other people!

He turned and went straight out into La Place d'Armes.
... the Place d'Armes was munificent around him ...
and he approved every motion, every gesture it made
now ... he tested each one ... and found none wanting
... each was relevant — fraught with meaning, with
danger, with potential. The low organic bas-relief of the
Providence Building dallied him, as he scaled the careful
crags to the top, like some wellbred mountain goat. And
then skyhopping ... passed to the well-fed balustrading
atop the brownstone stack beside ... balustrades that
distended in prime sirloin.... He pocketed the ironwork
of the clock, particularly the hour-hands ... and then he
was interrogating again the crest pedimenting the Mother
Bank of All Montreal: merchantman's Parthenon frieze
... whereon the heroes were sailor and yeoman-worker,

and Indian: it was a quotation from the Amurrican world of Currier and Ives — with this difference — it was in stone! It was in 3-D ... Currier and Ives for Cubes. And so aptly, atop the crest of Montreal itself ... the beaver — the Complete Canadian Cube ... the symbol of the state — substantial, diligent, sure, sombre, comestible (but only by the tail) ... and, of course, it could be fleeced — the Canadian Golden Fleece.

he was sucked over to the Bank ... and in, and endlessly voyeur mounted to say goodbye to the castors within ... to his legal guinea pigs: and as he expected, they had that look of men about to lose their maidenheads ... in fact of men who had lost their maidenheads, but didn't quite know how or why.... Somewhere they had been had. By him. But if they acknowledged it then they were lost to respectability — and they clung to that matriarch with all the diligent will of the foredoomed.

crossed La Place ... into the garden of the Church ... the snow kindly absolved the dirt of it — the evident sterility of its soil. Covered it and gave it back its beauty ... flowered the rows of chestnut trees that flanked it ... in the centre, a saint or other, wintered under a contraceptual bag. Some day this garden would flower again, would welcome the public again ... but only when the people wanted gardens again — perhaps the city would make it a tourist attraction for the Centennial Exposition — it was excuse sufficient. Meanwhile it remained a medieval close, curious analogue of the Place itself. He made his way to the flank of the Church ... up a back alley — the tower strode over him ... and seen from these abutments, it was immensely convincing — no mere Gothic revival façade ... and doubly so in that through the portcullised gate beside he could see the Mother Bank brooding over the Place: it was an unexpected dividend — and it sufficed him ...

He turned up the front steps of the Church ... past the huge cast-iron lamps in front, through the central of the three arches, into the Church ... he intended to visit the Church Museum — to see Jean Le Ber's frontal — but he stopped abruptly ... in a pew at the back of the Church. To rest a moment ... slowly it focused him ... drew him out again — he heard the thunder of the candles ... and again his eardrums were probed and penetrant — again he lost his male maidenhead ... he reeled, held tight, and then relented ... gave himself to the verity ... and as he did he felt his eyes palped by the entrelacings of the gilt pillars .. and he followed the line of gold, up to the gold florescence under the balcony — to the scallopings of wood frieze ... and he knew that he had to abandon himself to this ... had to give to this — give himself to this. There was no other viable alternative. No other way — not out — but in. No other truth. Everything else was shadow.

... for a moment the veil dropped again — threatened to drop — he tried to make his eye bounce back off the entrelacs ... briefly he succeeded — yet he knew that if the veil did drop, he was lost — that once again he was still-born.... He looked back at the writhings of the gold ... and as his eye turned to them, they shot in, under his guard, before he even knew what had happened ... shot into him, writhing and convulsing — the candles raged in him — again he tried to close down — to shut out this realization ... but now it was too late, gloriously, with absolute finality, too late ... his whole body soared from the pew — followed his eyeballs in with the entrelacings ... the roof lifted and he was adrift absolutely, afloat ... no longer was there any question of details, of itemization — all that had gone now ... he was confounded in utter conjugation with the body of the Church — it was militant in him. He turned — and staggered out ... the

Place d'Armes was outrageously alive in him ... detonating
everywhere, everything, in a profusion of knowledge
... suddenly every detail was searingly evident — each
outline blared in him, and the mass of the square raged
in him ... he saw the beaver again ... and as he did heard
the thunder of the candles ... his throat swole, his eyes
blazed ... ça crève les yeux, Pierre had said — he was right
— it stabbed your eyes out ... no in ... stabbed his eyes
back in.... He was haemorrhaging now ... could feel the
stream of blood blurting from him ... hideously alive.... La
Place.... The Place ... he could see the Place ... he started
to shout ... "La Place ... it's there ... don't you see ... La
Place ... Look...." And he started to run toward the statue
of Maisonneuve ... and his run became a dance, his whole
body vibrant, like the dancers in the nightclub, like the
old High Altar by Quevillon in the Church, that was (he
knew it now) the same altar as in his dream at home, as
sideboard of hospitality, like the commode in the Flesh
Market, like the sternum of the Lesser Sphinx ... out into
La Place, grasping Holy Host to place it in the very centre
of La Place. A pedestrian swerved.

"Drunken fool," he muttered, but Hugh took no notice.
He held the Host in La Place d'Armes, and the rest was
irrelevance ... into the very centre, and stood absolutely
mobile and saw that the whole Place was in dance and
that even the Mommy Bank had budged, and that even the
beaver on the frontal of the Mommy Bank was undulant
now, in this sudden tidal flow, boring through him, flowing
outrageously alive through him to fecundate this entire
Place while around him as he turned, the buildings all
vehement in his motion, he saw that the people had
stopped dead so that he started again to shout "Look ... La
Place d'Armes it is come alive for us, all of us" — but still
no one moved as he held his Host high up over La Place,

so that he knew that now there was only one possible solution, and taking the Host ate it alive till he embraced the Place and then turning to the first person he could see ran with his right hand outstretched, his forefinger out, to touch, to give this blood that spurted fresh out the open act as he ran to embrace them in this new life he held out at fingertip to touch they

phone George Carter - V1-7-3928
        (for drinks)

Luc - EM-4-1749 ... after 8

Rocker in Flesh Market
    - $185 (maple) - for Mary?

Yvon-Pierrot - MA-3 9275
        (till midnight - not Monday)

Sites to check - Notre Dame ✓
            - Marché Bonsecours ✓
            - Château de Ramezay ✓
            - B of M ✓
            - unknown statue
        Place Ville-Marie ✓
        Grey Nuns (old section)

Rick HE-6-3981 for dinner

Get - notebooks
    - scarf & sweater (army surplus)

Brief Biography of Scott Symons

Born   July 13, 1933, Toronto, of Loyalist stock, son of Major Harry Symons (author and gentle man) and grandson of Wm. Perkins Bull (author and rogue male). Married (between novels) and one son.

Education at home with five brothers, one sister

    at farm with 378 chickens, two goats, three dogs, seventeen pheasants ...

    at Pointe au Baril, Georgian Bay, for many summermoons

    as caddy at Banff

    as Cadet in RCN (erstwhile)

    in wine harvests at Margaux

    and by listening copiously to Edmund Cohu, Andy Lockhart, Donald Creighton, Philip Child, F.R. Leavis, Doris Krook, Uncle Tom, Owen Channon, Gabriel Marcel, Charles Moeller, Jean-Louis Gagnon, André Laurendeau, George Spendlove ...

    Certificates—Trinity College School

              Trinity College, Toronto (B.A., History)

              King's College, Cambridge

                (Gentleman's M.A. in Englit)

              Sorbonne (Diploma for foreigners)

    9 1/2 scholarships (total: $5,021.08)

Journalizm—Toronto Telegram (fired for insubordination)

    Quebec Chronicle Telegraph

    La Presse, Le Nouveau Journal, Montreal

        Montreal Men's Press Club Award

        Bowater Award for series on the French Canadian Revolution (1961: turned down by thirteen English Canadian newspapers as "irrelevant," "unnewsworthy," etc.)

Academicity—Curator of the Sigmund Samuel Canadiana Gallery, Royal Ontario Museum (of the Multivarsity of Tranta) and Assistant Prof. in Fine Art (after Canadian Art became a National Duty)

— fired for insubordination (told Director he was a eunuch)

Research Associate, Winterthur; consultant at the Smithsonian; post-graduate course at the Univ. of Pennsylvania.

Scholarly and Learned Publications: Nil.

Writing—two good bad plays, 20 vols. of wildly pertinent diaries, two novels of which this the first, and the second on Toronto finished.

Status—A Para-Canadian, released from any allegiance to the Canadian State but obsessively devoted to the Canadian Nation.

Future—Stormy.

Scott Symons in Toronto.